# HELIX

## ERIC BROWN

**SOLARIS**

First published 2007 by Solaris
an imprint of BL Publishing
Games Workshop Ltd
Willow Road
Nottingham
NG7 2WS
UK

*www.solarisbooks.com*

ISBN-13: 978 1 84416 472 1
ISBN-10: 1 84416 472 1

10 9 8 7 6 5 4 3 2 1

A CIP catalogue record for this book is available from the
British Library.

Designed & typeset by BL Publishing
Printed in the UK

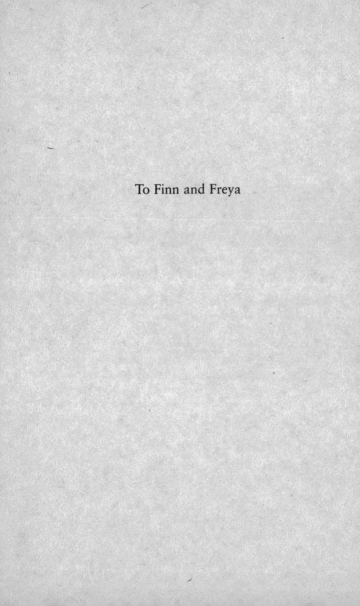

To Finn and Freya

# One /// Graveyard Earth

## I

THE YEAR WAS 2095 and planet Earth was dying.

That morning Hendry was working in the garden of the starship graveyard when his communications rig chimed. He moved back into the Mars shuttle and slumped down before the receiver. It was Old Smith, as usual, calling from across the straits in Tasmania to chat for a while. Smith said he'd lucked in on a radio station beaming out of Jakarta. The big news in Europe was a terrorist strike in Berne, at the headquarters of the European Space Organisation, with a dozen dead and hundreds injured.

"I thought I'd better get in touch, Joe," Smith said. "Doesn't your daughter—?"

Sweating, fear lodged like an embolism in his chest, Hendry cut the call short and tried to get through to Berne.

There was no reply from Chrissie. He waited five minutes then tried again. Okay, so she was out, working at the ESO headquarters. What time was it in Europe? He tried to work it out, but fear scrambled his thoughts. Australia was eight hours ahead of Berne, so it'd be around two in the morning in Europe.

Chrissie wouldn't be at work, then. She'd be sleeping, he told himself, and he didn't know whether to feel relief at the fact or renewed fear at the thought that his call should have awoken her.

He called her code again, and five minutes later gave up and left the shuttle.

He walked through the starship graveyard to the edge of the sea. Light-headed, trying not to dwell on Chrissie's lack of response, he looked over his garden, row upon row of peas and beans and potato plants, their lush foliage incongruous amid the rearing shapes of a dozen derelict shuttles and decommissioned tugs. Despite their dilapidated and broken-backed condition, there was something almost proud and defiant about these ships. They spoke of a time when humankind had not been afraid to explore, when the planet could sustain the luxury of space flight, before the cutbacks and the withdrawal of the moon and Mars colonies.

He passed between the two towering solid fuel boosters that formed the entrance to the graveyard, paused and took in the scene before him. The sea lapped listlessly at the scorching sands of the beach, but he saw only Chrissie's face in his mind's eye.

Thirty years ago Hendry had lived with his parents in the Melbourne suburb of Edithvale, now submerged twenty miles out to sea. This was as close to the stamping ground of his youth as he had been able to get, and the fact had disturbed him on his return in '90. He had known, intellectually, that Australia like every other landmass had been pared down little by little and reshaped by the creeping tides, but that the ocean had swallowed his childhood home he found inconceivable and shocking.

So he'd set up a base in the old starship graveyard, and started a garden, along with a dozen other like-minded, lost souls who over the following years had either died or moved away, driven by the encroaching sea or the increasing heat. Hendry had stayed on, despite the pleas from Chrissie to join her in Europe where civilisation was making a last stand against the worsening elements.

He had always resisted her offers of an apartment in Berne. He had his own life here, such as it was, and he could not face the prospect of living an artificial existence of pampered excess in some Swiss fortress enclave.

Now he wanted nothing more than to be with her.

He walked along the shoreline to the jetty, a tumbledown extension of rank lumber, which he had helped erect five years ago. He negotiated the treacherous, sun-warped boards, stepping over gaping holes, and came to the system of pulleys he'd rigged up last year. He hauled, and far below a ripped square of netting emerged from the sea bearing its usual meagre haul of small fish. He transferred the catch to a bucket and carefully retreated to the shore.

He moved along to the desalination plant, which was a grand name for the pile of shuddering junk that O'Grady had patched together two years ago, a parting gift before he bailed out and escaped north.

The plant was powered by a shield array of solar panels, coruscating blindingly in the morning sun. Beneath them the rusting pipes and engines throbbed, taking salt from the seawater and pumping the resulting clear, but foul-tasting, water back up the beach to the irrigation system that helped keep Hendry's vegetable garden alive. There were a couple of litres left over every day for Hendry's consumption, which he drank in the form of dandelion tea.

He checked the plant half-heartedly, going over the list of details O'Grady had warned him about before his departure. O'Grady had been the community's engineer, and his loss had been a grave blow—one from which they had never recovered. Stella had died not long after and her husband, Greg, had reluctantly left Hendry and sailed east in a home-made ketch. Hendry often wondered what had become of the meteorologist. Had he ever made it to New Zealand, and the mountainous land of promise they had heard myths about on infrequent radio broadcasts from Dunedin?

The desalination plant was doing fine, a testament to O'Grady's engineering skills. Hendry turned and walked back up the beach. He'd try getting through to Chrissie again now, and if he did so he'd celebrate with grilled fish and salad for lunch.

He hurried through the booster gateposts and was approaching the shuttle when he heard the chime of the incoming call. He arrived breathless and dived at the rig. "Hendry here. Do you read?"

It took a second for the picture on the screen to clear, and even then it was furred with atmospheric interference.

A smiling face looked out at him, and Hendry shot forward on the couch, relief flooding through him like a drug. "Chrissie! For Chrissake, I thought... The bomb—"

"I know. That's why I called. I've just heard about it."

"You okay?" he asked, inanely. He realised that his eyes were filling with tears.

She smiled out at him. "I'm fine. Don't worry. I'm not in Europe."

"You're not?"

Her smile widened, mischievous. "I'm in Oz, Dad. Sydney."

"You're kidding, right? Why on earth...?" If she were in Sydney, then the chances were that she'd be down to see him soon.

"I heard about the bomb," he said, "tried to get through to you. You can't imagine how worried I was when you didn't answer."

"It's okay, Dad. I'm fine," she said.

He sat back in the chair and laughed.

She said, "It was the Fujiyama Green Brigade. They claimed responsibility for the bombing." She looked away uneasily, perhaps wondering if she should have mentioned the Brigade for fear of opening old wounds.

He stared at her. "It was? My God..."

Chrissie smiled and changed the subject. "You look a sight, Dad!"

"I do?" He looked down at himself. He was wearing sawn-off denims, and an old shirt, through which his pot belly protruded. On his head an ancient straw hat protected him from the sun. "Well, not many people around here now, so I don't dress for dinner."

"How many, Dad?"

He thought about lying, but decided against it. "Exactly one."

Her round face, slanted eyes, registered shock. "You're all alone?"

"And doing okay, Chrissie."

He thought she was about to suggest, again, that he join her in Berne. Her calculating look was that obvious. To her credit she didn't even try, this time.

She leaned forward. The picture broke up briefly, then re-formed. "You remember how we used to talk about the future of humankind?"

He smiled. He had brought her up alone, after her mother had walked out. Chrissie had gone through a phase in her teens when the state of the world, and the future of humanity, became her overriding concern. She'd corner him and talk for hours on end about where the planet was going.

"I remember."

"And you were always the optimist, Dad."

"And you the teenage pessimist."

She laughed. "And now? You still optimistic?"

Hendry smiled. "Well… it's hard to be optimistic these days, you know?" He stopped there. He didn't want to sound like the Jeremiahs of his youth: Chrissie was still young; the future was hers, what little there was left of it.

"Dad," she said, changing tack, "do you think humanity carries within it the seed of its own destruction? I mean, was it destined to end like this?

Are we so corrupt on the personal level that that is inevitably mirrored in society at large?"

"What have you been reading, Chrissie?"

His daughter worked as a botanist, battling to save flora endangered by the harsh climatic conditions. As she'd emerged from her teenage angst, she'd turned into a happy young woman who, despite all the evidence around her, always argued that there was hope.

"Answer the question, Dad."

"Okay, okay," he smiled and thought about it, then shrugged. "That's a hard one, Chrissie. But in general I'd say no, nothing is inevitable. Many people are corrupt, but many are not. Some societies down the ages have prospered, and would have continued to do so without despoiling the Earth, if not for other societies who gained pre-eminence." He shrugged. "Does that make disaster inevitable? It depends a lot on luck, the right breaks." He decided he was waffling, and shut up.

"What you're saying is that if we had it all over again, Dad, then with luck it might work out differently?"

He nodded, wondering where this was leading. "Yes, I guess so."

She smiled, and the smile sent a terrible pain through him, for there was only one world, and it was dying, along with everyone upon it, even his beautiful twenty-five year-old daughter.

"Thanks, Dad. That's what I think, too." She leaned forward, so that her face almost filled the screen. "Something's come up at this end. It's all top secret, hush-hush. I can't breathe a word of it over the link. But we're flying down to Victoria for more training, and I've wangled an hour off to see you. I'll be there around noon, okay?"

He was stunned. "Can't wait, Chrissie."

"Love you," she said, and her image vanished as she reached out and cut the connection.

Hendry went about in a daze for the rest of the day. He'd last seen Chrissie two years ago, when she'd managed the arduous trip and stayed with him for a fortnight. Back then the community had numbered ten, and had a vitality about it, though he'd seen how shocked she was at his living conditions.

Since then they'd communicated every month or so, she trying to get him to relocate to Berne, he resisting, but later wondering why.

Maybe it was because he didn't want to become emotionally reliant on Chrissie. He'd been down that road fifteen years ago with Chrissie's mother, Su, and then she'd walked out, left him to join a commune of neo-fascist Greens bent on the systematic assassination of industrialists.

It had taken a long time to get over that, and a long time to come to terms with being alone again when, five years ago, Chrissie left their home in Paris to attend university in Berne. Hendry had thought of going with her then, but something had drawn him south, to the land of his birth.

Later he went out into the garden, watched the sun go down and then began hoeing between the peas. He normally slipped into a mindless fugue while working in the garden, but this time his head was full of Chrissie's optimism. Something had come up, she'd said, something hush-hush. She'd wanted to know if humanity carried the seeds of their destruction within them... And her mention of a new beginning?

He wondered if, like her mother, she'd been lured into some fanatical cult promising redemption.

But she would tell him all about it tomorrow. That was more than Su had ever done. She'd walked out after dropping Chrissie off at school one morning, left him a note saying that she'd had enough of being married to a spacer and was leaving.

Slowly, he'd worked to overcome his rage, his hatred. He'd hired the services of a private detective, who'd traced her to the headquarters of a back-to-the-soil cult in Tokyo, the Fujiyama Green Brigade. Hendry had tried to contact her, but his calls and emails had gone unanswered. He'd even visited Tokyo in an attempt to track her down, but the cult was expert at covering the traces of its converts.

A couple of years later the detective had called Hendry and told him that his ex-wife had been killed in a terrorist raid on the headquarters of the American Space Administration.

Hendry had tried to find within himself some iota of grief, without success. In his mind, Su had become a different person when she'd left him, an inexplicable cipher brainwashed by monomaniacs, and not the woman he'd loved and married in his early twenties.

As the evening cooled, he stopped weeding and looked up at the looming shape of the shuttle, dark against the sunset. The sight brought back a slew of memories.

Hendry had spent fifteen years working for Space Oceana, a smartware engineer on the ships that made the short-hop Earth–L5–Mars runs. Then the collapse of '88 had bankrupted Space Oceana and every other private enterprise in space, and the colonies had been recalled, the L5s emptied, and a flood of refugees had returned to an impoverished Earth, their expertise of little use in a world rapidly reverting to pre-technological barbarity... or so it had seemed to Hendry.

Over the past seven years, the majority of the world's population had succumbed to drought, rising sea levels and resource wars. Many of those who had survived had fallen, eventually, to plagues both man-made and natural. Terrorist groups, working on the assumption that it was better for no one to have anything than for a few to have a little, had released deadly pathogens into the water supplies of the mega-cities in America and China, killing millions, while seeding the air with lab-developed viruses. No one knew the present population of planet Earth. Some said it might even be as low as a dozen or so millions.

Added to which, the ozone layer was in tatters, and the sea was poisoned, and plant-life was withering in the rising heat...

He got down on his hands and knees to remove the weeds the hoe had missed. Minutes later he found that he was weeping, large tears falling straight onto the soil and rapidly soaking in.

It often hit him like this, inexplicably and for no apparent reason. He supposed, this time, it had something to do with Chrissie's futile optimism. His own end, his own death somewhere down the line, he could deal with. But he found unbearable the thought of his daughter's inevitable death, in a terrible future much worse than the present, without him around to hold her and tell her that everything would be okay.

He stood up, clapped his hands together to get rid of the soil, and berated himself for being so negative. For how long had he expressed the philosophy that he should live for the day, without thought for tomorrow? He had brought Chrissie up with this ideal. Live for the present, gain the maximum enjoyment from now, and the future would cease to exist; it would become but an unfolding series of moments to be savoured.

He moved back into the shuttle, fixed himself some fish and roast potatoes.

That night, sleeping fitfully, he dreamed for the first time in years of his wife. In the nightmare, Su flew to Berne and attacked the Space Agency's headquarters, blowing herself up and taking Chrissie with her.

He woke in the early hours, sweating in fear, and then remembered that his daughter would be with him at noon.

## 2

HE AWOKE LATE. It was almost ten by the time he rolled from his bunk and showered in the makeshift cubicle he'd erected under the nose of the shuttle. He breakfasted on the salad left over from yesterday, then rooted through the storage units for the last of the coffee. Chrissie loved freshly ground coffee, one of the many rare commodities in Europe these days.

He left the shuttle and made his way through the garden, seeing the regimented rows of produce through Chrissie's eyes and feeling proud of his achievement.

The sea was as sluggish as ever, scummed with a meniscus of something oil-based. Recently his catch of fish and the occasional crab had diminished. There had been a time when the daily haul had easily fed the community of ten; now there was barely sufficient for himself. He dragged up the net and inspected the catch. Two catfish, and a baby snapper, which he threw back. It was better than nothing, he supposed, and would provide the makings of a decent lunch.

He checked the desalination plant—it throbbed away contentedly—then made his slow way back to the starship graveyard.

He grilled the fish, then fixed a fresh salad. When he looked up it was almost midday. He went out and sat in his chair beneath the awning, staring out across the flat, parched landscape and wondering from which direction Chrissie might come.

He wondered too how she might have changed in the two years since he'd last seen her in the flesh; the com-link was no indication, with its distorting static.

It was after twelve when he roused himself from his daydreams. He looked at his watch: quarter past. In the old days, when society had been dictated to by clocks and timetables, he might have worried, but in these days of ad hoc transport systems a delay of hours was not uncommon.

It was almost one when he heard the sound of chopper blades stropping the air. He stood and scanned the shimmering horizon. The helicopter was coming in low from the north, nose down. He watched it settle about a hundred metres beyond the perimeter fence of the graveyard. A tiny figure jumped out and ran doubled-up through the rotor's downdraught, waving briefly to the pilot. The chopper lifted, turned and swept away.

Chrissie began walking towards the dilapidated fence. Hendry went to meet her, something expanding in his chest and forcing tears into his eyes.

They stopped and stared at each other. Then Chrissie ran through the gap in the fence. Hendry grabbed her, feeling her solidity, the reality of the first human being he'd held since her last visit.

She pulled away, dashing tears from her eyes. "Look at me... I can't help it. There I was, saying I'd be all strong and unemotional! It's great to see you, Dad."

She was so like her mother; she had inherited Su's Japanese features, though tempered by his Caucasian genes; she was taller than Su had been, but carried herself with the same confidence and assurance.

He took her hand. "Come on. Let's get inside. I've fixed lunch. Catfish and salad—with real coffee."

"Real coffee? Dad, how on earth did you manage that?"

"Well, I know an exclusive supplier in town..."

He took her through the garden, proudly showing off the potato plants, the beanstalks heavy with pods. She smiled, suitably impressed.

She looked around at the derelict reminders of humankind's dream of conquering the solar system. The ships hulked against the blue sky, massive and ugly and yet, for some reason, oddly beautiful. Over the years the sun had excoriated their paintwork, continuing the work started by solar flares and hard radiation during the vessels' long service between the inner planets.

"And you're here all alone?" Chrissie asked. "What happened to... I forget their names?"

"O'Grady, Greg? They left, moved on. Stella died."

"I worry about you, you know?"

"Don't. I'm old enough to look after myself."

She laughed and they climbed into the shuttle.

She looked round the long lounge. He wondered if she was comparing it to her luxurious apartment back in Berne.

She said, "I only have an hour. I'm sorry. They're pretty strict."

"That's okay. We can talk over dinner."

She helped him prepare the food and carry it outside. They sat beneath the awning and sipped the freshly ground coffee.

"Okay, now. Out with it. What's it all about? This mission, the training." He shook his head. "You look, I don't know... like the cat who's got the cream."

"Do I? I hope that doesn't mean smug, self-satisfied."

"No, just contented. What's going on?"

She took another sip of coffee, sighed with pleasure. "That's good." She paused, then went on, "I'm glad you think there's hope, that we aren't doomed to repeat our mistakes. I think we've learned from them, so that we can move on, build a successful society that doesn't consume resources."

He thought he knew where this was leading. "They've tried colonies, Chrissie. Look what happened on Mars, Luna. Neither of them could sustain themselves. They were both dependent on Earth." He looked at her. She was smiling at him, blithely. "You are talking about a colony, aren't you?"

She nodded. "Of course. Where else could we start again, anew?"

"Chrissie..." He was aware of the despair in his tone.

"Listen, Dad. This is different."

"One of the moons of Jupiter, Saturn? Harnessing the power of the planet's radiation...?" He stopped, realising how improbable this was.

She was shaking her head. "Try further out."

"Further out?"

She leaned forward. "Dad, the European Space Organisation has developed a starship, a colony ship, to take four thousand specialists out of Sol system."

Staggered, he opened his mouth to say something, finally managing, "Ah... And to where, exactly?"

"Another star system, in Ophiuchi to begin with. The mission will last hundreds of years, maybe even thousands, travelling at around half the speed of light."

He said, "A colony ship? What do they call them, generation starships?"

She shook her head. "Not a generation ship. The colonists won't be conscious. They'll be in cold sleep, suspended animation. They'll be awoken at journey's end, when a habitable planet's been found."

"That's some undertaking."

"A last, desperate measure." She shrugged. "I was approached over a year ago by the ESO. They wanted people with my specialism."

He felt something surge through his head, rocking him. His vision blurred. He tried to pull himself together.

"Dad," she said, "you don't know how hard this is for me... When they asked me... at first I said no. It felt like treachery, deserting a sinking ship. Why me? Why not thousands of other people? I had an okay life in Europe... But then I began to think about it. A new beginning, a chance to start again, and this time do it right. They wanted me, and thousands like me, because we were at the top of our fields. The more I thought about it, the more I knew I had to go. Then I thought about you."

Despite his fear, despite the inner voice saying that he didn't want to lose his daughter, he found himself saying, "You have to go. If you didn't... you'd never forgive yourself. I can't hold you back—that'd be selfish."

She nodded, tears sparkling in her eyes. She looked up. "I knew you'd say that. I know I have to go. But it'll be so damned hard."

He stood and moved around the table and took her in his arms, wanting to break down himself but instead rocking her and reassuring her that she was doing the best thing.

They resumed their seats. Hendry ate without tasting a thing and Chrissie told him about the training she'd been doing for the past nine months. "Basic stuff, survival in extreme conditions, medical procedures. I'll be specialising in plant biology when we reach a habitable planet." She stopped and shook her head. "I get an odd feeling whenever I say that."

"When do you... when's the launch?"

"Well, we board the shuttle next week and ascend to the starship. Then we'll be put into the deep freezer, or rather the cryogenic units. But the ship itself won't be launched for six months after that. The techs need to iron out the bugs, check the systems."

"So after next week, for the next six months, you'll be in suspended animation." He tried to think about that, his daughter frozen in orbit high above the Earth.

"And then for... who knows how long? Certainly hundreds of years."

He would be long dead by then, and Earth would be a wasteland by the time she awoke, no older than when she had set off.

He said, "I didn't think they had the technology."

"It's been developed over the past ten years, when it became obvious that things were getting bad here. The ship was constructed in orbit. The fact wasn't broadcast."

Hendry smiled. "The Fujiyama Green Brigade would take a dim view."

"They're suspicious, which is why they bombed the ESO headquarters."

Hendry shook his head. "They were always fundamentally selfish," he said, and wondered if by that he meant that Su was too.

"The paradoxical thing is, Dad, that the ship's named after Lovelock, the eco-philosopher. The colony will be founded on principles mainly promulgated by him and his followers. The Fujiyama Green Brigade should be championing what we're doing, rather than trying to blow us up."

"Terrorism might start out with principles," he said, "but it finishes by being driven by nothing more than egoism. They can't go themselves, so they don't want anyone else to go."

She stared across the table at him. "You know something, Dad? I thought you'd object, take it badly. I mean... you lost Mum, and now I'm going—"

"The two are completely different!"

"Well, yes, but the end results are the same. We left you."

"Chrissie, Chrissie... You've got to do it. I'll be so proud of you." He smiled. "You know something?

When I was up there, pushing those shuttles between Earth and Mars, there wasn't a shift went by when I didn't think about the stars, the planets out there, the opportunities just waiting. And now my daughter's going to the stars..." And Christ, how I'll miss you, he thought, how bloody hard this goodbye will be.

"We're going to succeed, Dad. We're not going to make the same mistakes. We might be human, but that doesn't mean we'll take our flaws to the stars— or if we do, then we'll have systems in place to ensure that they don't destroy us, or our new world."

They finished the meal, Chrissie describing her training, the other specialists in her team. He listened to her words without really hearing them. But he watched her, he stared at her as she spoke, and realised how incredibly beautiful she was, and how much he loved her.

The sound of the chopper blatting through the hot air came as a shock. Hendry started, wishing that the last few minutes could have been extended for ever. The helicopter landed beyond the perimeter fence, and the sudden silence when its engines cut was almost as shocking as the sound of its arrival.

They stood, facing each other across the table, then moved around it and embraced.

"Oh, Dad, I wish it didn't have to be like this. I love you so much."

He felt so weak, so vulnerable, but for Chrissie's sake he held himself together. "Love you too," he whispered.

"I'll call you by com-link the day before I take the shuttle, okay?"

"I won't go out," he managed to joke.

The pilot leaned from the helicopter's bubble fuselage and waved.

They walked to the torn perimeter fence, hand in hand. He paused there, but she pulled him after her.

Before the chopper, the ugly vehicle that would carry her away, they stopped and faced each other. "Dad..."

"Go on," he said. "Good luck. Name a planet after me. Discover an alien race..."

"I love you."

"Love you too, Chrissie. Go on..."

They held on tight, then she broke away with a sob, ran to the helicopter and dived inside.

It jumped into the air, blasting him. He backed off, waving.

Chrissie was a tiny figure next to the pilot, waving frantically at him.

The helicopter turned tail and fled, and Hendry watched it until it was a tiny comma on the horizon. Seconds later it had vanished from sight. He wanted to yell, "No!" and deny the fact that he would never again hold his daughter.

He returned to the shuttle, a pain like grief excavating a hollow in his chest. He kicked out at the shuttle's dented engine nacelle and cried out loud. There was so much he wanted to say to her, so much he had to tell her, so much left unsaid. He wanted an age in which to simply stare at the reality that was Chrissie Hendry. It was impossible to conceive that she would exist only in his thoughts and memories, now.

He moved into the shuttle and wept.

## 3

THE DAYS AFTER Chrissie's last visit were the bleak-
est of his life, emptier even than the empty days after
Su had left him. He'd had Chrissie then to fill his
time, his thoughts. Now he had nothing. He maintained the routine of his days through habit, but the
tasks which before had filled him with satisfaction—
the hoeing, the examination of his haul of fish—now
only served to point up the fact of his loneliness.

It tortured him to think that, soon, she would be
frozen for the duration of his life. In hundreds of
years, maybe even thousands, she would be awok-
en... It was not knowing what might become of her
that was so galling. She was his daughter, whom he
had spent a good part of his life protecting, ensuring her physical and mental well being. To lose
control of that, to know that at some point in the
future she would be in danger and he wouldn't be
around to help... This kept him awake long into the
hot early hours of the long nights.

Four days after her visit, the com chimed at nine.
Thinking it was Old Smith, he accepted the call and
sat back in the couch.

Chrissie's face materialised on the screen, hazy with static, and the sight of her took his breath away.

"Dad, I said I'd call."

"Chrissie…" He was totally unprepared, at a loss how to respond.

Her image wavered, flickered. The line was particularly bad tonight.

She appeared again, smiling. "I'm fine. Everything's going great up here."

"Up here? You're aboard the ship?" The knowledge, for some bizarre reason, distressed him. He had thought she was still on Earth, that there was still some geographical connection between them, however tenuous.

"I'm in the com-room of the *Lovelock*. I'm going under in…" She checked her watch. "In about two hours. I know it's painful for you, but I said I'd call one last time."

He smiled. He hoped that his image was as hazy as hers, for he was weeping again. "I'm fine. Shooting the breeze with Old Smith in Tasmania, growing my peas…"

"Dad, I love you…"

"And I…" He stopped. Her face vanished. He leaned forward in panic. "Chrissie!"

She appeared again. "The link's breaking up. I've almost had my allotted time. I'm thinking of you always. I love you…"

"Chrissie, take care. I—"

"Dad!" she cried, as her image fragmented. He had a last fleeting image of her, reaching out, the pink of her face rendered in tiny pixelated rectangles, a cubist representation of frozen anguish.

Then the screen blanked and Hendry leaned forward and called her name, attempting to re-establish the link.

He sat before the screen for a long time, hoping against hope that she would be able to contact him again, wanting it but knowing that it would only prolong the torture.

At last he pushed himself from the couch and stumbled outside. He sat in his chair beneath the awning and watched the sun set, its glare made spectacular by atmospheric pollutants. He recalled what she'd said, and looked at his watch. In a few minutes she would be put under, frozen in a suspension unit. He imagined her lying there, thinking of him, wondering about her uncertain future.

He glanced at his watch. She would be unconscious now, cryogenically suspended. When she woke up it would be as if no time at all had elapsed for her, while he would have lived his life and died long ago.

He looked up, into the deepening dark of the night sky, and searched for the tiny speck that would be the *Lovelock*. He should have asked her where it would be, so that he could have watched its daily orbit and then, in six months, raised a glass to her as the starship lighted out of Earth orbit and began its long journey to the stars.

He saw nothing that might be the starship.

That night he dreamed that Chrissie had died in her suspension unit, and he awoke in a sweat. All the next day he catalogued the myriad fates that might befall her. Every possibility, he realised, was valid when viewed in ignorance—and that was what tortured him.

The following day he didn't bother going down to the sea to fetch the fish and check the desalination plant. He didn't even venture out into the garden, the first time he had missed doing so in years. It all seemed so pointless. Why was he living like this, alone, in hardship, waiting out his days until incapacity claimed him and he died a slow and lonely, painful death.

But what was the alternative? He could venture out into the real world of people and communities, but that would only be to confront the ravaged mess the world had become. He had run away and come here to get away from all that... So why was he going on, day after day, living the same futile, repetitious existence?

That evening Old Smith called. They chatted for an hour, the old man telling Hendry in great detail how he'd built three new beehives that morning and transferred a queen to each.

Then Old Smith said, "Hendry... look, you're all alone over there. There's ten of us here. We're all getting on, and we have our bad days, but we're a good crowd, and things aren't too bad here. We have a big garden you could help keep up..."

Hendry smiled sadly, knowing that the haziness of the link would hide the quality of the smile: Old Smith might even interpret it as grateful.

"You know something, Smith? I'll think about it. Thank you. I could do with a change." But even as he said the words he knew he had no intention of ever leaving the shuttle.

Two days later, unable to rouse himself to check the desalination plant, or to fetch the fish from the jetty, he sat in his armchair and stared at the rotting salad in the bowl. The day was hot. The sun seemed huge, as if it had had enough of planet Earth, and man's folly, and was intent on burning it up. The garden, irrigated automatically from the pumps, flourished—but even this depressed Hendry, pointed up the fact of his isolation.

He moved into the shuttle and rooted around in a storage unit. He knew it was around here somewhere... O'Grady had insisted they kept it handy, in case of marauding strangers. They had never had occasion to use it.

He found the rifle and took it outside, along with a box of cartridges. He sat with the gun on his lap for a long time, the very image of a protective homesteader of old.

What did it matter if he ended it now, or if death came in some other manner years down the line?

Chrissie would never know, would not suffer grief at his action. His bones would have long crumbled, in situ, by the time she was awoken from suspension.

He broke the rifle and inserted two cartridges into the barrels. Then he sat a while longer, staring at the sun as it fell towards the horizon.

It would all have been different if Su hadn't been lured away by those green fanatics, if she had stayed loving him and his daughter. But she went for a reason, he told himself. She was lured away by something that he could not provide, some longed-for fulfilment of the soul.

He looked at the gun, tested the feel of it against his temple, but the act of having to hold it at arm's length in order for the barrel to touch his temple and his finger to find the trigger, seemed slightly ludicrous. With the barrels inserted into his mouth, in the classic method, the pose seemed even more ridiculous, some futile fellatio more comic than tragic.

He lowered the rifle and smiled to himself. It was as if the act of playing out the taking of his life had served as some form of catharsis. Bizarrely, he felt hungry. He realised that he had not eaten properly for days.

He set the gun aside and hurried into the garden.

A day later something happened which made him look back at the failed suicide and shudder with the thought that, if some tiny thing had been different, if some brain chemistry had been slightly altered, he would never have lived to experience this miraculous salvation.

## 4

IN THE MORNING he walked down to the sea and checked the net. The catch was the smallest yet, a stunted crab and a couple of small catfish. He tipped them all back and walked on to the desalination plant, which was throbbing away as steadily as ever. He made his way back to the shuttle, planning the vegetables he would pick for lunch and dinner. In the garden, unearthing a good crop of new potatoes, he thought about Old Smith and his offer last night.

The idea of sharing his emotions with the people in the Tasmanian commune, who would inevitably want to know about his past life, did not appeal. The lonely life suited him. He was through with the idea of becoming emotionally attached to anyone. That had only brought him pain in the past. He would tell Old Smith, next time they spoke, that he had worked too hard at making the graveyard viable to abandon it now.

Having come to this decision, he felt relieved. He could look ahead, perhaps extend the garden, try out a few new vegetables, the seeds of which he had stored in the cooler. He would while away his days listening to classical music and reading his way through the shuttle's extensive library, thinking about the good times he'd shared with Chrissie.

The heavy blatt of a helicopter's rotor blades startled him. He laid aside the handful of potatoes he was unearthing and squinted in the direction of the noise. It was coming in low from the north, the vehicle as far as he could tell identical to the one Chrissie had arrived in over a week ago.

His initial thought was that Chrissie had changed her mind, was not leaving Earth aboard the starship. His heart leapt, until his head gained control. She would have called to tell him of this decision, not arrived out of the blue like this.

He stood and moved towards the derelict perimeter fence, staring across the intervening fifty metres of scrub to where the chopper had set down, its stilled rotors drooping like palm fronds.

A suited figure climbed down from the fuselage, spoke briefly with the pilot, and turned to stare at Hendry. He walked towards the graveyard, clutching a slim black briefcase under his arm. The sight of such a dapper figure in this blasted landscape was at once incongruous and alarming.

Something's gone wrong, Hendry thought. The cryogenic process malfunctioned, killing Chrissie, and this suit has come to apologise on behalf of the ESO and offer statutory compensation.

The man was slim and very blond, and wore a pair of wraparound sunglasses that made his expression— aided by an unsmiling mouth—inscrutable.

He stopped before the fence, staring at Hendry. "You are Joseph Charles Hendry, date of birth 24th

May 2052?" The words, delivered in a harsh Germanic accent, seemed absurd.

"What do you want?"

"I am Gert Bruckner of the European Space Organisation."

"It's about Chrissie. What's happened?"

"This matter does not concern your daughter, Mr Hendry. She is fine." He turned his head to the left slightly, staring past Hendry to the shuttle. Perspiration stood out on his blond, reddening brow. "If we might get out of the sun…"

Hendry relented, moved aside and gestured Bruckner to follow him. When they reached the shuttle he indicated a chair beneath the awning, wondering what the hell a representative from the ESO might want with him.

He fixed a jug of cold camomile tea and sat across the table from Bruckner.

He poured and looked up. "How can I help you?"

Bruckner laid his briefcase on the table, unclipped it and withdrew a sheaf of papers. He leafed through them, concentrating on certain paragraphs, as if familiarising himself with details. He took a sip of camomile tea.

"Mr Hendry, you served with Space Oceana for ten years from '78 to early '89, a smartware engineer on shuttles."

"What about it?"

Bruckner glanced at a printed form. "You served with distinction, worked hard, even instituted design improvements on a couple of parallel systems—"

"It was my job, before things went belly up."

Bruckner nodded. For all the emotion he evinced, he might have been an automaton. "Those good old days of solid fuel," he said without emotion, and Hendry wondered if the line was a quote.

Bruckner went on, "How would you like that job back, Mr Hendry?"

Surprising himself, Hendry laughed. It was impossible, of course. Why would the ESO be starting up shuttle runs again? And to where? The Mars and Moon colonies were long abandoned... Unless there was a plan to recolonise. But it would never work.

"I don't understand. The colonies... I mean, why would the ESO be recruiting shuttle engineers?"

Bruckner stared at him, his expression neutral. "We aren't, Mr Hendry."

"In that case, will you please explain yourself?"

Bruckner nodded, took another sip of cold tea. He replaced the glass precisely upon the condensation circle it had formed on the tabletop. "Mr Hendry, the ESO in Berne suffered a terrorist attack two weeks ago. We lost a number of clerical personnel in the bombing, and five technicians."

"I heard about it. So..."

"So, we need to replace those technicians."

"But the ESO doesn't fly shuttles anymore," Hendry said. He saw himself reflected in Bruckner's lenses. The man stared at him, his mouth set.

"We need the engineers not for shuttles, but for a project that until now has remained—or so we thought—top secret."

Hendry thought he was about to suffer a coronary. Something tightened in his chest. He felt dizzy. "What project?"

Bruckner said, "The ESO is sending a starship, the *Lovelock*, on a mission to colonise the stars. It is—and this might be construed as a melodramatic way of putting it—Earth's last hope." For the first time, Bruckner smiled. "But I think your daughter..." he referred to his papers, "Christine, might have mentioned something about it?"

Hendry said, "How could she keep quiet when she would never see me again?"

"Well... perhaps now, if you accept the commission, your daughter *will* see you again."

His heart thudded. All this was happening too fast. It was as if his emotions had to play catch up with what his head was telling him.

"I... But why me? Why not any of the dozens of other younger smartware—?"

Bruckner cut in, "They're dead, in one or two cases not interested. Your credentials are impeccable. You are the logical choice."

Hendry just shook his head.

Bruckner went on, "We've recruited four specialists so far to replace the five murdered. One survived without injuries. The six, when the *Lovelock* lights out, will form the maintenance crew that will be resurrected from cold sleep at journey's end to run a series of checks on the smartware systems and to bring the ship down."

"This is incredible," Hendry murmured to himself.

Chrissie... Chrissie was not lost to him. If he accepted the commission, then one day, in the far future, they would be reunited. He tried to envisage her surprise and joy.

"This is for real, not some sick joke?"

In reply Bruckner took a metallic card from the breast-pocket of his suit and passed it to Hendry. He tried to read the print, but his vision blurred.

"My identification. You can access the relevant data if you have an up-to-date com-system."

"Okay... okay, so the *Lovelock* is heading for the stars. What are the chances of finding somewhere habitable? Surely pretty low?" Not that this, he thought, would be any deterrent to his accepting he job. His reward would be to have Chrissie again.

"The *Lovelock* will be heading for a star system a little over five hundred light years from Earth. Before the Mars colony was disbanded, radio telescopes gathered data on Zeta Ophiuchi, a blue main sequence star. We processed the data after the withdrawal, and discovered that the star possesses a planet, which, from spectrographic analysis, is a good candidate for habitation. This will be the *Lovelock*'s first port of call."

Hendry nodded, attempting to come to terms with what Bruckner was telling him.

A purpose to life, after so long without one. A chance to be with Chrissie, to build a colony out there among the stars...

"When do you need my reply, Mr Bruckner?"

The official indicated his card. "My details are there," he said. "If you contact me within the next two days, shall we say, we can send a helicopter for you. There will be a period of training in Berne before departure. Contractual details will be discussed in Berne, should you accept the offer."

Bruckner stood, inclined his head, and indicated a sheaf of paper on the tabletop. "Read through the mission synopsis before you contact me." He paused, then said, "Goodbye, Mr Hendry. I hope we meet again."

Hendry watched him go, step carefully over the remains of the fence, and cross to the helicopter. Seconds later the chopper took off, whisking Bruckner away. Hendry watched it, snickering over the parched brush, and wondered if he'd dreamed the conversation.

That night Old Smith contacted him again. "Well, given any more thought to the offer?"

"I thought about it long and hard, Smith. But something's just come up. My daughter wants me to join her."

"And you're going?" Old Smith looked crestfallen.

Hendry smiled. "It's an offer too good to refuse," he said.

"So you're going up to Switzerland?"

Hendry smiled. "Somewhere up there," he said.

They chatted a while longer before Old Smith waved a frail hand. "Good luck on the journey, Hendry. It's a long way…"

# 5

THE HELICOPTER FERRIED him as far as Sydney—now little more than a fortified military base—from where an ESO sub-orb ship carried him the rest of the way to Europe. Strapped into the acceleration couch behind the taciturn pilot, Hendry had the very real sense that he was indeed going to the stars. The chopper ride to Sydney had failed to bring home to him the fact of where he was going, merely what he was leaving. Now, cocooned by the high-tech apparatus of space flight, much of which was familiar but a lot of which had been developed since his days in space, he knew that what Bruckner had told him was, amazingly, true: he was going to be frozen in a suspension unit and fired off to the stars. The fact brought home to him the immense privilege of being saved like this, and at the same time what a small cog he was in the vast, impersonal machine of the European Space Organisation's colonisation mission.

The sub-orb ride took five hours. From an altitude of 40,000 feet, planet Earth looked little different from how it had appeared fifty years ago, a little greyer, perhaps, and the landmasses reconfigured thanks to the rising tides. But at lower altitude, after take-off from Sydney and when coming in low over southern Europe, the full effect of global warming could be seen: the sere land, denuded of vegetation, with not a tree in sight. The cities were static, roads broken like fragile threads, buildings derelict.

At the midpoint of the journey, as they were sailing high over Southern Asia and the Middle East, the pilot spoke for the first time. "That's India down there, or what's left of it. A billion dead. A country wiped out." He grunted. "Only the temples are left standing."

"Plague?" Hendry asked.

"And civil war, and drought."

A while later the pilot commented, "To your left. That was Israel, Jordan, Syria and all the rest. It's a no-go area now. Nothing lives down there, not after the nuke wars."

From the air, the devastated region gave the paradoxical impression of calm, a geographical serenity not matched by a century of conflict culminating in the mutually destructive war of '75.

Italy was a parched wasteland, its surviving population having fled north a decade ago. Only as the sub-orb screamed in over Austria did a kind of normality return—though that was deceptive. Despite the sight of lush green valleys down there, Hendry knew that Austria was no longer a functioning state; like eighty per cent of other European countries, it had suffered from civil wars, plagues, societal breakdown due to the more invidious malaise of mass unemployment as, one by one, services necessary for the smooth running of a modern industrial state had ceased functioning.

Switzerland was a fortified enclave populated by the rich and the privileged, and the lucky—those who had found themselves in the right place at the right time: Chrissie, for example. It was ironic that the Swiss state, for so long neutral and without an army, now possessed the largest fighting force in the northern hemisphere—employed to patrol the borders and keep undesirables out.

Hendry was taken by armed convoy from the spaceport to the ESO headquarters, a journey of some half a kilometre through what looked like a shantytown of ad hoc buildings and listless citizens roasting in the midday heat.

His driver saw him staring. "Mainly Italian and Greek refugees," he said. "They work in the factories, what few are still running."

By contrast, the ESO compound was an oasis of modern brick buildings equipped with air-conditioning. He was shown to an apartment overlooking a swimming pool, in which tanned, healthy-looking Europeans disported themselves.

He underwent a comprehensive medical check-up later that afternoon, conscious for the first time in years of his middle-age gut and general level of unfitness. "We'll soon knock you into shape," the medic joked. "Now let's have a look at your head." For the next hour he suffered tedious probes and prods as a neuroscientist checked the functioning of his implants, the sub-dermal receptor sites set flush to his skull that allowed him to interface with shipboard smartware. It had been one of his fears that recent developments in that area might have rendered his hardware obsolete—but the head-tech assured him that he had nothing to worry about. There had been **precious** few innovations in that area for **at** least ten years.

**The** following morning, at breakfast, he met Bruckner again. The man was just as impeccably attired, and still insisted on wearing his trademark wraparound shades.

He drank orange juice across the table from Hendry and gave an outline of what the new arrival was to expect over the next few days. He would undergo basic training—nothing that should prove too taxing, given his prior experience in space—along with a regime of physical exercise. Before all that, he would meet his five colleagues in the maintenance team. In a little under a week they would take a shuttle up to the *Lovelock*, where cryo-technicians would put them under for the long sleep.

"And you?" Hendry asked as Bruckner was about to rise and leave.

The official smiled and resumed his seat. "You mean, am I coming along?" He shook his head. "I applied but was rejected. Middle-management hacks are not in high demand for the colony the ESO plans for out there."

"I'm sorry."

Bruckner nodded. "But if you think I'm doing this out of altruism, well…"

Hendry wondered what possible reward there might be, other than job satisfaction, in working on a project like this.

Bruckner went on, "This is the low-down, Hendry. Switzerland as a functioning state is dead, kept alive artificially by the ESO. And even our time is finite. We have contingency plans, however; islands north of Denmark, where we've started self-sufficient colonies. When the *Lovelock* launches and things get too bad here, we plan to evacuate there and try to keep some semblance of culture alive." He shrugged. "For how long, I don't know. Put it this way, my wife and I don't plan to have children. And if that seems cynical... well, you think what it might be like to remain behind."

"Touché," Hendry said.

After breakfast he was introduced to Sissy Kaluchek and Lisa Xiang, respectively a cryogenics specialist and a pilot. They were in the gym, going through the series of set callisthenics devised by the physio. They broke off to come over, introduce themselves and chat awhile. The rest of the team, they explained, had been passed fit and rewarded with a day off.

Kaluchek was a tiny Inuit, whose wide dark eyes and high cheekbones—and the fact that she was perhaps fifteen years his junior—reminded him of Chrissie. He liked her immediately, something confiding in her hesitant smile and softly spoken demeanour. Xiang was in her late thirties, a muscular Taiwanese whose forthright manner struck Hendry, after so little human contact for years, as disconcertingly abrasive. "Welcome to the team," she said in a strong Californian accent. "We call ourselves the second-stringers. I mean, lucky, or what?"

Kaluchek rolled her eyes. "You call us the second-stringers," she corrected.

That evening they sat around a table beside the pool as waiters served them the finest food Hendry had eaten in years, and he met two further members of the team.

Greg Cartwright was a bright-eyed American pilot, impossibly young, who gave the impression of being overawed by the fact that he'd been being plucked from oblivion and sent to the stars, granted, as it were, a second chance. He chattered happily about the mission, going over the smartware programs with an enthusiasm the others found obviously amusing.

Friday Olembe, by contrast, was in his late thirties and taciturn—and the little he did say struck Hendry as cynical.

The African listened to Cartwright enthusing about what they might discover out there, then said, "So even if we do find a habitable planet, what's the chances of us not messing it up like we did this one?"

Cartwright opened his mouth to speak, but fell silent as Xiang looked up. "Haven't you read the mission brief, Olembe?"

"From beginning to end, boss." The way he emphasised the last word suggested to Hendry that Olembe had an issue with the Taiwanese woman's role as team leader.

"Then you obviously didn't take in the way we're going to go about building a new society, did you?"

Olembe stared at her. "So many words. I heard similar words from the UN about Africa, years back. And we got fucked over royally, even so."

Xiang shook her head. "There's a big difference now. No one else is in control. We are. Our destiny's in our own hands."

The African pulled a face. "Give me a break. You're beginning to sound just like the mission brief, Xiang."

Hendry noticed Kaluchek staring at Olembe with ill-concealed dislike. "And you," she said, "are full of shit."

Olembe was about to reply, but stopped himself as a tall woman walked to the table carrying a tray. She had an oval face, dark hair drawn back, and moved with the poise of a ballerina. She set her tray beside Hendry, nodding to him in greeting and said, "Carrelli, team medic."

Xiang said, "If you're so down on our chances out there, Olembe, why did you accept the position?"

Everyone around the table turned to look at him. Olembe simply shrugged and said, "You been to Lagos recently?"

The Italian medic sat back, watching the exchange. She said nothing, but calmly ate her meal. Hendry wondered how much her insularity was a personal characteristic, and how much the consequence of being the sole survivor of the terrorist bomb that had killed her five former team members.

That night Hendry sat beside the pool, alone. Over the past few years he'd never given much thought to the heavens, other than gazing once or twice at the full moon, and the red spark of Mars on the horizon. Now he stared up at the magnificent spread of the Milky Way and found it impossible to credit that soon—subjectively, at any rate—he would be out there among those burning points of light.

# Two /// Agstarn

## I

Ehrin Telsa left his mother's mansion and skated along the ice canal between the looming, monolithic buildings that crowded the centre of the city. Agstarn was quiet this early, just after dawn in the second month of deep winter, and few citizens braved the razor winds that sliced down from the surrounding mountains. Those who did venture out wore padding so thick they resembled globular summer fruit. The only creatures that could go abroad without some form of protection were the stolid zeer, great shaggy beasts used by the jockeys to haul carts and taxi-sledges. They plodded slowly along the canals, their breath misting the air like ectoplasm and their manure, dropped prodigally all along their route, melting the ice and creating hazardous potholes.

Ehrin kept an eye out for these pitfalls, but his thoughts were elsewhere. His mother had died a week earlier, after a long illness, though Ehrin had found it hard to mourn the passing of the woman whose heart had been as hard and unyielding as the glacial ice that surrounded the city in deep winter. It was what she had told him on her deathbed, and his subsequent discovery, that unsettled him now.

One week ago, hours from death, she had gripped his hand and raised herself with the fanatical strength of the dying and stared into his eyes. "Your father was a strong man, Ehrin. He had principles. But sometimes principles can be your undoing. He defied the Church to his cost…" And here, to Ehrin's exasperation, and despite his prompting, she had relapsed into a fitful sleep. She regained consciousness only once more, to rant incomprehensibly about vengeful Church militia, before her breath rattled like a ratchet in her throat and her eyes glazed like turned zeer milk.

During the days that followed, through his mother's bleak interment in the permafrost of the central cemetery and after, he had dwelt on her words.

The subtext was that Ehrin's father had defied the Church on principle, and suffered. But how had he suffered? He had owned the biggest dirigible company in the city, supplying the Church itself with the machines, and had owned a great mansion on Kerekes Boulevard overlooking the winter gardens. He had been a genial, happy man right to the end… He had died test-flying an experimental dirigible when Ehrin was ten, and the loss had affected Ehrin in two ways: he had experienced a physical pain as if something had been torn from the cavity of his chest, and mentally he had resolved to continue his father's work, to make the Telsa Dirigible Company even bigger and better.

Late last night, while going through his mother's hoarded belongings, he had happened upon a sheaf of letters from his father, which she had kept tied with string in a locked chest in the attic.

The return address of one particular letter had caught his attention and sent his heart racing. He had never known that his father had travelled beyond the confining mountains of Agstarn, but here was an envelope bearing the address of Sorny on the very edge of the western plains—and presumably delivered the two thousand miles to Agstarn by carrier hawk.

The letter had been surprisingly brief. Dated fifteen years earlier—just months before his father's death—it was barely a page long and described the living conditions in the town of Sorny, on the edge of the circumferential sea. But more interesting than the litany of hardships his father was undergoing was what he read in the final few lines: "I have neither the space nor the time to describe here the terrible things K and I have seen today. That will have to wait until I'm with you again. With all my love, Rohan..."

*The terrible things...* What can his father have meant? Ehrin had gone through the other letters his father had sent from Sorny, had discovered nothing other than the gruelling conditions suffered by the expeditionary force and the locals. Could it be this that his father referred to, the starvation, the attention of wild animals from the ice plains?

With his father dead, and now his mother, it would appear that the secret had died with them... but for that mention of K.

Could it be, Ehrin wondered, that the mysterious K was none other than Kahran Shollay, his father's business partner and now Ehrin's partner in the Telsa Dirigible Company?

As he took a sharp bend in the ice canal, heading for the foundry on the edge of town, Ehrin was aware of the letter in his jacket pocket, like a burning coal next to his heart.

The foundry occupied the last three blocks of a terrace of ancient mills on one of the oldest ice canals in Agstarn. His father had once explained that the foundry had to be positioned on the edge of town so that the dirigibles, once constructed, could be launched without the hindrance of surrounding buildings: the entire west-facing wall at the end of the terrace was a vast sliding door, through which the magnificent dirigibles were inched, with much pomp and fanfare, on the day of their maiden flights.

It was a dark, dour industrial area, the surrounding stonework stained with the coal dust of centuries. Against this, the bright fires of the foundry showed cheerily through doors and windows along the length of the building. Within the foundry, the tiny figures of workers could be seen going about their business, dwarfed by the smelting ovens, the mammoth crucibles and the rearing skeletons of the partially completed dirigibles.

Ehrin skated towards the entrance, kicked off his skates and hurried into the fierce heat of the shop floor.

He was sweating within seconds, perspiration running into his eyes and creating an impressionistic blur of half-naked workers toiling in hellish conditions. He tore off his padded jacket and climbed the wooden steps that gave on to the office area. Kahran was not at his desk this morning, and Ehrin wondered if he had fallen ill again. Approaching one hundred, Kahran was stubbornly proud of his health and fitness, though of late he had succumbed to a succession of viral infections. Ehrin had been unable to tell the old man to slow down, take it easy: Telsa Dirigibles was Kahran's life. While most men of his age had retired gracefully, Kahran refused to let up and came into work nine days of the week.

Ehrin passed through the offices and came to a second flight of stairs, which gave access to the long attic that for five years, since coming of age and inheriting the company, Ehrin had made his home. It was crammed with overstuffed armchairs and sofas, and lined with rickety bookshelves; many of the old tomes had been his fathers, dry engineering treatises alongside more readable accounts of adventures in the eastern and western plains.

A semicircular window looked out over the outskirts of the city and the towering peaks of the western mountains. Before it Ehrin had placed his favourite armchair, in which he spent most of his working day going over paperwork, checking blueprints and poring over the order books.

He smiled at the irony. As a boy he had dreamed of adventure, fancied himself as an explorer blazing a trail in one of his father's skyships, opening up the land to east and west... Instead, he had become an engineer, and not even a hands-on engineer at that; the responsibilities of running the family business had taken him from the shop floor, even from the drawing office, and tethered him to his father's desk, which he had lately abandoned for the more comfortable haven of his armchair. His younger self would have snorted in contempt.

He watched the occasional dirigible float over the city, proud that the majority of the ships were of his own, or his father's design. There was another airship company in Agstarn, run by an old rival of his father's, but their ships were inferior products, "Full of stale farts and bad technology," as his father had joked on more than one occasion.

He looked across the dim room, to the desk on which stood the black and white photograph of Rohan Telsa. He was dressed in a severe full-length summer coat, high white collar and stove-pipe hat, but the formal dress did nothing to quench the fire of geniality in the old man's eyes.

Ehrin, surprisingly, found himself choked with emotion. His father had died fifteen years ago, and he thought he had overcome his grief. Perhaps he was weeping for his mother, for the loss of both his parents, for the fact that he was now alone in the world. How proud his father would have been of him, and how they would have discussed their latest airships long into the early hours.

He chastised himself for his self-pity: he was not alone at all, for he had Sereth, his fiancée—and how she would have remonstrated with him at his display of piteous emotion.

He heard the door creak, followed by a discreet clearing of an old throat.

"Kahran, come in." He turned and watched the old man, bent almost double now, advance across the threadbare carpet. Ehrin indicated the second armchair, and beside it the decanter of spirit, and Kahran smiled at the invitation.

How age had ambushed his father's business partner, folding his spine and greying the fur of his face. His breath came in laboured wheezes as he took his seat and carefully poured himself a tot of spirit.

"To the Company," he said, and raised his glass high. Three fingers of his gnarled right hand were without nails, stumps that appeared obscenely naked. Ehrin recalled that his father's hands also bore testimony to his days on the shop floor of the foundry—doing the manual work that Ehrin, as the scion of the Telsa family, had been spared.

Ehrin smiled and said, "To the Company," and wondered at asking Kahran about his father's letter—and about what his mother had told him on her deathbed: that his father had defied the Church to his cost.

He was wondering how to frame the question when Kahran said, "When are you expecting the word, Ehrin?"

The question caught him unawares for a second, until realisation came: recent events, his mother's death and the discovery of the letter, had pushed from his mind the tender his company had put in to prospect the plains to the west of the central mountains.

"Today," he replied, "if indeed today is the thirty-third."

Kahran's thin smile hyphenated his sunken cheeks. "It is..." He paused, then said, "And if you win the tender?"

"If *we* win the tender," he corrected the old man gently. "Why, what do you think? We will go ourselves, on the adventure of a lifetime, and make the company even richer and greater than ever."

Old grey eyes watched him with a hint of censure. "And for ever be in the talons of the Church."

Ehrin shook his head. "The Church runs everything, rules everything, knows everything, Kahran. There's no getting away from that. Whatever we do, we are inextricably bound with the Church."

Kahran looked away. "How your father would hate to hear you speaking thus," he said with bitterness.

"I'm being realistic, Kahran. Perhaps it was different in my father's younger days. Perhaps the Church has gained in power over the past decades. The fact remains, I'm no pious worshipper at their totalitarian altar. I despise their methods as much as you do, but I'm in business and responsible for the livelihood of hundreds of workers, and if the Church sees fit to commission the expedition..." His shrug eloquently completed his statement.

"You'll take the commission, submit to the dictates of the Prelate, no matter what burdensome stipulations they impose upon the company?"

"Now you impute that which is not yet stated," Ehrin began. "What stipulations?"

The old man shrugged. "The Church will guide with a draconian hand, as is their way. They will demand an exorbitant share of the profits, or dictate exactly where you might prospect, and where is out of bounds."

Ehrin open his mouth to argue, but thought better. Here was the opening he needed to question his grizzled business partner.

"Kahran, years ago—back in 1265—you accompanied my father on an expedition to the eastern plains. Was this backed by the Church?"

The question was needless—the Church oversaw all travel beyond the central mountains.

"Of course. What of it?"

Ehrin gestured. "Then you went quite willingly, with no scruples about Church intervention?"

Kahran stared into his drink. "It was different, back then."

"The Church was less powerful?"

The silence stretched, and Ehrin sensed something. There was a tension in the air. It was as if Kahran wanted to tell him something, even though years of conditioning had taught him the wisdom of keeping quiet.

At last he said, "No, the Church was just as powerful then as it is now."

"So why didn't you object then?" Ehrin cried.

Bleak eyes, as grey as old snow, regarded him. "I did," the old man said in a small voice.

"And... ?"

"I voiced my objections to your father, in this very room. In fact, he was seated in the very chair you occupy now."

"My father was never a lover of the Church—but he argued against your objections?"

Kahran shook his head. "No, he agreed with me."

"I don't understand. In that case, why did he agree to go?"

Kahran took a mouthful of spirit, then said, "He didn't *agree* to go. Your father had no say in the matter. When the Church wanted to mount an expedition, they came to him. They requisitioned five ships, your father and myself, and we could only agree to go along."

"And if you hadn't agreed?"

Kahran shook his head. "Then it would have been the freezing frames for us, my boy. And even I, who loathed the Church and everything it stood for, didn't want my carcass stripped and lashed to a frame for all my detractors to piss on."

Ehrin let the silence stretch. He thought of his father's letter. At last he said, "What did you see, out there on the shore of the western plains?"

For a brief second, it was as if Kahran's opalescent irises saw not the glass he was clutching in his claw, but whatever they had beheld out there on the ice, fifteen years ago. Then he looked up and said sharply, "Who says we saw anything?"

Ehrin smiled. He had to tell the old man about the letter. He had come so far, got Kahran to open up about the Church—which he had been loath to do before now.

"Kahran, last night I read something in a letter, sent by my father from Sorny."

Kahran looked up, animated in way he had not been until now. "What did he say?" he demanded. "If it was incriminatory, then lose not a second and destroy the letter."

The old man's vehemence unsettled Ehrin. "My father merely wrote that he had seen something... something terrible. He mentioned you."

Kahran's eyes penetrated Ehrin like an ice-fisher's harpoon. "Did he say what he had seen?"

"No. That is, he merely said that you had both seen something terrible. He told my mother that he would tell her more when he returned."

"And that was all? No more?"

"No more. I swear."

Kahran nodded. "Good. That's good. Thank the mountains he was wise enough to keep his silence."

"Kahran, you're talking in riddles. What did you see that was so terrible?"

The old man's eyes time-travelled again, and then looked up and across at Ehrin. "As if you really think I would risk putting you in danger by telling you," he said quietly.

Ehrin nodded. He knew Kahran well enough to realise when he had pitched up against the oldster's stubbornness. He changed tack. "Before my mother died, she told me something. She said that he had defied the Church to his cost..." He paused, then asked, "What did she mean, Kahran?"

He should have known better than to think he could prise the truth from the old man's lips. Kahran merely turned on him a defiantly benign gaze, and said, "Who am I to fathom the dying words of an old and confused woman, my boy?"

Ehrin smiled to himself, accepting defeat for now, but swearing that he wouldn't leave himself in ignorance for long.

"Another drink, Kahran? We must discuss the plans for the new liner."

Kahran smiled, and nodded, and was reaching for the decanter when a tap sounded on the door.

Ehrin's secretary appeared at the far end of the room. "A messenger from the Prelate, sir. Shall I show him in?"

Ehrin was aware of his heartbeat, then told himself that a messenger would be sent irrespective of whether or not the tender had been won.

He ordered the messenger to be sent in, and a second later a young boy, garbed in the fanciful livery of the Church, slipped into the room and passed Ehrin a long envelope sealed with the jagged circle sigil of the High Church.

"Wait outside. I'll compose my reply immediately and send it back with you."

When they were alone again, Ehrin looked across at Kahran and raised the envelope. "What do you think?"

"I think we are the best company in Agstarn, and the Church will know this. They will offer the tender, but with strings attached."

"Well," Ehrin said, breaking the seal. "We shall see."

He read the short paragraph, etched into the parchment with an exquisite hand, then looked up at Kahran and read the missive aloud. "After brief deliberation, the Council of Elders of the Agstarn High Church hereby notifies Ehrin Telsa, Chairman and Director of the Telsa Dirigible Company, that the tender for the exploration and surveying of the western plains has been found satisfactory. Ehrin Telsa will present himself at the Church council chambers, at four o' clock on the 33rd day of St Jerome's month, for further instruction."

Kahran smiled. "Even when imparting news that one might find advantageous, the Church is parsimonious in its praise."

"I will go, Kahran, and learn what crippling provisos the Church requires."

The old man looked at him. "But you will assent to do their work whatever."

Ehrin smiled. "I am a realist," he said, and then recalled his father's words, *I have neither the space nor the time to describe here the terrible things K and I have seen today...*

# 2

THE COUNCIL CHAMBERS of the High Church were situated at the very hub of the city, from which radiated long, wide boulevards like the spokes of a cartwheel. It was, so the city planners of Agstarn had stated long ago, the microcosmic mirroring of the word itself: a great disc of land, which was the centre of the grey universe. More practically, Ehrin thought as he skated along the boulevard, turning his face away from the bitter southern wind, the positioning of the Church administration at the very centre of things signified the order of the world according to ecclesiastical edict: the Church was the fulcrum around which everything turned, whether it be affairs of the spirit or of the state.

That was the reality, and there was no gainsaying the fact. The Church was all-powerful, with representatives, both overt and covert, in all strata of society and in every level of business and administration. Such was the power of Prelate Hykell and his bishops that opposition was a pathetic affair, restricted to mutterings in closed drawing rooms, and even those mutterings circumspect lest servants, or even members of one's own family, related one's apostasy to the authorities. Opponents, those citizens foolish enough to openly defy the Church, had been known to vanish in the night or succumb to mysterious accidents, always fatal.

A palisade of high railings surrounded the council buildings, within which was a cobbled courtyard. Unlike the other byways of the city, this area was kept free from ice by a team of workers whose job it was to pick the forming ice from the cobbles, leaving them pristine and dry for the tender feet of the Church officials. The ice-pickers stood about, leaning lazily upon their tools, watching the citizens, come to petition Church Elders, with the superciliousness of the privileged workers they thought themselves to be.

Ehrin unfastened his skates, slung them over his shoulder and made his way across the dry, hard cobbles towards the imposing double doors, each the height of three men, fashioned from rare ironwood.

Before citizens reached the massive doors, however, it was necessary to pass down the approach avenue; at one time in the past, this would have been a journey to strike fear into the heart of even the most pious citizen. The avenue was flanked by great timber crosses, set out like so many letter Xs, the freezing frames upon which many a heretic had met their end. There had been no public execution for almost fifty years, but even so the time-worn freezing frames were a grim reminder of the power of the Church, a silent warning that the High Council would not balk at reinstating capital punishment if they deemed the circumstances warranted such measures.

Ehrin averted his gaze as he passed the multiple shadows of the frames, keeping his eyes on the cobbles but even so feeling the symbolic weight of the timber cruciforms on his conscience.

In the early days of his courtship with Sereth, he had been wary of stating his opposition to Church thinking and teaching. Sereth was, after all, the eldest daughter of Bishop Jaspariot, a doddering old fool put out to pasture as the chaplain of the city penitentiary, but dangerous nevertheless in that he had the ear of Prelate Hykell. Sereth was a believer, like the majority of Agstarnians—her credulity understandably reinforced by the views of her father. Despite their mutual attraction, each found the other's views somewhat shocking, a novelty that had enhanced the frisson of amorous excitement in the initial stages of their courtship. Latterly, however, Ehrin had come to find his fiancée's unquestioning parroting of Church dogma more than a little frustrating, while Sereth professed alarm at his heresy.

The fact was that he loved the fey, beautiful Sereth, and knew that in time she would come to view the universe as he did... though he would have to exercise caution in how he articulated his more radical theories.

Two uniformed Church guards stood beside the double doors, which were opened by a liveried flunky. Ehrin passed in to a vast entrance hall fitted in ostentatious luxury with great ironwood panels polished to a fiery lustre. His palms were sweating already—the council chambers were kept as hot as the foundry, only adding to his belief that the Church Elders were a clique of pampered sybarites.

At a reception desk he proffered his letter to a disdainful clerk, and was told to climb the stairs and take a seat outside chamber eleven.

He was kept waiting twenty minutes, uneasy beneath the imperious gaze of a scarlet-clad guard who stood to attention beside the council chamber's entrance. He wondered if it were the heat that caused his flushes, or the thought of the imminent scrutiny of the Church Council. He entertained the ludicrous notion that word of his heterodoxy had found its way to the Elders, and that his summons here was not to ratify his tender but to pass sentence on his views.

Interrupting his thoughts, the door opened and a clerk stepped out and spoke his name. Ehrin stood and hurried after the clerk, moving from the gaze of the guard to the more imposing regard of the three Church Elders seated behind a solid ironwood desk, their grizzled heads silhouetted against the stained glass window set into the wall behind them.

The clerk indicated a low seat before the desk, and only as Ehrin sat down did he realise, with a jolt of shock, that the central figure of the trinity was none other than Prelate Hykell himself. He felt a rash of fresh sweat break out on the skin of his palms.

The Prelate was leafing through a sheaf of documents, fastidiously scrutinising certain passages and affecting disinterest in Ehrin.

The two bishops to either side of the Prelate gazed at Ehrin with all the interest of bookends.

All three wore the scarlet ceremonial robes of the High Elders, while the Prelate himself wore the chain of his office, bearing the heavy grey boss depicting a circle circumscribed by jagged teeth—the valley of Agstarn and the surrounding mountains. Behind them on the window, the boss was repeated, this time set upon a circle of blue—denoting the sea—on a field of grey, the outer universe.

Ehrin thought that the Church's cosmology was even more ludicrous when stated symbolically like this, a view he had expressed to Sereth on more than one occasion, arousing her flustered ire.

A movement to his left made him aware of a fourth figure in the room, a man seated on a high-backed chair against the wall, garbed in scarlet robes. The fur of his face was grey, and balding in patches with great age, and the look in his iron-wood eyes was of unrelenting austerity. Ehrin returned his gaze to the stained glass window, uncomfortable.

Prelate Hykell looked up from his papers and stared at Ehrin. He was a middle-aged man, severely thin, his black fur greying only slightly. He had about him an air of dignity, of gravitas that, despite himself, Ehrin had to acknowledge.

He found himself wondering if this well-educated man really did believe that the city of Agstarn, and all around it, floated on a platform amid endless wastes of grey nothingness.

"Ehrin Telsa," Hykell said. "It is gratifying at last to meet the man behind such a fine proposal. You are to be congratulated on such a thorough petition."

Despite himself, Ehrin swallowed and nodded his gratitude.

"I am especially impressed by the comprehensive manner in which you have costed the mining project, and assessed the putative profits that might arise."

Ehrin murmured something self-depreciatory, wishing that the Prelate would get the niceties out of the way so that he could hurry across town and inform Sereth of the good news.

"But tell me, Mr Telsa, aren't the running costs of the flight a little on the conservative side?"

Ehrin smiled. "We would take only two dirigibles, and they would be piloted by myself and one of my employees. Our staff would be minimal; it is after all the surveyors and engineers who will be the important personnel on this expedition."

For the next thirty minutes they traded talk of a technical nature, the Prelate betraying his ignorance with a series of questions that Ehrin answered with ease.

The catechism came to a close; the Prelate shuffled his papers, and Ehrin assumed that he was about to be dismissed. He was surprised by Hykell's next question.

"I hope you don't mind my asking if you share the philosophical views of your late father, Mr Telsa?"

Ehrin opened his mouth, at a loss, then gathered himself before the Council noticed his lapse. "Philosophical views? I was ten when my father died."

"Quite," Hykell said, "and a great tragedy and loss it was, too. However, your father was known for his headstrong opinions regarding matters of theosophy."

Ehrin was quick with his reply, "That might have been, but if so he failed to debate them with me."

"Debate," Hykell said, "is not the only way to disseminate opinion. Children are susceptible to subtle influence. If he reared his children in a god-less household, he would not necessarily need to preach anti-establishment views in order to inculcate his children in godless ways."

The Prelate's piercing grey eyes fixed Ehrin with something like accusation.

After a second, Ehrin composed his reply. "My mother was a pious and God-fearing citizen, your Excellency. The matter of rearing children was entrusted to her—my father was too busy expanding his business concerns, and undertaking expeditions for the Church, to give his time to my welfare." Which was not quite the truth, but it would suffice for the probing Prelate.

Hykell inclined his head in feigned understanding. The bishop to his left, a wizened grey specimen with the mean face of a mountain ape, cleared his throat, and the Prelate gestured for him to have his say.

"If indeed your mother versed you in the ways of God and the Church, then it would appear that your belief has, let us say, lapsed somewhat of late."

Ehrin felt three pairs of eyes staring at him—four pairs, including those of the silent Elder in the corner—as the Elders awaited his response. He nodded and replied, "It would appear that you have access to my innermost thoughts," and instantly regretted rising to their bait.

Hykell smiled. "We are not mind-readers, Mr Telsa. We need not resort to such magical methods when mere observation furnishes us with the facts. I refer, of course, to your absence from Church ceremonials—not merely weekly services, but monthly commemorations and thanksgivings."

"Like my father," Ehrin responded evenly, "I am a busy man. My work gives me little or no time to pursue outside interests. I put in a ten-day week at the foundry—"

"The pious," Hykell said quickly, with what sounded like a stock response, "can find time to give thanks to the Lord and the Church which mediates between this realm and the next."

Ehrin remained silent, his palms prickling with sweat. He wondered where this was leading. They had as good as given him the commission—unless they were about to cruelly withdraw it. He knew he had to tread carefully; it would be folly to jeopardise the expedition by sticking to his principles.

He said, "I work hard building my company for the good of the people of Agstarn and the glory of the Church. I do find time, in my own way, to give thanks to the Lord for his munificence." He looked from one official to the next—and then across at the unsmiling Elder in the corner—but there was no telling whether they had been mollified by his lies.

Prelate Hykell lowered his gaze to the paper before him, then looked up and said, "My information is that you are engaged to be married to the daughter of Bishop Jaspariot."

"That is so."

"The bishop must be proud of his daughter's choice of the most eligible, not to say one of the richest, young men in the land."

"He has not said as much," Ehrin replied, disliking the Prelate's imputation that the match had been made on little more than mercantile grounds.

"I am sure he is," Hykell went on. "However, I know that he would favour the match even more if, shall we say, you were to make a more overt display of your alleged piety."

Ehrin felt a tight knot of anger form in his chest, but said nothing. Was this a threat, he wondered: attend Church services for all the city to witness, or Bishop Jaspariot might have second thoughts about giving Ehrin the hand of his only daughter?

Prelate Hykell was squaring off the sheaf of documents with a gesture that indicated the meeting was almost over. He paused, then peered over the sheaf and added, "There is one more thing, Mr Telsa. As a concomitant to the Church granting the charter to explore the western plains, we must insist that a representative of the High Council accompany you on the expedition. I hope you do not have any objections to this measure?"

So this was the proviso that Kahran had foretold. A spy aboard the dirigible, the better to observe his godless conduct. "Of course not. An Elder would be most welcome."

Hykell gestured across the room, to the dour, silent personage seated on the upright chair against the wall, who inclined his head minimally.

"Velkor Cannak," Hykell said. "My secretary and personal assistant."

Cannak fixed Ehrin with a grey, unsmiling gaze. "Our collaboration will be productive, I trust," said the Elder in a voice as dry as cinders.

Ehrin nodded in return. "I trust so, too," he said, but could not repress a shudder of revulsion at something about the man's austere demeanour.

Cannak inclined his head, as if in grudging acknowledgement of Ehrin's sentiment. "This will not be the first expedition I have undertaken with a

Telsa," the Elder said, something like a warning note in his dry, colourless voice. "In 1265 I accompanied your father and his business partner, Kahran Shollay, to the shores of the western sea."

Ehrin kept emotion from his voice as he said, "Our party will make you welcome... and perhaps we might discuss that expedition, at some point."

Cannak made no direct reply, but said, "I will anticipate crossing swords, so to speak, with Shollay. I take it he will be accompanying you, as your business partner?"

"I have not yet finalised the personnel," he said, intrigued by Cannak's choice of words. *Crossing swords...*

"May the Lord's light illuminate your footsteps," Cannak said by way of farewell. He rose, bowed to the Prelate and the bishops, inclined his head towards Ehrin and strode from the room.

Prelate Hykell said, "The matter is settled, then. Church lawyers will be in contact to draw up a working contract. You mentioned a putative starting date of the sixth of St Janacek's month, just one week from today?"

"That will give me more than enough time to make the final preparations."

"In that case all that remains is for me to wish you God speed. May the expedition bring glory on the Church, Agstarn and your illustrious company."

Ehrin nodded. "I will do my best to succeed," he said.

He rose, bowed and made his way from the council chamber.

He walked along the corridor and down the wide central staircase. So the expedition would go ahead—Ehrin anticipated the adventure with excitement, after a life led in the confines of the mountains—and who knew what marvels they would find on the mysterious and little-explored plains of the west. And they would be accompanied by the stern Velkor Cannak, who had crossed swords with Kahran, and presumably with Ehrin's father, on that first expedition. Perhaps, in time, Ehrin might even find out what exactly had occurred fifteen years ago to occasion so much rancour on both sides.

He was still daydreaming about the voyage as he passed from the portals of the council building. The sudden appearance of a figure, emerging from the shadow of a freezing frame, startled him. It was Cannak, his fur as grey as the ancient timber and his eyes just as cold. He swooped on Ehrin and gripped his arm with a trenchant claw.

Ehrin could only cower at the severity of the onslaught and peer timorously up at the official's thin grey face. He noticed that the fur around Cannak's forehead was bristling, a clear indication of his rage.

"You are no doubt very satisfied with proceedings so far," the Elder spat.

"I... I have no idea what—"

Cannak's grip tightened. "Assume disingenuousness at your peril, Telsa. You might think you have convinced Hykell of your piety, but be warned—the Church is all-seeing and all-powerful."

Ehrin gathered himself and pulled his arm from Cannak's painful custody. "And if the Church conducts all its business with the subtlety of your approach, then the Church is all-stupid."

Cannak's lips thinned even further, and he barked a sudden laugh. "There is a line in the sacred texts, to the effect that the sins of the father will be perpetuated by the foolish son. I can see much of your father in you, Telsa, and I don't like what I see."

Ehrin stared at the quivering Elder, considering a reply, before reasoning that the best reply of all would be to smile graciously and withdraw. He would gain nothing by further angering the old fool.

He inclined his head. "I will see you on the sixth," he said, and turned to go.

"Your father was a heretic," Cannak barked after him. "The family name is stained forever with the dishonour of his ungodliness."

Ehrin stopped in his tracks, and turned slowly to face the sanctimonious Elder. "The family name is one that makes Agstarn great," he said. "My father's beliefs, or lack of, are of no moment beside the fact of his achievements."

This sent the Church official into a spitting ferment of rage. Ehrin smiled and turned on his heel.

"You deserve to meet the same end as your blasphemous father!" Cannak called by way of a parting shot. "Verily, he reaped what he sowed."

Ehrin strode on, then stopped. He turned. Perhaps five yards separated him from the Elder. He said, "My father died bravely working for the good of the city and the people."

Cannak's response was surprising, and at the same time unsettling. He merely smiled, a self-satisfied expression foreign to such austere features.

Not trusting himself to remain in the vicinity of the Elder, Ehrin hurried across the cobbles, strapped on his skates, and pushed off down the ice canal at speed. The image he retained of Cannak was of a tall figure standing upright before the freezing frame, as bleak as the tenets of his Church.

He pumped his legs, working off his anger as he sped down a main boulevard and whipped around a corner into a residential district of tall mansions. The grey cloudrace overhead was darkening towards night, bringing a premature end to the short winter day, and the temperature was plummeting accordingly. Not many citizens were abroad, and even the occasional zeer beast seen on the canal was harrumphing in protest at the icy chill.

Ehrin skated towards Sereth's mansion, or rather the building in which she shared a penthouse suite with her father. He had planned to tell his fiancée of the good news anyway, but now he found himself in need of her affection, as if to banish the vitriol of Cannak's words.

A liveried doorman let him into the foyer, and removing his skates and hanging them around his neck, Ehrin hurried up the six flights of stairs to Sereth's room. He imagined her tired after a day's lectures at the university, curled on the divan with a steaming beaker of tisane.

He knocked on the door and entered, eager now to tell her of the good news.

She was standing by the window, looking out of the darkening city, and turned quickly at the sound of his entry.

They had been together three years now, and the sight of her still quickened his pulse. She was tall and slight, her blue pelt lustrous with youth and health. Her eyes, set wide apart, gave her an expression of infinite compassion and at the same time a childlike wonder.

He moved into her arms and stroked her cheek with his.

"You've won the tender," she said. "I can tell. You're like a child promised the run of the sweetmeat arcade."

He laughed. "And that's exactly how I feel, Ser. Can you imagine—to explore the western plain? How many people have ventured beyond the mountains?"

Her smile was indulgent. "How many? You tell me—it's you who always has your nose in accounts of desperate travels by footloose souls."

"Two dozen, maybe a few more," Ehrin said. "Think of it, two dozen travellers in what, five thousand years of documented history?"

She pulled him to the divan, and watched him with that mischievous twinkle in her eyes. "And perhaps there have been so few for a good reason, Ehrin the Impatient Explorer?"

He grunted. They'd had this debate before. "We're curious beasts," he said. "It isn't in our nature to remain imprisoned in this mountain fastness. The very fact that we're running out of iron and gas from the mountains impels our outward exploration. Even your benighted Church recognises that!"

She swiped at him. "Such blasphemy! If Prelate Hykell could hear you!"

"My little pious bishop's daughter," he jibed. "You'd rather we stay in Agstarn, learn nothing of the outer world?"

He knew she did not think this; she was too intelligent to take the isolationist view, but at the same time there remained in her a core of fear at what lay beyond.

She stroked the fur of his cheek. "Of course not," she said softly. "We must expand if we're to prosper, materially and intellectually. It's merely that..."

He squeezed her hand. "It's because we're enclosed, shut off from the universe, in more than one way: the mountains enclose us, and above our heads the grey clouds hide the realms beyond."

She shivered. "Don't," she said. "The very thought..."

"The very thought," he said, "fills me with awe. Have I told you," he went on, knowing that he had never mentioned it to her before, "that I dream of penetrating the sky?"

She pulled away and looked at him. "Don't you do that already, with your skyships?"

He laughed. "I mean, I dream of taking a ship—an adapted ship, mind—higher than the sky, to *beyond* the sky, to chart whatever might lie out there."

Her expression flickered between indulgence and indignation. "But Ehrin, there's *nothing* beyond the sky. At least, nothing that might sustain life. The Church—"

"The Church knows absolutely nothing about the beyond! Their conjecture is merely formulated to keep the populace frightened and in their place."

"You dispute the idea of a platform world, floating in the grey void?"

He said, exasperatedly, "I dispute nothing. That might very well be the case. But just as logically, any other theory is just as tenable."

"And you'd like to take a skyship and leave this world behind you!"

He grinned, "Well, why not?"

"Oh! My darling Ehrin! This is why I love you, because you're so like an impatient child!" She attacked him, tearing off his jerkin and biting his pelt. He responded by pulling off her robe. They made love in the bedchamber, beneath the sloping roof window that looked up into the everlasting greyness.

Later, as midnight approached, they lay in each other's arms and stared through the thick glass. After a long silence, he whispered, "My piety was called into question at the council meeting today."

She started. "What?"

"Prelate Hykell asked if I held the views of my father."

"I hope you lied!"

"Of course—do you think I'd jeopardise the mission on a point of principle? Anyway, a martinet called Cannak doubted my word. He accused me of impiety to my face. Unfortunately, he'll be accompanying us on the expedition."

"Cannak..." Sereth said. "My father knows him. I think they worked together. He's a hardliner, and close to Hykell."

"He's a fool," Ehrin said. "He accosted me in the courtyard after the meeting." He stopped, wondering whether to tell Sereth what had passed between them then. "He... he more or less told me that I deserved to die like my father."

Sereth stiffened in his arms. "You should be wary of making an enemy of a man as powerful as Cannak."

"He doesn't worry me, Sereth. I… just wonder what turned him against my father."

"Isn't that obvious? Your father was a disbeliever. Cannak is a fervent servant of God. The two aren't compatible, to say the least!"

Ehrin shook his head. "It's more than that… They were on the '65 expedition together. Something happened there. My father saw something." He told her about the letter his father had written to his mother. "I'm sure that that's what turned Cannak so against my father."

After a short silence, Sereth hugged him and whispered, "Be careful, my darling. Be careful."

He thought about what Hykell had said about Bishop Jaspariot allowing his daughter's hand in marriage to a disbeliever, and the implied threat of his words. He shared everything with Sereth, but this threat he would keep to himself.

Later, he said, "There is a place on the expedition for you, if you wish to come with me. Think of the research opportunities…"

Sereth was a linguist, whose speciality was the dialects of the remote mountain peoples. They had discussed how her research might be advanced by studying the language of the scattered tribes, which populated the western plains.

She squeezed him. "I still don't know, Ehrin. I want to come. I want to be with you. But the thought of leaving behind all that I know, and venturing into the unknown…"

He silenced her with a kiss. "You have a week to think it over, okay?

She kissed him. "I'll think about it, Ehrin," she said.

In the morning Ehrin made his way to the foundry and discovered Kahran at his desk. The old man looked up, weariness in his eyes. Ehrin guessed that he had been in the office since the early hours, filling his time in the only way he knew how. Ehrin wondered if that was sad, or commendable... or perhaps both.

Kahran said, "And was I right? The Church imposed swinging restrictions, or declared an exorbitant tax?"

Ehrin smiled. "You were right, Kahran. But nothing as bad as that. Come upstairs. We'll talk about it over a drink."

They made their way upstairs, Ehrin walking slowly behind the oldster as Kahran climbed the stairs with the painful precision of the infirm. They sat beside the semicircular window and Ehrin poured the drinks.

He told his partner of his meeting with the Council. As soon as he mentioned Velkor Cannak's name, the old man stiffened.

"What did he say?"

"He was with you in '65. He said you 'crossed swords'." Ehrin waited, then said, "Are you going to tell me about it?"

Kahran looked up, into the younger man's eyes. "And risk the militia finding out that you know? And risk their torturing you..." He held up his right hand, displaying the thin fingers bereft of nails.

"They did that? But I thought—"

"That, and worse."

Ehrin winced. "And to my father?"

Kahran nodded and took a mouthful of spirit. "I don't want to see you suffer the same fate."

Ehrin felt anger swell in his chest. He said, "The proviso, Kahran—the Council are sending an agent along with us, to keep us in check."

The old man looked up, understanding in his eyes. "Tell me," he said.

Ehrin nodded. "Velkor Cannak."

Kahran was silent for a while. At least he said, "You asked me, months ago, if I'd care to accompany you on the journey."

"And you refused, claiming age and infirmity."

Kahran fixed him with his grey eyes. "Well, claiming the prerogative of the old, I've changed my mind. If the offer is still open, I would like to come along. I don't like to think of you alone with the likes of Cannak."

Ehrin was of a mind to protest that he could handle himself in any situation, but said instead, "Of course it's still open, you old fool."

"To think, Velkor Cannak, after all these years," Kahran said, his eyes misting as he recollected the past. He looked up. "It should," he said, "prove an interesting expedition."

# Three /// Ice World

## I

THE *LOVELOCK* BEGAN to disintegrate while cruising at just under the speed of light. An explosion sheared the main drive from the starboard sponson and seconds later the port drive blew. The starship hurtled through the emptiness of space, breaking up and shedding a hail of debris in its wake.

Hendry was dreaming about Chrissie when he came awake. He called her name, experiencing an aching, elusive sense of loss.

The crystal cover of the cryo-catafalque lifted above him and he sat up quickly, overtaken by a swift dizziness. His last memory was of the smiling tech who'd put him under, and it came to him that the woman, and everyone else he'd known on Earth, would have been dead for generations now.

He thought of Bruckner and wondered if the dapper German ever made it to the ESO island sanctuary north of Denmark.

Only then did the wailing alarms and the shriek of the stressed superstructure penetrate his consciousness. Stuttering halogens blitzed his vision and across the aisle the sloping panel of the V-shaped cryo-hive had collapsed, revealing thrashing cables and banks of smouldering circuitry.

His stomach flipped. He wanted to vomit, but his last meal had been digested—and its remains cleaned from his system—centuries ago.

Further along the aisle he made out dark figures, their movements jerky in the failing strip lighting. Friday Olembe carried his bulk like a drunken quarterback, barging the corridor walls in a zigzag lurch towards the command unit. Behind him was the tiny bird-like figure of Lisa Xiang, tottering to keep her feet.

The ship bucked and pitched. Hendry gripped the cold frame of the catafalque and rocked back into its padded cushions.

"Joe! Let's move it!" Sissy Kaluchek was already on her feet, punching Hendry's shoulder as she passed. In her wake was Gina Carrelli, and Hendry was amazed by the expression on her face. She was calm, for pity's sake. The ship was breaking up around them, Christ knew how many light years from Earth, and the Italian medic wore a look as beatific as a nun on judgement day.

He hauled himself upright, rolled with the yaw of the *Lovelock* and launched himself in the direction of his colleagues.

He was the last into the cramped confines of the command unit, choking on the reek of burned-out electrics. Through the smoke and the jittery half-light he made out Greg Cartwright, already in the co-pilot's sling, telemetry needles locating the bare skin of his arms and burying themselves under his flesh. As Hendry watched, swaying on the threshold, Lisa Xiang swung herself into the pilot's sling. A dozen hypodermics arrowed towards her and seconds later she was integrated with the shipboard matrix, eyes rolling and whitening as she snapped out a litany of diagnostics.

"Slowing," she said. "Main drives ruptured. Running on auxiliaries. Greg?"

"Copy. Sweet Jesus, how did this happen? Joe, AI status? Joe, for Chrissake!"

Hendry moved himself, squeezing past Olembe at his station. He slipped into his cradle and slapped a series of dangling leads onto the receptor sites across his skull. He closed his eyes and concentrated, but achieved only a staccato integration with what remained of the ship's smartware matrix.

He felt as if half of his own senses were missing, a loss almost physical in its pain. His awareness should have been flooded with information from all quarters, a virtual schematic inside his head showing him the status of the starship. Instead, vast areas were dark blanks, and what did get through was scrambled, unintelligible.

He called out, "Primary AIs down, getting nothing here."

He glanced at Kaluchek and Carrelli. Kaluchek, as the cryonics engineer, could do nothing in the command unit. Carrelli too was surplus to immediate requirements. They hung on to the pressure seal of the entrance, swaying like workaday commuters. Kaluchek at least looked scared, whereas Carrelli was still damnably calm.

"Friday?" Cartwright said.

The African engineer grunted. "Like the lady said, main drives blown. Auxiliaries running the show. For now." He glanced at the screen bobbing on its boom before him. "Thirty per cent efficiency, and falling. They been hit by whatever knocked out the main drives."

"Any guesses what that was?" Carrelli asked.

"No way of knowing. Malfunction, sabotage? Who knows?"

Sabotage, Hendry wondered. The Fujiyama mob had got to know about the project and killed five of the original maintenance crew. Might they have succeeded in smuggling a bomb aboard the ship? How his wife would have laughed at his predicament...

He reached out, ran fingers over the touchboard. He shut down the failed primary AIs, brought up the secondary banks and waited till they'd downloaded sufficient information to apprise him of current status.

He concentrated and felt the patchy data seep into his sensorium.

"Okay," he said. "I have limited secondary capability."

Cartwright glanced across at him, and Hendry thought he saw pathetic relief in the American's college-boy blue eyes. "What gives?"

"We're just over five hundred light years from Earth," he said. As he pronounced the words, the reality sank in. "Which means... we left Earth around a thousand years ago."

Carrelli said, "So we must be somewhere near the destination system."

Beside him, Olembe shifted his sweating bulk. "Your secondaries capable of sorting out this shit and getting us flying again?"

Hendry shook his head. "Data stacks only. The flight secondaries are as dead as the primaries."

"Oh, Jesus," Cartwright said, almost weeping.

Hendry glanced past him, towards the dead wallscreen that should have relayed an image of deep space, had the telemetry been working. He didn't know exactly why, but he would have found a sight of the stars comforting.

He concentrated on the erratic data flowing into his head, trying to winnow vital information from the white noise of the failing system.

How long before the starship blew, he wondered, killing him and his colleagues along with the four thousand peacefully sleeping colonists? And Chrissie...

How could it all have gone so wrong?

Then he caught something, a line of garbled code he pounced on and deciphered. "Lisa, you get that?" He hardly dared hope, but the spark sent his pulse racing. "Last operation before the primaries blew."

"Check. Destination program, based on observed data." The pilot screwed round in her sling, smiling at him through her tears.

Sissy Kaluchek said, "What? What is it?"

"We're heading for a planetary body," Hendry said, "approximately a parsec away when we blew."

"Destination system?" Kaluchek asked.

Hendry said, "It must be."

"But is the fucking place habitable?" Olembe snapped.

Hendry sifted through the data, a sleet of maddening code like a migraine in his head. "No way of knowing. Any port in a storm."

"Je-sus!" Olembe shouted, hitting the padding of his station with a fist like a lump hammer.

"Got it!" Cartwright said, swinging in his sling. Again that pathetic note of relief, foretokening an optimism Hendry found oddly unsettling.

"Check," Lisa said. "We're coming down fast, too fast. Ship wasn't built for this kind of stress. Approaching a gravity well. A big one."

Cartwright screamed, "Atmosphere suits, for Chrissake! Everyone suit up!"

Kaluchek dashed back into the lateral corridor and returned seconds later with an armload of orange crashpacks. She doled them out like a kid at a Christmas party, the bucketing of the ship not helping the accuracy of her throws. Hendry retrieved his pack from the floor and pulled on the suit. He activated the filter and, after the smoke-thick fug of the command unit, felt the cold, clean air cut up his nasal passage and down his throat.

"Greg, hold her steady while I suit up," Xiang ordered.

She squirmed into her suit in seconds, then took control as Cartwright struggled into his own suit and resumed his sling.

Hendry found the straps and crossed them over his torso, securing himself to his cradle. Behind him, Kaluchek and Carrelli were frantically grappling with their own straps.

He thought of Chrissie, asleep in her cryo-unit and oblivious to the danger. He preferred to have it that way, rather than having her with him, facing the very real possibility of death on an alien world.

Then he thought of the blow-out, the destruction of the main drive, and something went very cold within his chest as it came to him that whatever destroyed the engines might also have accounted for the cold-sleep hangars.

He closed his eyes, feeling hot tears squeeze out and down his cheeks, and tried to sort through the storm of garbled data for some record of the sleep units.

"Hitting the upper atmosphere in ten seconds and counting," Lisa Xiang reported.

"Here it comes," Cartwright said.

Hendry opened his eyes and found himself laughing. How many times had he and his team practised this emergency manoeuvre during that week in Berne, with Lisa and Greg battling ersatz Heaviside storms in the simulator? And afterwards, in the bar, Greg buying the beers, all bright blue eyes and ginger buzz-cut. He'd bragged about his success in that loud college boy way that Hendry had found oddly endearing.

The image flashed through his mind's eye, and then was gone, ripped away by the reality of the drop and the fact that even now Chrissie might be dead somewhere way back in deep space.

The *Lovelock* tipped suddenly, precariously nose down. Something screamed behind Hendry, and his first thought was that it was Carrelli, losing her sangfroid. But the noise went on and on, and he knew it was the ship; some tortured lateral spar bending in a way not envisaged in the blueprints. Added to that was a constant, underlying thrum and intermittent explosions as bits of the ship were sheared off by the stresses.

He found himself drenched in sweat and knew that fear was only partly responsible. The heat in the unit was climbing steadily as they plunged through the planet's upper atmosphere. What would get them first, he wondered? Asphyxiation as the ship blew apart or cremation as the ceramic tegument lost its integrity and turned the unit into an oven?

Cartwright was swearing steadily as he wrestled with the controls, and beside him Xiang kept up a running commentary to herself in Mandarin.

Hendry tried to access the failing AIs, but banks were going down by the second, and what remained made little sense.

Xiang called out, "Five hundred metres and falling fast. We're nearly there. This is it. Hold on back there. It's going to be one hell of a—"

The impact seemed to go on forever. They hit something—that much was obvious from the rending scream of a million tonnes of starship fetching up against something just as implacable. Hendry was anticipating an explosion that would end it all, but as the *Lovelock* planed across the planet's surface the scream continued, punctuated by a series of concussive detonations as the auxiliary engines blew one by one.

Then the lighting failed and darkness like he'd never experienced before added to the terror. The ship hit something and flipped. Hendry was ripped from his webbing and felt himself falling. Someone screamed, the cry close to his head. He struck a surface with his shoulder, painfully. There was a deafening explosion, and instantly the searing heat was sucked out of the unit to be replaced by a bone-numbing cold.

Seconds later, miraculously, the *Lovelock* came to a halt and silence filled the unit. Except, he realised as the seconds elapsed, the silence had been only relative. He heard the ticking of contracting metal, the uneven breaths and curses of his colleagues.

The command unit had come to rest the right way up. Hendry was folded upside-down beneath one of the pilot's slings, his weight resting painfully on his bruised left shoulder. In the darkness he attempted to right himself, the operation hindered by shards of bulkhead that had punched through the fabric of the unit like so many deadly blades.

He felt something warm pouring onto his chest, imagined some hydraulic leak dousing him with flammable oil and shuffled backwards to get out of the way.

"Okay," he called out. "Okay, so we're down. Everyone okay? Sissy?"

He felt his heart lurch as a second elapsed, before the Inuit said weakly, "Here. I'm fine. A little shook up."

"Lisa?"

To Hendry's right, Lisa Xiang said, "Here. I'm fine."

"Gina?" he said. "You okay, Gina?"

It was Sissy who replied. "She's right here, beside me. She's unconscious, but I think she's okay."

"Olembe?"

"Here. I'll live."

"Greg?" Hendry said next. "Greg, you did a great job getting us down. Are you okay?"

A silence greeted his words, followed by the sound of someone moving around in the rear of the unit. Kaluchek said, "I'm trying to find the emergency power supply, get the lighting up and running."

Hendry reached up and felt the fluid coating his chest. It was coagulating in the intense cold. He lifted the same hand, towards the source of the drip, and came up against the underside of the pilot's sling, split like the rind of a ripe fruit.

Kaluchek succeeded in rigging up the emergency lighting. Actinic brightness flickered, blinding Hendry and filling the unit with a harsh glare that picked out the wreckage in stark detail.

A jagged section of the ship's outer skin had imploded, slicing the co-pilot's sling in two and with it Greg Cartwright. Hendry looked away, his stomach turning. It wasn't only blood that had leaked. He scraped the mess off his chest, retching.

Lisa Xiang was staring at Cartwright. "He brought us down. Without him I wouldn't have been able…"

Hendry gripped her hand, silencing her. Through the rip in the nose-cone of the ship he made out darkness, and distant stars, and what looked like a plain of ice glittering silver in the spill of the emergency lighting.

He looked back along the length of the unit and saw Olembe and Kaluchek, just staring in silence at the remains of their dead colleague. He found the expression on their faces oddly more moving than the lifeless body in the bisected sling.

Olembe was the first to react. "Okay, let's move it!" He hoisted himself out of his station and helped Kaluchek drag the unconscious Carrelli from the unit.

Shivering, suddenly aware of the intense cold, Hendry upped the temperature of his atmosphere suit and extricated himself from the tangled wreckage, following Xiang out of the unit and along the twisted corridor. They passed through the cryo-hive and into an elevator, then rode up to the crew lounge situated on the brow of the starship. Sunken sofa bunkers dotted the floor, and on three sides rectangular viewscreens would have looked out over the ice plain, but for the titanium shutters that had maintained the chamber's structural integrity during the voyage.

Olembe powered up the lighting and Hendry crossed to the forward viewscreen, leaning back to compensate for the pitch of the floor. He palmed the controls and to his surprise the shutters inched open, revealing an inky darkness relieved by a sparse pointillism of scattered stars.

He stood and stared. Something about the arrangement of the distant points of light, the unfamiliarity of the constellations, brought home to him the fact of their isolation.

He peered down the brow of the ship. From this vantage point, little of the destruction of the *Lovelock* could be seen. He tried not to think of the hangars which contained Chrissie and the other colonists.

While Kaluchek broke out a medikit and attended to Carrelli, Olembe swung himself into a workstation to assess the extent of the AIs' failure. Hendry slipped into the station next to the African and attached the leads to his skull. He closed his eyes. At a quick guess, ninety-five per cent of the ship's smartware was down, and the rest was firing fitfully.

He tried to assess the damage to the hangars. The program routed to the cryogenic system was inoperable.

He looked across at the African.

"My guess is the fault's in the relay," Hendry said. "If we can reconnect the matrix, maybe we can get something worthwhile up and running."

Kaluchek looked up from where she was applying a bandage to Carrelli's head. "You really think we can survive in this place?"

Hendry let a second elapse, then said, "You saw outside?"

The Inuit nodded, and with a wry grin said, "Reminded me of home, and I left home at sixteen, swore I'd never go back."

Olembe grunted. "Didn't remind me of home. Never saw snow before Berne."

Lisa Xiang knelt beside Carrelli and stroked the unconscious medic's cheek. She looked up. "Winters were bad in Taipei. We survived minus twenty for months and months."

Olembe glanced back at the screen. "What little telemetry we have says it's minus *forty* out there, and falling fast."

"What about atmosphere?" Xiang asked.

Olembe concentrated. "It's breathable. Almost Earth-norm. A little oxygen rich, a touch more nitrogen and argon."

Brightening, Lisa Xiang said, "A breathable atmosphere is a start."

"A start," Olembe said. "But where do we go from here? When I was picked for this mission I expected some kind of Eden, man. We sure as hell can't get this crate up and running again. We're stranded here. You're saying we can colonise this ice cube?"

Hendry said, "We might have come down in the planet's polar region, Friday."

Olembe was shaking his head. "I don't think so... Hendry, access the back-up file coded 11–72–23."

Hendry touched in the code and watched the figures slide down the screen.

"What is it?" Kaluchek asked.

Hendry said, "A scan program got a little of the planet as we came down. Not much, but enough to tell us where we landed. And it isn't a polar region."

Kaluchek opened her mouth to speak, but instead just shook her head.

Xiang, still caressing Carrelli's pale cheek, closed her eyes as if in silent prayer.

Olembe snorted. "If you want to know the truth, we came down smack on the planet's equator." He jabbed a thumb over his shoulder. "That's as warm as it gets out there, sweethearts."

Hendry turned to the screen, going through what little remained intact of the ship's smartware matrix.

Xiang looked from Olembe to Hendry, something piteous in the size of her sloping eyes. "So... what do we do?"

"We do the best we can," Hendry said without taking his gaze from the screen.

"Which is?" Olembe said.

He thought about it. "We assess the damage. We go out there and see what's left. With luck, if the power plants are still functioning, and if the engineering stores are intact... maybe we can set up a colony, of sorts."

"That's a lot of ifs," Olembe said.

Kaluchek said, "Just two," and smiled across at Hendry.

"I'm a realist," Olembe said. "The way we came down, my guess is there's jack shit left back there."

"The first thing we need to do is assess the damage to the hangars," Hendry said, thinking about Chrissie. "Our most useful assets now are the colonists."

Olembe laughed. "They might be a liability, man. You thought of that? I mean, how easy will it be to survive out there? It'll be hard enough for the five of us, never mind another four thousand."

Hendry stared at the African. "I'm confident we can build some kind of viable colony, no matter what the conditions." Even as he said the words, a small, treacherous voice was nagging away at the back of his mind, suggesting he was talking bullshit.

Kaluchek said, "So what next?"

Olembe shrugged. "It's over to you, boss," he said, smiling across at Lisa Xiang.

She was sitting next to Carrelli, stroking the Italian's cheek. She looked fearful, then, like a frightened animal. "I don't know. I think Joe's right. We can't give in. Perhaps it's not as bad as it seems."

Olembe sneered. "So much for your leadership qualities." He looked across at Hendry. "You're the senior party here. How do you feel about taking on the responsibility?" Was there a hint of a challenge in Olembe's question?

He felt three pairs of eyes on him, waiting for his reply. He wasn't a man of action, still less a leader. "We all take the responsibility. We assess each situation as it comes, talk it through and then come to some consensus decision, okay?" He looked across at Lisa Xiang. "Does that suit you, Lisa?"

She nodded, looking relieved.

Olembe nodded. "Sounds fine by me."

Kaluchek nodded in tacit agreement. "Fine, Joe."

"So first," Hendry said, "how about we try to assess the damage to the cryo-hangars?"

**2**

HENDRY, OLEMBE AND Xiang upped the temperature of their atmosphere suits, broke out strap-on illuminators from stores and set off through the maze of fractured corridors towards the cargo holds, which stretched the length of the *Lovelock*. Kaluchek stayed behind with the still unconscious Carrelli.

Hendry led the way along the first lateral corridor, viciously bent out of true by the impact. As he made his cautious way forward, his headlight picking out buckled corridor floors and walls, it came to him that Chrissie was dead, along with who knew how many other colonists.

The disc of his headlight played over a sheared section of decking and a truncated section of corridor wall. He felt a wave of something ice-cold against the chest panel of his atmosphere suit and realised it was the wind from outside.

This was as far as the lateral corridor went. The rest of it was gone, sheared off in the crash-landing. He came to a halt on the threshold of the alien world a couple of feet beneath him, and waited for the others to catch up with him.

Olembe established radio contact and said, "There's no other way to get to the hangars. We'll have to cross the ice."

Hendry turned his head forward, playing the beam across a mess of mangled metal, much of it smouldering and glowing in the aftermath of the impact. The ice stretched beyond, pocked with dark gouges and blackened sections of what had been the *Lovelock*.

His heart thumped as he stepped down awkwardly and looked for the cryo-hangars. His boots crunched ice, the sharps cracks reminding him that he was the first human ever to set foot on extrasolar territory. If only the occasion had been a little more auspicious...

Olembe pointed to the starboard sponson, or rather to what remained of it. Far to the right was a snapped spar, ending in a fused mass of metal. Hendry turned, looking for the port sponson. It too had been sheared off. The sponsons had held the main drives, and he knew that with their loss went any hope of establishing the cause of the accident.

A thought occurred to him. "What were the chances of losing both sponsons?" he asked the engineer.

Olembe nodded. "Saboteurs could have got at both drives—but then again we might have lost one to a blow out in space, and the other during entry. There's no way of knowing." His voice sounded tinny, distant in Hendry's earpiece.

"Wouldn't saboteurs have bombed the *Lovelock* before take-off, to satisfy themselves that they'd wrecked the mission?"

Olembe shrugged. "One group did try, but security caught the bastards. Maybe this was their back-up plan."

Hendry thought about it. "But what were the chances of the bomb or bombs detonating just as we arrived here?"

Olembe said, "Pretty good, if the bomb was set up to be triggered by the activation of the AIs when they came online approaching the destination system. It's possible."

Accident or sabotage, Hendry thought. He'd rather it be the former—the alternative, that the mission had been thwarted by jealous protestors, filled him with futile anger.

Olembe set off, picking his way through the debris. Hendry and Xiang followed.

He thought he saw something a hundred metres ahead, where the first of the hangars should have been. He stumbled, cursing the tight beam of his headlight. The only illumination, other than the three bobbing discs, was from the scant stars overhead.

But he could see enough to tell him that the hangar was intact, if dented in either the initial explosion or the subsequent crash-landing.

They came to a stop together, dwarfed by the flank of the cryo-hangar. A vast painted numeral told Hendry that this was Hangar Two, and something withered within him. Chrissie was in Hangar Three.

"Lisa," Olembe said, indicating the hatch. "Get in there. Run a systems check."

The pilot nodded, cycled herself through the hatch and moved into the hangar, disappearing from sight. Olembe signalled Hendry to follow him.

It was obvious that the metalwork holding the hangars together had not survived the crash-landing. The spars had snapped and buckled on impact, sending the cryo-hangars and cargo holds tumbling across the ice like so many casually scattered dice. A hundred metres beyond Hangar Two, the broad monolith of Hangar One squatted in the darkness.

They hurried towards it. Olembe entered the code into a panel beside the hatch and seconds later it sighed open. They stepped inside and automatic lighting sensed their entry and flashed on, dazzling them.

They were standing on a raised platform above the floor of the hangar. Below them, a thousand catafalques lined the aisles with reassuring, geometrical precision. Olembe was tapping at a touchpad set into the padded gallery rail.

He scanned the screen and turned to Hendry. Even behind the faceplate, Hendry could see that the African was smiling. "They're okay, Joe. They survived."

Without replying, Hendry turned and almost stumbled from the hangar. In slow motion desperation, careful not to lose his footing on the ice, he moved into the darkness. There were two more cryo-hangars somewhere, and one of them contained Chrissie.

He was aware of movement beside him: Olembe, keeping pace. He felt a strange concern that the African shouldn't be aware of his desperation.

Something loomed up ahead, the black shape of a hangar. He made out a tall white number Three stencilled across the corrugated flank. Beside it was another hangar, this one a smaller provisions store.

Hendry indicated the storage hangar. "We need to see what provisions we've got, okay? You do that, I'll check in here."

Olembe looked at him, the expression in his eyes registering Hendry's need to do this alone. He nodded.

Hendry turned to the hatch and tapped in the entry code with clumsy gloved fingers.

The hatch cracked and sighed open, easing outwards on lazy hydraulics. He paused on the threshold. A vast fear stopped him from taking that first important step. He wanted to know so much, wanted confirmation of Chrissie's survival, that he was too afraid to initiate the movement that would bring him the knowledge, one way or the other.

Like someone afraid of water and facing a vast ocean, he took a deep breath and stepped forward.

The automatic lighting failed to respond to his presence, and he knew.

He stumbled over to the com-screen set on the gallery rail, and with shaking fingers initiated a diagnostic routine.

The screen pulsed to life and a second later flashed up three lines of script. The words were in English, yet his brain refused to acknowledge the meaning of the simple message.

He read it again, then again, and felt grief fill his chest like something physical, as hard and cold as ice.

TOTAL PRIMARY SYSTEMS FAILURE.
AUXILIARY PROGRAM INOPERABLE.
LIFE-SUPPORT MECHANISMS
DYSFUNCTIONAL.

He swung his headlight around the interior, and a second later saw it. Across the chamber, where the banks of self-regulating fuel cells should have been, was a jagged, gaping hole in the corrugated wall revealing the darkness beyond.

He pushed himself away from the gallery rail and stumbled down three steps to the deck of the cryo-hangar. Maybe there was still hope. If the malfunction had occurred on crash-landing, and the resurrection program had already kicked in, then perhaps there was still a chance.

He stopped, swept his beam across the ranked catafalques. He found the third row and set off along it, counting the cryogenic units as he went. Chrissie was in Unit Seventeen. She had always claimed seventeen was her lucky number.

He approached Unit Fifteen and slowed, trailing a hand across the cold surface of the catafalque. His footsteps clicked on the ceramic floor, loud in his ears.

He came to Chrissie's unit and stopped.

He should have turned then, walked away. He should have saved himself the sight that he would never, to the end of his days, forget. But a tiny futile hope pushed him forward. He reached out and took the lip of the crystal cover, and raised it, briefly.

His daughter was blue, and still, and when he reached out and touched her cheek it was frozen as hard as marble.

He wanted to lift her, to cradle her in his arms. He had the irrational desire to tell her that everything was all right, that she had nothing to fear, as he had done countless times in the past.

Instead he closed the lid, then turned and fled, following the crazily spinning disc of his headlight. Once on his way back to the hatch he stumbled painfully into a hard, unyielding unit. He fell to the floor, hauled himself upright and continued.

He emerged into the cold dark night and stopped, grabbing the frame of the hatch for support and taking deep breaths. For the first time he became aware of the wind, keening through the skeletal remains of the destitute starship.

He looked up. Fifty metres away across the ice was another cryo-hangar, this one marked with a giant number Four. As he watched, a small figure emerged from the shadow of its flank and approached him, growing larger. Olembe signalled with a wave.

"The sleepers in Four are fine," he called out. "But the stores are badly damaged. The fliers are wrecked. A couple of the trucks are operable, but..." He stopped, peering closely at Hendry. "Joe?"

It was all Hendry could do to shake his head, but the gesture conveyed all the meaning necessary.

"Christ, man. All of them?"

"All of... A thousand. All dead. Chrissie..."

"Christ." Olembe gripped Hendry's arm in a gesture both consoling and supporting. "Come on. Back to the ship."

He allowed Olembe to take his weight and somehow, his feet trailing through compacting ice crystals, they made their way back towards the towering structure of the *Lovelock*'s distant nosecone.

Halfway there, Hendry made out Lisa Xiang's small figure waving and running towards them. She skidded once or twice and almost lost her footing, before finally coming to a halt before them. "I was in the hangar—"

Olembe interrupted. "They're dead, right?"

Wide-eyed behind her faceplate, Xiang shook her head. "They're all fine. But while I was in there... I heard something."

Hendry was hardly aware of what the pilot was saying. He could only think of Chrissie, and the fact that of the four cryo-hangars only hers had malfunctioned.

"...So I came out. I was going back to the lounge when I saw it."

"Saw what, Lisa?" Olembe said.

She shook her helmeted head, as if in wonder. "It was... I don't know. A being... an extraterrestrial being." She looked from Olembe to Hendry, her expression behind the faceplate ecstatic. "It was over there, behind the microwave relay." She pointed to a downed antenna, perhaps twenty metres across the ice.

Hendry turned to look, his heart beating fast.

"We've been dreaming about this event for years, centuries..." She laughed, a little nervously. "Maybe... I don't know. Maybe they can help us. If they can survive in this climate, then perhaps—"

Olembe cut in, "Get real. Any creature making this their home is adapted, right? They've evolved to the hostile conditions. We couldn't live here, even with help. And anyway, what makes you think they'd help us? What makes you think they'd understand a fucking thing about us?"

Xiang stared at him. "This is a momentous occasion, Olembe. Need you be so cynical?"

"I'm being practical, sweetheart."

Xiang turned to look at Hendry. "What do you think, Joe? Should we try to make contact?"

He wanted to tell her that he was in no fit state to make such a decision. His head was too full of what had happened to Chrissie to contemplate the enormity of the fact that they were not alone in the universe.

He just shook his head, mute, and for some reason he recalled a book he'd read as a boy. It had been billed as an epic of first contact, and told the story of humanity's discovery of an alien race, and how the contact had brought humankind to another level of understanding...

It had awed him at the time, and later it had been one of Chrissie's favourite novels.

First contact... If it weren't for the nascent grief burning in his chest, he would have rejoiced.

He found his voice, "Perhaps Lisa's right. Perhaps we should try to establish some form of communication. We might learn from them. I don't know... perhaps they're technologically advanced. They might be able to help us repair..." He gestured around him at the wreckage, hopelessly.

Olembe snorted. "Look, we can talk about this all you want when we get back inside. Come on."

Hendry moved towards the nose-cone.

"Stop!" Xiang yelled. She was looking across the ice, pointing.

Hendry wheeled, made out a movement perhaps twenty metres away. Something emerged from behind the microwave relay, paused and regarded the three humans.

He made out a vague, silvery form, starlight coruscating in bursts from the angles of its attenuated limbs.

For perhaps ten seconds—though it seemed an eternity to Hendry—human and alien stared at each other across what was at once merely a matter of metres, and also a chasm of wonder and ignorance.

Without warning, Lisa Xiang stepped forward. She moved towards the alien, step by slow step, and raised her right hand in greeting.

Olembe said, "For Chrissake, Xiang! Get back here!"

"It's okay, Olembe. I know what I'm doing..."

Olembe snatched something from amid the wreckage beside him—a length of metal, which he held like a club.

Xiang paused, midway between Olembe and the alien, then adjusted the radio controls on the epaulette of her atmosphere suit. Her voice, when it issued from her helmet, carried across the ice to the extraterrestrial. "We come in peace," Xiang said. "We are from Earth, and we come in peace."

She would go down in history as the first human being to establish verbal contact with a member of an alien species.

And it was the very last thing she would do.

The alien moved.

Later, Hendry would have plenty of time to look back on what happened then as if it were a nightmare. An overwhelming terror eclipsed his grief, and the moment seemed to go on forever. He and his colleagues were transfixed, rendered powerless.

The alien advanced with lightning speed and was upon Xiang before she had a chance to flee.

It was over in an instant. There was no time to register surprise or fear as the thing approached. One second Lisa Xiang was standing, knees flexed as if frozen in the act of flight, arms still outstretched, and then she disintegrated.

Hendry saw sections of body explode in every direction. Almost instantly she was no longer where she had been. In her place, stilled now and facing them, was her killer.

Hendry had the fleeting impression of something insect-like, bristling with a dozen scintillating blades, a glimpse that lasted a fraction of a second before Olembe acted.

The African leapt forward and swung his improvised club, and the metal made ringing contact with Xiang's killer. The creature moved, its retreat as swift as its attack. Hendry blinked and it was gone. Then he saw it again, fifty metres away, blades snickering the night air.

Olembe grabbed him. "You saw how fast it moved! Let's get out of here!"

Hendry was ten metres from the crumpled opening of the lateral corridor, though it seemed a mile away.

Olembe sprinted. Hendry scrambled over the ice after him, falling and crying out in panic. He climbed to his feet and took off frantically. It seemed an age before he reached the mouth of the crumpled corridor and passed into its shadow. He chanced a backward glance, heart thudding, fearing what he might see. The thing was still out there, watching them. It could attack at any second, cover the distance between them in an instant.

He sprinted along the uneven surface of the corridor, Olembe ahead of him. They came to a bend and Hendry almost wept with relief as he made out an open hatchway. Olembe dived through, grabbing Hendry and pulling him inside. He slammed the hatch shut and both men collapsed against the wall, breathing hard.

Olembe swore.

"What?"

"The fool! The fucking stupid, idealistic fool!" Hendry looked at the African, and realised that he was weeping. "I told her, Hendry, I fucking told her! I should have stopped her!"

"You weren't to know, Friday. Christ, I said maybe we should communicate with the thing,"

"First contact," Olembe said. "What a fucking disaster! First contact. It's been written about for centuries, the glorious day when we'd meet sentient aliens—"

Hendry said, "That thing was *sentient*?"

The African stared at him. "You didn't see those choppers?"

Hendry shook his head. "I honestly don't know what I saw."

"It was armed to the gills, man. It wore armour. The mother meant big business. Sentient aliens, with manufacturing capability, and they welcome us like that." He slapped Hendry's shoulder. "C'mon."

All Hendry could think about, as they made their slow way back along the tortured passageways, was how they were going to break the news to Kaluchek and Carrelli. A thousand colonists dead, and Lisa with them—and they were imprisoned within a dysfunctional starship surrounded by a race of homicidal extraterrestrials on a planet that made Antarctica seem hospitable.

They reached the elevator pad and rose to the lounge.

Carrelli was sitting up, talking to Kaluchek. The women had found a stash of brandy and were holding squeeze tubes to their lips. As the pad lifted him into the chamber, Hendry pulled down the hood of his atmosphere suit and breathed the warm air.

Kaluchek indicated Carrelli. "Look who's back in the land of the living."

Carrelli smiled. "I'm fine. It was nothing. I'll be okay."

Hendry stepped off the pad, followed by Olembe. Silence filled the room like ice.

Kaluchek stared across at them. "What?" she asked, sensing something.

Carrelli stood and asked urgently, "Lisa? Where's Lisa?"

Hendry shook his head.

Olembe eased past him, walked down the sloping chamber and grabbed a tube of alcohol from the storage unit. He took a slug, ignoring the medic.

"Joe," Kaluchek said, "where the hell is Lisa?"

Hendry shook his head, words refusing to form.

Olembe snapped, "She's dead."

Hendry had never seen a face pantomime such incredulity as Kaluchek's did then. "Dead? How—?"

"Her breathing apparatus failed?" Carrelli said. "The atmosphere *is* deadly?"

Hendry just shook his head.

"Listen up," Olembe said. "We're not alone on this fucking ball of ice. We were attacked. Lisa was attacked."

Kaluchek raised fingers to her lips. Carrelli said, "What happened?" in barely a whisper.

Hendry had second thoughts about the brandy. He took a tube and drank. The liquid burned a path down his gullet. He fell into a sunken bunker and said, "Something... it looked like some kind of insect, armed with... I don't know, swords of some kind. It came at us faster than—"

Olembe interrupted. "Lisa approached the thing. She actually moved towards it and said..." He stopped.

Hendry finished, in a whisper, "She said that we were from Earth, and we came in peace."

"And then the fucker," Olembe said, "tore her to pieces."

Hendry looked from Carrelli to Kaluchek. Their faces were masks of shock, blood-drained and open-mouthed. "If it wasn't for Friday we'd both be dead."

The African shook his head. "I acted on instinct. Grabbed a piece of wreckage and hit the bastard. It gave us time to get back inside."

Dazed, as if she hadn't fully taken in what the men had told her, Kaluchek said, "It killed Lisa? Where is she? Maybe Gina could—"

"Sissy," Olembe said with pained precision, "imagine a samurai on speed, armed with a dozen scimitars. Lisa didn't stand a chance." Olembe paused, then said, "That isn't all."

Hendry's throat was sore with the effort of clamping back a sob.

Carrelli said, "What? What is it, Joe?"

He shook his head, words impossible.

With a gentleness Hendry found surprising, Olembe said, "The colonists in Hangar Three... Joe found them. Chrissie was in Three."

"They're all...?" Carrelli said.

"The remaining three thousand are okay," Olembe said.

Carrelli moved quickly to his side. "Joe, I can give you something. A sedative, something to take the pain away for a while…"

Hendry stared at his brandy and shook his head.

She glanced around at the others. "If you need to be alone, Joe…"

"No." It came out faster than he'd intended, but he meant it. Right now, the last thing he wanted was to be left in the chamber by himself, prey to visions of the past.

He took another long drink, felt himself drifting. The conversation went on around him. He heard the words as if at a great distance.

At one point, Sissy Kaluchek said, "So… what now? What do we do?"

Olembe snorted, "There's precious fucking little we can do, sweetheart. The planet out there isn't exactly paradise, and the natives are hostile."

Kaluchek stared at him. "You don't think those *things* can get in here?"

Olembe looked across at Hendry. "Fuck knows. We'd better arm ourselves."

"And then what?" Kaluchek said.

"Well," Olembe grunted, "we can't get the ship up and running and fly out of here. We gotta face the fact, we're stranded, and there won't be no more starships coming thisaway, at least not human starships."

Carrelli said, "So we give in. Sit here and drink ourselves into oblivion. Is that what you're saying?"

The African turned and stared at her. "You got a better idea?"

Hendry found himself saying, "We could always go back into cold-sleep, set to wake in a thousand years..." The prospect was appealing.

Olembe laughed. "And what good would that do, Joe? We'd wake up, and what would have changed?"

Hendry shook his head and took another mouthful of brandy.

"We haven't explored the place," Carrelli said. "We have arms, technology. If this place has daylight..." she shrugged. "You never know, we might make a go of it yet."

"Strike up a pact with the friendly aboriginals," Olembe sneered. "Come on, Gina."

Carrelli faced down his stare. "I find your attitude very unhelpful," she said, her Italian accent suddenly very hard. "We're facing a bad situation, okay, and all you can do is give in."

"Hey, sweetheart, I ain't giving in."

"It sounds like it to me, Olembe," Kaluchek said.

Olembe shrugged. "Look, all this hot airing isn't gonna solve a thing. Right now it doesn't look too good. I'm a realist."

"So you're giving in," Kaluchek pressed. "You can't see a way out of this trap, right?"

Olembe stood and took a tube of brandy from the wall unit. "As of now, I can't see a way out." He moved up the incline to the far end of the lounge and slumped into a workstation, frowning at the screen.

Kaluchek watched him go, shaking her head. "Jerk," she said under her breath.

Hendry said, "Go easy on him, Sissy."

"Why the hell should I?"

Hendry shrugged. "He says what he thinks. He doesn't hold anything back." He looked from Kaluchek to Carrelli. "Admit it, he said what we were all thinking, but we didn't want to come out with it."

Kaluchek shook her head, staring into her brandy. "I don't give in. No matter what. No matter how bad things seems. There's always a way out, an answer."

Carrelli backed her up. "We'll survive. I know we will. All we need is knowledge. We can do anything if we have a full understanding of the situation we're in."

"I hope you're right."

The medic stood and moved to a vacant workstation. "I'll try to find out what we have left in the way of medical supplies."

Kaluchek watched her, then looked across at Hendry. "You should really have taken something from Gina, you know. Alcohol isn't the answer."

He ignored her. They drank in silence and stared out through the viewscreens at the dark night, the occasional star twinkling through the frigid atmosphere.

Hendry saw Chrissie lying in the catafalque, beautiful in death. Then the image was overlaid by the vision of Lisa Xiang, stepping forward, hand raised in peaceful greeting. He could not banish from his mind's eye her bloody and futile death.

His thoughts drifted, back to Earth, to Chrissie.

He said, at last, "It's strange..." and stopped there.

"What?"

He shrugged. "I was reasonably content, back on Earth. I lived alone." He told her about the Mars shuttle and the starship graveyard. "I talked to Chrissie every month or so, saw her every couple of years." He smiled. "It was enough to know that she was there, that sooner or later I'd see her again. Then she came and told me about the mission. She was going to the stars, leaving me for good. The painful thing wasn't so much being on my own, or even the knowledge that I'd never see her again—though that was bad enough—but not knowing what would happen to her. She'd live out her life among the stars, thousands of years after I was dead... and I wouldn't know a thing about it." He smiled. "Maybe I was a typical father. I wanted some control over her life."

Sissy smiled and shrugged.

"And now she's dead. It seems so damned pointless, so random. Why her? You know something, I was so looking forward to when she woke up and found me here."

"I'm sorry, Joe."

He stared at his brandy. "She was so fired up about the mission. She believed in this project. She wanted to build a world out here that worked, that didn't repeat the mistakes we made on Earth."

Sissy said, "We'll do it, Joe. Somehow, we'll—"

He said, bitterly, "Perhaps it's just as well she didn't survive. I mean, what are our chances—?"

"That's grief talking, Joe. We'll pull through."

A while later he said, "Did you leave anyone on Earth?"

She shrugged, looked uncomfortable. "Not really. I split up with a guy a year before I was selected for the mission."

"Parents?"

"Mom left when I was ten, ran off with some guy. Dad died a few years later. I had a sister I never saw. My kid brother... we *did* get along. He was killed in the cholera epidemic that swept through Canada a few years ago." She laughed, unexpectedly.

"What?"

"Listen to me. A 'few years ago'! All that happened *hundreds* of years ago!" She stopped, then said, "Wonder what happened to Earth? Do you think anyone survived?"

He thought about Old Smith, the people he'd lived with on the commune, Bruckner and all the other admin staff at the ESO... long dead and forgotten. Well, almost forgotten.

"If humanity did survive... a thousand years is a long time... who knows what might have happened. Maybe some groups did struggle through, build a better place."

She looked at him. "But you doubt it, right?"

He grunted. "Yes, I doubt it. We'd wrecked the planet. Left a nice mess for the generations who followed, if any did."

He looked across at her, her brown eyes reminding him so much of Chrissie. "Who do you blame, Joe?"

"Blame? You mean the politicians of the twentieth, early twenty-first century? The industrialists?" He shook his head. "They were just human, and greedy. They'd inherited systems and infrastructures it was almost impossible to change and break out of. I don't blame anyone."

"Human and greedy? We're human and greedy, Joe. Does that mean there's no hope?"

"I had the same conversation with Chrissie. Do we carry with us the seeds of our own destruction?

She had faith in the ultimate success of the project. We were starting from scratch, we'd learn from our mistakes."

"I think I would have liked Chrissie," Kaluchek said. She sipped her drink, staring across the room. Hendry took another tube of brandy. He lay back in the bunker and thought about his last meeting with Chrissie, the pain he'd felt when he'd said goodbye.

He slept eventually, and dreamed, and in his dreams Chrissie was five again, and they were playing snakes and ladders, Chrissie bewailing her luck when she landed on a snake...

He woke up suddenly, cut to the core by the realisation of his daughter's death. He sat up. Sissy was comatose across the bunker from him, sprawled out with a brandy tube clutched possessively to her chest. Carrelli was curled in a far bunker, quietly sleeping. At the far end of the lounge, Olembe sat hunched over a screen.

Chrissie was dead: all his time with her was in the past, now. The future he'd envisioned, with his daughter a major part in it, would remain nothing but a dream.

He looked up, and only then did he realise that it was no longer night-time beyond the viewscreen. While he'd slept, daylight had come to the planet. A weak, watery daylight, granted, but nevertheless a light that perhaps betokened some small measure of hope.

He stood and crossed to the viewscreen, realising as he did so that he would be the first human being to witness sunrise on an alien world. He looked out across a vast white-blue ice plain, as smooth a regular as the surface of a mirror. He scanned the horizon, looking for the sun—then lifted his gaze.

Zeta Ophiuchi was a small point high in the sky, almost directly overhead. He tried to work out the physics of so rapid a sunrise, and then gave up.

Then he saw something, but couldn't quite work out what he was looking at. He had never seen anything like it before, and it was as if his brain was having difficulty processing the unfamiliar data relayed by his staring eyes.

He leaned forward, gripped the rail and tried to make sense of the celestial display above him.

Weakly he called out, "Sissy. Sis, look at this."

He heard a tired, "What?"

He said, "Get yourself over here."

He heard her climb from the bunker and pad towards him. He glanced at her, not wanting to miss the look of wonder that spread across her face.

"Gina!" Sissy almost screamed.

Olembe looked up from his workstation, then hurried over. Across the lounge, Carrelli woke up and stretched. She joined them and said, "What is it, Sissy?"

Olembe could only stare, eyes wide, before he began to laugh.

Carrelli smiled quietly to herself, her optimism vindicated.

Hendry gazed through the viewscreen. "Salvation?" he said to himself.

## FOUR /// THE WESTERN EXPEDITION

**I**

THE LAUNCH OF a dirigible never failed to fill Ehrin with excitement.

As a child he had watched from the launch berths, hand in hand with his father, as the magnificent beasts nosed their way from the hangar into the open air, huge and ponderous and some of them far vaster than anything in creation, larger even than the central city blocks. To his infant eyes they had seemed to fill half the sky, the gaudy ellipses of their envelopes the only splash of colour against the permanent grey overcast.

As the years progressed, and the launches and his attendance became more frequent, he never lost that strange inward thrill recollected from childhood. Then there came the time when he piloted the dirigibles on their maiden flights, and in his twenties he was transported back in time, was a child again watching with pride and awe as his father regaled him with the fascinating details of each new skyship.

Now he was at the controls of the *Expeditor* as it left the foundry hangar and inched out over the city, the thrum of the multiple engines conducting a thrilling vibration through his bones. Kahran was beside him, monitoring the controls; they would pilot the skyship turn and turn about over the next few days. Sereth, as excited as a schoolgirl—this was only her second time aboard a dirigible— curled in a window seat and stared out through the thickened glass windows that lined the gondola, commenting from time to time at the sights she could see far below.

Ehrin smiled as he gazed down at the city, reduced at this elevation to the appearance of an architect's scale model. The monolithic city blocks were foreshortened, dark cubes against the long slashes of silver that were the ice canals. He saw crowds lining the canals, tiny beetle-like figures gazing up at the skyships and waving. He had no doubt that they were cheering, too. A public holiday had been announced to commemorate the auspicious launch of the Western Expedition, as the Church had titled it. The authorities made much of the fact that the expedition would return with the information necessary to begin mining operations beyond the fastness of the central mountains, and it was as if the crowds below were celebrating their triumphant return ahead of time. The sight of the two dirigibles, the smaller lead ship piloted by Ehrin followed by the gigantic red liveried freighter, must have made a stirring sight as they processed slowly over the city towards the pass notched in the ramparts of the western mountains.

The events leading up to the launch had not been without incident. While Prelate Hykell stood on the platform and gave a dull, sententious speech, Ehrin and Kahran had busied themselves with the pre-flight sequences. It was while they were in the control gondola that none other than Velkor Cannak had burst through the swing door carrying his travel case, incensed that Ehrin had allocated him a berth in the freighter. He would, he said, be accompanying them in the lead gondola. Ehrin had exchanged a silent glance with Kahran, but said nothing. There was a spare berth aboard their ship, though the journey would have been pleasanter without Cannak's dour presence. Diplomatically, Ehrin had asked Sereth if she would be kind enough to show Elder Cannak to the spare berth, and there he had remained throughout the launch. Perhaps, Kahran had quipped as they left the hangar, the official suffered from airsickness.

Now they climbed higher, ascending to the elevation required to safely negotiate the mountain pass. Agstarn receded below, so that the buildings lost individual definition and became mere dark shapes against the grey bowl of the valley. The city came to resemble a great circle like an archery target, though one shot through radially with the grey filaments of the ice canals. Ehrin increased speed, and they gradually left the city in their wake and approached the snow-draped foothills. Ahead, he made out the isolated villages clinging to the valleys that striated the flanks of the mountains, the inhospitable hamlets inhabited by zeer breeders and hunters. Ehrin had never looked upon these sequestered collections of mean dwellings, observable from the luxury of his insulated loft, without wondering at the type of people who would gladly make these places their homes.

"Look!" Sereth cried, pointing.

Far below, like a silver river in full spate, a herd of perhaps a hundred zeer was being driven down the hillside towards Agstarn, bound for the slaughterhouses on the outskirts of town. Soon even this was lost to sight, dwindling to a faint ribbon, and then disappearing completely against the snow as the *Expeditor* rose higher and higher and edged towards the gap between the jagged peaks ahead.

Ehrin ducked slightly, the better to view the rear mirror mounted on the flank of the gondola. Behind them, the freighter—its vast scarlet bulk filling the oval of the mirror—was rising even higher than the *Expeditor* in order to ease itself through the pass. The freighter carried a crew of three pilots, four engineers and as many geologists, as well as the requisite drilling equipment and machinery to carry out the preliminary boring operations.

They came to the pass, a great gap between the peaks 20,000 feet high, scoured of snow by the constant winds. It was incredible to think that people had actually traversed this treacherous route on foot. In the days before dirigibles, the occasional expedition had set forth from Agstarn, returning after years with tales of adventures among the wild tribes inhabiting the vast western plain.

Ehrin eased the skyship between the grey facets of rock, aware as he did so that he was exploring territory new to him. He had travelled around the city by dirigible in the past, going as far as the bulwark of the mountains, but no further. This, below, was terra incognita, and the thought brought a smile to his lips. He exchanged a glance with Kahran, who nodded as if reading his mind. To him, Ehrin thought, this would be nothing—Kahran had travelled as far as Sorny, on the shore of the western plain, a distance almost unimaginable to a mind conditioned by the puny dimensions of Agstarn.

Sereth came up beside him, slipping an arm around his waist and staring through the window at the depthless grey wastes ahead.

A sound issued from along the corridor at their backs, that of a cabin door opening and closing. Kahran muttered something under his breath. Unsteady footsteps negotiated the corridor—the gondola was swaying with a slight pendulum motion—and Velkor Cannak emerged into the control room and cleared his throat.

"Elder Cannak," Ehrin said, determined to be civil. "Please take a seat. Can we get you a tisane?"

"Neither will be necessary," Cannak said. "I merely wish to issue you, as the *secular* leader of this expedition, with this." He held out a long envelope to Ehrin, who looked into the Elder's face as he took the letter. Cannak's expression gave nothing away, as cold as the slabs of rock passing by outside.

"I will be in my cabin if you have anything to discuss relevant to its content," Cannak said as he turned and left the control room.

"This should be interesting," Ehrin said as Cannak's door closed behind him. "Any guesses as to what it might be?"

"A written apology for his conduct the other day," Sereth laughed.

Kahran spluttered. "Believe me, Cannak is not the kind who offers apologies gladly."

"Then some kind of pre-payment from the Church," Ehrin joked. "A cheque for a million monits."

"More like a summons to appear before a court of heresy upon your return," Kahran said.

"Open it and find out!" Sereth cried, attempting to snatch the letter from his hand.

Ehrin slit open the envelope, slipped out the single sheet of parchment and began reading. He looked up.

"Well?" Kahran said.

"An order from none other than Hykell himself," Ehrin said. "Brief and to the point. Here." He passed the letter to Kahran, who scanned the page and read the relevant passages aloud.

"...hereby entrust Officer Cannak with the spiritual and physical well-being of all those embarked upon the expedition to etc., etcetera. In this capacity, Cannak's opinion in all matters relevant to the success of the mission is to be sought at all junctures. Cannak's word is final and is to be obeyed as that of the High Church. Any instances of insubordination will be dealt with by the High Council upon the return of the expedition, etcetera... Signed, Prelate Hykell."

Kahran looked up, shaking his head. "'All matters relevant to the success of the mission'..." he said. "What does Cannak know about the technical side of the mission, anyway? There was nothing of this in the contract!"

"I wouldn't let it get to you," Ehrin said. "We reach the plains, the geologists and engineers do their drilling, and we move on... What can Cannak order us to do, other than go down on our knees and pray three times a day?"

Kahran snorted. "Let him try."

Sereth said reasonably, "The Church had to produce something like this, just to show us that they think they're in control. Ehrin's right. It means little."

"But the insult in thinking that he can dictate—!" Kahran began, flapping the parchment. He moved off, heading for the corridor at a shuffle. "I'm going to have a quiet word with him."

Ehrin reached out and caught the old man's arm, shocked at how the slack flesh shifted on the bone. "Leave him be, Kahran. Conflict would only suit him. The response that would most rile the Elder is no response at all. We will act as if we haven't read the missive."

Kahran stared into his eyes, and finally nodded. "Very well. You're right. But allow me one futile gesture of protest..." And, not waiting for Ehrin's response, the old man crumpled the parchment in his fist and tossed the ball across the control room.

The *Expeditor* had moved beyond the mountain pass. Below, sheer slabs of rock fell away in a drop that seemed to go on forever and made Ehrin's stomach clench with vertigo. He stared ahead and made out a great plain spreading in all directions save one. After the confines of the tiny plain on which Agstarn sat, this one seemed illimitable, its very extent inhospitable. Who or what could safely make their home here, without the shelter of enclosing mountains to shield them from the razor-sharp winds?

They would find out, he knew. For a fact, tribes did inhabit the plain, though it had been decades since explorers had last made contact with the tribespeople. What kind of lives these people lived, what language they spoke, and even what gods if any they worshipped was something that the expedition might in time discover.

Ehrin eased the dirigible down the mountainside, glancing in the rear-view mirror to ensure the freighter was right behind them. Its colourful bulk hove into view, eclipsing the dark V of the pass. Ehrin accelerated, set the controls to automatic and took a swivel seat before the pedestal.

The plan was to continue at top speed for the remainder of the day, landing at nightfall to make camp—or rather to moor the ship and sleep in the gondolas. It was deemed too dangerous to sail by night, when the winds of the plains were known to become gale force. In the morning they would continue, the geologists surveying the terrain for what seemed to them a suitable drilling site.

Then they would make camp while the engineers erected the bore, and wait upon the success or otherwise of the prospecting. If the engineers struck lucky, then they would mark the site and the expedition would return triumphant to Agstarn. Ehrin hoped that the first few test drills discovered nothing, to give them longer out here on the plain.

If they came upon villages or settlements, then Ehrin fully intended to explore, make contact with the tribes and learn as much as he could about their lives. If, that was, such a venture did not fall within the proscription of their ecclesiastical chaperone.

Kahran brewed a pot of tisane and they drank the steaming cups, from time to time Ehrin casting an eye over the controls.

Kahran busied himself with a bulky camera he had set up beside a window. "I won't let the opportunity pass to get a record of *this* journey, Ehrin."

Sereth said, "*This* journey?"

"In 1265," Kahran said, "my photographic plates of the expedition to Sorny were confiscated by the Church. They no doubt destroyed them all."

Sereth was wide-eyed. "But why would they do that?"

"Spoken like a true bishop's daughter," Kahran said, but with a smile. "The Church is careful with what it allows its citizens to understand of the universe out there."

Ehrin, who had been watching Sereth, now saw her expression freeze as she looked beyond Kahran to the corridor.

Velkor Cannak stood in the doorway, staring at Kahran as he fussed about the camera, oblivious. The Elder's face was tight-lipped, as if he had been forced to suck on a bitter-fruit.

"As ever, Kahran puts his words ahead of rational thought." His rasping tone startled Kahran, who jumped minimally before regaining his composure and resuming his fiddling with the lens. He muttered something to himself.

"The Church, as you say, is careful when it comes to ensuring the well-being of its citizens," Cannak said. "If indeed your photographs were impounded, then it would be for good reasons. It would not do to spread images of the barbarous ways of the tribes of the western plains."

Kahran opened his mouth to reply, but bit back whatever rejoinder was on his lips and said instead, "There, that should do it." He looked at Cannak. "I take it that the Church will allow me to photograph safe images of clouds and landscapes, Elder?"

Cannak seemed oblivious of the implied criticism. "Aesthetic images of the journey will no doubt look well upon the walls of city mansions."

Sereth intervened, as if to lighten the mood. "Would you care to take a cup of tisane with us, Elder, and admire the view?"

Ehrin looked for the crumpled missive, where it had fetched up against the timber panelling of the window seat, but it had vanished. He noticed the bulge in the pocket of Sereth's jerkin.

Cannak inclined his head. "I think I will do just that," he said, seating himself next to Sereth and accepting a pot of scented water.

She traded small-talk with the Elder for the next fifteen minutes, while Ehrin busied himself needlessly with the controls and Kahran composed a series of photographs.

At length, Cannak looked up and addressed Ehrin. "I take it that you have had time to cast an eye over the edict from Prelate Hykell?"

Ehrin feigned a complicated adjustment of the starboard rudder, and answered casually, "I have."

"And I take it that you have no objections?"

Ehrin hesitated, wondering how to word his reply. Before he could speak, however, Kahran interrupted. "Just what is it that you fear, Elder?"

Cannak manufactured a wide-eyed expression of surprise. "Fear? What do you mean by *fear*?"

"What is it that the Church doesn't want its citizens to know about the expedition? Surely, if all is God's creation, then all should be known?"

Cannak replied quickly, "All is God's creation, but God in his wisdom decreed that the Church should act as arbiters in the welfare of the people of Agstarn. That is why, for thousands of years, the city has prospered peacefully, while the people of the lands beyond the mountains have lived lives little better than wild beasts."

Ehrin said, "And it is the influence of these so-called wild beasts that the Church wishes to keep from the eyes and ears of the gentlefolk of Agstarn?"

Cannak regarded him evenly. Ehrin wondered if the Elder would recall the remark for future censure. "The Church rules with strict principles," Cannak said, "which have suited us well down the centuries. There are those subversives among our society who would stir ferment at the slightest excuse in an effort to destabilise the status quo."

"But I still don't understand," Ehrin pressed, despite a warning glance form Sereth, "how knowledge of the lives of so-called savages might bring about such destabilisation."

Kahran eased himself upright beside his bulky camera, massaging the small of his back. He looked at Cannak and said, "Or is it more than wild beasts that the Church fears, eh, Elder?"

To his credit, Cannak took the jibe evenly. "And quite what do you mean by that?" he enquired.

Ehrin looked at the old man, aware of a sudden tension in the control room. Kahran hesitated, then said, "I can only assume, taking everything into account, that the only thing the Church fears from the expedition is that we might stumble upon something that could contradict the teachings of the Church, contravene holy text, and sow the seed of doubt in the minds of the people of Agstarn."

Sereth, seated next to the Elder, raised a quick hand to her throat and slid a glance towards Cannak.

The Elder smiled. "I am resolute enough in my faith to know that no such findings could contradict the word of God as handed down in the Book of Books."

"We're going around in circles," Ehrin laughed. "If the Church has nothing to fear, then why the heavy-handed proscriptions?"

Kahran continued, "Like I say, it is my opinion that the Church knows more than it feels safe to vouchsafe. Perhaps the very story of Creation might turn out to be, if we explore far and wide enough, a tissue of myth."

Cannak could barely control his anger. "Such blasphemy has been dealt with harshly by the High Council."

"Cannak, I am an old man, near the end of my life. Do you really think that I fear anything at this stage, especially threats from the High Council?"

Cannak smiled. "I should have known that the years would have done nothing to temper your cynicism."

Kahran waved in disgust. To Ehrin he said, "The Church fears, most of all, not so much the possibility that its tenets will be proven to be lies, but the resulting loss of power if the truth were to be disseminated."

Ehrin turned to Cannak. The Elder replied evenly, "And the truth, of which you speak so confidently, is what?"

"Why," Sereth interrupted, flustered and attempting to pour balm on troubled waters by offering more tisane, "what truth could there be, other than God's truth, that God created Agstarn and the mountains, and the platform on which all is based, which floats in the limitless sea of the Grey?"

Ehrin smiled at his fiancée, loving her all the more for her naivety.

Cannak said, inclining his head towards Sereth, "The first sensible words addressed to me so far on this trip. The Church would fear losing power only in so far that it would fear the chaos that would ensue, and fear too the wrath of God for allowing such chaos."

Ehrin was torn between asking Kahran what might be the truth he spoke of so confidently, and saving Sereth's feelings. Of the feelings of Cannak, and the possible consequences once they returned to Agstarn, he gave little thought.

"Upon which note," Cannak concluded, "I will wish you good evening. And I hope that the morning will bring good sense and temperate sentiments to all aboard this ship."

He swept from the control room and pulled the communicating door shut behind him. Into the resulting silence, Sereth said, "I honestly don't know why you baited the old stickler. Surely silence would have been a virtue, as well as common sense.

Who knows what he will tell the Prelate when we return!"

"Sereth, we can't let the sanctimonious fool dictate to us how we should conduct ourselves on this mission."

Kahran turned to Sereth and said harshly, "Sereth, fifteen years ago I suffered greatly thanks to that pious bastard. Ehrin's father suffered even more. You will be lucky not to see murder committed before journey's end."

Giving a sharp gasp, as much at Kahran's tone as the content of his promise, Sereth rose and hurried from the room.

Kahran watched her go, shaking his head. "Ehrin, I'm sorry."

Ehrin ignored the apology and said, "What happened, Kahran? Why did my father suffer? And the truth you speak of?"

Kahran stared with rheumy eyes at the younger man, but finally shook his head. He pointed across the room at the control pedestal, and at first Ehrin thought he was trying to divert his attention. Then Kahran said, "The freighter. They're sending a message. We'd better attend to it."

The system of mirrors, which terminated in a flashing disc on the control panel, was relaying a message from the larger ship. Ehrin stepped across to the pedestal and gave his attention to the series of flashes.

The message was simple: "Building observed below. Should we land and investigate?"

Ehrin peered through the starboard window, and seeing nothing crossed the gondola and stared through the port panels. There, far below, dim in the gathering twilight, was the foreshortened shape of what must have been a vast edifice standing isolated on the snow-covered plain.

Ehrin glanced at Kahran. "Shall we incur the wrath of Cannak even more and take the ship down?"

Kahran grinned. "Nothing would give me greater pleasure."

Ehrin opened the relay to the following ship and signalled: "Affirmative. Follow us down."

For the next ten minutes, Ehrin worked the controls so that the *Expeditor* lost altitude and circled around the summit of the building below. As they dropped, the edifice came into clearer view.

Ehrin looked at Kahran, his own sense of awe reflected in the eyes of the old man.

The building was like nothing he had ever seen before, either in terms of architectural design, size or the stuff from which it was manufactured. It was constructed in a series of great steps, so that it towered over the darkling plain to a height of perhaps a thousand yards, and in the dying light of the cloudrace it glimmered with a dull lustre as if fabricated from bronze.

Ehrin brought the skyship to ground twenty yards from the rearing flank of the building and cut the engines. He stared out in the ensuing silence, but even if he pressed his face to the glass of the window he was unable to make out the summit of the ziggurat.

There was a sudden commotion from the corridor. Sereth hurried from her cabin, followed by Velkor Cannak.

"What's happened?" Sereth asked, coming to Ehrin's side.

"Why have we landed?" the Elder wanted to know.

Ehrin pointed. Cannak stared through the window, the look of shock on his features perhaps the most animated display of emotion the Elder had shown so far.

"May the Lord preserve us from all that is most unholy," Cannak intoned to himself.

## 2

FOR THE NEXT fifteen minutes, Ehrin prepared the party to leave the ship. He broke out the padded suits and four gas-lamps, while Kahran suggested they arm themselves.

Velkor Cannak watched the proceedings in silence, until he could stand no more. "Have you considered the wisdom of venturing out so hastily? The wisest course of action would be to wait until morning."

"The building appears uninhabited," Kahran responded. "There are no other dwellings apparent nearby. Why waste time until morning, eh, Ehrin?"

Ehrin stared across at the Elder. "The Church has no objections to a little exploration, I take it?"

Cannak bit his lip and ignored the jibe, turning instead and staring at the ziggurat through the window.

"You will join us, Elder?" Sereth asked.

"For the sake of an objective record of the journey, necessity dictates that I must," said the Elder and struggled into a padded suit.

Five minutes later they were ready. Ehrin broke the seal of the hatch and stepped into the gathering darkness. A flensing wind pounced, surprising him with its combination of noise and ferocious cold.

The freighter had come to rest a hundred yards away across the permafrost, and even its vast bulk was dwarfed beside the stepped monolith of the ziggurat. Two engineers were making secure the gondola with guy ropes; Ehrin and Kahran did the same for their ship, firing a series of spikes into the tundra from which they affixed the hawsers that would keep the *Expeditor* steady in the raging wind of the plain.

Ehrin moved away from the skyship, then gestured to the others to follow him. The personnel of the freighter were issuing from its gondola in ones and twos, staring up at the edifice in wonder. Ehrin found Sereth, bundled in her padded suit, grasped her hand like an excited schoolchild and hurried her across the snow towards the ziggurat.

They walked the length of its flank, examining the sheer wall of the base block for any sign of a portal or entry. The bronze surface of the ziggurat appeared to be formed from sections, but joined without bolts or rivets. The fact that the joins were seamless, quite apart from the feat of engineering necessary to have constructed such a tower, suggested a level of technology far superior to that achieved in Agstarn.

For the first time, giving way to his initial excitement, Ehrin began to feel apprehensive.

They came to the corner of the base block and turned. Perhaps a hundred yards ahead he made out a shadow in the side of the building. As they approached, the shadow resolved itself into a long opening, giving access to the first floor of the ziggurat. Ehrin felt Sereth's hand tighten in his.

They arrived at the opening. A groove ran the length of the threshold, to accommodate a great sliding door twelve feet high, which emerged slightly from the wall closest to Ehrin. In the face of the door was a window, perhaps the length of an arm above Ehrin's head.

They walked towards the open entrance, the others close behind them, and peered inside. The gargantuan scale of the outer ziggurat was reproduced on the inside. Ehrin wondered what manner of giants were responsible for the manufacture of such a place.

Beside him Sereth gasped.

Strips of illumination had activated as they approached the threshold, revealing a long chamber of sloping brass-coloured walls, of the same metallic substance as the outer walls. The difference here was that scored across the walls were lines of what appeared to be text, but in an alphabet unknown to Ehrin. Sereth let go of his hand and slowly approached the sloping wall, staring in wonder and reaching out to trace the arcane hieroglyphs with her fingers.

The others, with Kahran in the lead, passed him and approached the far end of the chamber. He knew he was probably wrong, but it was hard not to think of this place as some kind of Church: there was the long aisle, and at the end what could be construed as an altar—a raised area at the back of which was an oval plate or portal. He smiled to himself at his lazy assumptions.

Beside the knot of engineers at the far end of the chamber, the tall, black-clad figure of Velkor Cannak stood as if in stupefaction, gazing about open-mouthed. He clutched the small, red-bound Book of Books to his chest and murmured a silent prayer.

Ehrin wanted to confront the Elder, to demand from him some explanation of how this building fitted into Church lore, which had the people of Agstarn as the enlightened, chosen ones of an omniscient and beneficent God. But something stopped him. He was loath to call it compassion for the Elder in his time of mental turmoil—he felt nothing but contempt for Cannak and his beliefs. Perhaps, though, it was some subconscious form of self-preservation: Cannak was dangerous, or at least he would be when they returned to Agstarn, and there was no more dangerous beast than a zealot whose beliefs were under threat.

Sereth returned to his side.

"Can you read them?" he asked.

She shook her head. "Not a word. They're like nothing I've ever seen before." She looked around her, taking in the vaulted ceiling high above. "What is this place? It's vast. Everything is on such a massive scale, as if it were designed for..."

"For giants?"

She just stared at him. At last she said, "The Church teaches that we were created, alone in the grey, on a platform sufficient unto itself, and given a safe city surrounded by hostile climes. We were the chosen ones. The others, the tribes of the plains, were unenlightened, but would see the true path in time when the way of the Agstarnians was brought to them..." Tears appeared in her eyes. "That's what father told us, when my sister and I were small, and sat upon his lap before the fire at night. I believed him."

Ehrin took her hand and squeezed.

There was movement further along the chamber. Cannak had turned in a rush and swept towards them. Ehrin at first feared that the Elder was about to attack him, verbally if not physically—for the look upon the old man's face was as cold as the wastes without—but to his relief Cannak hurried past and headed for the exit.

Sereth looked into his eyes. "Why did you bait him back in the ship, Ehrin? And why is Kahran so hostile?"

Ehrin stroked away the tears that spangled her fur. "I can't believe in what the Church teaches, Sereth…" He hesitated, then said, "Years ago, Church Inquisitors tortured Kahran and my father for their beliefs, or lack of—and Cannak was responsible. Can you grant Kahran his rancour, knowing that?"

Sereth turned away, staring about her with wide eyes.

Kahran was approaching them from the far end of the chamber. The old man had a spring in his step that Ehrin had not seen for years, and when he drew close he could see a matching vitality in his eyes. Kahran's expression was one of triumph barely contained.

The old man exited the chamber, and Ehrin and Sereth followed. By now darkness had fallen and the night winds risen. As they stepped outside, Sereth leaned into him and said, "My father, Ehrin? What shall I tell my father when I return?"

Ehrin considered the harmless old cleric. "I can appreciate how you feel." He shrugged. "Perhaps say nothing. Your father is old. The truth can often be cruel."

They leaned into the wind and made their way along the frontage of the ziggurat, turning into an even fiercer wind as they rounded the corner and slogged across the snow towards the swaying sky-ship.

They were about to board the gondola when a deputation from the geologists approached. The lead man was Kyrik, who Ehrin had known socially for years. "Ehrin, we've discussed it among ourselves and the opinion is that we might as well make this our first test site and set up the bore. If we work through the night, we should have some results by midday tomorrow."

Ehrin nodded. "Why not? We're, what, only fifty miles from where we first planned to test drill, aren't we?"

"Something like. It makes sense, in terms of economy and time, to take the opportunity to drill."

Ehrin touched the geologist's shoulder. "Good luck. We'll talk in the morning."

Sereth was already climbing aboard. Ehrin joined her. After the flesh-numbing cold of the plains, the atmosphere of the gondola welcomed them with warmth and the scent of tisane.

The gondola was split into three sections. Forward was the control room, behind which was the corridor which gave on to the small sleeping berths. To the rear was a lounge approximately the size of the control room, but more luxuriously appointed: padded sofas formed a U-shape around occasional tables, upon one of which stood a steaming samovar.

Kahran was brewing tisane, and to Ehrin's surprise he saw that Cannak was there too, clutching a cup in both hands and staring sightlessly through the enfolding window.

Kahran was saying, "So where does this leave your theology, Elder?" in a gloating tone.

Sereth rolled her eyes and retreated a little way into the corridor. She squeezed Ehrin's hand. "I can't take any more arguments. I'll see you later, Ehrin."

They kissed. "I'll ensure they don't come to blows," he said, and joined the two men in the lounge.

"We're staying here till midday tomorrow," he said, and relayed the geologist's reasoning.

Cannak turned in the window seat and said, "Is that wise? What if the people who built that... that monstrosity should return?"

"You mean the giants?" Kahran said. "The advanced race your Church would deny ever existed?"

"The sacred texts make no such denial. They merely state that the people of the plains are heathen and godless. Such a state does not preclude the accomplishment of sophisticated technological feats such as we witnessed out there."

"You have an answer for everything," Kahran murmured.

"Study of the Book of Books supplies the diligent scholar with the knowledge to refute the ignorance of disbelievers," Cannak responded.

Something lit Kahran's eyes. "Then how do you explain what we beheld at Sorny and beyond in '65?"

The men locked gazes, for all the world like a pair of bull zeer in mating season. Cannak said, "You suffered for your rashness then. You can suffer again. And be warned, others besides yourself might suffer also."

Kahran said, "Have you not even one tiny grain of doubt in your soul, Elder?"

Cannak drew himself upright. "I have faith. Faith is strength. I know the work of God, and though I admit that not all things might be clear at times, I know that God has his purpose which will in time be made obvious to the righteous."

After a long silence, during which Kahran stared with ill-concealed loathing at the Elder, he said, "Rohan Telsa was a fine man, Cannak. He was the finest man I have ever known. What the Church did can never be forgiven."

Cannak stood. "Be careful, Shollay. Be very careful."

Kahran stood, too, facing the Elder, then spat upon the carpet of the lounge, turned on his heel and retreated to his sleeping berth.

Ehrin stared after him, then turned to the Elder.

Cannak said, "It would be wise to forget you ever overheard that exchange. I hope you understand?"

Cannak swept from the lounge and down the corridor before Ehrin had time to reply.

He sat alone for perhaps ten minutes, nursing a pot of cooling tisane and contemplating his thoughts. He recalled Kahran's forecast, back in Agstarn, that the expedition would prove to be very interesting, and his later avowal that murder might be witnessed by the end of the journey. One thing was for sure, Ehrin thought, and that was that the events of the voyage would have disturbing repercussions on their return to the capital city.

He made his way to the sleeping chamber he shared with Sereth, undressed and climbed in beside her. She embraced him, her nakedness and warmth reassuring.

At one point during the night, as the wind howled through the hawsers outside, she whispered into his ear, "Ehrin, even if the Church is wrong... that doesn't mean to say that there is no God, does it?"

He held her tight. "Of course not, Ser," he reassured, and wondered at his lie.

## 3

BEFORE BREAKFAST THE following morning, Kyrik arrived at the *Expeditor* and informed Ehrin and Kahran that the test drill had proved fruitless. He suggested that they move on to the next site, two hundred miles to the west, and Ehrin concurred.

When the geologist had departed, Kahran dragged his photographic apparatus from his cabin and asked Ehrin, "Any sign of Cannak?"

"He's still in his cabin."

Kahran folded the legs of his camera and fitted a protective canvas hood over the lens. "In that case, I'll get a little photographic evidence of the ziggurat."

"Be quick. We'll be underway in an hour or two."

Kahran nodded, hoisted the camera onto his shoulder and elbowed his way through the door. Within seconds his padded shape was lost in the swirling snowstorm.

Ehrin moved to the lounge and prepared a breakfast of eggs and flat cakes on the griddle, then brewed a gallon of tisane in the samovar to see them through the day.

Five minutes later Sereth joined him, looking bleary-eyed and sleepy. He often thought she looked at her most beautiful before she had prepared herself for the day, elemental and animal-like with her snout still wet before the application of powder.

"Sleep well?" He passed her a pot of tisane, which she accepted as she slumped into a divan.

"I dreamed of finding a giant's temple in the wilderness, and a nasty row between Kahran and the Elder." She looked up at him and laughed.

"It's the freezing frames for me and Kahran when we get back."

She winced. "Don't. That isn't a bit funny."

Ehrin doled out a portion of egg and cake, and they ate while the wind battered the gondola and the snowstorm reduced visibility beyond the windows to less than five yards.

Ehrin was wondering whether to venture outside and fetch Kahran when the hatch burst open. Ehrin made out a figure in a padded suit and hat. At first he thought it was Kahran, come to report some amazing discovery. Then the figure leaned into the cabin and he made out the geologist, Kyrik.

He had the sudden intimation that something had happened to Kahran, and he felt a sweep of relief when Kyrik said, "You'd better come, and Sereth also. She might be able to work out what they're saying."

"What *who* are saying?" Ehrin began.

"We have visitors," Kyrik said, then turned and hurried back out into the snowstorm.

Ehrin exchanged a glance with Sereth. "Stay here. I'll send someone if it's safe for you to come out, okay?"

She nodded mutely and watched him go.

He felt his heart begin a laboured pounding as he stepped into the teeth of the gale. He turned in the approximate direction of the freighter, his breath stolen suddenly by the ferocious wind. He looked for Kyrik, but there was no sign of the geologist. Visibility was down to a yard or two, a little further when the wind let up briefly. In one lull he made out the scarlet envelope of the freighter, blooming against the grey overcast. Then he saw Kyrik, battling his way across the snow towards the great dirigible.

He headed towards it, leaning into the wind, his every step an effort.

Minutes later he caught up with Kyrik, who gripped his arm and led him around the front end of the gondola. Here, protected from the wind, half a dozen geologists and engineers huddled, staring into the snowstorm.

Perhaps twenty yards away, like something from an ancient chiaroscuro print, Ehrin made out a phalanx of twenty men mounted on zeer, or what at first appeared to be zeer. On closer inspection, the animals were bigger, shaggier, than their urban cousins.

That went, also, for their riders.

As Ehrin stared, wondering whether to hold his ground or turn and run, a zeer detached itself from the line and approached slowly. The other riders held back, as if awaiting the outcome of this encounter. As the great beast approached, Ehrin gained a better view of its rider.

The man was bulky, but not with the expected padding. In fact he wore very little, other than a harness across his shoulders, which supported an ancient, though nevertheless lethal-looking, blunderbuss. His bulk was made up of fur, long black hair that gave him the barbaric appearance of a wild animal. Ehrin wondered at the hardiness of a people able to tolerate the sub-zero temperatures, and the lacerating wind of the plains, practically naked.

The man shouted suddenly, the gruff words incomprehensible.

Kyrik leaned towards Ehrin and said, "They've been calling for five minutes. We don't understand a word."

"At least they haven't drawn their weapons," Ehrin said.

On impulse, he stepped from the shadow of the gondola and raised a hand in a gesture which he hoped might appear conciliatory. "Greetings. We are from Agstarn, beyond the mountains."

The leader of the group inched his zeer forward, finally halting three yards from where Ehrin stood.

At closer quarters, other differences to the city dwellers became obvious: the man's snout seemed longer, his eyes set closer together, producing an overall effect that looked both ugly and hostile.

He barked another gruff sentence, and this time Ehrin made out what he thought might be the word *trade*...

"We have not come to trade," he said. "We are explorers, from beyond the mountains."

The leader's expression remained hostile. He grunted, gesturing to this freighter, then back towards the other tribesmen mounted on their zeer.

Ehrin glanced back at Kyrik. "Go and fetch Sereth."

He returned his attention to the tribesman, taking in the workmanship of the leather bridles and halters strapped about the zeer's great muzzle. He gestured and said, "Zeer? We have zeer in Agstarn..." The words elicited no response from the tribesman, except perhaps a mystified furrowing of the man's vast brow.

By now, other tribesmen had overcome their hesitancy and joined the first, staring up at the swelling belly of the freighter's scarlet envelope. They looked nonplussed, and exchanged baffled growls amongst themselves.

Ehrin guessed that the tribesmen were on average half a head taller than his own people, and more muscular. They wore their head fur crested and coloured, a fashion that would seem outrageously confrontational in the city.

If they were to turn bellicose, he thought... if they were to interpret our motives the wrong way, and decided to attack first and question their actions later...

His thoughts were interrupted by Sereth's arrival. She peered out from beneath the padding of her cap, her eyes widening at the sight of the tribesmen.

Ehrin said, "They've spoken, but we don't understand a word."

Sereth nodded, stepped forward and said, "Greetings, from the people of Agstarn."

The rider grunted something in reply. Ehrin glanced at Sereth, who gave an encouraging smile.

"I got about half of that. They speak our language, or rather what would have been our language... what, a couple of hundred years ago?" She cleared her throat and spoke. Watching her, listening to her, this woman he had known for three years, he could only feel a swelling of pride at her achievement in communicating with the tribesman.

The rider smiled, a broad grin welcoming their mutual comprehension, and let forth a volley of guttural sounds.

Sereth replied in kind. The other tribesmen hunched forward in their saddles, the better to hear the exchange.

She turned to Ehrin. "They call themselves the people of the ice-henges, and come from a village or settlement ten miles east of here. They saw our cloud-ships, as they call them, and came for a closer look."

She addressed the rider, who replied with an affirmative nod and a long diatribe.

Sereth relayed his words. "They are traders. They have limited contact with a tribe who live in the foothills of our mountains, though on this side of the range. These other people have dealings with villagers on the outskirts of Agstarn. The people of the ice-henges have heard stories of our city, and our cloud-ships. They thought they were legends, fairy stories."

She turned to the rider and spoke again.

When he replied, she said to Ehrin, "They wish to know if we have anything to trade. I said that we were not traders, but explorers. I don't think they understand the concept. Trade is the only way of life they know, as far as I can make out."

"Ask them if they know who constructed the ziggurat."

Sereth nodded and relayed the question.

The rider gestured, flinging an arm to the cloudrace and shouting a short reply.

Sereth said, "He says that it's the work of God."

"That's very helpful," Ehrin said.

But the rider was going on, his words becoming louder, more insistent, his gestures more extravagant. Sereth nodded, screwing her face up as she attempted to follow what he said.

At last the leader paused, and Sereth said, "He says that God made the temple when he made the world. He made it for the ice-henge people, who celebrate the bounty of their God every year with a gathering in the temple. Non-believers, he said, are not welcome at the temple."

The rider leaned forward on his mount and addressed Sereth.

At length she reported, "I'm not sure I understood all of that... but he said something along the lines of... well, that their God still watches over them, protects them. This is the bit I'm not sure about: he claims that the hand of God, or maybe the arm, reaches down from heaven every so often and touches the temple, thus reassuring his people that he is still there, caring for them." She shook her head. "What would Kahran say about that?"

Ehrin smiled. "He'd probably consider it as ludicrous as Cannak's beliefs. Sorry, Ser."

The rider was speaking again. Sereth leaned forward, battling with the competing wind to hear his words. The tribesman finished his speech with a flamboyant gesture, both arms describing great circles as if miming an explosion.

Sereth said, "Once, in living memory, the ice-henge people angered their God. They... I think they strayed from their nomadic path... anyway, their God was angry, and the next time his arm appeared in the heavens it held a fiery torch which so frightened his people that they returned to the path of their ancestors."

One of the riders stirred his mount and edged up beside the leader, conferring in hushed tones. The leader heard him out, his expression serious, then replied briefly.

"What are they saying?" Ehrin whispered.

Sereth shook her head. "I didn't get much. The odd word. Something about trade again."

The leader spoke to Sereth, leaning forward and bracing his bare arms on the pommel of his saddle. He flicked his head to one side, in a gesture Ehrin took to indicate the second dirigible moored beyond the freighter.

While the tribesman spoke, for longer this time, Ehrin realised that despite his padded clothing he was beginning to feel the cold. He looked along the line of the tribesmen, not one of them wearing anything that might be considered protective clothing. They appeared not to be discommoded by the cold in the slightest.

He felt Sereth grip his arm. "I'm not sure I understand this... I think I'm missing something." She fired a series of guttural calls to the head tribesman.

He replied, grunting shortly.

She turned her cold face to Ehrin, shaking her head. "I was right. I didn't mishear."

"What?"

"They're traders. They trade with the people of the near mountain, as they call them."

"I don't see—" Ehrin began.

Sereth cut in, "It's what they trade in that's... alarming, Ehrin. I thought I couldn't possibly be interpreting correctly at first, but I clarified the fact. They trade in people."

Ehrin echoed the word, staring at her.

"Slaves. They keep slaves. I think they're people from smaller, weaker tribes to the west. They have little use for them, being essentially nomadic, but they trade them with the people of the near mountain, who put the slaves to work in their villages. In return, the people of the ice-henges receive food during lean times and the occasional zeer."

"Great. So they wanted to trade us food for slaves? Tell them that we don't work that way."

He stopped. Sereth was shaking her head. "They don't want food. They want to know if we have slaves to trade. They'll give us zeer, and sell on the slaves to the mountain people."

"In that case inform them, in the politest possible way, that we're all out of slaves today. Maybe next time."

Before she could relay this, the tribesman spoke.

Sereth nodded and said, "He seems to think that we do have slaves. He's saying something about the lesser cloud-ship. He's asking if the people within it are for trade."

Ehrin was tempted to say that the tribespeople could take Cannak for nothing, but restrained himself.

Sereth spoke to the leader, then reported to Ehrin. "I've told him that we are all together. Our friends aren't for trade. He... I don't think he likes the sound of that."

The leader was scowling and talking hurriedly to the riders on his left and right.

"If it looks like it might get nasty, tell them that we have other things to trade. Gifts."

Sereth nodded, waiting for the leader to finish his conference with his companions.

Ehrin turned and saw Kyrik and the others, watching him. "I don't know how much of that you heard, but I think we'd better board the ships. Prepare for immediate flight."

Kyrik turned and gestured to the others. Quietly, they filed away around the prow of the gondola, slipping through the falling snow like ghosts.

Despite the chill, Ehrin was hot.

Sereth spoke to the leader, more than the usual questions or short statements this time. She stopped and said in a whispered aside to Ehrin, "I've offered them food and knives. They don't seem interested. They're convinced we have people to trade."

The leader barked something.

Sereth looked stricken. "God in the Grey," she intoned. "They want people, and won't leave till they get them."

Ehrin nodded. "Okay…" His throat was dry, and his legs felt suddenly weak. "Listen. Tell him that we might have someone… Tell him that we'll return to the skyship and bring them out. Ask him to give us five minutes."

Sereth nodded, fear stark in her eyes, and turned to the leader. As she spoke, Ehrin watched the rider closely, trying to decipher his reaction.

He heard Sereth out without expression, his gaze cold as he stared at the small city woman.

Sereth paused, and the tribesman flicked his head in a quick gesture and barked his reply.

"What?" Ehrin asked.

She was smiling in relief. "He's agreed. We can go. They will wait five minutes, then meet us back here with two zeer in exchange for... one of us."

Ehrin took Sereth's hand and edged around the gondola, fear prickling the nape of his neck. He almost dragged Sereth the last few yards to the *Expeditor* and bundled her inside. Cannak was in the lounge as they entered. He looked up from his tisane as they hurried through to the control room. "There you are. I was wondering..."

The rest was lost as Ehrin pushed through the swing door into the control room and busied himself at the control pedestal. Cannak was not to be deterred. He followed Sereth and Ehrin, enquiring fussily, "If you care to tell me what—"

"Not now, Elder. With respect, we've got to get out of here."

Sereth took Cannak to one side, explaining the situation. Ehrin heard the Elder say, "Little more is to be expected from those who live a godless existence."

He was about to start the engines when he remembered Kahran with a sickening lurch in his stomach. "Sereth, where's Kahran? Check his cabin."

She hurried aft, returning seconds later. "He's not there."

Ehrin cursed. "That's all we need."

Cannak had taken a seat. He looked up quickly. "Where is he?"

Ehrin ignored the Elder and powered up the engines. The dirigible was still moored to the ground, but he had little time to worry about that. The speed of their lift would remove the spikes effectively enough.

The dirigible rose, came up against the pull of the hawsers and strained. Ehrin accelerated. A hawser snapped, and then a second spike came flying from the ground and struck the gondola. The ship lurched forward suddenly, freed from its moorings.

The gondola swayed, bringing a cry of alarm from Cannak as he attempted to save his tisane.

Sereth was beside Ehrin. "Kahran?"

"With luck he'll still be in the ziggurat. I'll come down right outside it and hope he's somewhere close by."

Sereth pointed through the window. Ahead, the freighter was rising slowly and turning ponderously on its axis. Below it, Ehrin made out milling tribesmen staring up the dirigible in fright and consternation.

As he watched, someone raised a weapon and fired. He saw the quick squib of its detonation, and a spark flew from the coachwork of the freighter. The dirigible lost no time and ascended.

Seconds later the *Expeditor* was racing above the heads of the tribesmen. They scattered in a mêlée of snorting zeer, but not before firing on the fleeing dirigible. The metal of the gondola rang with the impact of their bullets.

If they were to aim higher and damage the engines or the envelope... Ehrin tried not to dwell on this as he lofted the dirigible and made out the bulk of the ziggurat to starboard.

He set the dirigible on a course around it, hoping that Kahran was still indeed within the building. If he had ventured out, alerted by the noise of their departure... Sereth was kneeling on a window seat, pressing her snout against the window and giving a running commentary. "They're following the freighter, Ehrin. The trouble is, the freighter's following us..."

Ehrin swore to himself. He had his hands full with directing the dirigible, without signalling to the freighter to make its own course away from the ziggurat.

He cut the engines and the *Expeditor* dropped, buffeted by the gales that raged around the ziggurat. Below, the base block loomed. He set the dirigible down with a clatter that jarred his bones and set up another protest from the Elder. The *Expeditor* settled, but without the stabilising hawsers it swayed in the gale like a child's balloon.

"Stay here. I'll be right back. If he isn't there..." He had meant to say that if Kahran was nowhere in sight, then they'd leave without him, but the words stuck painfully in his throat.

He dashed to the hatch, hauled it open, and plunged out into the blizzard.

He was mere yards from the long opening at the base of the ziggurat. He ran through the raging gale, blinded by snow, and entered the relative calm of the giant chamber. The wind ceased its keening wail, and he was enveloped in sudden stillness. He stared up the length of the chamber, sure he'd see Kahran there.

There was no sign of the old fool.

"Kahran!" he yelled, his voice echoing eerily from the walls, repeating his cry with diminished urgency.

He ran a hundred yards, impelled by desperation. There were no niches in the sloping walls where Kahran might have been, and the space at the end of the chamber—where the altar would have been, had this really been some kind of temple—was open and offered no place of concealment.

Ehrin turned, calling Kahran's name again, and knew for certain now that the old man had left the ziggurat.

He ran back to the entrance, going over and over his decision to flee the tribesmen, and wondered if he might have handled the situation any differently.

He emerged from the ziggurat into the full force of the blizzard, his breath snatched from his lungs.

To his right, the *Expeditor* swayed back and forth, only the weight of the gondola anchoring it to the ice. Even as he watched, the wind dragged it little by little away from the ziggurat. It was only a matter of time before it toppled, ripping the envelope.

He peered into the blizzard, but saw neither the freighter not the pursuing tribesmen.

He was about to run for the skyship, all hope gone, when he heard a feeble cry to his right. It came again. "Ehrin? Is that you?"

His heart leaping, he peered into the raging storm.

A figure emerged, dragging his bulky camera. "Ehrin! You should have seen it! Amazing! I caught it all—just minutes ago!" He emerged from the snow, beaming like an idiot, tears streaming from his rheumy eyes.

Suddenly, beyond Kahran and the bobbing shape of the *Expeditor*, Ehrin made out the swelling envelope of the freighter. Below it, charging towards them in a stampede of snorting zeer were the tribesmen.

Ehrin grabbed Kahran without ceremony and, almost pulling him off his feet, dragged the oldster towards the dirigible, the legs of his tripod clattering across the iron-hard tundra.

"You should have seen it!" Kahran was saying.

Only then, as they approached the open hatch of the dirigible, did Kahran perceive the danger. The tribesmen were a hundred yards away and closing. For a second, Kahran's eyes registered shock, before Ehrin yanked him inside and slammed shut the hatch.

He ran to the pedestal, powered up the engines, and yelled for everyone to hang on as they surged into the air, the gondola swinging wildly as the engines screamed in protest and carried them ever further from the plain and the pursuing tribesmen.

Sereth came to him and buried her face in his chest, while Cannak gripped a handrail with a shocked expression. Kahran was seated on the floor, his short legs sticking out before him as he cradled the precious bulk of his camera.

Ehrin, despite the fear still sluicing through his system, or perhaps because of it, laughed as he stared at the oldster.

He oriented the dirigible, found the freighter to starboard and signalled for it to follow. Down below, the tribesmen were lost to sight in the concealing snowstorm.

Kahran looked up at him. "I was leaving the ziggurat when it happened, Ehrin. I heard a sound, louder even than the wind. I looked up. What I saw..." He shook his head and stared across at Elder Cannak. "How can your religion explain this, Elder? I saw a great column sweep through the air, a silver tentacle wider than any city block, and miss the summit of the ziggurat by yards." He patted the timber cabinet of his camera. "I have it here, Ehrin. Proof of what I saw. Whatever it might have been..."

Ehrin looked at Sereth. "The tribesmen's arm of God," she murmured.

He adjusted the steering, and the *Expeditor* headed west at speed.

## Five /// The Ziggurat

**I**

THEY STOOD BEFORE the long viewscreen and stared up into the morning sky.

High overhead, forty-five degrees above the horizon, was what looked like a thin, cloud-shrouded ribbon. Hendry followed its progress to the west and saw that it described a vast parabola through the sky, curving down until it was lost to sight to the left of where the *Lovelock* had crash-landed.

Sissy Kaluchek peered, then pointed like an excited child. "There! There's another one above the first, but still beneath the sun."

Hendry strained his vision and saw that she was right. Another ribbon, or tier, curved high above the original. As he tracked its course through the sky, he saw that it joined the first in what appeared to be a vast celestial spiral.

"It's like a great spring wound around the sun," he said. "We haven't landed on a planet—we've landed on a... a helix."

"The lowest tier of a helix," Olembe said.

"Or the highest," Kaluchek put in. "Depends on how you look at it."

Olembe shrugged dismissively. "Whatever. But there's something I don't get," he said. "ESO told us we were heading for a planet in the Ophiuchi system, right? They said nothing about a helix."

"Maybe they didn't know about it?" Kaluchek said.

"Yeah, right," Olembe said. "Think about it. That thing out there is massive. How much light would it reflect from the sun? My guess is enough to make the sun, when seen from Earth, look far too bright for its spectral type. They would have noticed that back on Earth, believe me."

"The fact is," Hendry said, "that no one noticed it, not the ESO, nor earlier astronomers. Why the hell not?"

Olembe said, "There is one answer. The light from Zeta Ophiuchi takes just over five hundred years to reach Earth, okay? So maybe this thing was... *built* less than five hundred years ago."

"Built?" Kaluchek echoed. "You mean that thing... this helix... didn't evolve naturally?"

Olembe laughed. "Get real. It'd defy all the cosmological laws known to man. Something as complex as the helix just couldn't *accrete*."

The only sounds in the lounge were the steady bleeps emitted by the workstations.

"And if it was built," Olembe went on, "then it was built for a reason." He laughed. "Looks to me like we've stumbled on one of the wonders of the universe."

They stared out through the viewscreen at the spiral display.

Olembe said, "Okay, so there's a possibility we just might get out of this mess alive. But we'll have to leave the ship, move up that damned spiral till we come to a warmer region. Joe, get on a station and see if telemetry can tell us anything about this place."

Hendry left the viewscreen and slipped into a seat, attached the monitors to his head and attempted to access the relevant systems.

Olembe said, "I'll be back in a second."

"Where you going?" Kaluchek asked.

"Breaking out the weapons," he said as he hurried from the chamber.

Hendry patched through to the limited telemetry recordings made by the *Lovelock* during the crash-landing, then directed the scopes towards the spiral high above.

Carrelli slipped into her own station, head bent as she worked. Sissy Kaluchek remained before the viewscreen, staring at the helix in the sky.

A minute later everyone looked up when Olembe pushed into the lounge carrying an armload of laser rifles. Hendry pulled the leads from his skull, watching the African hand out the weapons. Sissy Kaluchek grimaced at the rifle thrust into her hands. "I've never fired one of these things before," she said.

"Dead easy," Olembe said. "Press the red activate pad and point it in the general direction of the enemy. They're heat-seeking."

"And what if the things that killed Lisa are cold-blooded?" Hendry asked.

The African grinned. "Good point. In that case, just make sure you hose the laser around plenty."

Kaluchek looked across at Hendry and pulled a sarcastic thanks-a-bunch face. Hendry smiled in sympathy.

Carrelli accepted the laser as if accustomed to the idea of toting around a deadly weapon. She checked the charge and nodded, laying it across her thighs with all the ease of a bored mercenary.

Hendry took his laser and propped it beside the console, something about the sleek black weapon making him uneasy. The rifle was a physical reminder that, if they were to leave the wreck of the *Lovelock*, they would first have to venture outside and make their way to the storage hangar.

Kaluchek said, "What about the colonists?"

Olembe moved to a workstation and began typing. "I'll set up a revival program for the back-up team in Hangar One. They'll be awoken in a year, if we haven't returned by then. I'll download what's happened, where we're heading."

"A year?" Kaluchek said. "Will they be okay? I mean—"

The African laughed. "They've been under for a thousand years. One more won't do them any harm."

She stared at him with ill-disguised loathing. "I wasn't thinking about a systems failure," she said, "but whether or not the things that got Lisa might find some way in."

"My theory, for what it's worth," Olembe said, "is that the thing killed Lisa out of some territorial imperative. We invaded its territory, and it responded."

"You make it sound like some kind of primitive," Kaluchek said.

"It's weaponry wasn't exactly sophisticated. A bunch of swords and lightning speed. It didn't eat Lisa, and it hasn't tried to get in here for us—so I guess it doesn't see us as a potential food source. So it probably wouldn't assume the hangar is full of frozen protein snacks."

"Christ," Kaluchek said, turning away.

Hendry said, "We'll come back, get the colonists, make sure Greg and Lisa have decent burials." And Chrissie, too, he thought.

Olembe nodded. "Amen to that." He looked around the group, business-like. "Okay, Joe. What you found?"

Hendry regarded the screen before him. "I patched into the ship's limited observational telemetry system and programmed it to scan the helix."

"And?"

"Its findings are pretty basic, but still amazing." He looked at the three faces staring at him. "Okay, it worked out that there are four twists of the helix below the sun, and four above. We're on the bottom tier, farthest from the sun, which accounts for the Arctic conditions outside."

"If the helix has eight tiers," Kaluchek said in awe, "then the thing must be massive."

"Vast," Hendry said. "According to the data, there's sufficient landmass in the entire helix to contain over ten thousand planets the size of Earth."

Kaluchek was shaking her head. "But how does that work? If it's one continuous strip of land all the way up and around..." she gestured outside, at the faint sun riding high in the sky, "then how do you account for the fact that the sun *rose* about an hour ago?"

Hendry nodded. "This is where it gets even more amazing. Each curving tier is made up of thousands of individual worlds—only they aren't spheroids like planets as we know them. They're more like barrels, or a better analogy would be like beads on a rosary, each world turning not on a vertical axis, but on a horizontal axis."

Kaluchek just shook her head, staring at him.

Hendry went on, "It gets even more interesting. Between each one of these turning worlds is a strip of sea, around a thousand miles wide. And according to telemetry, each world is unlike its neighbour in terms of atmosphere, geography, meteorology..."

He stopped, and the silence stretched. He thought of Chrissie, and how she would have relished the situation they found themselves in now.

Olembe slapped his rifle. "We've wasted enough time talking. Let's get moving."

"One moment," Carrelli said. She indicated her screen. "I've been going through the secondaries' telemetry. It picked up some images of the planet when we came down. I found this."

She pulled at her screen and swung it around so that everyone could see the image.

Hendry made out a grainy picture of silver-grey land, with a square, blurred shape at its centre. Carrelli magnified the image and the blur resolved.

It appeared to be the aerial view of a blocky building, foreshortened by the elevated perspective.

Carrelli said, "It's the only sign of anything *constructed* on this world."

Hendry said, "Where is it?"

"About two hundred kilometres up-spiral from us." She looked across at Olembe. "We'll be heading that way, so why not make it the first port of call?"

Olembe nodded. "That makes sense. Okay," he said. "Let's do it. Keep close. I'll cover the front, Sissy and Gina the flanks. Joe, you cover our backs."

Hendry nodded, aware of the thudding of his heart as he rose and followed Olembe, Carrelli and Kaluchek from the lounge.

## 2

THEY RODE THE elevator plate down to the crushed lateral corridor and picked their way through the tortured debris. Hendry had brought along a softscreen, loaded with all the telemetry available from the *Lovelock*'s smartware matrix.

He upped the temperature of his atmosphere suit and filled his lungs with cool, clean air. He felt a little dizzy at the prospect of venturing out again. He kept his gaze focused on Sissy Kaluchek's slim back in the orange atmosphere suit as they approached the end of the corridor.

Ahead, framed by the jagged perimeter of the corridor's shredded walls, he made out watery light and a blinding expanse of snow marred by the charred wreckage of the starship.

Olembe paused, unshouldering his rifle. "You all set?" When he received acknowledgement from the others, he said, "Okay. Let's go."

Olembe stepped onto the ice, followed by Kaluchek and Carrelli. Hendry activated his rifle, followed the others and turned rapidly, stepping backwards and covering the rear with his levelled laser. He had a sudden memory of doing something similar as a boy in the outback, playing a heroic part in the Asian wars of the Fifties.

In the cold light of day, the damage to the *Lovelock* appeared even more devastating than it had seemed last night. The ship lay in a scatter of fractured sections, highlighted by the barren wastes all around. The only intact part of the ship, other than the hangars, was the leaning wedge of the nose-cone, and that had been excoriated and blackened in the crash-landing.

Seconds later something caught Hendry's eye and he drew a sudden breath. To his right, a bright slick in the snow provided the only splash of colour in the otherwise monochrome landscape. Lisa Xiang's blood had flash-frozen as it spilled across the ice in an eerily symmetrical pattern like a Rorschach blot. He looked for any other sign of her remains, but saw nothing. He found himself wondering at Olembe's assumption that Lisa's killer hadn't eaten her.

He swung his gaze left, and his laser with it. Approaching the blood, from behind the microwave antenna, was a series of stark asterisks, a hundred divots chipped into the ice where the creature had advanced on pincers like ice picks.

He was sweating. He felt as if the creature—or more than one of them, who knew?—was watching the frightened huddle of humans, biding its time before making its deadly approach.

He heard an enraged call in his ear-piece. "Joe! For Chrissake!"

He turned. The others were ten metres ahead. Olembe had paused for him to catch up. Hendry ran, turned and resumed his rearward guard. They were approximately midway between the nose-cone and the storage hangar, with around another hundred metres to go.

He flicked his gaze left and right. Beyond the scatter of the *Lovelock*'s wreckage, the plain was flat and featureless. It seemed impossible that anything could conceal itself in that horizontal waste, other than if it burrowed into the permafrost. There was one alternative, of course: the creature might be hiding somewhere among the debris of the ship.

To his right was the low, dark shape of Hangar Three, and he thought back to what he'd found in there. It seemed more than just twelve hours since he'd found Chrissie dead. Maybe some component of his grief, or his denial, was playing tricks with his memories, stringing out his time sense in a subconscious act of self-preservation. He felt tears sting his cheeks and tried to push images of his daughter to a place where they wouldn't haunt him.

Just a few weeks ago, subjective time, he was sitting beneath the awning in the starship graveyard, staring out across his vegetable garden...

He fetched up against something and gasped, then felt a hand slap his shoulder and turned to see Sissy Kaluchek grinning at his funk. They were standing in the shadow of the storage hangar and Olembe was tapping the entry code into the hatch sensor.

The hatch sighed open and they tumbled inside, Olembe securing the seal behind them. He pulled off his faceplate and grinned. "Round two to the human race."

Hendry gazed around him at the tumbled mess of machinery filling the chamber. The complement of six fliers had come loose from their shackles and bounced around the hangar, not only wrecking themselves but flattening other vehicles and storage units. Four ground-effect trucks were write-offs, though two had come through the crash-landing unscathed.

For the next hour Hendry and Kaluchek went through the operating systems of the two surviving trucks, big tracked vehicles built to carry a crew of eight, while Olembe and Carrelli checked the trucks' mechanics. The on-board smartware was in good working order. Hendry spent thirty minutes downloading all the functioning AI programs from the ship's secondary caches.

They stocked each truck with canisters of food supplies. Olembe said, "And when we run out... let's just hope we find something edible on the next world."

"And if we run out of fuel?" Kaluchek asked.

Olembe slapped the flank of the truck with affection. "They run off mini-nuclear piles, and they're virtually everlasting."

"What about when we get to the seas?" Hendry asked.

"The poor bastards who put the mission together even thought of that, Joe. These beauties are amphibious. Okay," he looked around at his colleagues, "we'll split into two teams of two. Any preferences, anyone?"

Kaluchek said, "No offence, Olembe, but I'll take Joe."

"No offence taken, sweetheart." He grinned at Carrelli. "It's you and me, Gina."

Olembe would take the first vehicle, Hendry and Kaluchek the second, keeping always within visible distance of each other. At night they'd sleep together in one truck, taking turns to mount an armed guard.

Kaluchek said, "And how long before we come across a habitable world? Christ, we'll have to travel a hell of a way to reach anywhere halfway warm."

Hendry had performed a few basic calculations back in the lounge. "According to telemetry—and it's pretty theoretical guesswork, at best—if we take six weeks to cross the face of each world, and calculating a half degree increase in the temperature per world, then it'll be in the region of five years before we hit a habitable region."

Olembe said, "Of course, then we have to find a world that checks out Earth-norm."

Carrelli smiled. "We've got time, my friend. We have plenty of time. The sleepers are going nowhere."

"I'd like to find Eden in my lifetime," Olembe said. "Okay, let's get going."

They climbed into the pressure-sealed cabs, Hendry drawing shotgun duty while Kaluchek drove. The engine kicked into life and Kaluchek manoeuvred the truck into line behind Olembe's. They rolled towards the hangar doors, which eased open as they approached, and passed out into the vapid daylight.

Hendry peered through the sidescreen at the remains of the *Lovelock*, a pathetic scatter of twisted debris, with only the nose-cone upstanding like an accidental epitaph to the colonists who had died. He averted his gaze from Chrissie's hangar and looked ahead, across the featureless expanse of the ice-bound plain.

Overhead, he made out the vast parabola of the tier immediately above theirs, and above that one, even fainter, the next swing of the helix, a tortuous road to the promised land.

## 3

FOR THE FIRST hour of their journey, Hendry was scrupulous in scanning the expanse of icy wasteland stretching out on either side of their two-truck convoy. A screen set into the padded dashboard relayed the rear view, showing the parallel imprints of the trucks' wide tracks. Long ago the dark irregularity of the crashed starship had dwindled into the whiteness, its disappearance opening up within Hendry a hollow sense of loss.

Ahead, the first truck was a dark beetling shape, spraying snow.

There was no sign of the creature that had killed Lisa. He thought back to the attack, the utter randomness of the event. If not for Olembe's quick thinking, then he too would have fallen victim to the crazed alien... He shook the vision of Lisa's spilled blood from his mind's eye and looked ahead.

As the minutes passed and it became obvious that there were no alien assailants within kilometres of the trucks, Hendry relaxed his guard, checking their flanks and rear only every few minutes.

Kaluchek slouched in the driving seat, one hand adjusting the controls from time to time. She was still in her atmosphere suit, but had removed the hood and let her black hair fall to her shoulders. She had the round face of her people, the embedded slit eyes that gave her a look of withdrawn brooding. Since the crash-landing, she and Hendry had found themselves forming a strange bond of tacit understanding, in subtle opposition to Olembe's machismo and Carrelli's aura of quiet control. Not for the first time he found himself wondering at Kaluchek's overt dislike of Friday Olembe.

He tipped back his head and stared through the truck's clear canopy. Like this, he had a perfect, three-sixty degree view of the helix. It corkscrewed up above him, its vast arcs getting ever thinner and fainter as it went. For the first time, he realised that each succeeding tier was a little wider than the last, so that the helix described not so much a spring whose arms were equidistant from the sun, but an oblate spiral.

He stared at the tier directly above and made out the shape of clouds, and occasionally the very faint smudge of what might have been a mountain range. He found himself smiling in awe at the simple magnificence of the construct.

Kaluchek looked across at him and said, "So... what do you make of the rest of the team?"

He smiled. "Who in particular?"

"Carrelli first."

He shrugged. "I can't work her out. She gives nothing away. Even back in Berne she was inscrutable. I just put it down to her having lost five friends in the bombing. What do you think?"

Kaluchek considered. "She's a tough one, Joe. Did you see her back there? We were shitting ourselves, and she was as cool as ice. Did you get to know her at all during training?"

"We exchanged small-talk, but she never gave anything away. I don't even know if she had a partner, kids. You talk to her?"

"I tried, but got nowhere. I got the impression she was watching us, trying to work us out, our group dynamic."

"An amateur psychologist," he began.

"I don't think there's anything amateur about her, Joe. I think as well as being a medic, she's a shrink. Think about it—it'd make sense to have a trained psychologist along. And have you noticed how placatory she is, how she's defused a few tense situations since we hit this lump of ice?"

He smiled. "You don't miss a trick, do you?"

"What do you think I did as a kid, isolated in bug-fuck nowhere, Iceville, but watch people and try to work out how they ticked?"

He was tempted to ask Kaluchek what she made of him, and why she'd chosen to partner him ahead of any of the others, but thought better of it.

Instead he said, "And Olembe? Why don't you like him."

She smiled. "That obvious, is it?" She paused, thinking about it. "Look, I know things about Olembe's past that I don't like..."

He looked at her. "Such as?"

She shook her head. "Later, Joe. Okay?"

He nodded and fell silent. He remembered with a stab of guilt to check the surrounding land for marauding extraterrestrials. The ice was a blinding empty sheet on all sides.

A few minutes later Kaluchek said, "Hey, you know, if you need to talk at any time, about what happened back there, your daughter and all…"

He nodded quickly. "Sure, I'll remember that. But I'm fine, really." Even as he said the words, he realised what a ridiculous statement it was.

He was saved further embarrassment by the sharp tone of the truck's communicator. Olembe's voice filled the cab. "Hey, Joe, Sissy, you seen what's up ahead?"

Hendry took up the receiver, at the same time scanning the wastes ahead of the first truck. "What is it?"

"Two o'clock, about three kilometres away. Check it out on your mag-screen and get back to me."

Kaluchek was already thumbing the controls.

The central section of the viewscreen opaqued for a second, then cleared. Revealed within its rectangle was the magnified image of what Olembe had spotted.

"What the hell?" Hendry began.

"Looks like a city to me," Kaluchek said under her breath. "A city made of ice."

Hendry made out a series of silver pyramids and minarets scintillating in the weak sunlight. Kaluchek was right. It looked like a city, not constructed from metal and glass but from the only available material, a low skyline of blocks hewn from the ice and erected to form a sanctuary from the sub-zero temperatures that lashed the land.

Hendry reached for the receiver. "Olembe, we've got it. What do you think?"

The African grunted a laugh. "What do I think? I think we should leave well alone. You not seen them?"

Hendry's heart lurched. "Seen what?"

"Our friends, the homicidal aliens. They're teeming around to the right of the central minaret."

Kaluchek adjusted the controls and zoomed in on the ice-tower. In its shadow was a crowd of angular, skittering extraterrestrials. There were perhaps a hundred of them and they appeared to be armed like the first one they had encountered.

Armed, he thought—or were those flashing blades merely a part of their biological armature? He wondered what they were doing, massing there before the minaret—observing some rally, a religious ritual? Or perhaps gathering for attack?

Ahead, Olembe's truck veered left, taking a detour away from the alien city. Kaluchek followed.

"You think they've seen us?" Hendry asked.

"If they have, they're showing no indication of giving chase," Kaluchek said.

Hendry gripped his laser, wondering how effective his weapon might be against a horde of sword-wielding berserkers. He peered through the sidescreen as the minutes ticked by and they moved ever further from the city.

"Five kay, Joe. I think we're okay this time."

He nodded, breathing a little easier. The material of his gloves was soaked with sweat.

Kaluchek relaxed visibly. "You know, chances are that we'll encounter other races on our way up-spiral. Let's hope that they're not all as unfriendly as those bastards."

He didn't reply, but considered the journey ahead, and the possibility that they might indeed encounter other alien life forms.

This moved him to consider Chrissie, and how she would have faced this opportunity with elation. As a teenager she had been obsessed with the idea of extraterrestrial life, filling her computer with images of aliens she had created herself.

He was still dreaming of his daughter when the communicator sounded again.

"We're about three kilometres from the building Gina found," Olembe said, "and look. Ahead, ten o'clock." He cut the connection. Olembe's truck was making a slow left turn, its tracks spraying snow.

Kaluchek followed suit and Hendry peered through the viewscreen.

There was no sign of the building, but something appeared to be suspended in the air approximately three kilometres away. Hendry peered, then remembered the magnification and adjusted the screen. The image expanded, and Hendry sat back and whistled.

A long grey filament or column rose vertically into the air, arcing in a graceful parabola and disappearing from sight high above.

He got through to Olembe. "Any ideas?"

"Beats me," Olembe replied. "It's some feat of engineering, whatever it is."

Hendry returned the screen to normal view and the filament dwindled. Kaluchek accelerated, drawing alongside Olembe and Carrelli. Ahead, the building from which the column rose was coming into view, at first a dark irregularity on the horizon, but growing rapidly as they approached.

It was vast. Hendry had not known what to expect, going by the blurred aerial shots Carrelli had produced—but it was not this awesome edifice.

It was a ziggurat, a series of ever-smaller blocks set atop each other and rising hundreds of metres into the air. At its summit, a complicated construction—which looked at this distance to be a baroque metal framework—anchored the end of the filament to the uppermost block.

Hendry tried to crane his neck in order to chart the filament's destination, but it dwindled to a vanishing point long before it reached the tier above—if it ever did so.

The first truck pulled ahead and raced down a kind of approach boulevard demarcated by a series of regularly placed blocks to right and left. Kaluchek followed, and a minute later they drew into the shadow of the ziggurat, the trucks made insignificant by comparison to the base block of the construction, like beetles at the foot of a pyramid. They drew alongside Olembe's truck and cut the engine.

They had halted before what appeared to be the ziggurat's entrance. A long, recessed slab of what Hendry thought might be brass, set into the metal from which the ziggurat was constructed. Even at this distance he could make out rococo scrollwork etched into the door panels. The whole effect, he thought, was eerily alien.

He glanced across at Olembe, who signalled ahead and started the engine. Kaluchek followed at a crawl and approached the looming entrance.

The trucks halted again, side by side. Hendry pulled on his faceplate, upped the temperature control of his atmosphere suit and swung himself down from the cab. Olembe and Carrelli were already standing before the imposing doorway, looking up. Hendry followed their gaze. Overhead, the filament whipped vertiginously into the sky. He became aware of the cold wind, whining around the ziggurat.

Kaluchek joined them. "What I don't understand," she said, "is why we didn't see the filament in the aerial pix. I mean, it would have been big enough to be visible."

Olembe looked at her. "Perhaps we didn't see it because it wasn't there."

"What the hell do you mean by that?"

"Think about it, Sis."

"I am thinking," she snapped, "but it still doesn't make sense."

Hendry said, "You mean, it connected since the shot was taken?"

Olembe nodded and pointed at Hendry. "That's what I mean, Joe."

Carrelli was inspecting the carved fascia of the vast doorway. "Here. There's a viewplate."

They hurried over to her, standing on tiptoe and pressing their faces into the misted transparency of a horizontal viewplate. Hendry made out a great hallway, diminishing in perspective, its walls sloping to form a wide aisle at the end of which stood a tall oval plate the same bronze shade as the doorway.

Carrelli was already searching for some means of entry. Olembe joined her, scanning the pillars that stood on either side of the doorway.

Beside him, Kaluchek whispered, "What the hell is it, Joe?"

He shook his head. He had a wild idea, but he didn't want to raise her hopes.

He was returning to the truck for his softscreen, intending to record images of the ziggurat to its memory, when he stopped and stared out over the plain of ice they had crossed just minutes before.

"Friday!" he yelled.

The African came running. "Great," he said, following Hendry's gaze. He turned to Carrelli and Kaluchek. "If you can find a way inside, girls, and pretty damned quick, I'd appreciate it."

Hendry found himself raising his laser at the phalanx of extraterrestrials approaching across the ice. They were perhaps half a kilometre away, fleeting silver forms coruscating in the sunlight as they advanced like a plague of silver-grey, upright locusts. There could be no doubt, he thought, that they were heading for the ziggurat.

"I estimate we have three, maybe four minutes," Olembe said.

Hendry glanced back at the doorway. The women were frantically searching the portal for a means of entry.

"You think we'll be safe in the trucks?"

Olembe glanced at him. "You saw what the fucker did to Lisa. What do you think?"

The aliens were closer now. Hendry could make out individual blades, glinting as they came.

"Carrelli! What gives?" Olembe yelled. He hoisted his rifle and levelled it at the approaching horde.

Hendry glanced over his shoulder. Carrelli and Kaluchek were standing beside the doorway, slapping a series of engraved panels. As he watched, Kaluchek made a stirrup with her hands and

Carrelli stepped into it, reaching up the side of the pillar to slap a high panel.

A sound from the ice plains made him turn. The aliens were much closer, and perhaps more disturbing than the sight of them was the sound that accompanied their advance: the thin high keening of chitinous blades and pincers, as if stropping each other in anticipation of the imminent slaughter.

"Joe!" Kaluchek called, and when Hendry spun round he saw, with a kick of joy, that the doorway was sliding slowly open.

Olembe was already in the truck. "Get up here!" he yelled.

Hendry dived into the cab and Olembe revved the engine, speeding towards the gap created by the slowly sliding panel. Hendry thought they were sure to scrape the sides as they sped through. They made it with centimetres to spare.

The women were already inside, inspecting the pillars for the device that might close the doors behind them. Hendry screwed around in his seat. The aliens had reached the far end of the approach avenue and were swarming up it, silver pincers semaphoring a fair imitation of hostility.

The first alien was ten metres from the doorway when the thick bronze slab began, with grinding slowness, to roll shut.

Seconds later, with the creature a metre away, the gap narrowed to nothing.

Kaluchek rushed to the door panel and peered through the viewscreen. "Take a look at this, Joe."

He joined her. The remaining truck was surrounded by a hundred skittering aliens, hacking into its coachwork with claws and pincers. Perhaps a minute after the attack began, the truck was a skeletal framework and the area around it strewn with a mess of wiring and sectioned panels.

An alien turned. Hendry made out waving eye-stalks beneath a bony ridge like an ossified mushroom cup. In the blink of an eye the thing sprang, covering the distance between the truck and the viewplate in a fraction of a second. It hit the door with a thud, followed by a raging rattle of chitinous pincers. Its eye-stalks waved dementedly, peering at them through the viewplate.

Hendry backed off, sweating, and looked in sudden alarm for the others. Olembe and Carrelli were slowly walking along the length of the chamber, approaching the tall oval plate at the far end, like supplicants in a cathedral.

He turned to the viewplate. The sound from outside was growing louder, a frantic scrabbling and scraping as more aliens joined the first and sought to force their way inside.

"Oh, Christ. Let's just hope the doors hold," Kaluchek said. He took her arm and they hurried up the aisle towards Olembe and Carrelli.

"Our friends still trying to get intimate?" Olembe asked.

"Christ knows how long that thing'll hold," Hendry said.

Carrelli was staring at the bronze oval before them. "Long enough," she said with infuriating calm, "to allow us to work out what this thing is."

Hendry gazed up at the portal set into the stonework. The bronze oval was perhaps ten metres tall, with a pattern of arabesques decorating its surface.

"Maybe," he found himself saying, "it's the entrance to some kind of transporter." He wondered if he was making wild assumptions again. "That's why the filament wasn't in the aerial image: it connects briefly when the station on the facing tier is geo-synchronous."

Olembe said, "You're reading my mind, Joe. Question is, how brief is briefly? My guess is very brief. Presuming this thing's connected to the world at the other end, and both worlds are turning, then the period of connection can't be that long. I reckon we don't have much time before disconnection."

Carrelli said, "Then it would be another day— however long a day is on this world—before it reconnects."

Olembe smiled. "And I don't want to spend a day locked in this place with those critters baying for our blood."

Carrelli stepped forward, almost hesitantly, and laid a palm on a patterned section of portal. Instantly the oval panel began to slide open, surprising Carrelli who stepped back with a gasp.

"How the hell did you do that?" Olembe said.

Carrelli shook her head. "That symbol," she said, pointing to a vaguely fish-shaped hieroglyph. "It was similar to the one that opened the outer door."

They stared into the revealed chamber, awed and silent. Hendry made out a vast space, dimly lit.

At last Olembe said, "Okay, get the truck."

Hendry hurried back to the truck with Kaluchek and hauled himself aboard. Outside, the aliens were still scraping at the doorway. He glanced at the viewplate, and wished he hadn't. Frantic claws had excavated a deep gouge in the material.

Kaluchek revved the engine and steered towards the chamber. She braked before the entrance while Olembe and Carrelli climbed aboard.

They stared into the chamber.

"Okay, let's do it," Olembe said at last.

She started up the truck. It rolled slowly forward, crossing the threshold. A second later the portal eased shut behind them and Kaluchek cut the engine. All was silent for a second or two, and then Hendry became aware of a faint but definite vibration, as if the vehicle was still in motion.

Olembe opened the door and swung from the cab, climbing down onto the deck and laughing. "We're going up," he said.

Hendry joined him, followed by the others. He stood very still, feeling the vibration that ran through the soles of his feet and up his legs. At the same time, his stomach seemed to be floating. He recalled the sensation from elevators back home, but found it hard to believe that he was really riding some kind of transportation system between the tiers.

"The air's breathable in here," Olembe said, looking up from his softscreen.

Hendry pulled off his faceplate, breathing in warm air tinged with a sharp, metallic note. He moved to the edge of the floor, where scrollwork tiles segued seamlessly into an identically patterned wall. The chamber was oval, like the inside of an egg, one with the colour and design of the ziggurat's interior panelling.

He reached out and touched the warm metal, and felt a distinct thrumming beneath his fingertips.

Kaluchek said, "Do you think the same beings built the elevator and the helix?"

"It'd make sense," Olembe said, "to have a transport system between the tiers. The alternative would be some form of space flight, which might be costly, or else it's the long haul up the spiral."

"There was no sign down there of the beings who built this," Hendry said. "Unless those aliens are the devolved ancestors of the original builders."

"What a terrible thought." Kaluchek shivered.

"The builders must exist somewhere," Carrelli said, smiling at the notion. "I imagine them as an incredibly ancient, wise race. Anyone who had the capability of constructing the helix must have been around for a long, long time."

"How romantic," Olembe said. "And what if your wise ones turned out to be ichor-dripping fascist lizards?"

Carrelli chose to ignore him. They returned to the truck and shared out the rations.

As they ate, Carrelli said, "I've been thinking. This can't be the only elevator on the helix. There must be others, no?"

"Don't see why not," Olembe grunted.

"So maybe there will be a series of elevators, connecting each tier of the spiral at certain intervals."

Hendry said, "Well, that'd make the task of finding a habitable world a little easier."

"If you're right, Gina," Kaluchek said, "then we might find somewhere in a matter of days. Imagine the reaction of the colonists when we wake them with the good news."

Olembe pointed at her. "Always assuming, Sis, that the worlds we find aren't already inhabited."

Hendry was considering this when the chamber seemed to bob. He rocked in his seat, his stomach flipping. The sensation was as if he'd been spun quickly head-over-heels and returned to his original position.

Kaluchek said, "Midpoint, right? We turned in the tube, and now we're heading down to the next tier, the one above the first?"

Carrelli looked up from her sectioned plate and nodded. "My guess too, Sissy. We should be reaching the next tier in about ninety minutes."

They wondered aloud at what they might find on the next tier, and whether it might be warmer than the last, and habitable—or inhabited.

Hendry imagined finding some temperate, habitable and vacant world, and then returning to the *Lovelock* and leading the colonists, via the filament, to their destination. Surely the colonisation of the helix would not prove to be that simple?

Or perhaps they had experienced the worst of the mission so far, and the rest would be plain sailing.

He climbed from the cab. He wanted to be on the deck when they touched down, not confined in the truck. He crossed to the wall and touched the scrolled patterning of the bronze tiles, wondering if the design was merely aesthetic or possessed some inherent meaning. Lost in thought, he moved slowly around the chamber.

He recalled the last time he had seen Chrissie, at the starship graveyard in Melbourne. They had held each other as they said goodbye. She had been so real in his arms, so solid and vital—and if he closed his eyes he could feel her again.

Kaluchek said, "You're miles away."

He opened his eyes. "I was thinking... weeks ago, subjectively, I was facing a future on Earth without

Chrissie." The instant he said it, he wished he hadn't. It had sounded so self-piteous.

She looked at him. "Joe, I'm sorry..."

They were silent for a time, staring at the curlicues and whorls that adorned the tiles. Kaluchek glanced back at the truck.

Hendry said, "Why the downer on Friday, Sissy? You said—"

She wrinkled her nose. "Because the guy's a shit," she said.

He shrugged. "He seems to have done a decent job so far, taking charge and all."

She looked at him. "I know you're going through hell with what happened back there, but don't let it blind you to what Olembe's doing."

"He's doing his best to lead us to safety." He hesitated, then said, "Back in the truck, you said something about Olembe's past."

"Yeah..." Unexpectedly, she took his hand and said, "Joe, listen—back in Berne, while I had some free time, I did some research on the folks I'd be living with for God knew how long."

"And?"

She asked, "What did he tell you about himself?"

"Not much, just that he had a wife, kids."

"He didn't tell you what he did for a living?"

"I assumed he was a nuclear engineer."

"He was. He worked at the big N'gombe plant near Abuja. But before that he was a colonel in the West African Army."

Hendry shook his head, at a loss to see where this was leading. "So?"

"He was in charge of the unit that took five hundred hostages in the war with Morocco six years ago. Five hundred men, women and children. They were held for ransom. The WEA wanted a mass release of its prisoners from jails in Rabat and Casablanca. They threatened to kill the hostages—women and children first."

Hendry looked back at the truck. Olembe and Carrelli were in the cab, sitting side by side without speaking.

"And? I didn't keep up with world events back then."

Kaluchek stared up at him. "The Moroccan government held out, and Olembe was as good as his word. He ordered the murder of the hostages. All five hundred were killed and buried in a mass grave in the Sahara."

Hendry shook his head. "Christ. Sissy... you sure about this?"

"Unlike you, Joe, I did nothing but keep up with world news five years ago, wondering where the hell we were going. I took a big interest in what that bastard did. He was never arrested, never tried. The five hundred were just another set of casualties in wars and famines and other disasters that'd claimed the lives of millions. When I got to Berne, I thought I recognised Olembe. I did some checking on what's left of the web. When I knew for definite, I got hold of Bruckner, asked him if he knew he was employing a mass murderer."

"What did he say?"

"He prevaricated, but I pressed him and he admitted that ESO was aware of Olembe's past."

"And they were turning a blind eye because they were desperate for competent engineers so close to launch?"

Kaluchek was nodding, her face hard. "You got it, Joe." She looked across at the cab. "Now you know why I don't like the bastard."

Hendry nodded, lost for words. Kaluchek went on, "I don't like the idea of someone like Olembe benefiting from ESO's largesse. More than that, I don't like the idea of starting anew with a mass murderer in our midst.

"Sissy, don't do anything foolish like confronting him."

"Don't take me for a mug, Joe. I'll wait till things have sorted themselves out, till we've found a world we can settle and got the colonists up there... then I'll tell the authorities what I know and they can take it from there."

Hendry nodded. "Fine. That sounds like the best thing."

"So anyway, as I was saying, be aware of what he is when he's issuing all those commands, okay? Don't trust the bastard an inch."

Back at the crash-landing site, out on the ice when the alien had attacked, what Olembe had done had effectively saved his life... Of course, Olembe had done it to save his own life, too, but nevertheless Hendry had felt then some debt of gratitude for his actions.

He wondered what had driven Olembe to order the murder of five hundred innocent men, women and children.

He looked at Kaluchek. "And while you were checking up on your travelling companions, what did you get on me?"

She shook her head. "Not much. I know about what happened to your wife. I couldn't help noting the irony."

He nodded. "You mean, the Fujiyama Green Brigade's responsibility for killing the five members of the original maintenance team? Had that not happened, I wouldn't be here now. I'd be a thousand years dead."

"Life's strange, Joe. And if it was the Brigade who managed to sabotage the *Lovelock*..."

He closed his eyes. What might his wife have said about the Brigade's actions bringing about the death of her only daughter? How might she have justified that act of terrorism? The frightening thing was the thought that she would do just that, claim that personal sacrifice, no matter how bitter, was of little consequence beside the accomplishment of the Brigade's objectives.

Kaluchek was saying, "I also tried to find something on Carrelli, but you know what? I couldn't find a thing. Not one thing. It was as if everything about the woman had been wiped from the files, or as if she'd never existed."

Hendry said, "If you're right about her being a shrink, then maybe she's an ESO plant. They recruited her, gave her a new identity..."

"Yeah, that's what I thought, Joe. But why?"

They were interrupted by a shout from the cab. Olembe was leaning out, grinning. "Hey, you two lovebirds paired off already? Breeding starts only when the colony is set up."

"Jesus!" Kaluchek said, quickly withdrawing her hand from Hendry's.

They moved around the chamber, Hendry staring up at the arch high above.

Five minutes later, just as he was beginning to wonder if they would ever come to the end of the ride, the pitch of the vibration change subtly. "Feel that?"

Kaluchek nodded. "Christ, this is it. I don't know whether to feel elated or shit scared."

Olembe called out from the truck again, "Okay, I suggest we put the masks back on. We don't know what the atmosphere will be like outside."

Kaluchek pulled a face at Hendry. "Talk about stating the fucking obvious!"

Kaluchek made her way to the truck, but Hendry remained where he was, staring at the oval portal as the vibration conducted through the decking diminished. He pulled on his faceplate and felt the sudden tightness of apprehension in his chest.

Minutes later the sense of being afloat ceased; then the chamber jolted, ever so slightly. Slowly, the portal slid open, revealing a chamber identical to the one they had left behind. Hendry stepped from the elevator, then paused and stared down the length of the aisle.

The design on the sloping panels to either side was so similar to the ziggurat below that it might have been the very same building. The only difference was that the sliding door at the far end of the aisle was open to reveal darkness beyond.

He looked back into the chamber. Olembe turned the truck, spinning it on one track so that it faced the exit. The others peered through the windscreen, watching Hendry.

He pointed to himself, then signalled towards the exit. Olembe gave him the thumbs up.

He moved along the aisle, at once curious and apprehensive as to what he might find. He came to the great doorway and peered out into a blizzard of swirling snow. A fierce wind raged, and he was suddenly thankful for the protective warmth of his atmosphere suit. He raised his laser, stepped cautiously across the threshold and peered around him.

The ziggurat stood on a great snow-covered plain. A grey cloudrace surged overhead. He looked up at the shadowy shape of the transport filament rising into the darkness. He turned and raised a beckoning arm.

The truck grumbled to life and accelerated down the aisle and out of the ziggurat. It braked beside him and Kaluchek jumped down, followed by the others.

"Just like the tier we left." Kaluchek's voice sounded tinny over the radio link.

Olembe consulted his softscreen. "It's twenty degrees warmer. Positively tropical."

Kaluchek stepped forward, then halted. She pointed, indicating something in the snow before them. Hendry made out an area that had been disturbed, a patch of scuffed snow and the unmistakable shape of footprints.

They approached as one, knelt and examined the prints.

"My guess is that whoever made these are bipedal and walk upright," Olembe said. "But they're much smaller than us."

They were pondering his words when they heard a sound in the air. Hendry tried to identify it. A deep, throaty, thrumming sound... like some kind of primitive engine.

He looked up, and the noise was explained.

Riding high in the air, perhaps a kilometre to the
east and just beneath the level of the cloudrace, he
made out the shapes of two dirigibles heading away
from the ziggurat.

## Six /// The Zorl

**I**

THE SNOWSTORM CLEARED towards midday and the wind abated, and the dirigible enjoyed a calm passage high above the rilled snowdrifts of the western plain. Ehrin was at the controls, with Sereth seated on the divan, making notes of her dialogue with the tribesman.

At one stage she looked up and said, "Wait until I return to college with this, Ehrin. There are things here that will turn accepted thinking on its head. For instance, the old school assume that the tribes of the plain speak a different language completely. But what I heard out there proves that both come from a common root, suggesting that at one point in the past the ancestors of the modern-day tribes left the city for the plains—or even the reverse, that they left the plains for the city." She looked up, across to where Elder Cannak was sitting with his sharp nose in the Book of Books.

"That would accord with Church thinking, wouldn't it, Elder?" she asked. "The tribes and the city dwellers are all one people, created by God and placed upon the platform to do his will."

Cannak looked up, a spatulate fingertip marking his place in the text. "It is reassuring that one of you at least subscribes to the word of God. You would do well to pay heed to your fiancée, Mr Telsa."

Ehrin chose not to reply, but said instead, "That we are all one people seems patently obvious to me, Sereth. What is more mysterious is the provenance of the ziggurat, and who might have built it? What purpose did it serve, and when? There are a thousand questions I want answering!"

Sereth said, "What does the Church say on such matters, Elder?"

Cannak looked up from his book. "Logic dictates, since we are the only sentient race on the platform, that therefore we, long ago in the distant past, must have ventured out upon the plain for whatever reasons and constructed the edifice. Perhaps it was erected to the glory of God?"

Ehrin glanced at the Elder. "And the silver column Kahran witnessed, and of which the tribesman spoke?"

Cannak gave a disarming smile. "Perhaps it was conceived as some form of corridor to heaven," he said half-facetiously.

"It seemed to be coming the other way, Elder," Ehrin pointed out. "From heaven to the land. Perhaps God wishes to come down from time to time and walk amongst us?"

"And woe betide the heathen sinner if He does," the holy man said.

Sereth said, "But seriously, what can the ziggurat be? And why is it so large? It's as if it were constructed not by men, but by giants."

Ehrin said, "No doubt the Church will have it that we were taller in the days of old, eh, Elder?"

"Your atheistic jibes fall not on deaf ears, Mr Telsa, and are duly noted." He hesitated, then went on, "And anyway, we have only the word of Shollay that the column existed. He might have hallucinated it in his delirium."

"We'll have proof enough when he develops his photographs," Ehrin said.

Cannak elected to maintain a dignified silence. Sereth pulled a face at Ehrin, at once anxious and irritated at his childish jibes. Ehrin winked at her and turned his attention to the snow-covered plains below.

He had kept a sharp eye out during the past four hours for any sign of habitation or life down below. Other than the occasional wild zeer, and smaller beasts he was unable to identify from this altitude, the plain was bereft of a living thing. This fact, he reasoned, was not all that surprising, given the inhospitable nature of the land. He saw no trees in the wilderness, not the slightest hint of grass or shrub, and nothing in the way of cover from the relentless wind. How the tribesmen survived, let alone flourished, in such hostile climes was beyond him. And yet by the appearance of the lead tribesman and his cohorts, they seemed as strong and healthy as any pampered city dweller.

Just then his attention was drawn to a curious feature on the ice. He peered, and made out a series of trenches or ditches that appeared as short, dark strips cut into the permafrost far below. There were perhaps a dozen of them, each one approximately three hundred feet long and fifteen wide, arranged in a stepped line across the landscape. Ehrin wondered if they were a natural feature—surely not?—or something created by tribesmen, for whatever reason.

Fifteen minutes later the freighter signalled to suggest landfall. Ehrin replied in the affirmative and throttled back the engines. Their dinning tone dropped and the gondola rocked as they descended to the plain.

Cannak looked up. "We are landing?"

"The geologists want to set up another test bore. We'll be here for another day, at least."

"Then let us hope that this stop is less eventful than the last," the Elder said.

Five minutes later the *Expeditor* came to rest, with the freighter close behind. Kahran still had not emerged from his cabin, which was temporarily doubling as a dark room while he developed his photographic plates. Rather than disturb him, Ehrin dug out a new set of spikes from the storeroom and ventured outside. For the next fifteen minutes he made the dirigible secure, thankful that the snow had not returned and that the wind was manageable.

A hundred yards away the engineers were hauling the drilling rig from the hold of the freighter and beginning the laborious process of setting up the bore.

When he returned to the gondola, Sereth had prepared a tureen of stew, and he joined Cannak and his fiancée for lunch in the lounge. The conversation was stilted—Ehrin made awkward small-talk about what the geologists hoped to find this far west. He was grateful when a cabin door opened in the corridor and Kahran hurried out, flapping a series of prints.

He spread them on the table, almost knocking over pots and bowls in his enthusiasm. He sat down and pointed. "The quality isn't up to what I'd hoped, but look, here and here, see—the column."

The prints showed the dull shape of the upper reaches of the ziggurat, blurred by the snowstorm, against the grey backdrop of the sky. In two of the prints, a bizarre tentacular shape could be seen, hanging in the air above the summit, but short of the complex array of girders by about ten yards.

"It hung in place for perhaps fifteen minutes," Kahran explained, "before rising and sweeping off through the air. I received the impression that the thing was fabricated from some metallic substance, and worked somehow on the principle of a telescope, with jointed segments retracting into its length... But I allow that the visibility was poor, and as to the actual mechanics of the device..." he spread his hands, "well, I'm only guessing."

Cannak hardly spared the prints a glance before returning to his stew. Sereth was frowning at the blurred images, a worried expression on her pretty face.

Ehrin stared at the prints in wonder. Had he been told a couple of days ago that the voyage would prove so eventful, so soon, he would have scoffed.

He was in danger, now, of becoming inured to the wonders discovered on the plain. Kahran's photographs restored that sense of awe.

To his old friend he said, "As a boy, I dreamed of exploring the world with my father, or discovering all the answers to the big questions: how and why we are here, where exactly *here* is..." He traced the outline of the column with a fingertip. "This... I don't know, but this seems to make all those unanswerable questions valid again. Nature isn't as we perceived it once upon a time." He looked at Kahran. "Everything is changing, and we are here to witness it."

Kahran stared at him, shaking his head.

Elder Cannak laid his Book of Books upon the tabletop and tapped it with a thin forefinger. "Gentlemen, all the answers you will ever require are to be found in here, and one day you will be granted the wisdom to acknowledge the truth of my words."

Kahran merely smiled, gathered the prints and moved to the other side of the room, where he sat in silent contemplation of his handiwork.

Sereth pulled Ehrin to his feet, "Come on, before you two get into another futile argument. Excuse us, Elder. I will educate my erring fiancée by reciting poetry."

"Poetry?" Ehrin goggled as Sereth pulled him from the lounge.

"Shh!" She dug him in the ribs with an elbow and laughed as she kicked open their cabin door and turned to embrace him. "Ehrin, forget all about the uncertainties for a while, please, and make love to me, hm?"

He carried her to the bed where, mindful of the berth's thin partitions, he did his best to obey her.

An hour later, as he lay on his back and held Sereth to him, he heard the drill start up and the shouted commands of the engineers.

Sereth said, "Have you thought about what might happen when we return home?"

"Yes," he lied. "We arrive in Agstarn triumphant, having struck oil and gold; we'll have made our fortune and discovered wonders little dreamed of by the hidebound philosophers back home. Then we'll marry and build a vast dirigible to take us as far as the circumferential sea."

Propped on one elbow, she stared at him. "We will? You never told me that?"

"Well, it's only just occurred to me that it would be a wonderful thing to do."

"What, to marry—or to sail the circumferential sea?"

He grinned and kissed her. "Both," he said.

She sighed. "Do you want to know what will really happen?"

"I have a depressing feeling that you're going to tell me."

"We'll return to Agstarn and you'll be arrested by the militia for unholy conduct. You might escape a jail sentence, but you'll have your company assets confiscated. And, worse, I'll be forced to renounce you and marry some clerk of the Church."

He pulled her to him, kissing her snout. "Ser, come on... Old Cannak is a fool. Hykell, despite his position, is more enlightened than that. Just so long as I don't try to proclaim my atheism to all and sundry, I'll be allowed my freedom. You don't think for a minute that they'd take the company from me? The city relies on Telsa Dirigibles for its prosperity."

"You don't think they'd be able to find someone else, just as young and ambitious, but religious, to run the company?"

He blinked. "They wouldn't do that, would they?"

She stared down on him, stroking the fur of his cheek. "If you keep baiting Cannak, he'll do his best when we return to bring you to your knees. Go easy on him, Ehrin. Ignore him rather than risk incurring his wrath, hm?"

He was silent for a long time after that, while Sereth napped on his chest and he stared up at the low ceiling, her dire prophecy overlaying his own dreams with images of gloating Elders and stark freezing frames.

He thought of Kahran, and what he and his father had discovered on the expedition to Sorny... Then the Church had done all in its power to silence the men, and certainly in Kahran's case they had succeeded. A handful of mangled fingers, and much rancour, testified to the fact.

No wonder that now, face to face with Elder Cannak, and the reality of the authoritarian regime of Agstarn so far away as to seem of little threat, Kahran was bent on exacting his own small, perhaps futile, revenge on the representative of the High Church.

Perhaps he should take Sereth's words seriously, and cease his criticism of Cannak and his beliefs?

Later they stirred themselves and climbed out of bed. The others were no longer in the lounge, having retired to their own cabins. Ehrin left Sereth with her notes, pulled on his padded jacket and ventured out onto the plain.

He found Kyrik beside the test bore, supervising the work of the dozen engineers and fellow geologists. They had erected a small cabin beside the rig, and the workers took it in turn to step out of the wind and warm themselves in the shelter with mugs of tea.

The noise from the drill, added to the howling wind, made conversation almost impossible. Kyrik clapped him on the shoulder and pointed to the freighter, and the two men crossed the snow and entered the looming cavern of the dirigible's hold.

"We've hit a seam of iron." the geologist reported. "At this stage it's hard to tell how extensive it is, but we're hopeful. We're going deeper, and the test should be in within the hour. If it's high grade, and there's enough of it, then the expedition's exceeded all expectations."

"Good news." He shook Kyrik's hand. "Let's keep hoping…" he said by way of farewell.

"And praying, Ehrin. Let's pray we bring glory to the Church in the eyes of God."

Ehrin, wearing a fixed smile, nodded and feebly echoed the geologist's sentiments. "Let's hope so, Kyrik."

He stepped out into the wind, watched the drilling for five minutes, then looked around—a great three-sixty degree sweep of the plain—at the desolate and forbidding landscape. He thought of Agstarn, the heated mansions, the bountiful markets… and the repressive regime of the Church. Shuddering, he made his way back to the *Expeditor*.

That evening, as darkness fell across the land, they ate a meal of meat pastries and boiled vegetables in the lounge, the notable absence being Elder Cannak who elected to dine alone in his cabin. Ehrin for one was relieved. The continual presence of the prim, upright Elder—censorious to a degree—made Ehrin want to goad the man. In light of Sereth's earlier warning, Ehrin had decided to think twice before confronting Cannak; even ignoring the man would be preferable to getting himself deeper into trouble.

The three ate well, the conversation helped along by a bottle of summer-fruit wine. Kahran, growing maudlin, told them of his childhood in the slum outskirts of Agstarn, and then his apprenticeship at the foundry, where he had soon formed a strong working partnership, then friendship, with his boss, Ehrin's father.

"They were great days, Ehrin. The company was small, but ambitious. Together we designed and developed some of the airships that would become great—the Telsa 17b, the Arrow, which grew into what is now the Telsa cargo freighter. I don't know, but it seemed that the Church left us alone back in the early days, didn't interfere with what we did. Perhaps it was just that we were a small concern, but now that we're big, well, the Church wants its grubby finger in the fat pie."

Sereth said, "Were you never religious, even as a boy?"

Kahran smiled into his wine. "My father always said that religion for the poor was but another form of repression, while for the rich it was merely another means of wielding power." He laughed.

"With a father like that, how could I have grown up pious?"

"It's no wonder that you became fast friends with my father, Kahran."

The old man tipped his glass, then dabbed a droplet of wine from his greying snout. "We were like this," he said, meshing his fingers. "We made Telsa Dirigibles what it is today. Later," and he laughed a little drunkenly here, "Agstarn became too small for us. We craved adventure. We conceived an expedition, west to the outpost of Sorny." He stopped, then said, "I look back and wonder whether I regret venturing there. It made me what I am today, forged my view of the world... but the sacrifices..." He terminated his recollections by draining his glass and reaching for the bottle.

"More wine!" he cried. "Drink has charms to soothe the troubled spirit!"

Sereth smiled. "I've had enough for one day, Kahran." She hesitated, and Ehrin saw that she was considering asking Kahran about Sorny, and he shook his head warningly.

Later, perhaps when they were back in Agstarn, he would ply Kahran with wine and try to learn the truth for himself.

A little later, a knock sounded at the hatch. Kyrik entered, apologising for the interruption, and reported good news. The lode they had discovered was huge—enough to supply the needs of Agstarn for at least five years, at a conservative estimate. The plan was to continue drilling through the night, to assess the true extent of the seam, and then discuss the situation in the morning. One body of opinion among the geologists was that they should return immediately to Agstarn so that the development of the site might be initiated as soon as possible.

Ehrin said that they should discuss the possibility at first light. When Kyrik departed, he said to Sereth, "So we might yet return to Agstarn in triumph."

Sereth was about to reply when an explosion like thunder, but sharper, cracked above their heads. Sereth shrieked and grabbed his hand. Ehrin started, almost knocking over the table, while Kahran swore pithily and then excused himself to Sereth.

"The rig!" Ehrin cried, jumping up and grabbing his padded jacket.

Cannak emerged from his cabin, looking alarmed. "By all that's holy, what was that?"

Ehrin rushed for the hatch, ignoring the Elder, while behind him Sereth explained that perhaps something had happened to the test bore.

With Kahran not far behind him, Ehrin left the *Expeditor* and hurried over to the rig. The geologists and engineers were gathered outside the cabin, staring at the darkening southern horizon. Ehrin looked to the rig, saw nothing amiss, then found Kyrik. "What the hell was that?"

In reply, Kyrik pointed.

High in the sky to the south, the deepening darkness of the overcast was bisected by a fiery line, which vectored towards the plain perhaps five miles away.

Kahran grasped Ehrin's arm and hissed, "Your father had a theory—if any airborne vessels were to exceed the speed of sound, then they would create a... an acoustic explosion, I think he called it. Don't you see!"

Ehrin felt a little dizzy, at once relieved that the rig was undamaged, but having to come to terms with what Kahran was telling him.

As he watched, whatever it was that had streaked through the heavens came to ground to the west; he awaited the resulting explosion, but none came.

The geologists, conversing among themselves, returned to work on the bore. Kahran was still gripping his elbow. "We can't just stand here like stuffed zeer! We've got to go and investigate."

His heart thumped. "What do you think it was?"

"Whatever it is, the bastard Cannak would proscribe our investigations."

"We needn't tell him." Ehrin thought about it. "Kahran, we'll take the freighter. Tell Kyrik what we're doing—make some excuse along the lines that the Elder is sleeping so we can't take the *Expeditor*. I'll go and tell Sereth."

Kahran nodded and rushed off to find the geologist. Ehrin, excitement creating a delicious pressure in his chest, made his way back to the dirigible.

Sereth and Elder Cannak were in the lounge, and both looked up when he entered. "Well?" Cannak asked querulously.

"I don't know what it was," he said. "We're taking the freighter up, to get a better look over the area. I suspect it was nothing more than a freak meteorological effect. We'll probably find nothing."

Cannak gave him a dubious look, as if he suspected Ehrin of concealing the truth. "Do you need an extra pair of hands?" the Elder asked.

"There's no need. I'm taking Kahran."

Sereth stood. "Take care, Ehrin."

He managed a laugh. "There's nothing to worry about. Brew some more tea. We'll be in need of it when we get back."

He kissed her, nodded towards the Elder and slipped from the lounge.

Kahran met him beside the double hatch of the freighter's gondola. "I'm surprised Cannak didn't try to stop you."

"I said it was probably thunder, but that we're taking the freighter up for a look."

Kahran laughed. "All set?"

While Ehrin settled himself at the controls and started the engines, Kahran moved around the freighter pulling up the spikes. Five minutes later he joined Ehrin in the control room as the freighter rose, turned slowly, and moved off to the west.

Ehrin kept the dirigible low to the ground, the better to see... whatever was to be seen, wreckage or debris of some kind, perhaps. He looked across at Kahran. The old man was staring through the forward window, his watery eyes alert.

"If it were something... a craft... that flew faster than sound..." He shook his head. "We don't have such technology, Kahran."

The oldster nodded, not taking his eyes off the plain below. "It's a big world, Ehrin. Agstarn does not comprise its extent. What lies over the horizon, and beyond even *that*?"

Ehrin stared at him. "Sorny," he whispered.

Kahran grinned. "Try even further than Sorny, my boy."

Before Ehrin could beg an explanation, Kahran cried out and pointed. Ehrin slowed the engines and peered through the window, heart hammering.

Down below, dark against the pale ice field, he made out a deep rut scored across the plain; it ran for perhaps two hundred yards, terminating in a wedge-shaped object half-buried in a frozen bow-wave of snow.

He felt dizzy, and a hot wave of nausea swept over him. He clutched at the controls to steady himself, then throttled down the engines and brought the freighter to hover over the crash-landed craft.

*Craft...* something manufactured, flown here for a reason, by people with a technological sophistication far in advance of anything in his wildest dreams.

The thought was at once terrifying and irresistibly alluring.

"Take the crate down," Kahran said. "I'll make it fast. Then..." He looked at Ehrin, reached out and gripped his hand. "Then we'll go for a closer look."

Ehrin nodded, something constricting his throat. He lowered the freighter, bringing it to rest on the plain fifty yards from the downed vessel. While Kahran hurried from the cabin and secured the hawsers, Ehrin settled the engines and stared out through the window.

Little could be seen of the craft from this angle, other than the piled snow it had pushed up with its precipitate landing. The superstructure that was visible glowed a dull gold in the dying light. Nothing moved, other than a curl of steam rising from its carapace.

Kahran appeared at the hatch. "Ready?"

Ehrin laughed nervously. "To tell the truth, I'm not sure. What if it... if they're..." But Kahran was already moving away from the dirigible. Ehrin swallowed his fear and stepped from the cabin, pulling his hood up against the wind and following Kahran through the snow.

They paused a few yards from the craft, side-by-side, and stared.

The vehicle was small—a little larger perhaps than the gondola of the *Expeditor*, but far more streamlined and... alien. This close, Ehrin made out an array of six rear-mounted engines, their nacelles glowing red hot.

In the flank of the craft was a triangular window and—Ehrin found this alarming—there was a faint white light issuing from within.

He looked at Kahran. The old man wore a wide-eyed, shocked expression, the fur of his face standing upright with what might have been fear or alarm. Ehrin wondered if he himself looked as stricken.

Kahran took his arm. "Shall we take a closer look?"

Ehrin thought of Sereth, back at the dirigible, of the good citizens of Agstarn going about their daily business in complete ignorance of this momentous event...

He stepped forward, Kahran shuffling by his side, and approached the flank of the craft. Even above the keening of the wind he could hear his boots crunching the iced snow.

A yard from the triangular viewscreen, he could see what appeared to be black leather padding within, and small lights on what might have been an overhead console.

He felt his stomach clench as he stepped forward, aware of Kahran right beside him, and peered into the craft.

What he saw made him gasp and back away in fright, Kahran clutching his arm in alarm. Like schoolchildren they approached again, Ehrin's curiosity overcoming his apprehension.

A being lay almost horizontally on some kind of padded couch; its head was twisted towards the viewscreen, but the being was either dead or unconscious. Its left leg was bent at an awkward angle, as if broken with the impact of landing.

It wore a silver one-piece suit, which was strange enough, but the oddest thing about the creature was its face. It was black and very wrinkled, its features scrunched, and totally without hair. It looked at once naked and fearsome without facial hair, vulnerable and yet paradoxically aggressive.

Kahran was staring in at the creature, his snout pressed against the glass.

"Is it dead?" Ehrin asked.

Kahran shook his head. "No. See, its chest is rising and falling. Just injured, I suspect."

"We ought to be careful. If it regains consciousness and sees us, it might be hostile."

Kahran smiled, more to himself than to Ehrin. "It isn't hostile," he said.

Ehrin looked at him. "How do you know that?"

Kahran ignored him; he was moving along the flank of the craft, searching for something. Ehrin followed, Kahran's words, and now his actions, mystifying him. "Kahran?"

They came to the outline of a hatch, flush with the skin of the craft. Inset was a lever, which Kahran grasped and turned clockwise. There was a sudden hissing sound from within, and the rectangular hatch seemed to levitate from its housing. It sighed towards them quickly, swinging outwards and upwards, and revealed the interior of the craft.

Kahran stepped through first. Ehrin, panicked, said, "Do you think this is wise?"

Kahran turned to him. "Believe me, we have nothing to fear."

Ehrin followed the old man into the alien ship, wondering what Elder Cannak might have to say if he could see them now.

A short corridor took them to the cramped control room where the creature lay, still unmoving. All was in darkness, the only illumination provided by the tiny sequencing lights on the various consoles that surrounded the being.

Kahran knelt beside the creature and felt for its pulse. He looked up and nodded. "He's alive."

Ehrin could only stare. In the flesh, the creature seemed even more alien and ugly than when seen through the viewscreen. Also, it emanated a pungent body odour that Ehrin found unpleasant.

Kahran reached out and shook the creature's arm, gently.

Ehrin found his voice. "You said it wouldn't be hostile. How can you be certain?"

"They aren't," Kahran said.

"They?"

"They call themselves the Zorl," he explained, casting his eye over the creature's silver uniform. "They're a peaceful race."

Ehrin leaned against the wall of the control room, then found himself slipping onto his haunches. He shook his head. "How the hell..." he began, then stopped. "The expedition to Sorny," he said with sudden realisation. "The Zorl are from the western plains, from Sorny?"

Kahran looked up. He shook his head. "Try again. Try from across the circumferential sea."

Ehrin opened his mouth, but no words came. At last he echoed fatuously, "From across the circumferential sea?"

Every child in Agstarn was taught that the world was a platform, which floated in the grey void. At the very edge of the platform was the circumferential sea, beyond which was a continuation of the grey, which went on forever without end. As a boy, Ehrin had tried to envisage eternity, grey without end, going on forever and ever, but the concept had dizzied and frightened him.

Now Kahran was telling him that another platform existed beyond the sea, and that this strange creature hailed from there...

"But how do you know? I thought you said you went to Sorny—"

Kahran smiled at him. "Your father and I paused at Sorny, then ventured beyond. Hard though it is to imagine, we went with the blessing of the Church. Velkor Cannak and a colonel in the Church militia accompanied us."

Ehrin held his head in his hands and stared at his old friend. He had known Kahran for so long, and yet had hardly known him at all. "Beyond Sorny," he mouthed in wonder. "Tell me..."

Kahran smiled. "We flew over the sea, to another world—"

"Another platform?"

"Ehrin, we don't live on platforms. Imagine..." He stared into space, attempting to summon a suitable analogy. "Imagine a series of beads on a bracelet. Each bead is what we think of as a platform, except it isn't a flat plain but a cylindrical bead. There are many of these beads side by side, and between each one is a sea."

Ehrin felt his pulse pounding in his forehead. He was aware of his facial fur standing on end. "A cylindrical bead... But that must mean—let me think about this... But that means if you travel far enough in one direction, then you'll eventually arrive back where you started!" He laughed aloud at the astounding concept. His mind was in a spin. "And how many of these other worlds exist out there, on this great bead in the grey?"

Kahran shook his head. "That I don't know. We only ever travelled to the next one, to Zor as the natives called it. For all I know there might even be a dozen or more. The Zorl we met spoke of at least two others they were aware of..."

Ehrin stared at his friend. "And you told no one about this?"

Kahran's smile was sad. "How could I, with the Church threatening me with death if I so much as breathed a word?"

Ehrin closed his eyes, his head filled with bizarre visions. To think of it, that his own father had actually stepped onto the soil of another world...

"Why did the Church want to visit this other world? What did you see, Kahran?"

The old man shrugged. "The Church was led by a different Prelate back then. He was as much a bastard as Hykell, in fact a bigger bastard, but he at least had curiosity. He wanted to know if what the Church taught was the literal truth. Hence the voyage. As to what we found beyond the sea." He looked up, into Ehrin's eyes, and his expression was bleak. "We found an advanced civilisation of beings..." He gestured to the unconscious alien on the couch. "The Zorl. But their world was devastated. They had fought a war between themselves with weapons so powerful and terrible that we cannot imagine their like, weapons that laid waste to entire cities, killing millions in one strike, and which left a lingering illness in the air which eventually accounted for the survivors." He shook his head. "The sights we saw, your father and I, the devastation, the piled remains of beings long dead in the ruined cities that lined the coast... There were survivors, pitiful souls living like savages among the debris. We communicated with them as best we could, but of course they didn't speak our language. We found..." he paused, then went on, "we found strange flying machines, and what we took to be the weapons of annihilation, tall columns that we guessed were launched like firework rockets. My lasting image is of the people who survived, who lived among the objects of their world's downfall. They were as pitiful as animals, Ehrin."

Ehrin recalled what his father had written in the letter to his mother, fifteen years ago. *I have neither the space nor the time to describe here the terrible things K and I have seen today...*

"My father wrote to my mother, hinting at the things you saw..."

Kahran said, "Imagine, Ehrin. We were no young pups, wet behind the ears. We were learned men of the world. For all our experience, however, we knew nothing. Imagine discovering the truth about the universe, that we were not alone, and then discovering a race that had all but destroyed itself?"

Ehrin shook his head. "I cannot begin to imagine what it must have been like to witness at first hand." He looked up. "And then you returned, and the Church swore you to secrecy?"

Kahran nodded. "We protested, of course. We argued that the truth had to be told—if for nothing else, then as a warning to ourselves what the folly of power might wreak upon civilisation. But the Church wanted none of that; it had power, and supposed knowledge, and anything that subverted that knowledge with contrary facts of course threatened to weaken that power." He looked down at his right hand, from which the fingernails had been ripped, and Ehrin was shocked to see tears in his old friend's eyes.

He looked away, and his gaze rested on the creature—the Zorl—on the control couch. He took in the array of consoles that filled the craft, the sleek workmanship, the baffling instruments. "And now this," he murmured. "A Zorl from across the circumferential sea has come to our backward world."

"A return visit, as it were," Kahran said.

"But if its world was devastated as you said…"

"Perhaps they have rebuilt, or areas of it survived annihilation."

"Are you sure that this creature is a Zorl? Could it not be from a world beyond Zor even?"

Ehrin stopped and stared, for the creature, perhaps disturbed by their words, was stirring, attempting to lift itself into a sitting position upon the couch. It blinked huge black eyes at Ehrin and said, "We are Zorl," in a thick, almost incomprehensible dialect.

Ehrin found himself backing away, pushing himself even further against the wall, the hackles on the back of his neck bristling with fear.

Kahran was staring at the creature. "You... you speak our language?"

The being looked from Ehrin to Kahran. Its crumpled, wrinkled features were expressionless. It possessed eyes, nose, a mouth and ears, as did Ehrin's people—but its nose was a squashed affair, mere nostrils on the surface of its face, while its ears were small and flattened against the side of its head. Ehrin had never seen anything as ugly in his life, and that included the wild mountain zeer.

It spoke again, a gravelly rumble. "We have been watching you from afar. Some of us studied your language."

Ehrin wanted to ask why, and what the Zorl wanted here, but something stopped him. He stared at the pilot, down its silvered length to the buckled mess of its right leg.

The Zorl followed his gaze, its liquid black eyes focusing on the limb. He gestured to Kahran. "There. On the wall. Pass me the..." He said a word Ehrin didn't understand, but he was pointing at a square of material as black as the rest of the ship's fittings.

Kahran detached it from the wall and passed it to the Zorl.

Ehrin watched as the alien, grunting in pain, managed to straighten the broken limb. Then he took the dark material and wrapped it around his injured leg; it appeared to tighten, compress, and the Zorl lay back with a sigh of relief.

He looked from Ehrin to Kahran, then reached out and touched something on a console to his right.

Beyond the corridor, the hatch eased shut with a hiss.

Ehrin's heart skipped a beat.

"A precaution only," said the Zorl.

Ehrin found himself nodding, as if to placate the alien. If its physical appearance were not alarming enough, Ehrin found the advanced technology it had at its disposal even more disturbing.

The Zorl moved its huge eyes between Ehrin and Kahran, and said at last, "Are you in the employ of the Church?"

Ehrin could only shake his head. "Why... why do you ask?"

The Zorl stared at him. It moved its lips in an odd grimace. "I need to know my enemies," he said.

Ehrin exchanged a glance with Kahran. To the alien he said, "You... your enemy is the Church?"

The Zorl did not reply, but instead pulled something from the breast pouch of his silver suit. The device was small, square and flat, like a slate. From its glossy black surface depended two thin wires.

If it were a weapon, Ehrin had never seen its like before.

The Zorl inserted the end of the wires into an inlet in the arm of his suit, then held out the black plate to Ehrin. "You. Touch this when you reply to me. Do you understand?"

Ehrin nodded, his mouth suddenly dry.

"Now," said the Zorl, "are you in the employ of the Church?"

Hesitantly, Ehrin reached out and rested his fingertips on the plate. It pulsed with a slight heat. He said, "Technically, we have been hired by the Church to explore the western plains. But..." Here he looked at Kahran, as if for support. "But we are opposed to the Church and its regime in Agstarn."

As he spoke the plate grew warmer.

The Zorl pulled another of its odd lip-grimaces, and said, "You speak the truth, friend."

Ehrin stared at the plate. A device that could divine truth from lies...?

The alien said, "How far are we from your capital city?"

"Perhaps six hundred miles—a long day's flight from here." He stopped, realising the stupidity of his words. "But your ship could do it in a fraction of the time."

"The ship, my friend, is incapacitated. Even such a short journey is beyond it."

Kahran leaned forward. "You wish to go to Agstarn? For what purpose?"

Ehrin stared at the alien, wondering at the reaction of the Church to the arrival of the Zorl in the capital. He felt a thrilling pressure of excitement in his chest.

The alien was silent for a time, then replied with a question of his own, "Can you help me reach the capital city?"

Ehrin gasped and looked at Kahran, who said, "That depends on your mission there, my friend."

"My mission," the Zorl said, "is to locate a weapon your Church took from my world, a weapon of terrible capacity. Then I will destroy it."

"A weapon?" Ehrin echoed.

The Zorl continued, "My world fought a terrible war in the recent past. We who survived, we who rebuilt our world, renounced violence... But your Church took something from us, and if they were ever in a position to use it," the alien closed its fist in a gesture that had meaning only to itself, "then the Zorl would mourn anew."

A silence followed his words. Ehrin looked across at Kahran, who was staring into space, his mouth open as if in shock.

"Kahran?"

As if in a daze, his friend mouthed, "The deathship?"

The alien stared at him. "You know!"

Ehrin shook his head. "What? How do you know? A deathship?"

"Fifteen years ago, my friend," Kahran said, addressing the alien, "I came to your land, saw the destruction. We were led by agents of the Church. We found the deathships, only one of which was functioning." Kahran looked at Ehrin. "The Church coerced your father into working on the ship, fathoming its mechanics. While I was returned to Agstarn, your father remained on Zor until the ship was airworthy once more. Then he flew it to Agstarn."

"My father...?"

"He had no say in the matter." Kahran addressed the alien, "The Church, as you might know, is a force of evil on our world."

The Zorl made its lip-grimace again. "The fact that it possesses the deathship fills me with dread," he said. "I must reach Agstarn and destroy it."

Kahran leaned forward. "I can help you, my friend. The Church has a hangar in the mountains, where they keep the deathship."

The Zorl reached out with the truth plate, offering it to Kahran. "You truly know where the deathship is located."

Kahran reached out and touched the plate. "I know where it was fifteen years ago. I see no reason why the Church would have moved it."

The alien lay back on the couch, gripping the padding with its hairless black fingers. "Then all that remains is for me to reach Agstarn and find the hangar..."

Ehrin looked at Kahran. He said, "We could take him back in the freighter, conceal him in the hold, and then hide him in the foundry until it's time to find the deathship hangar."

Kahran nodded. "Very well. But what about this craft?" he asked the Zorl.

"Leave it here. It has served its purpose."

Ehrin stared at the alien. "But how... how will you get back to Zor? I mean, once you've destroyed the deathship, how will you...?"

The alien was staring at him with an odd intensity. "My return was never calculated in the scheme to destroy the deathship," he said simply.

Ehrin closed his mouth and nodded, his mind racing. "We could learn so much from this craft," he said in a small voice. "Why, it's years, decades ahead of anything we might create..." He puffed his chest. "I run a dirigible factory, designing many of the ships myself."

"This is an *interworld* ship," the Zorl said. "It can fly into space, through the vacuum, to the worlds on other levels."

"Other *levels*?" Ehrin repeated.

The alien lip-grimaced again. "Later, I have much to tell you about the universe beyond your present understanding," he said. "Meanwhile, if you would help me reach Agstarn, then the ship is yours."

"Mine?" Ehrin could only gasp. He turned to Kahran. "I have a suggestion. Hear me out. We take both the Zorl and the ship back to Agstarn…"

Kahran stared at him. "The ship too?"

"It will be easier to hide the alien in the ship, and the ship in the hold of the freighter, than to conceal the alien in the hold without him being discovered." He turned to the Zorl. "You can lock the hatch, and somehow cover the viewscreens so that it's impossible to see inside?"

The Zorl reached out, and the viewscreen beyond his head turned as black as the surrounding fittings.

Kahran said, "There is the little difficulty of getting the craft aboard the freighter, Ehrin. And how do you propose to keep the geologists from telling Cannak about the craft?"

"I'll talk to Kyrik. If he wants to hire the Telsa ships at much reduced rates in future, I'm sure he'll agree to keep quiet." He turned to the alien. "You said the ship is incapacitated… Would it move just a little, a matter of yards? We have a transporter nearby, with a cargo hold large enough to take the ship."

"The secondary drives are working—enough to allow the ship to hover. It's a component in the primary drive that suffered damage."

"In that case, if I position the freighter closer to the ship, can you manoeuvre it into the hold?"

The alien reached out, touching a series of glowing panels on a console above his head. Disconcertingly, the craft lifted quickly, bobbing in place perhaps a yard from the ground. He hit another panel and the hatch opened with a hiss.

"Before you go," the alien said, gesturing to his chest. "My name is Havor."

"I am Ehrin."

"Kahran," said the old man.

The alien grimaced again and inclined his head. Ehrin nodded to the alien, then hurried from the cabin. He jumped to the ground, assisting Kahran, and arm in arm they leaned into the wind and trudged back to the freighter.

Minutes later they stood side-by-side at the controls as Ehrin lifted the dirigible into the air and eased it fifty yards across the plain so that it sat before the hovering Zorl ship.

Kahran touched his shoulder. "Ehrin... what we are doing, if the Church found out, you do realise what they would do to us?"

Ehrin stared at his friend, and nodded. "I'm prepared to take that risk, Kahran. And you?"

"What do you think?" Kahran smiled. "You remind me so much of your father, Ehrin."

They left the gondola and stood side-by-side in the wind-driven snow as the Zorl ship eased itself slowly into the hold. They followed it in; the alien settled the ship in the far corner of the chamber, where it occupied a quarter of the floor-space.

They boarded the interworld ship again and crouched before the alien. "Is there anything you need? Food, water? You'll be shut up in here for a day or so, until we get back to the foundry."

"I have sufficient supplies to last me months," the Zorl said.

"We will meet again in two days from now. And then..." Ehrin grinned. "And then you can tell me more about the universe."

The Zorl reached out and took Ehrin's hand in an unusual gesture. "The pleasure will be mine."

They hurried from the hold, secured its double doors, then returned to the control cabin and hauled the freighter into the air, its engines whining at the increased load.

Ten minutes later Ehrin set the freighter down beside the *Expeditor* and took a deep breath. "I only hope Cannak doesn't see through our lies, Kahran."

"Allow me to do the talking, Ehrin."

"I'll find Kyrik and tell him about this ship," Ehrin said.

They left the freighter. The geologists and engineers gathered about the rig, talking animatedly among themselves. Kyrik saw them coming and waved. "Great news—the bore's yield exceeds anything we might have reasonably expected. We could head back home in the morning, if that suits you?"

Ehrin nodded. "We've had good luck too." He told the geologist they had found something on the plains. Inspired, he said that he thought it was a gondola from one of his father's old test dirigibles. Kyrik was too full of his own success to consider the likelihood of this.

Leaving the workers to their celebrations, Ehrin and Kahran crossed to the *Expeditor* and stepped into the warmth of the lounge. Sereth stood up when they entered. "Ehrin! You were an age! I thought you'd crashed, or lost your way."

He held her. "We're fine, Ser."

Cannak looked up from the Book of Books. "You were gone long enough."

Kahran grunted, "I wanted to find a crashed alien starship on the plains," he said, silencing a startled Cannak. "But all we did find was a mangy herd of wild zeer."

Ehrin suppressed a laugh and sat with Sereth, taking the pot of tisane she offered and warming his hands. He wanted to tell Sereth everything, but that would have to wait until their return to Agstarn.

And then, how to explain that he was harbouring an alien being bent on destroying Church property, albeit property stolen from its inventors?

In the morning, the engineers dismantled the test rig and stowed the equipment in the freighter's hold. An hour later they were in the air, Kahran at the controls and Ehrin staring out through the forward window at the driving snow as they headed east.

Elder Cannak was in his own room. Sereth was still sleeping.

Ehrin glanced across at Kahran, formulating the words to express what he had been thinking. "Kahran, did my father talk to you about the deathship after he'd returned to Agstarn?"

Kahran looked up. "We met only once, and we discussed it briefly."

"Did my father guess what a powerful weapon it was?"

Silently, Kahran nodded. "He knew, by the time he had worked on it and flown it back to Agstarn."

"But he still did the bidding of the Church?"

"Ehrin, you can't blame him. They threatened him with death. How was he to know that—" He stopped suddenly, and stared through the window.

Ehrin looked up. "Know what?"

Kahran turned tragic eyes on Ehrin. "How was your father to know that they intended to kill him anyway?"

Ehrin's stomach seemed to lurch, as if the dirigible had dropped ten metres. "My father's accident...?"

Kahran nodded. "Church militia planted a crude explosive within the ship's engine."

Ehrin felt tears sting his eyes. He looked at his old friend. "And yet they allowed you to live?"

Kahran stared down at his mangled fingers. "They tortured me to learn what I knew," he said. "I managed to deny that your father told me anything about the deathship..."

Ehrin stared ahead, seeing nothing.

Kahran placed a hand on his shoulder. "We will prevail, Ehrin. Be assured of that."

**I**

HENDRY DREAMED HE was back on Earth.

He was in the starship graveyard and, with the surreal displacement common to dreams, the five year-old Chrissie was living with him. In the dream he experienced an overwhelming love for this beautiful child, a love that was almost a melancholy ache, as if informed by her death a thousand years later.

He awoke suddenly and sat up, struggling in the confines of the inflatable sleeping bag. He shuffled back and leaned against the sloping wall of the chamber, staring across the floor to the squat shape of the ground-effect truck. Carrelli was sitting in the passenger seat, reading a softscreen. There was no sign of Olembe. Kaluchek, he noted with surprise, lay cocooned in her sleeping bag beside him.

He stared at her face, innocent in sleep of all expression, and marvelled at her similarity to his daughter. A sudden wave of grief broke over him, reducing him to silent sobs.

He worked to control himself. He lifted a hand and stared at it, then beyond the splayed fingers at the vast echoing emptiness of the chamber.

He experienced a sense of unreality, a sensation of mental remoteness from the physical fact of his presence here. He was on a distant world—no, an artificial construct built by an alien race—a thousand years after he had left everything he had known on Earth. He felt an uneasy dissonance with the reality around him; everything was strange, threatening, other than the three human beings who accompanied him. He felt a sudden surge of affection for his companions then, even Olembe, the prickly, aggressive mass murderer, if Kaluchek was to be believed; even Carrelli, the cool Italian whom it seemed impossible to get to know. And as for Kaluchek... He stared at her, and realised that he felt something for her beyond the obvious fact that she reminded him of Chrissie.

They were human beings. They were all he had in this inimical, alien landscape; the only points of emotional familiarity with which to orient himself. These three disparate humans, and the three thousand sleeping colonists back on the first tier, constituted a measure of hope in an otherwise hopeless situation.

Beside him, Kaluchek had turned in her bag. She laced her hands behind her head and smiled up at him. She had removed the hood of her atmosphere suit so that her jet hair fell round her face.

"Olembe ran a check," she explained. "The air in here's breathable. I double-checked, just to make sure. Even odder, the air outside is almost Earth-norm, too."

Hendry lowered his faceplate and unfastened the hood. "Where's Olembe?"

She pointed to the great bronze door. "He went for a walk a couple of hours ago."

He recalled the airships they'd seen last night. "He ought to be careful. After our first encounter with aliens down there..."

"Don't worry. He took a laser. He'll no doubt kill first and ask questions later."

He eased himself from the sleeping bag and stood, stretching. "Hungry?"

"Could eat a horse, or even an alien equivalent."

They crossed to the chamber and Hendry took a couple of self-heating food-packs from a stack in the back of the truck. Carrelli looked up from her softscreen, smiled and nodded to them, then resumed whatever she was doing.

They ate, sitting on the floor beside the truck. Kaluchek looked up from her food at one point and smiled. "I'll tell you something, Joe. I've been trying to come to terms with what's happening to us."

"Join the club."

"I remember when I was eighteen. I left home for the first time. All I knew was the town I'd grown up in. University was frightening. I was a loner, found it hard to make friends. After Alaska, LA was..." she laughed, "alien. I longed for flat, empty landscapes, people who didn't say much instead of talking all the time. Everything was different. I withdrew into myself. It was a kind of psychological malaise. I'm not explaining it very well."

"It's okay. I know what you mean. It's the same thing here, right? I crave... I don't know... a world of sun and sand and blue sea, where we can create utopia."

She gave him a wonderful warm smile. "That'll do me, Joe. I want to be surrounded by familiar things, even people."

He laughed. "And you, the loner."

She gripped his hand, raised it to her lips and kissed it, and Hendry felt the sudden urge to hold her in his arms.

Across the chamber, the sliding door ground open, startling them. Kaluchek dropped his hand quickly, looking guilty, and stared at the gap in the entrance. A swirl of snow cascaded in on a gust of icy wind, followed by the bulky figure of Olembe in his orange atmosphere suit.

He closed the door behind him, pulled off his hood and crossed to the truck. He joined Hendry and Kaluchek, hunkering down beside them, and unfastened a softscreen from where he'd rolled it for convenience around his left forearm. Hendry watched the African, wondering at the pressures that had made the man give the orders all those years ago.

Carrelli climbed from the cab and joined them, sitting cross-legged on the floor.

Olembe powered up his softscreen and pointed to the image of an eight-tier spiral coiled about a central sun. Two flashing asterisks marked positions on the lowest tier and on the one above it.

"That's where we came down," Olembe said. "This here, on the second tier, is where we are now.

I reckon, going by the temperature increase from that tier to this, that the fourth tier will be habitable. Mediterranean, even."

"And we reach the tier above us by this," Carrelli gestured vaguely at the surrounding ziggurat, "umbilical elevator."

Olembe nodded. "Good name for it, Gina. I don't see why not. It's got us so far, why not all the way up?"

Hendry looked at the softscreen and said, "I've been wondering... We've happened across two alien races so far, and presumably there are even more on the thousands of other worlds. My question is, why? Why was it built, where did these races come from, and for what reasons?"

Carrelli frowned. "My theory, for what it is worth, is that the races we've so far discovered, and no doubt many others, were brought here by whoever built the helix, for whatever reasons."

A silence settled over the group, as each of the four digested the import of Carrelli's words.

Then she said, "I've been looking into how the umbilicals might work." She placed her own softscreen beside Olembe's. The screen showed a schematic of the first three tiers, and a representation of the ziggurats on each.

"The first ziggurat on the lower tier was equipped with an umbilical, giving access from one to two. I think it would be mechanical redundancy to have this ziggurat," she gestured around them, "equipped with an umbilical. My theory is that the next umbilical is on the third tier's ziggurat, and swings down to connect to the second tier at every rotation—that is, every planetary day."

Hendry was shaking his head. "The feat of engineering to produce those things…"

Olembe grinned. "We're dealing with some advanced critters here, Joe."

Carrelli continued, "So if the last connection was between tier one and two, then it follows that the next will be between three and two. All we have to do is sit tight and wait."

Olembe pointed a thumb over his shoulder. "I went out there earlier and planted a surveillance cam on the plain, focused on the top of the ziggurat." He tapped the sidebar of his softscreen and a grainy image appeared on the screen, showing the upper block of the edifice, lashed by snow. "We'll get everything stowed in the truck and prepared, and when the link is made we'll head for the elevator."

He stood and stretched. "I could kill a coffee. Anybody for the reconstituted swill ESO gave us?"

For the next couple of hours they sat around the softscreen and chattered desultorily, getting up from time to time to stretch their legs with a walk around the chamber. At one point Hendry moved to the viewscreen in the door, staring out at the grey overcast that seemed to be this planet's default meteorological condition.

Kaluchek joined him. "Thought you might want this." She held out another mug of the ersatz coffee, reminding him of how much Chrissie had loved the real thing.

He took the mug and gestured with it to the world beyond the viewscreen. Daylight had arrived while they'd been talking, a minimal lighting of the grey. "I wonder if this is it, perpetual grey with no sight of the sun?"

Kaluchek frowned. "That's possible... I was try-ing to work it out. If the planets on the helix turn on a central axis, like beads on a string, then there'd be no inclination that produces the sea-sons on Earth. There'd be only a progression of day and night, with no seasons and therefore no years."

"So the weather conditions out there would be constant; snow and blizzards and continual grey cloud cover."

She shook her head, sipping at her coffee. "I won-der what the natives are like? What kind of life might have evolved on such a hostile world?"

"It only seems hostile to us. To the creatures of this world it'd seem normal." When speaking to Kaluchek like this, gently correcting her ideas with his own, it was as if he were with Chrissie again.

She said, "One consequence of living on this world, if the cloud cover is constant, would be that they might not know anything about the helix."

He considered a race of beings ignorant of the wonder of the universe about them. What kind of society might *that* produce?

They stared through the viewscreen at the pointil-listic flurry of snow reducing visibility to a few metres, each lost in their own thoughts.

Kaluchek said, "I was going through the data Olembe collected about this place on his screen."

"And?" He sipped his coffee and grimaced. It was hot, which was about all that could be said in its favour.

"The temperature varies between five below zero at night, and two or three above during the day. It's habitable out there, unlike the first world."

"We'd need an extensive system of hydroponics to grow enough food to feed three thousand colonists," he said. "Things will be better on the next tier."

Kaluchek nodded. "I was just thinking worst-case scenarios—what if the worlds of the next tier prove uninhabitable?"

"Then we'd move on to the next."

"And if that were uninhabitable?"

He looked at her; she was grinning at him over the horizon of her mug. He said, "You're playing the devil's advocate."

"I was just thinking about how lucky we've been so far, in that the atmospheres on the two worlds we've happened across have been breathable. I mean, fortunate or what? That might not hold for the next tier."

He nodded, considering her words. "It is a stroke of luck," he said. "And it can't have been accidental."

She frowned at him. "How do you mean?"

"Well, these worlds were constructed, designed. The atmosphere was put here, as it were. My guess is that the tiers were developed expressly for air-breathers, who were then brought here, if they were brought here, perhaps as some kind of experiment."

She considered this, sipping her coffee, then said, "But it doesn't mean to say that all the levels are alike, which was my original point. The next one might have been designed for methane breathers, for all we know."

He smiled at her. "We'll find out in time."

She was quiet for a while, watching him. "I was thinking..." she said, then stopped.

"Go on."

"Carrelli. She knows a lot for a medic. Her back-up specialism is smartware systems—but she knows a hell of a lot about everything."

"Well, she was part of the original maintenance team. They had a year or more in training."

"Do you know what I think?"

He laughed. "You already have her down as a psychologist—" he began.

"I think she was selected by the ESO as the embedded team leader. Listen, it makes sense. Lisa Xiang was the nominated leader, and she was strong, opinionated, but she was only a pilot and a secondary nuclear engineer. She didn't have Carrelli's breadth of knowledge, her intuition."

Hendry closed one eye and looked at the tiny Inuit. "So... are you complaining?"

"Far from it! If I'm right, and Carrelli is the boss, then that's one in the eye for Mr Olembe."

He laughed. "But only if Olembe was aware of Carrelli's position. She's so embedded it's not noticeable." He reached out, suddenly, and touched her cheek.

She smiled at him. "You think I'm dreaming all this?"

"I don't know. Let's give it time, okay, and see what happens? I might be eating humble pie before long."

"And big helpings of it, Joe." She reached for his hand and held it.

Two minutes later Olembe called out from across the chamber, "Hey, this is it. Here it comes!"

They hurried back to where Olembe and Carrelli were sitting cross-legged, leaning over the softscreen. Olembe was manipulating the touchpad, refining the image. The screen showed the summit of the ziggurat, and approaching it as if in slow motion the tentacular length of the umbilical.

Carrelli was saying, "The engineering is truly amazing. Once it docks, as it were, it's connected to both the ziggurat here and the one on the tier above. By the very nature of the worlds' rotation, that means the ziggurats will be moving away from each other all the time, though very slowly. The umbilicals must have some form of telescopic or elastic capacity."

Kaluchek said to Carrelli, "Any idea how long they'll remain connected?"

Carrelli shook her head. "It's hard to say. Technically, maybe only minutes while the transfer from the portal to the umbilical is achieved by the travellers. After that, my guess is that it disconnects so the umbilical is trailing through space, tethered only to the destination world." She shook her head in wonder.

"It's almost there," Olembe said.

Hendry watched as the terminus of the umbilical swept through the air above the ziggurat. He felt a sudden apprehension: soon they would be aboard the umbilical, rising to the next tier, and whatever they might find there. The truck was packed; all that remained was to jump aboard.

The umbilical hovered briefly above the summit of the ziggurat, then passed on, whipping through the air a good ten metres above the top block.

Olembe swore. Kaluchek asked, "So what happened?"

Hendry watched the umbilical move ever further from the peak of the ziggurat, taking with it any real hope of easily ascending to the next tier.

Carrelli shook her head, at a loss for words, and stared at the screen.

Olembe was hunched over the softscreen, muttering angrily to himself and tapping the touchpad. He stilled the picture, played it back, then magnified the image. He froze the scene and pointed. "Look..."

The end of the umbilical was a mess of tangled and shredded metal, blackened and twisted. It's interior could be clearly seen, a silver honeycomb diminishing into the length of the column.

"Looks like there's been some kind of explosion," Kaluchek said.

"What the hell might have caused that?" Olembe muttered.

"Whatever," Carrelli said, her expression impassive, "it rules out attaining the next tier the easy way..."

Kaluchek was staring at her. "And the hard way?"

Olembe laughed. "Think about it, sweetheart."

Kaluchek turned to the African, glaring. "If you call me that one more time—"

He raised both hands in a mocking pantomime of fear. "Hey, cut me some slack, lady. Back off, okay?"

Carrelli said, "Squabbling will do nothing to help the situation."

"Well, tell that fucker to stop patronising me."

Carrelli turned a warning glance towards Olembe, who rolled his eyes with a *who? me?* expression.

Hendry laid a clandestine hand on the small of Kaluchek's back and applied pressure. She shot him a glance, smiling.

"Very well," Carrelli said, looking around the group. "The only thing we can do in the circumstances, if we wish to ascend to the next tier, is to make contact with the alien race that inhabits this world. Agreed?"

Olembe nodded. "Makes sense to me."

"They have obviously reached a rudimentary level of technological innovation," Carrelli said. "Who knows, with our know-how and their manufacturing capabilities, we might be able to rig up some means of getting to the next tier."

Hendry said, "And if not," he smiled bitterly, "then it's the long haul up-spiral."

With this sobering thought they boarded the truck and prepared to leave the sanctuary of the ziggurat.

## 2

THEY ROLLED OUT onto the plain of ice. The blizzard had ceased and the snow had stopped, revealing a flat, frozen landscape, featureless and without even a hill to break the iron-grey monotony that stretched out before them. To the right, in the distance, could be made out a faint line of black, snow-capped mountains.

Olembe was in the driving seat, Carrelli next to him. Hendry sat in the back with Sissy Kaluchek. Olembe braked the truck. "Okay, which way? Do we head for where the airships were coming from, or going to?"

Hendry said, "The dirigibles we saw were heading towards the mountain range. Would it make sense to follow them?"

Olembe tapped a touchpad and brought up the windscreen's magnification facility. The far range sprang into startling view, a jagged array of cold peaks. There was no sign of the airships.

"I don't see any habitation that way," Olembe said. "No cities, villages."

Kaluchek spoke up, "What did you expect, a string of streetlights spelling out 'Welcome'? In my experience, cold communities conserve energy."

Olembe restrained himself. "No sign of buildings, roads, anything like that."

"Anyway," Kaluchek said, "I think Joe's right. Let's make for the mountains. What do you think, Gina?"

She considered the question. "Perhaps the mountains might provide some limited form of protection from the elements," she said at last. "In which case, a settlement might be found there. That's making a lot of assumptions, however."

Hendry said, "We're in a situation where that's unavoidable."

She nodded. "Then shall we turn right?"

"The mountains it is," Olembe said, revving the engine and slewing the truck away from the ziggurat, accelerating over the hard-packed ice.

A minute later, Kaluchek said, "What if there is a settlement, but it's on the other side of the mountain, and airships are the only way to reach it?"

"We could always attempt to attract the attention of a passing ship," Hendry quipped.

The tracked vehicle ate up the kilometres. The grey of the day was about as bright as a Melbourne twilight, Hendry thought. He stared through the sidescreen, willing some feature to appear and break the monotony. The only thing that moved was the loose snowfall on the ground, wafted into wave patterns by the incessant wind. The central section of the windscreen showed the mountains, and he found himself staring at them in an attempt to discern anything that might signal habitation.

The heat inside the cab increased, inducing somnolence. Kaluchek closed her eyes and let her weight ease against Hendry, her head against his shoulder. He was pitched back twenty years, to when he and Chrissie had travelled on shuttle buses in France during his leave from space, heading off on holidays to the Normandy coast. Inevitably she would fall asleep, the pressure of her body against his inducing in him a sense of peace and contentment.

Now he wanted to stroke Kaluchek's jet-black hair, to show her some small gesture of affection. He was sure that she would not object, and yet he found himself holding back, afraid for some reason he could not quite fathom of escalating the degree of their relationship.

He was dozing when Olembe called out, "Hey, what was that? Over there, ten o'clock."

He slowed the truck. Hendry jolted awake and likewise Kaluchek beside him. He realised that his heart was hammering and peered through the sidescreen, wondering what the hell the African had spotted.

Then he saw it, or rather them.

They were dim at first, obscured by the fall of snow that had started up again: faint, humped shapes in the grey, white against the snowfield. He was reminded of yaks, though these creatures were half as large again as their Terran equivalent.

Olembe slowed the truck to a crawl, turned and approached the herd of a dozen or so passive creatures.

Passive, Hendry thought—but he nevertheless felt in the footwell for his laser.

Kaluchek placed a hand on his leg and leaned across him, grinning like a child at the zoo as she stared out at the herd.

"They look harmless enough, Joe."

He nodded, aware that his first contact with an alien race had prejudiced his reactions to this encounter. Olembe braked the truck a few metres from the animals. They looked up at the truck, large eyes incurious, then bent their thick muzzles to root again through the snow for whatever morsels of food might be found.

"They appear bovine," Carrelli said, "and built for the climate. Look at those pelts."

Grey fur hung to the ground in soiled tassels. Most of the creatures sported four horns, emerging at right angles from massive heads. Despite the proximity of the truck, the herd had lost interest. Hendry suspected that the task of foraging for food in this hostile landscape was perpetual, and it was a wonder they found anything at all in the snowy wastes. Their backs were encrusted with mantles of frozen snow, which, along with their immobility, gave them the appearance of statues.

"Seen enough?" Olembe asked.

Hendry could have stared at the odd beasts indefinitely, fascinated by the fact of their existence on this cold and lonely world.

No one objected, and the truck roared into life again. The noise moved the animals to lethargic flight, and then only a few metres before they bent once again to nuzzle for elusive food.

The truck cruised towards the mountains, crunching over the tundra at a steady fifty kilometres per hour. At one point Olembe manipulated the touchpad and said, "The range is around five hundred kays distant. I reckon we'll make the foothills in around ten hours or so."

Carrelli said, "I'll take over the driving in a while, okay?"

Hendry stared at the magnified mountains, looking for a pass or cutting that might allow them through. There was no sign of habitation in the rucked foothills. He wondered where the dirigibles had been heading, and imagined some ice-bound mountain fastness inhabited by who knew what bizarre species of extraterrestrials.

He found himself taking Kaluchek's hand and gripping hard. She squeezed back, smiling up at him.

A while later she said, addressing everyone, "This reminds me of my childhood in Alaska. Miles and miles of snow. Long journey to get anywhere." She sat up, leaning forward without letting go of Hendry's hand, and said to Carrelli, "Where were you brought up, Gina?"

"Me? Oh," the Italian sounded surprised at the question. "Naples, until I was eighteen. Then I went to college in Rome." She turned in her seat and smiled. "It was nothing like this, I can assure you of that." She fanned her face. "The heat! You wouldn't believe it." The gesture, Hendry thought, made her seem human.

"You studied medicine in Rome?" Kaluchek asked.

The Italian nodded. "Five years of general studies, then I specialised in neurology for three years."

"When did you join the ESO?"

"Five years ago, when I was thirty. They were recruiting for medics to work on the ground in

Berne. Then three years ago I was approached by Bruckner and told about the expedition."

Kaluchek smiled. "You must have jumped at the chance?"

"Actually, no. I asked them to give me time to think it over. I mean, to leave everything familiar for an uncertain future..."

"You had family, loved ones?"

Carrelli shook her head, her expression hidden by the back of the seat. "I had no one. My parents were dead. I was an only child. I had a lover until a few weeks before the offer of a place on the mission, but she left me, so..."

At this, Hendry saw Olembe turned his head and glance quickly at the medic.

Carrelli shrugged. "So, there was nothing really to keep me on Earth, except perhaps fear of the unknown. I thought about it over the days, tried to overcome my fear, and then contacted Bruckner and accepted."

Kaluchek said, "And you haven't regretted it?"

Carrelli turned in her seat and smiled at the Inuit. "Of course not. It was the best decision of my life. To experience what we have experienced, what so few humans have experienced... that is truly wonderful, no?"

Kaluchek's gaze slipped past the medic to the mountains. "I acknowledge that intellectually, Gina, but in reality... I don't know. Had anyone told me what we were going to experience, I would have considered it amazing, but now that it's happening to me—the fact that it's *me*, here, undergoing this amazing experience... to be honest, I can't help feeling it's all a bit mundane. I hope that doesn't sound ungrateful, or small-minded, but it's true…"

Gina smiled at her, reassuringly. "I understand what you mean. It's a surprisingly common reaction to individuals in extraordinary circumstances. They close down, concentrate on the small-scale. It's one way of combating the fear." The medic looked at Kaluchek, glanced down to her hand gripping Hendry's. "You are afraid, aren't you, Sissy?"

For a second, Hendry thought the woman beside him was about to tell Carrelli to go to hell, but what she did say made Hendry admire Kaluchek even more. The Inuit nodded her head minimally and said, "Afraid as hell, Gina," and she squeezed Hendry's hand all the tighter.

Carrelli said, "Don't worry, you're not alone. We are all a little scared of what the future might hold, aren't we, gentlemen?"

Hendry laughed. "Ever since those things back there got Lisa… I've been wondering what might happen next. Sure I'm scared."

Carrelli turned pointedly to the driver. "Friday?"

The African gripped the wheel, eyes straight ahead. "I've seen a lot, Gina. I've been through hell in Africa. What happened to Lisa back there, sure, it was god-awful but I'm not scared of anything the future might throw at us. The worse that can happen is that we die, right? I'm not afraid of dying."

Kaluchek said, "There's worse things than dying, Olembe. How about dying slowly, and knowing you're going to die?"

The African took his attention from the screen and turned to glare at the Inuit. "I've been there, Kaluchek."

She was about to say something, but Hendry frowned *no* at her, and to her credit she restrained herself.

Hendry looked at Carrelli. She had closed her eyes, head against the rest, in a fair imitation of sleep. But she wore a satisfied expression, and he wondered how much she had learned about her fellow travellers.

Thirty minutes later, with Kaluchek asleep beside him, and Carrelli breathing evenly in the passenger seat, Olembe looked at Hendry in the rear-view and said, "How about that, Joe? We're shacked up here with a dyke and a shit-scared Eskimo. You were just going along with all the fear stuff to make the women feel cosy, yeah?"

Hendry smiled. "Wish I was, Friday. But it's true, and I don't mind admitting it. Maybe I led a sheltered life the past five years, but I wasn't expecting anything like this. Of course I'm afraid. It's a natural human reaction."

Olembe shook his head. "We'll be fine, Joe. Have faith. I'll see us through. Okay?"

And the way Olembe said this, with a touching belief in his own abilities and without a trace of macho bravado, made Hendry wonder if he would ever truly understand the outwardly surly nuclear engineer.

He closed his eyes and was asleep in minutes.

Then, all the more shocking for coming so unexpectedly, the truck hit something and pitched forward, slamming the passengers against their restraining harnesses and waking them instantly.

**3**

"CHRIST, OLEMBE!" THIS was Kaluchek, hanging forward in her harness as the truck tipped nose-down, its tracks screaming as they churned uselessly through the air.

Olembe cut the engine and yelled, "Quit it, Kaluchek. I didn't see the fucking thing! A mist came down about five minutes ago."

In the silence that followed, Carrelli said, "Every-one is okay?"

Hendry massaged his neck. "I'm fine."

Kaluchek said, "I'm okay. What the hell hap-pened?"

The view in the central section of the windscreen, still set on magnification, was blurred, but the glass to either side showed a wall of ice a metre from the windscreen. Hendry peered through the misted sidescreen. The truck had pitched into some kind of trench or ravine.

"Okay," Olembe said. "It's no problem. We've fallen into an ice trough or whatever. We can dig a way out in front of the truck and drive on."

"Hope you brought some spades along," Kaluchek said.

"There was a set in the truck's storage unit," Olembe said. "I'm going to crack the hatch, okay?"

They pulled up their hoods and sealed the face-plates of their atmosphere suits. Hendry upped the temperature against the imminent cold and unfas-tened his harness. Olembe climbed out, followed by Carrelli.

The wind buffeted Hendry as he opened the hatch and peered out, assessing the drop from the truck's step. The ice appeared to be level, perhaps half a metre below the track. Hendry climbed down, then turned to help Kaluchek out.

The grey gloaming, which passed for daylight on this world, was light enough for them to make out the feature that had impeded their progress. The trench was perhaps a hundred metres long and five wide; it came up to Hendry's shoulders.

Kaluchek was staring about her, frowning at Hendry through her faceplate. "Strange," she said.

"What?"

"This. I mean... I know all about ice and snow, Joe. But this doesn't make sense."

He felt a prickle of unease migrate the length of his spine. "How so?" He glanced at Olembe, who was lifting a hatch on the side of the truck and handing out the short-handled spades.

"Maybe I'm being paranoid," the Inuit said, "but this doesn't look natural to me."

Olembe looked at her. "Hey, sweetheart, we're on an alien world light years from Earth. This isn't the North Pole here. Things are different, yeah?"

Kaluchek pointedly ignored him, turned her back and examined the side of the trench. She reached out and touched the face of the ice, tracing something with her gloved fingers.

Hendry crossed to her. "What?"

She was shaking her head. "If I didn't know better, I'd say that the ice had been cut."

Olembe was standing beside the front of the truck, staring at where its snub nose was embedded in the wall of ice. Using the bonnet as a step, he climbed up, then hoisted himself onto the plain of ice and looked down at them. Even at this distance he appeared a faint ghost in the mist that had suddenly descended.

"Okay," he called. "I suggest we start digging up here. If we excavate a ramp, starting around five metres back... the four of us should have it done in no time."

He moved away, out of sight across the plain. They heard the crunch of Olembe's spade as it bit into the ice.

Hendry looked at Kaluchek. Her expression, framed in the rectangle of her faceplate, was worried. Carrelli was about to join Olembe by way of the truck's bonnet, but stopped to say, "Are you two okay? Joe? Sissy?"

Kaluchek shook her head. "This isn't right, Gina."

Standing in the ice pit, with the wind raging above his head like a banshee, Hendry felt suddenly desolate and very afraid.

They all heard Olembe's cry, a sudden grunt followed by a truncated exclamation—and then silence. Carrelli jumped onto the truck's snout, peering over the edge of the pit and across the plain.

"Friday!" she called.

Hendry joined Carrelli, hauling Kaluchek after him. The hood dinted under their combined weight. They stood unsteadily, gripping the lip of ice before them and staring at ground level across the plain.

There was no sign of Olembe.

Only then did Hendry realise that he'd left his laser in the truck.

"Oh, Christ," Kaluchek wept beside him.

Hendry opened radio communication and hailed Olembe. Silence greeted his call. "Olembe, for Chrissake, are you reading?"

"What happened to him, Joe?" Kaluchek sobbed.

Hendry reckoned that he could see for about five metres, though the depth of visibility was hard to judge; it was impossible to focus on the grey mist before them.

Carrelli said, "He fell—he must have fallen into another ravine like this one."

Before Hendry could stop her, she had hopped up onto the ice. She squatted for a second, taking in the scene ahead, then stood and strode into the mist.

Hendry said, "Gina, switch on your radio, okay? Keep in contact."

Through his headset he heard a crackle, and then her voice. "Okay, Joe."

They looked over the edge of the ice, watching Carrelli peer ahead into the mist. She was perhaps fifteen metres from them now, moving cautiously forward, a step at a time.

Hendry was not sure what happened then. He heard a quick cry, almost an exclamation as if the medic had slipped. She fell onto her back, heavily, and seemed to be dragged forward through the mist. It was over in seconds. She was there one instant, gone the next.

"Gina!" Hendry yelled.

"I... I'm being—!"

Silence.

Kaluchek cried, "The lasers! I'm going to get the lasers!"

She dived from the bonnet, slipping on the ice then scrambling on all fours towards the slanting tracks of the truck. She used them as footholds to climb, then hauled open the hatch and pulled herself inside.

Hendry was about to start after her—gripped by a sudden fear of being left alone—when he felt something fasten tight around his neck, then a quick vicious pressure around his upper arms. Something was forced over his head and he was aware of being yanked from the pit and dragged across the ice.

He yelled, a cry inarticulate with terror. He felt something crash into the side of his head, the pain unbelievable for a split second. Then, thankfully, before either the agony became unbearable or the awareness of what was happening to him increased his terror, he slipped into unconsciousness.

# 4

"Joe?"

Hendry groaned and tried to lift his head. His skull throbbed. He let it drop and stared into the greyness. He was aware of heat, and a terrible stench.

"Joe? You okay, man?" It was Olembe, speaking as if from a great distance.

His awareness faded. He was alive, at least. And so was Olembe. He was suddenly taken by the need to know that Sissy was safe, the desire overwhelming, but he could feel himself drifting back into unconsciousness.

Later, he was aware of voices. He was sweating, and the stench was just as strong, and this time he felt movement, a constant jolting sensation as if he were aboard some kind of rapidly moving vehicle. He kept his eyes closed, listening.

"They'll be okay." This was Carrelli.

"What about Kaluchek?" Olembe asked.

"I don't think her skull is fractured, but she's concussed. She'll pull through okay."

Hendry felt relief flood through him.

Olembe was saying, "… reckon they'll do with us?"

A silence, then Carrelli responded. "If they wanted us dead, they would have killed us back there. They're taking care of us, after a fashion."

"How the hell do you make that out? First of all they beat our brains out, then tie us up in the back of a sledge—"

"And they have supplied us with pelts, to keep us warm."

That explained the stench, Hendry thought, and the cloying heat. He was weighed down by a great animal skin, and his atmosphere suit was still set to combat the freezing temperature of this world.

"Wonder where the hell they're taking us?"

Carrelli said, "To their leaders, in some town or other? These people obviously have some degree of organisation."

"People?" Olembe half-laughed. "You call those things *people*?"

"Whatever," Carrelli said. She seemed too tired to argue the point.

Olembe grunted. "Just hope their leaders show more humanity than these bastards." Then he laughed at the irony of his words.

"We will find out," Carrelli said, "in time."

Hendry gathered his strength, pushed off the stinking animal skin and struggled into a sitting position, his head throbbing.

Olembe helped him. "Hey, take it easy, okay? You'll be fine. They clobbered you on the head, but Gina took a look and said you'll be okay."

Hendry blinked. They were sitting in some kind of open cart, which was sliding at speed across the ice. Olembe was sitting across from him. Carrelli sat beside Hendry, cradling Sissy Kaluchek's head in her lap.

"Sissy?" Hendry managed.

Carrelli said, "She took a bad blow to the back of her head, Joe. I think she'll be okay. Don't worry."

He looked at Sissy. Her expression appeared serene behind her faceplate. The hood at the base of her skull was discoloured with blood.

"The truck," he said, more to himself.

"We've lost everything, Hendry," Olembe said. "The truck, the softscreens, lasers, provisions…"

He glanced at Olembe. A dark stain covered the material just above his faceplate and rivulets of blood had run down the sides of his nose like tears.

He looked at Carrelli. "You okay?"

She smiled. "They spared me their clubs, just tried to strangle me into unconsciousness."

He tried to move his legs, and only then realised that his ankles were shackled by some kind of leather thong, which was attached to metal rings set in the central timbers of the cart.

Olembe said, "I've tried to unfasten them. No way—they're frozen solid."

Hendry shuffled into a more comfortable position, his back against the cart's sloping side timbers. From here he could see that a team of six shaggy animals—identical to those they had seen earlier—was drawing what seemed to be a sledge, judging by the hiss of runners on ice.

All around, he made out more of the animals, dozens of them, with hunched figures mounted upon their backs. The closest was perhaps five metres away, indistinct in the descending twilight.

The creature riding the bovine-equivalent was small, and Hendry was unable to tell whether the pelt that covered its arms and legs was some kind of protective cladding or natural fur.

He tried to make out its face, desperate to know what kind of being had captured them, but at this distance all he could see was a faint, dark blur.

"We're heading for the mountains." Carrelli pointed ahead, and Hendry was surprised to see that the jagged peaks, which earlier had been hundreds of kilometres distant, now loomed close, their stark summits jet black against the perpetual grey sky. The sledge was approaching the foothills, a series of folds in the ice perhaps five kilometres away.

He looked at the medic. "You think the trap was set deliberately? They saw us coming and dug the trench?"

"Either that, or it was one of a series already dug, perhaps to capture the animals they use. They probably herd them towards the trenches, as prehistoric man did on Earth."

"But these creatures are more advanced than prehistoric man, right?"

She nodded and indicated the rings in the floor. "They have metals, and we know that others of their kind have airships."

"You think they're the same people?"

"I wonder if two sentient races would be brought to the same world?"

Brought to the same world, he thought. "What kind of being would construct a helix and then populate it with sentient extraterrestrials?"

Olembe grunted. "Beings, Joe, who have the ability to do so."

"Perhaps that was the wrong question," Hendry said. "I should have asked, why?"

Carrelli gave her graceful shrug. "Who knows that, Joe? Perhaps only the Builders themselves."

"The Builders," he said. "At least now they have a name. You've christened them, Gina."

She smiled, "Unoriginal, but it will suffice, for the time being."

He looked around, attempting to assess the numbers of riders escorting their sledge. He could see a dozen or so, but occasionally became aware of more as their forms drifted in and out of the rapidly descending twilight.

He said, "Sissy was right. We should have listened to her."

"Huh?" Olembe grunted.

"She said the trenches weren't natural. If we'd thought about it, gone back for the lasers…"

"She was right," Carrelli said, "but we didn't act. There is nothing we can do now but attempt to appeal to these peoples' higher authorities. If they have airships, some kind of sophisticated civilisation… perhaps they might be amenable to reason."

Olembe laughed. "Sophisticated civilisation and amenability doesn't always follow, Gina. Look at the Nazis, the Moroccan fascists this century."

She considered his words. "My guess is that these people, or at least the makers of the airships, are progressive, curious. I think they will want to know more about the universe, their place in it… But look at this overcast. I think they know nothing about the helix. Perhaps we are their first visitors. We can tell them a lot about the universe, if they are willing to listen."

"That's a big if," Olembe said. "And you've forgotten one thing—we don't speak their language."

Carrelli smiled at him through her faceplate.

Hendry considered where this was leading. "But even if we can communicate with their leaders in some fashion, what's the chances of them being able to help us get to the next level? Dirigibles are one thing, space-going vehicles quite another."

"They have the basis of a sophisticated technology," Carrelli said. "With our instruction, they could perhaps help us develop a simple rocket to take us into space."

"Great idea," Olembe grunted, his tone suggesting he thought it highly unlikely.

"We've overlooked one thing," Hendry said. "Perhaps each level has more than one ziggurat? For all we know there might be dozens of them dotted around each tier."

Carrelli nodded. "There is that possibility."

Sissy Kaluchek, her head in Carrelli's lap, groaned and flailed an arm. The medic restrained her. "Take it easy," she soothed. "You'll be okay, Sissy. Lie back and rest."

Kaluchek opened her eyes, stared up at Hendry. He smiled and reached out for her hand, took it and squeezed. Her eyes registered nothing but surprise and mystification, before she closed them again, her lips moving silently.

Carrelli felt for her pulse, attempted to judge her temperature by placing her hand against the brow of the Inuit's atmosphere suit. "It's good that she came round so soon," she said. "I think she'll be okay."

Hendry retained his grip on Sissy's hand, aware that Olembe was staring at him. He rested his head against the hard timbers and closed his eyes.

The feel of her hand, even through the layers of their atmosphere suits, reminded him of the time in Paris when Chrissie had fallen from her bike and cracked her head on the pavement. She'd been unconscious for hours, then rushed from the local hospital to a clinic specialising in head injuries. There, Hendry had been told that there was a possibility that, even though Chrissie would come round, she might have suffered some degree of brain damage. The next four hours, sitting beside her bed with her small hand gripped in his, had been the longest of his life. Chrissie was seven, and Su had left him a few months previously, and he'd wondered if things could get any worse than this.

Then Chrissie had blinked herself awake, and smiled up at him, and a Thai surgeon had checked her over and told him that she was going to be okay.

Sitting in the back of the alien sledge, Hendry wept as it came back to him... along with its corollary: Paris and the smiling surgeon, everything he had known on Earth... a thousand years gone, now.

"Hey!" Olembe's exclamation brought his reverie to an end. "We've got company."

Hendry opened his eyes and sat up. He heard the snort of the bovine animal first, as it shuffled up to the side of the sledge. The stench that was ever-present from the animal pelts increased with the approach of the living article. The sharp reek of ordure, urine and sweat hit his sinuses like a driven spike.

He turned awkwardly, hampered by the ankle shackles, and stared at the beast and its rider.

"We were captured," Olembe said with disgust, "by monkeys."

"Hardly monkeys," Carrelli corrected. "More like... lemurs. But we can't let ourselves be prejudiced by appearances. The fact that they captured us suggests a certain level of sophistication."

Hendry stared at the creature perched upon the back of the beast of burden, and it stared back at him. It was mounted like a jockey, knees drawn up, small bare paws gripping an arrangement of leather thongs connected to the beast's dripping nostrils.

The creature was small, perhaps the size of a ten-year-old child, and wore only a bandoleer across its torso. Hendry found something about its spindliness unsettling, but its face was more disturbing still. It was covered in blue-black fur and dominated by a sharp, vicious snout, above which were two big, black eyes. Obvious intelligence was at work behind those unfathomable eyes as it stared at Hendry and the others.

A weapon of some kind—an old rifle of polished wood and brass—was strapped to its back. At least, Hendry thought, it showed no inclination to use it.

The creature leaned forward and spoke in a series of high, protracted yips; rows of tiny sharp teeth showed, and Hendry could not stop himself from imagining the creature ripping into raw meat like some primitive animal.

Hendry looked across at Carrelli, who raised a hand and smiled. Olembe said, "And peace be to you, friend."

The creature yipped again, the words ending in a cachinnation, which shot a hail of spittle towards Hendry; it froze on the way and tinkled against his faceplate.

The creature reached down for something on the other side of the beast, and hauled up what looked like an animal skin wobbling with a full load of fluid. Without ceremony it hurled the skin into the sledge, then urged its mount forward until they were lost in the mist.

Hendry stared at the animal skin sloshing at their feet.

Carrelli said, looking across at Olembe, "More evidence that they don't mean us harm. Why give us fluid if they were going to kill us, Friday?"

He grunted. "They're keeping us alive until they can butcher and eat us, for all we know."

Hendry smiled. "Need you be so optimistic?"

Olembe shrugged. "I think a healthy degree of scepticism about these bastards' motives might be in order."

Hendry reached out and lifted the animal skin. It was heavy and rolled awkwardly in his grip. He deposited it in his lap and examined a small nozzle, manufactured from metal and worked by a tiny tap.

He looked up at Carrelli. "Would it be safe...?"

"If we had a softscreen, then we could analyse its content." She shook her head. "The fact is that sooner or later we must eat and drink, if we are to survive."

"I think I'll hold off until we reach civilisation," Olembe said, "if we ever do."

"Pass it to me, Joe," Carrelli said. "I'll play guinea pig."

He passed the skin to the medic and watched as she unsealed her faceplate. She lifted the skin to her mouth and worked the tap. Clear liquid trickled out, spilling over her chin. She closed the tap and made a thoughtful face as she swallowed, then nodded and deposited the skin on the boards of the sledge.

"Water. Just like anything you'd find on Earth, with a slight taste of some mineral."

"Let's see how long you keep it down," Olembe said, dubiously eyeing the skin as it shivered at their feet.

Hendry was aware of how thirsty he was, and then how hungry. It seemed a long time since he'd breakfasted on rations back at the ziggurat. He glanced at the chronometer set into the sleeve of his suit: they had left the ziggurat almost ten hours ago.

He stared ahead, through the mist darkening with the approach of night. The mountains were much closer now, a looming bastion that filled the horizon. They had left the ice plain and were climbing into the foothills along a well-worn track cut through rock. Their escorts paraded before and after the sledge. Ahead, he made out perhaps twenty riders, before they were lost in the twilight, and the same number to the rear.

Kaluchek stirred. She gripped Hendry's hand. "Joe?"

He smiled down at her. Her face, behind the visor, looked so young. "You're going to be fine. Relax."

"What happened? I was in the truck, going for the laser..." She frowned, recollecting. "Something dragged me out. That was the last thing..."

"We're okay, Sissy. We'll be fine."

Olembe grunted. "We've been captured by a troupe of fucking monkeys, Kaluchek."

Carrelli said, "They have given us water."

Kaluchek tried to sit up, but the pain in her head stopped her. She winced, collapsed back into Carrelli's lap. "Where are they taking us?"

Olembe said, "To their leader, girl. Where else?"

Kaluchek laughed. "I'm dreaming, right?" She smiled up at Hendry. "What are they like?"

It was Olembe who replied, before Hendry could think of a suitable description. "Imagine monkeys, with big eyes, rat-like snouts and lots of little pointy teeth. Your average nightmare aliens, Kaluchek, even though Carrelli here thinks they're born altruists."

"Not altruists, Friday," Carrelli answered evenly, "just not the primitives you take them to be."

"Carrelli, they attacked us and beat our brains out. I don't call that friendly."

Kaluchek rolled her eyes to look at the medic above her. "If they wanted us dead, they would have killed us back there, right?"

"That was my reasoning, Sissy," Carrelli said.

Hendry shifted his position, the hard timber beneath his buttocks at last becoming unendurable. He dragged a noxious pelt towards him, arranging it behind his back. Kaluchek smiled up at him.

Thirty minutes later he noticed lights in the darkness. They were approaching a settlement of squat, stone-built dwellings that climbed the hill to their left, one above the other like stacked beehives. The points of light were lanterns, held aloft by individuals who had braved the freezing night to greet their fellows.

"What's happening?" Kaluchek asked as the sledge ground to a halt. She struggled upright, this time determined to make it, and sat beside Hendry.

More locals emerged from the cone-like dwellings and approached the sledge. They were too short to see over the side, but stood on the incline at a distance of some metres and stared at the heads and shoulders of the strange captives.

Hendry noted a difference between the aliens who had captured them and the mountain-dwellers, and he wondered if the former were native to the ice plains. The mountain-dwellers appeared a head shorter than their cousins, and wore considerably more clothing: padded suits and caps that covered their heads and necks like balaclavas.

The two camps met and appeared to be in discussion, the aliens from the ice plains explaining their find to three mountain-dwellers, who at one point approached the sledge and inspected its content.

Olembe said, "So this is civilisation, folks. Look, I think we need a plan of action if things start getting violent."

Kaluchek looked across at him. "We're shackled, Olembe. We have no weapons. I'm feeling like shit. I couldn't fight off a kitten."

"We'll be unshackled at some point. Then, if things start looking bad, I say we attack and grab their weapons. They're puny bastards—they wouldn't stand a chance."

Carrelli was shaking her head. "Violence only as a last resort, okay? Until then we sit tight and see what happens."

Olembe opened his mouth to speak, thought better of it and merely shook his head in disgust.

It appeared that some decision had been made. From further up the track, a team of six draft animals appeared hauling a sledge.

"We're being transferred, Carrelli," Olembe said. "This might be the only opportunity."

The team of animals was led down to the track by a mountain-dweller, where it was halted alongside their own sledge, facing downhill.

Hendry said, "I don't think they're transferring us. It wouldn't make sense to take the risk."

"Then what—?" Olembe began.

From a nearby building, half a dozen mountain-dwellers, working in pairs, carried what looked like heavy sacks and perhaps a dozen skins of liquid. They deposited them in the second sledge and returned for more, halting only when the sledge was laden.

Carrelli laughed. "We're being traded. Apparently we're worth twenty sacks of grain and a dozen skins of wine... or whatever the local equivalent might be."

Kaluchek said, "And if these folk think we're worth that much, then I don't think they mean to kill us straight away." She looked across at Olembe, challenging.

The animals hauling the second sledge were prodded into action. The plain dwellers moved off down the hillside on their stolid mounts, but not before one of their number paused his mount beside Hendry and the others.

He wondered if it was the creature that had given them the water-skin earlier; it was impossible to tell. It merely stared at them, one after the other, its snout moving as it talked to itself. How alien we must appear to this creature, Hendry thought. The being made a quick movement with its snout, flicking it in the air—a valedictory gesture?—then rode off into the night.

Seconds later the sledge started up and they continued on their way, this time escorted by a team of mountain-dwellers, a dozen smaller aliens—six fore and six aft—riding their own shaggy mounts.

"My guess is that their capital city lies somewhere beyond the mountains," Carrelli said, "which is where the dirigibles were heading."

"And that's where we'll be imprisoned and tortured as the invaders we're assumed to be," Olembe said.

"Or where," Kaluchek returned, "we might be treated as honoured guests." She nudged Hendry. "What do you think, Joe?"

He smiled. "Despite the evidence of the pain in my head, I think we'll be accorded some degree of civility—though I don't doubt they'll be naturally suspicious of us. It can't be every day they're visited by ugly, furless giants."

"I'll remind you optimists of this when the bastards bring out their thumbscrews, or whatever else they use to extract confessions."

Carrelli said, not without humour, "Go to sleep, Olembe."

The African laughed and pulled a pelt towards himself.

An alien detached itself from the rearward group and rode alongside, staring at the strange cargo its people had purchased. Other than its smaller stature, and the fact that it was padded like a lagged boiler, it resembled the plain dwellers with its hostile snout and large, inscrutable eyes. Hendry shifted uncomfortably under its penetrating gaze.

They climbed, the track becoming narrower as it passed between sheer walls of ice towards a distant pass in the mountains. At last the passage became so constricted that the alien rider was forced to abandon its inspection and ride on ahead, to Hendry's relief.

He rearranged the pelt so that he could lie down, and Kaluchek joined him, resting an arm across his chest.

Like this, jolted to and fro as the sledge climbed through the alien night, Hendry and his fellow travellers slept.

**5**

HE WAS AWOKEN, hours later, by the light.

He opened his eyes and stared up at the featureless grey, wondering how the lemur-creatures of this world survived the endless, drear days without a hint of sunlight. The answer was obvious: they had no conception of the existence of anything like the sun. The sight of the fiery primary, if and when that happened, would be a revelation.

The others were talking. Kaluchek noticed his movement and shuffled towards him, helping him to sit up. "You've been out for hours, Joe."

He reached out and took her hand. "Are you okay?"

"Apart from a sore head," she smiled, "I'm fine."

Hendry looked around at the passing landscape. They had left the mountains behind them and were coming down the other side. Behind the sledge, the dark peaks reared, cold and hostile, while ahead...

It was the sight ahead of the sledge that occupied Carrelli and Olembe. They were pointing out various features and discussing them in lowered tones.

With Kaluchek's help, Hendry managed to shuffle to his knees and peer over the front edge of the sledge.

"What do you think?" she asked.

He had expected, going by what he had seen so far of the aliens' civilisation, something rudimentary by way of a township, a primitive collection of stone-built dwellings similar to the village they had seen on the other side of the mountains, though perhaps on a grander scale. Even the fact that the aliens obviously had a manufacturing capability had not prepared him for the sight of the city that sprawled before them in the bowl of the mountains.

It was vast, and consisted of great blocks of buildings that reminded him of the architecture of Earth's nineteenth century. It had evidently been constructed from the centre outwards, built along great boulevards radiating from a hub of grand buildings, which dominated all the others. Between the buildings, the wide streets were silver with ice, along which citizens skated in ones and twos, and draft animals hauled carts not dissimilar to the one in which they were travelling.

The sight of the city was impressive enough, but what made it truly a thing of wonder were the airships that sailed above it. Hendry counted fifty of them, all sporting brightly coloured balloons—globular, oblate and cigar-shaped—before giving up. They criss-crossed the grey skies without colliding, a veritable feat considering their number. Some made short hops across the city, putting down on rigs erected on top of buildings, while others ventured out to the foothills. They flew at various levels, at differing speeds, creating a dramatic kaleidoscopic effect when seen from the elevated vantage point of the mountainside, the polychromatic aerial display contrasting with the monochrome drabness of the city beneath.

"What's amazing," Olembe was saying, "is that we travel five hundred light years through space to find a race which functions on principles similar to those of Earth a couple of hundred years ago. They have wheels, carts, sledges, skates, airships…"

Carrelli considered his words, then said, "Perhaps it's not so unusual. They're a bilateral, carbon-based, upright species, after all. It would be surprising if during their evolution they had not discovered the things you mentioned."

"You mean," Kaluchek said, "that things like sledges and skates and everything else, they're the most efficient devices for the particular environment, so it's inevitable that they would have been developed?"

Carrelli nodded. "No doubt we'll find many things peculiar to this race, adapted for the type of beings they are, but it isn't surprising that we have so much in common."

Hendry said, "Is it surprising that the two species we've discovered have both been upright and bipedal?"

Carrelli shrugged. "That's hard to say, Joe. The sample is too small to make a judgement. Perhaps we're an anomaly, and life in the universe will prove to be very different. Or the reverse: perhaps all life in the universe is similar to ourselves." She paused, then went on, "There is always the possibility that whoever built the helix populated it solely with air-breathing bipeds."

They were silent for a time, considering this possibility.

"The more pressing question," Olembe said, "is what these bastards intend to do with us."

Kaluchek looked across at him. "You sound frightened, Olembe."

"Not frightened, sweetheart, just let's say concerned. It's best to consider all possibilities. You pacifists might be right, and the monkeys might turn out to be angels in disguise, but we need a plan of action if they decide to turn nasty."

Carrelli looked at the African for a second or two, before nodding reasonably. "I don't disagree, in principle. What do you suggest?"

Olembe looked surprised. "Well... the advantage we have over them is that we're bigger. We could take them by surprise and overpower them easily, grab their weapons and take it from there."

"If we do need to act," Carrelli said, "then we must do so after having agreed the action amongst us, is that agreed? There should be no action without consultation, no lone heroics. If we can do so, we avoid taking life—is that agreed? We haven't travelled five hundred light years to kill members of only the second race we've discovered." She looked round the group, receiving affirmative nods from everyone including, somewhat reluctantly, Olembe.

"Okay," he said, "but I know in my bones that these guys have it in for us."

He had the last word, and in the following silence they all gazed ahead at the city.

They were approaching the sprawling outskirts now, meaner dwellings and larger buildings that overflowed from the valley bowl and crept up the hillside. The road between the low, granite-grey buildings consisted of churned slush for the last sloping kilometre into the city, but it became a mirror-smooth canal of ice when they reached the valley bottom. The draft animals hauling the sledge seemed at home on the ice and proceeded at a brisk trot.

Their passage had attracted the attention of locals: at first one or two passers-by had dawdled to take a look at the curious cargo, but now the word had spread and a posse of thirty or forty padded citizens trailed the sledge, kept back by the dozen mounted mountain-dwellers. Hendry felt uneasy beneath the scrutiny of these strange beings, and wondered if alien crowds had the same propensity for unheeding reaction as had their counterparts on Earth. All it would take was one hothead to incite the crowd to violence against the bizarre off-worlders...

They came at last to the sanctuary of a four-square building within a walled compound, situated on the edge of the city. The sledge passed through great iron gates, which were hauled shut behind them, effectively barring the curious crowd. Hendry's relief was tempered by the thought of what might lie ahead.

The entourage of mountain-dwellers remained guarding the sledge. One of their number dismounted and hurried across a cobbled courtyard to the door of the building. He passed inside, watched by everyone including Hendry and the others, and emerged a minute later trailing perhaps a dozen beings in black uniforms.

Kaluchek looked at him, and he wondered if she was thinking the same thought. It was the black uniforms, and not so much the fact that the creatures were armed with primitive rifles, that struck fear into his heart. He wondered if dark uniforms symbolised the brutality of authority on this world, too.

The armed aliens, evidently some form of police or militia, surrounded the sledge, and one of their number yipped a high command. Seconds later another dozen militia hurried from the building and took up positions next to their comrades, rifles levelled.

It was impossible to tell from their facial expressions how they were reacting to the presence of aliens in their midst, but their body language suggested unease, even fear. They appeared skittish, fidgety. At a movement from Carrelli, easing herself into a more comfortable position, they backed off and raised their weapons nervously.

Carrelli said, under her breath, "No heroics, Friday, okay? They have us surrounded, and those weapons might look like antiques, but I don't want a head full of buckshot."

"Yes, ma'am," Olembe muttered.

One of the mountain-dwellers was in conversation—a frantic exchange of high yelps and barks—with one of the militia. While the militiaman spoke, he never allowed his eyes to stray from the sledge and its human cargo. He flung his head back once or twice, made side-wise chopping gestures with his paws. It was impossible, Hendry thought, to guess what might be passing between the creatures.

The exchange ended and the militiaman made a slow, cautious circumnavigation of the sledge, staring at the humans one by one. It returned to its original position beside the mountain-dweller, then yipped an order to one of the armed militia who hurried across the cobbles to what turned out to be a garage.

A minute later an enclosed cart was hauled out and dragged across the courtyard to stand beside the sledge. It appeared too small to contain all the humans, but Hendry guessed that this was its purpose. Yet another transfer, another destination, their fate deferred for a while yet.

Olembe whispered, "They've got to untie us, yes? If we're gonna make a move, that would be the time to do it."

"And risk getting our heads blown off?" Kaluchek said. "Forget it."

Carrelli said, "There's no need to take risks yet, Friday. Let's see what happens, okay?"

Olembe swore. Kaluchek reached out and took Hendry's hand.

He watched as one of the militia swung open the doors of the enclosed truck.

Olembe was right in that the transfer necessitated their being unfastened from the sledge, but how the aliens went about it was ingenious. The militia leader yelped at an underling, who shouldered its weapon and approached the sledge with caution. Instead of climbing into the cart, as expected, it ducked beneath it and scrabbled across the cobbles. The iron rings in the middle of the boards began to turn as screws securing the rings to the sledge's timber floor were unfastened. A minute later the rings came loose. The humans were free of the sledge, but their ankles were still shackled by the leather thongs. It would be impossible to move at much more than a constricted shuffle.

The leader approached the sledge, yelled at them. Behind him the militiamen gestured with their rifles, and one of them pulled down the sledge's tailgate.

Olembe first, followed by Carrelli, Kaluchek and Hendry, climbed from the back of the sledge and approached the prison wagon. Hendry winced at the pain in his back and legs, his muscles unused for so many hours. He glanced left, then right. Their progress was watched by the militia, weapons levelled vigilantly.

He watched Olembe, fearing that the African might ignore Carrelli's warning and attack the militia. He could see that Olembe took the indignity of capture with bad grace, but to his credit he kept his head and climbed dutifully into the wagon.

Hendry was the last aboard, Kaluchek turning to help him, and as he stepped into the confines he winced, expecting a blow to the back of his head.

He seated himself next to Kaluchek, taking her hand, as the doors were slammed shut and barred. In the darkness they could hear preparations being made to transport them onwards. A team of draft animals was attached to the wagon, and minutes later they lurched into motion across the cobbles and out into the ice canal.

"Where now?" Kaluchek asked.

Hendry said, "Maybe this was a militia outpost. We're being taken to the headquarters. We'll soon be meeting with the people in control."

"Yeah," Olembe said, "the bastards who say whether we live or die. We should have tried to escape when we had the chance."

"For fuck's sake shut it, Olembe, okay?" Kaluchek yelled. She was, Hendry sensed, close to tears. He gripped her fingers.

"Temper, temper," the African replied in the darkness.

The wagon slid across the ice, its motion rapid, throwing the humans from side to side. Hendry felt Kaluchek's face against his upper arm, felt the silent sobs that shook her body.

"At least we know one thing," Carrelli said.

"Which is?" Olembe asked.

Into the silence, Carrelli said, "The water is safe on this world."

"If that's supposed to be funny, Carrelli..." Olembe said.

Ten minutes after setting off, the wagon slowed. The transition from ice to cobbles was made again, the wagon jolting for a minute before it came to a halt.

"This is it," Olembe said.

A minute elapsed, then two. Hendry wondered if this was some sophisticated form of torture in itself.

Then the doors opened, and the grey light—dazzling after the absolute darkness of the wagon—flooded in, blinding them for a moment.

Only then did they see their reception committee.

Hendry was dragged from the wagon by means of a pikestaff that snared the thongs at his ankles. He yelled, fell painfully to the cobbles, and was aware of the others tumbling out after him.

Then, before they had time to get up, twenty uniformed militia armed with clubs and rifle butts set about rendering them incapable of opposition.

Olembe cried out—something about how wrong you bastards were—before a crunching blow silenced him.

Kaluchek screamed Hendry's name, as if pleading for his help, and the last thing he saw was a rifle butt falling towards his head.

## EIGHT /// THE TRUTH

**I**

IN THE EARLY hours of the morning following their return to Agstarn, Ehrin left his room in the attic of the Telsa foundry and hurried down to the shop floor. There, in the shadows of the great silent crucibles and furnaces—usually alive with noise and fire—Kahran hailed him, and they left the foundry and moved quickly through to the hangar.

In the illumination of the gas-lamp that Ehrin held before him, the rearing shapes of a dozen dirigibles filled the hangar, ranging from the small one-man skyships to the mammoth freighters. The hangar was silent, like a museum, and for a second Ehrin imagined far future generations looking back and smiling at these exhibits of a backward technological age. He had never thought that before—had always assumed that the dirigibles were the leading edge of scientific innovation—but Havor's inter-world machine had changed all that. How primitive all this must seem to the strange alien pilot!

They had made the return journey to Agstarn without incident. Ehrin's fear that a curious geologist or engineer might question their story about the alien ship, or worse actually try to board it, had proved unfounded. He had refrained from entering into any further theological argument with Elder Cannak, but something the Elder had said on parting had sent an icy shiver up the fur of Ehrin's spine. "I have noted our conversations, Mr Telsa, Mr Shollay, and, notwithstanding the success of the mission, I will be forced to make a report upon your conduct, and philosophical views, to the relevant bureau."

"Mere words," Kahran had said once the Elder had departed, but Ehrin had seen the shadow of doubt in the old man's experienced eyes.

They hurried across the oil-stained hangar floor to the looming shape of the freighter. Ehrin had earlier taken the precaution of locking the cargo hold, and now he turned the key with fumbling fingers and hauled open the double doors.

They crossed the hold to the streamlined shape of the golden ship, and Ehrin rapped on the triangular viewscreen.

Seconds later the hatch hissed open.

They passed down the corridor and entered the control room. Havor was lying upon the couch, staring at a screen above him. He glanced at Ehrin and Kahran and grimaced in greeting. "I've been assessing the damage, which isn't as extensive as I first feared. I've managed to repair a relay system, but the main drive suffered physical damage on re-entry." He looked from Ehrin to Kahran. "I'll need to replace a component if I want to get the ship running again. And then…"

"The deathship," Ehrin said.

Havor inclined his great head. "The deathship indeed," he said, grimacing.

"How can we help?" Kahran asked.

"I will need a precisely tooled part, which should not be beyond your capability to produce."

"We will do what we can," Ehrin said.

"And if Kahran might describe in detail the whereabouts of the Church's mountain hangar, I will leave here and do what I must do."

"Better than that," Kahran said, "I'll come with you, guide you to exactly to the where the Church keeps the deathship."

"And if Kahran comes," Ehrin said, "then I will come too. The ship will hold three?"

Havor grimaced. "Capacity is not the problem, my friend." He looked at them with his inscrutable black eyes. "I must warn you, there will be danger involved in the mission. If the Church has studied the weapons systems aboard the deathship, even the secondary systems, then they might have their stronghold well defended against even aerial attack."

Ehrin asked, "You call it a deathship, and speak of terrible weapons…"

By way of a reply, Havor said, "My friends, what is the most fearful weapons your race possesses?"

Ehrin looked at Kahran, who shrugged and said, "Perhaps the projectile cannon. It can hurl a shell which detonates on impact, killing dozens."

"The deathship," said Havor, "is well named. One strike from its primary weapons system could destroy a city the size of Agstarn, and all in it. The secondary system is defensive, something similar to your cannons, though it can fire a dozen projectiles a second."

"And your weapons?" Kahran asked.

"A similar projectile capability," Havor said. "I trust that half a dozen strikes on target will destroy the Church's hangar and the deathship."

Ehrin glanced across at Kahran. "I would still like to accompany you," he murmured, and Kahran nodded his agreement.

Havor pulled an even uglier grimace, and held out his big, hairless hand for Ehrin and Kahran to touch.

"And then?" Ehrin said. "What are your plans once the deathship is destroyed?"

The alien turned its head from side to side. "I do not plan beyond the attack. That has my sole attention."

"You spoke of other worlds," Ehrin said, tentatively, "other *levels*..."

Havor made a rumbling guttural sound, which Ehrin took for a laugh. How ignorant he must seem to this otherworldly being! How young and ignorant!

Havor said, "Later, my friend. First, I will show you the damaged component, which perhaps you might replace..."

Havor led the way from the ship. In the light from Ehrin's lamp, they moved along the golden flank, Havor pausing from time to time to lay an affectionate palm on various hieroglyphs and decals.

Ehrin noticed that the alien was walking without even the slightest limp, and marvelled again at the miracle of Zorl technology.

Havor indicated a panel in the flank of the ship, blackened as if scorched by a blowtorch.

"A burn-out on re-entry," Havor explained. He reached up and touched the panel, which ejected itself slowly from the body of the ship. Ehrin made out a mass of burnt-out wiring and charred metal.

Havor inspected the damage, then reached in and extracted the remains of a silver cylinder, perhaps nine inches long. He held it out for Ehrin and Kahran to inspect. "I can replace the circuitry and some of the other damaged components, but not the compression duct."

Ehrin took the cylinder, turned it over and passed it to Kahran, who inspected it and said, "I don't foresee a problem. It's finely turned, and the threading at this end is finer than we usually need," he shook his head, "but we can do it."

"How long will it take?"

Ehrin said, "What? Half a day… a little less. If we start right away, then I'll deliver it before midday. And then…"

The alien grimaced. "You are eager to learn more of the strange universe out there."

"Eager would be an understatement, Havor."

The alien looked at him. "To live on a world where the sky is forever grey, hiding the stars and the levels beyond…"

"Stars? Ehrin echoed. "Levels?"

Havor grumbled his distinctive laugh again, and slapped Ehrin on the back, a blow that almost sent him flying. "I will return to my ship, and await your return."

Reluctantly, Ehrin left the freighter's hold with Kahran, carefully locking the doors behind them.

For the rest of the day they worked on a lathe to reproduce the failed part, discarding their first effort as clumsy and concentrating even harder on the second. As he worked, Ehrin thought of the alien in the freighter—and the people of Agstarn going about their normal, routine business as if nothing had changed, as if there were no strange being in their midst who had promised to reveal the secrets of the universe.

The work of the foundry went on around him, work which usually would have absorbed his attention. Now it seemed almost futile, the fussing of so many ants working to build that which, to more advanced life forms, would seem banal and backward. He wondered if anything in his life would ever be the same again.

They had almost completed the second cylinder when the factory foreman approached and, above the noise of the foundry, announced that Ehrin had a caller: Sereth. He felt a momentary pang of resentment, and then guilt. He told the foreman to show her up to his rooms, then reluctantly left the last of the work to Kahran.

Wondering what Sereth might want, Ehrin left the factory floor and climbed the stairs to his attic rooms.

## 2

SERETH WAS PACING back and forth before the semi-circular window when Ehrin pushed open the door. She looked up quickly and with a shriek ran across to him, embracing him fiercely. "Ehrin, my love. Strange, terrible things have been happening today!"

"Ser, calm down. What strange things?"

"I don't know where to begin—"

"Begin," he said, "by sitting down and taking a drink. Tisane?"

"Something stronger. Do you have spirit?"

He guided her to the sofa beside the window, poured two stiff measures and sat down beside her. "Take this. Slowly. Now, calm down and tell me what's wrong."

It could only be something to do with Elder Cannak, Ehrin thought. The Elder had reported them to Prelate Hykell...

Sereth held the glass in both hands and took a restorative swallow. She coughed a little and composed herself. "Very well. First of all, you are in danger. That's why I had to come over straight away and warn you."

"Cannak?" he said.

She nodded. "When I came back from college today, father was in a flap. He'd attended an extraordinary council meeting. Velkor Cannak had called it, to discuss certain matters arising from the expedition to the western plain. He claimed that it was a matter of urgency, and wouldn't be put off."

Ehrin's mind raced. A matter of urgency? Had Cannak learned about Havor and the interworld ship? Kyrik, he thought—the pious geologist. He had seen the ship in the hold, become suspicious and informed Cannak.

"Your father was at the council meeting?"

Sereth nodded. "His attendance, as a bishop, was compulsory."

"And he told you what Cannak said?"

"He was most upset. Cannak recounted the journey to the western plains, and read verbatim from notes he had taken during the trip. These were to the effect that you, Ehrin, and Kahran had indulged in irreligious dialogue bordering on the sacrilegious. My father admitted that, if Cannak was to be believed, then what you said was beyond the acceptable."

Ehrin sat back and laughed, much relieved.

Sereth stared at him. "Ehrin, have you taken leave of your reason? Cannak has reported you to the High Council, for mercy's sake!"

"Is that all?"

"Is that all? Do you realise what punishment the High Council can inflict?"

"Velkor Cannak is an old fool. Even the High Council wouldn't take his words seriously."

Sereth was staring at him, shaking her head. "But they have! Cannak laid before them the facts and requested your immediate arrest."

His initial impulse was to scoff. So what if they arrested him, and charged him with sacrilege? What might be the repercussions?

He said, "And if we are arrested?"

Sereth stared down at her hands, clasped around the glass. "You'll be questioned by the Inquisitors of the High Council. They will learn the truth."

"That, Sereth, sounds like a euphemism."

She looked up at him. "My father has only harsh words for the Inquisitors. He's a moderate, as you know. He has no time for Hykell's methods."

And if the Inquisitors did torture him, might they extract from him more than the mere fact that he was a heathen disbeliever?

"So I will admit, before they bring out the thumb-screws, that I find their cult a farce."

"Ehrin, you fool! Can't you see the danger you're in?"

"What will they do to me, Sereth, if they do learn the truth, that we did indulge in 'irreligious dialogue'?"

She just stared at him. "Ehrin, you are a public figure. You are respected in the community. If word was to get out that you held sacrilegious beliefs, you'd be shunned, disgraced. And, if Cannak has it his way, then word will get out—he wants it made public record that you are to be arraigned to stand before the High Council."

Ehrin nodded. "What did the other bishops say?" he asked. "I take it they arrived at a decision?"

She shook her head. "The Council was split. Three for the motion, three against. That means Hykell has the casting vote, and will decide later today."

"In that case Kahran and I had better prepare ourselves for a grilling."

She reached out and took his hand. "My father advised me to find you. He gave instructions, which I had to pass on. He says that when you are arrested and questioned, you must admit the offence and claim extenuating circumstances: he said that you are to claim you were drunk at the time of speaking with Cannak. We did drink much summer-fruit wine, Ehrin. As the only other witness, I will be called, and I will testify that this was so."

"And this will get me off the charge of sacrilege?" Ehrin said sceptically.

"My father thinks that it might be seen as a mitigating factor, and that your punishment might be therefore less severe."

"Only five hours on the freezing frame instead of ten?"

"Ehrin, how can you joke about something as serious as this! My father said that the Church might satisfy themselves by imposing a heavy fine, and that you might even get away without it being made public."

"And I should be grateful for the Church's leniency?"

"You should be grateful that the Church won't impose a prison sentence—though that isn't out of the question."

He closed his eyes and rubbed his temples wearily. He wanted to laugh at the Church and their petty rules, their bigoted perspective on reality. Instead, to appease Sereth, he reached out and squeezed her hand. "Very well, Sereth. I will do as your father suggested. Please thank him for me."

She looked at him for a long time, something unsettling in her gaze. "What is it?" he asked. "I've said I'll kow-tow, haven't I?"

She replied evenly, "Ehrin, I sometimes wonder about you. About us. We have everything. We are affluent and privileged; we are at the peaks of our respective careers, and out of pig-headedness you run the risk of ruining both our lives."

He kept his anger under control. "Sereth, it isn't pig-headedness. It is a profound hatred of the Church and everything it stands for."

Her reaction was surprising. He had expected a tirade, a torrent of abuse. Instead, she just bent her head and sobbed. When he attempted to take her shoulder, she batted his hand away and wailed, "Once, not long ago, Ehrin, everything was so certain. I knew what the world was, that the Church was always right, that if we followed the righteous path, then we would be rewarded both materially and spiritually..." She looked up, and her expression was stricken. "And now, now everything is in chaos!"

He had the paradoxical urge to tell her that, just because he disbelieved, it should not necessarily undermine her own system of belief.

She looked up. "What is happening, Ehrin?"

He looked at her. "Happening?"

"I told you that terrible, strange things had happened today."

"But I thought..." he began.

"My father had some other news. He tried to tell me in such a way as to reassure me that he was not concerned... but I know my father. I know when he is troubled."

"Sereth, you're talking in riddles."

"My father said that there was a rumour going around the penitentiary. He had it from a reliable source that a number of... of strange beings had been captured on the western plains and were now languishing in cells." She stopped, looked up at him, and went on, "They are unlike any other creature ever seen, according to my father. I could see that he was deeply troubled."

Ehrin shook his head. Even more aliens? He wondered if other Zorl beside Havor had made the crossing between worlds.

He reached out and took her hand. She said in a small voice, "What's happening, Ehrin? What is true? The Church says that other worlds do not exist, that this is God's only world. But I could see in my father's eyes the light of doubt..."

He held her hand as she wept. "We live in uncertain times, Sereth. But the one thing you can be certain of is that I love you. That might not be much, but it's the only consolation I can offer."

She looked up, tears melting her brown eyes, and smiled at him.

"I must go. I told my father that I would stay with him tonight."

He went with her from the attic and down the stairs to the foundry, quiet now that the shift had finished and the workers had returned to their homes.

He embraced her at the door. Sereth said, "Promise me you won't be foolish if the High Council comes for you? Promise me, Ehrin."

He nodded and kissed her. "You have my word," he said.

He watched her as she fastened her skates, waved forlornly and set off along the ice canal. Soon she was a tiny figure lost in the crowds, and Ehrin felt a strange sadness at her turmoil, and at the same time a curious sense of excitement.

What light might Havor be able to shed on the stories of aliens from another world?

He crossed the empty factory floor and found Kahran buffing the cylinder. "Ready?"

"As ready as it will ever be. Let's hope that our craftsmanship is sufficient. How's Sereth?"

Ehrin smiled. "She is disturbed by the fact that Cannak wants us arrested for committing 'irreligious dialogue'." He told his friend the gist of her warning.

Kahran grunted. "Perhaps it would be best to claim we were pissed as zeer."

"She also told me that there's a rumour of alien beings discovered on the western plains."

Kahran looked up. "Has someone found out about Havor?"

Ehrin reassured him. "These are other aliens, if the rumours are to be believed." He clapped Kahran on the back. "We are experiencing mysterious times, my friend. I only wish that my father could have been around to enjoy them."

"I'll raise a drink to that." He held the cylinder up before his face. "Let's deliver this to Havor and see if it does the trick."

They hurried from the foundry and crossed the silent hangar. Ehrin opened the lock on the freighter's cargo hold and slipped within, closing the door tight after Kahran. In the light from his gas-lamp, the elegant, golden interworld ship glowed like a jewel.

Ehrin rapped on the hatch, which swung slowly open. Havor stood on the threshold, and Ehrin was struck anew at the evidence of the creature's alienness, his dissimilarity to any living being he had seen before. He tried not to stare at the Zorl's naked black face, the parallel lines of oversized white teeth, as Havor gave his habitual grimace and said, "You have the part? Come, let us test it."

Havor led them along the flank of the ship and opened the panel, then took the cylinder and inserted it into the housing. He tampered with it for several minutes, then gave it a look and nodded his satisfaction.

"Will it suffice?" Ehrin asked.

"We will find out shortly," the alien replied.

They returned to the hatch and climbed inside. In the control room, Havor slipped into the horizontal couch while Ehrin and Kahran stood and watched. The alien was reaching up to a console above his head, tapping at a series of tiny panels, which responded with sharp musical notes. Lights glowed in a sudden array, and Ehrin heard something humming deep within the interworld ship.

Havor looked at them and grimaced. "So far it is functioning as it should."

He reached up and pulled something from a recess in the ceiling of the cabin, a black frame which he gripped in both hands. The frame was scattered with small lights, and arrays of tiny panels, which Havor tapped quickly with his fingertips.

"Hold on tight, now."

They did as instructed. The ship rose rapidly and stopped, then seemed to bob in place like a boat on a river.

Havor was staring at a square of glowing material embedded within the frame. Tiny letters and numbers rolled down the flat surface.

"One, check. Two, check..." This went on through to six, at which point Havor turned to them. He was wearing his biggest grimace yet. "Thanks to you, my friends, the ship is airworthy once more."

Ehrin felt a flood of emotion, and it came to him how proud his father would have been at this moment.

Kahran was saying, "When do you plan to make the strike?"

"Sooner rather than later, my friend. It would be folly to wait even a day or two. Perhaps tonight, in the early hours, when all Agstarn sleeps."

Kahran turned to Ehrin and said, "The interworld ship leaving from the foundry might give the Church even more evidence against us. I have an idea. We take the freighter out in the dead of night, fly from the city, and only then launch the ship."

"That makes sense," Ehrin said.

Havor agreed. "You are already on bad terms with the Church?"

Ehrin laughed. "Well, that's one way of putting it," he said, and went on to tell the alien about the High Council's extraordinary meeting to discuss their fate.

Havor heard him out, then said, "It is always detrimental to society to allow a group of people, who believe in one way and one way only, to come to power. The first casualty of autocracy is the common man, the second is the truth."

"The truth," Ehrin echoed. "For so long the truth had been the word of the Church, but perhaps now that is coming to an end."

Kahran said, "For centuries the Church has taught that there is but one world, one platform in the grey, even though latterly they knew that to be a lie. Then I travelled to your world and discovered to my amazement that other beings beside ourselves existed in the grey." He looked at Havor. "And how many others might exist out there too?"

The alien grimaced and touched Ehrin on the shoulder. "Did I not promise that I would tell you what I know of the universe, though of course perhaps my understanding is but partial."

Ehrin shook his head. "So much has happened of late that my head is spinning..."

"Where to begin?" Havor said. "Perhaps I should ask what you know already of your world?"

Ehrin told the alien what his people believed. "Though," he went on, "I often wondered if there were other platforms out there, despite Church teachings. And then Kahran told me that we were but one of many platforms or worlds, strung out on a chain through the grey."

Havor grimaced, and Ehrin knew that the alien found his ignorance amusing.

The alien pointed to the lamp that Ehrin still gripped. "Pass me the lamp."

He handed it over, and Havor settled himself cross-legged on the floor. Ehrin and Kahran hunkered down. Havor set the lamp between them. "Now... may I borrow your beads, Kahran?"

From around his neck Kahran lifted his chain of brown beads and passed it to the alien. Havor unfastened the tiny clasp so that the chain hung straight.

"Kahran was right, in a way," said Havor. "The worlds we inhabit are strung out on a kind of chain, though the chain does not pass through a sea of limitless grey, but," he went on, "is wound about a central sun, like so..."

Ehrin watched in amazement as Havor, holding one end of the chain beside the oblate glass cowl of the gas-lamp, proceeded to wind it around the glass so that, by the time it reached the top, the chain with the tiny beads upon it described a helix.

"The flame within the lamp," Havor said, "is equivalent to the sun, which gives us light. The sun is a star, and far beyond our helical system there are millions of other stars, burning bright..."

Ehrin found his voice. "And they too have helical systems, with other worlds, strung about them too?"

Havor inclined his head in assent. "We have no reason to suspect otherwise, though my kind have not travelled to them."

Ehrin asked, "And where are we upon the chain? At which level?"

Havor indicated the second level of eight that wound about the lamp. "We are here."

Ehrin nodded, staring in awe at the model of his solar system.

Kahran pointed to the helix. "There must be hundreds of worlds in existence around the sun!"

Havor made the deep, guttural sound that indicated his amusement. "I am sorry, but this demonstration is not so very accurate. There are many thousands of worlds strung out on the helical chain, my friends."

Ehrin leaned back against the bulkhead, overcome with dizziness. "Thousands? Thousands of world just like this one?"

Havor lifted a hand. "Not just like this one, Ehrin. They are vastly different. Some are barren, without sentient life. Others bear life in various stages of evolution. My race has explored a handful of neighbouring worlds, and discovered three bipedal peoples, all technologically inferior to the Zorl."

"With ourselves," Kahran said, "being one of them."

Havor inclined his head. "But you, if it is of any satisfaction, possess a greater technology than the other two races we have so far discovered. We have taken it upon ourselves—considering our experience in these matters—to monitor the progress of these races; to act, if you like, as moral guardians. Though I admit that there are dangers in such interventionist tactics."

Ehrin thought about it, then said, "Havor, if other beings came to our world, then it would suggest a level of sophisticated technology, am I right?"

"To a varying degree, yes. They might possess the equivalent of your flying machines and hale from neighbouring worlds on the same level, or interworld vehicles if they came from the levels above or below."

He told Havor about the rumours of aliens from another world.

"Did Sereth describe them?" Havor asked.

"Her father did not witness them himself. If it is true, then they are held in the Church penitentiary in Agstarn."

Kahran shook his head and said, more to himself, "We need to overthrow the Church's despotic regime."

The alien said, "I will aid you in so far as destroying the deathship will rob them of a fearsome weapon." He returned the beads to Kahran, then stood and moved to the control couch. "I have preparations to make, if we are to strike in the early hours."

Kahran stood also. "We had best prepare the freighter, Ehrin."

In a daze, shocked at his own rebellious thoughts, as well as by the momentous reality Havor had just opened up for him, Ehrin climbed to his feet and picked up the lamp.

With a nod to Havor, he led the way from the interworld ship and hurried from the freighter's cargo hold. In the fitful light of the lamp, the scarlet envelope of the freighter bulged above them. Soon, he thought, he would be embarking on a mission that might just spell the beginning of the end of the Church in Agstarn. The notion filled him with delight and dread.

They were making for the entry hatch of the freighter's control room when Kahran halted him with a hand on his arm. "Shh! Did you hear that?"

Ehrin cocked his head, heart pounding. "What?" he hissed.

"I thought I heard footsteps, on the foundry stairs."

Ehrin listened. He did hear something, then. Voices, coming from beyond the hangar doors.

He heard shouts. There were people in the foundry. His first thought, which struck him as ridiculous in retrospect, was that the factory was being burgled.

Then the massive door to the hangar swung slowly open, and a dozen uniformed men carrying rifles and torches filed into the chamber.

He froze, aware of Kahran's hand still gripping his arm.

The intruders wore the feared sable uniforms of the Church militia. "Halt there!" the cry came from a militiaman who stepped forward confidently, brandishing a pistol.

Kahran hissed. "We could drop the lamp and run for it, through the side door and into the canal. We could return and set off with Havor in the early hours."

"And if they have the place surrounded?" Ehrin said. "And anyway, we'll be released soon enough, and then we'll go with Havor." Arrest was not to be feared—he was confident that they would be let off with a stiff fine, at worse a suspended jail sentence.

"Let's play along with the bastards," he said to Kahran. "Let them think we've given in."

He placed his lamp on the ground, then raised his hands. "We're here. Lower your weapons and we'll come peacefully."

He stepped forward, and instantly he was surrounded by a swarm of militia, surprised and not a little shocked by the force with which they dragged

him across the hangar. He had expected courteous-
ness, at least, even when being arrested, not this
casual brutality.

Behind him, he could hear Kahran struggling and
cursing in protest.

He was hauled from the foundry and tossed into
the back of a zeer-drawn prison wagon, and seconds later Kahran unceremoniously joined him.

They untangled themselves in the darkness and
sat upright as the zeer team started up and dragged
the wagon along the ice canal.

Despite himself, Ehrin was shaking with fear.

I

ONLY GOOD FORTUNE saved Sissy Kaluchek from being beaten unconscious by the alien militia. Joe was the first to be dragged from the wagon and set about with clubs and rifle butts. The rats came for Kaluchek next, and after the first blow—a glancing strike which ricocheted off the side of her head and crunched into the control panel of her atmosphere suit, positioned like an epaulette on her left shoulder—she lay face down on the ice-cold cobbles and feigned unconsciousness. It took an effort of will to quell her rage and tell herself not to fight back. In any other situation she would have fought like a tiger. Now she knew for certain that her life was at stake, and her act worked. After kicking her in the ribs, her tormentors moved on. Kaluchek heard Olembe shouting in fury, his grunts as he flailed out, and then the high yelping of the rat-like creatures as they dealt with his attack. She kept her eyes shut tight, petrified. She heard another crunch, and then Carrelli's moans, and then an ominous silence. It was broken only, seconds later, by the sound of the quick, excited respiration of the rats—as she'd decided to call them, even though they were technically more like weasels, or even lemurs—and then a rapid exchange of yips.

When her fear that they were gong to be beaten to death diminished, she became aware of the cold. Until now her atmosphere suit had kept the planet's killing temperature at bay. Obviously the blow to its control panel had smashed the smartware system. Her immediate fear was not another attack from the rats, but the sub-zero temperature.

Surely, she thought as she maintained a rigid position on the cobbles, the rats wouldn't leave their captives out in the open air to freeze to death.

She was answered minutes later when she felt hands grab her arms and legs. She was hoisted unsteadily and carried, the pinch of claws digging into her flesh making her want to cry out in pain and revulsion. The stench of the creatures was unpleasant too, a faecal reek that made her want to retch. She kept her eyes shut and flopped in their grip, as she imagined an unconscious body might, and felt herself borne from the cobbles and evidently into a building. The temperature increased, though only slightly, and her captors' footsteps echoed along what might have been a stone-paved corridor. More than anything she wanted to open her eyes, but self-preservation urged caution. There would be time later to satisfy her curiosity.

Her body tipped—she was being carried down steps—and then levelled out. Seconds later she heard the rattle of bars, and a squeal of hinges. On the way into the cell, her hip struck stone and it was all she could do to stop herself from crying out.

They dropped her—what had she expected, that they might set her down with care?—and she managed to maintain stillness and silence as the others were carried into the cell. She heard them drop like sacks of meal, and then felt something strike her. It was an arm or a leg, its weight pressing unpleasantly across the small of her back.

After a scuffle of retreating footsteps, a door clanged shut and was locked. She listened intently, but heard only the breathing of her colleagues. Cautiously she opened one eye—her right eye, nearest the straw that covered the stone-slabbed floor. She made out Joe against the far wall, face up, blood trickling from his forehead and down inside his faceplate. Next to him Carrelli lay on her side, her back to Kaluchek. That meant that it was Olembe who was pressing against her rump.

She closed her eyes and found herself weeping.

After a long minute, she opened her eyes and moved her head. They were in a barred cell, which fronted on to a short corridor. Across the corridor was a small timber door. She could see no sign of the rats.

Olembe's arm pressed down onto her, and now she could smell him, the reek of sweat which his suit had done nothing to lessen. She felt a second of involuntary panic, and the ludicrous anger provoked by the idea that even now, insensate, he was violating her.

She prayed that there were no rats around to see that she was conscious, and squirmed from under the African. She shuddered, sitting up and backing away as if in panic. She reached Joe and lay down beside him, easing him into a more comfortable position and feeling his warmth strike through her suit.

With Joe between herself and Olembe, she felt safe again.

She reached a hand around Joe's torso, felt the corrugation of his ribs beneath her hand. His heartbeat was even, his breathing regular.

It was odd how she had felt an immediate attraction to Joe back at Berne. He was much older than her—fifteen years older, she calculated—and looked care-worn, with his long, lined face and greying hair. But she had warmed to his softly spoken, self-effacing manner, his easy smile and warm laugh. He had the demeanour of someone who had seen a lot in life, not all of it nice, but had struggled through and not let adversity defeat him.

They had got along well in Berne, and since reawakening out here they had gravitated to each other. She felt for Joe Hendry what she had not let herself feel for another man in a long time.

She wondered if her sentiments had been returned, or if Joe had responded to her merely because he needed human contact after the death of his daughter.

Now she held Joe to her, comforted by his warmth in the freezing cell, his nearness, and stared over his chest at Olembe, face down on the straw and staring at her, she thought irrationally, even though his eyes were shut. She felt the weight of his arm again in her imagination, and a wave of revulsion swept over her.

Why couldn't the rats have hit Olembe a little harder and killed the bastard?

She was weeping again, which she hated. It came over her like this, at the strangest times, and she hated it because it was a sign of weakness that ran counter to the tough-girl exterior she tried to adopt. She hated it, too, because it was an indication that, no matter how well she thought she had dealt with what had happened all those years ago, she knew that it was still to deal with—that she had to have some form of closure so that she could put the past behind her and face the future unburdened.

And she hated it because every time she wept, Friday Olembe scored another point in his victory over her.

She shivered, despite Joe's warmth. She closed her eyes and dozed, and perhaps inevitably—with Olembe so much in her thoughts—she had a brief lucid dream of that night in LA.

She came awake in quick panic. She had the dream often, so vivid it seemed she had time-travelled, and always she awoke feeling the same breathless panic she had experienced back then.

She had been eighteen, and just in the big city from Nowheresville, Alaska, and still full of the wonder at the bright lights, the towering buildings, the bustle and vitality of LA. She had been wide-eyed and naive and innocent, but the city had taken all that away from her. Or rather a bastard called Olembe had done that.

A sound from the corridor cut into her thoughts. She froze. The door opposite the cell was being unbolted. She closed her eyes, then opened the left one a slit and made out three armed guards slip into the corridor followed by another rat, this one dressed not in the tight-fitting black uniform of the others, but in a long red robe with a pendant—some kind of circle surrounded by triangles—hanging around its neck.

The robed rat stepped forward cautiously and peered in through the bars, staring at the prisoners. It was impossible to read its expression—just as it was impossible to read human emotion into the face of an animal—but its jaw opened a little, and its eyes widened, and Kaluchek wondered if it was experiencing revulsion or amazement, or both.

So this, perhaps, was a representative of the authority in whose hands their fate now rested.

The rat remained staring at them for perhaps two minutes. At one point it gestured towards the closest human—which happened to be Olembe—and spoke to one of the militia. Kaluchek willed it to order the removal of Olembe...

If the rats killed the African, she would be without the continual reminder of the past that his presence provoked. But she would be without, too, the opportunity to make Olembe face what he'd done to her back then.

It was a paradox that the thought of confrontation filled Kaluchek with terror, for it was something she had dreamed about for years.

The robed rat backed away from the bars, gestured with a clawed hand and shrieked at a guard. The guards opened the corridor door and the rat hurried out, trailing its robe, followed by the guards. The door thundered shut and Kaluchek breathed with relief.

She looked across the cell at the unconscious Olembe, and felt revulsion.

A little over twelve subjective years ago, after a month in LA, she had attended a fancy-dress party to celebrate the Democrats' election to government. It had been a time of optimism—a last-ditch attempt to party in the face of global collapse. Kaluchek recalled feeling that perhaps there was hope in the election to power of a party whose foreign policy included the desire to ensure the continued survival of the world, rather than retreat into the isolationism that was Republican policy.

So the party was a celebration of the future, which in retrospect struck Kaluchek as kind of perversely ironic.

She had met a big guy dressed as the devil—and how ironic was that?—and they had chatted and moved out into the college garden. She'd gone to the party as Betsy Pig, a popular holovision character at the time, and kept the mask on while they chatted, for which she was eternally grateful.

The devil had come on strong, nothing offensive at first, just a whisper in her sow's ear that they could fuck each other senseless in the long grass beyond the pond... but Kaluchek had smiled uneasily beneath the mask and tried to change the subject. She didn't have anyone at the moment, and wanted the first time to mean something... But the devil had pressed, taking her by her waist and pulling her to him, so that she could feel the hard ridge of his erection beneath his Lycra tights. And instead of having the desired effect of turning her on, she had felt sick, physically sick and psychologically sickened that the bastard was resorting to physical coercion.

She had pulled away, unable to speak, and started walking back to the party. He'd yanked her to him with a physical force that was shocking, hit her across the head and dragged her into the copse that skirted the lake. She had tried to fight him off, but she was a tiny pig and he a strapping devil, and he'd just hit her across the face, again and again and again, until she was almost unconscious, almost... but still able to feel what he was doing as he thrust her into the grass and ripped off her leggings and raped her.

And he left her bleeding and sobbing in the grass, feeling beyond what any definition of being violated might suggest, feeling abused to the core, and powerless, for how could any authority on earth do to him what he had done to her? And she felt, too, a shame—and hated herself for feeling this—a shame that she had been weak enough, stupid enough, to let it happen.

Panic had made her gather her wits, pull on her leggings, and stagger away from the campus. She feared he might return, pull off her mask to identify his victim, or worse, drown her in the pond. So she went home and sobbed herself to sleep in a rage that took months to diminish.

She told no one, but decided to deal with what had happened in her own way. Over the next few days she made enquiries, and learned that there had been two devils at the party that night. She effected a meeting with Satan number one, and discounted him immediately—a tiny Mexican student with poor English. Then, with a fear she found hard to control, she befriended a friend of Satan number two, and in time met the African nuclear engineering major, and knew from the tone of his voice, rich, superior, American accented, that this was her man, Friday Olembe.

All she had to do then was to plan her revenge.

Except, Olembe dropped out of college a month later—someone said he'd returned to West Africa—and Kaluchek had experienced an impotent renewal of her initial rage, anger that his flight had denied her revenge, closure.

After that she had thrown herself into her studies, worked hard, to prove to herself that she could do it, and not let what the bastard had done blight her life and stop her succeeding. She'd studied around the clock, letting her social life go by the wayside, and ignored all attempts to date her by students who called her, behind her back, the Ice Queen, the Frigid Bitch of the cryonics lab.

She'd graduated with honours, got a top job at a government research station on Luna, then suffered the disappointment of the recall to Earth eight years later. Almost immediately she landed a post with ESO in Berne, a top-secret assignment that offered hope to the blighted Earth: the colonisation of the stars.

She had never forgotten about a devil called Olembe, but he no longer haunted her dreams. At one point, accidentally, she discovered that he was working on the N'Gombe fission plant near Abuja—she'd come across a paper of his while researching potential fuel sources for the starship's cryo-hangars—and it was as if a door to her old life had been opened. Over the following week, the pain returned, and with it the realisation that he'd escaped punishment and made a very comfortable life for himself back in Africa. Thoughts of revenge had surfaced, briefly, before common sense made her see reason.

Then, just a year ago, she had missed out on the final selection for the *Lovelock* mission, and disappointment had hit her hard.

In a moment of weakness, she had allowed the seed of hate to grow again, and it took root, became almost an obsession. She would go to Abuja, confront Olembe... During her most despairing and anger filled moments, she even dreamed of killing him.

Then, months before the *Lovelock* was due to light out for the stars, terrorists had struck mission control, killing five of the six maintenance team. Amazingly, the tragedy became the opportunity for Kaluchek to fulfil her dreams. She was summoned to Director Bruckner's plush office and asked if she still wanted to go to the stars. Light-headed, not believing her luck, she had said yes.

Then, a couple of days later, an odd thing happened.

In conversation with Bruckner beside the pool, he had let slip that the replacement maintenance team was complete but for two places—a smartware engineer and a top person in fission nucleonics.

Almost without thinking, guided by her subconscious, perhaps, she had found herself saying, "Actually, I've heard there's a good man in Africa, Friday Olembe."

Bruckner dropped by a few days later and told her, casually, that her suggestion had been acted upon. ESO had checked out Olembe, and he was now part of the team.

For the next few days, before they were due to meet for the first time, Kaluchek wondered if she had been horribly mistaken. Wasn't it best to let sleeping dogs lie; wasn't forgiveness the way to move on, not revenge?

She wondered what had provoked her suggestion. Perhaps it was the thought of leaving him on Earth, of allowing him to live out his life without restitution for what he had done to her. Paradoxically she had granted him an extended future—for the sole purpose of extracting some form of yet-to-be-planned revenge.

Then they had met—five new recruits around the pool at Berne—and Kaluchek had experienced an almost heart-stopping fear. As she gazed across the table at Olembe's broad, well-fed, arrogant face, she knew hatred as never before. Olembe was a beast, a macho thug whose arrogance in maturity she had extrapolated from the student she had briefly known. She had managed to tolerate his company for about five minutes, before making some excuse and slipping away.

She had willed herself to act calmly in the days that followed, to behave normally in his company, even though the sight of him filled her with panicky terror.

Over the course of the following week, she had worked out what she would do.

Beneath her, now, Joe coughed, gasped in pain and tried to sit up.

After so many negative thoughts, after all the pain and hatred, the fact of Joe Hendry coming to life filled her with pleasure.

She stroked his head and smiled. "Hey, Joe. Take it easy, okay? You'll be fine."

He blinked up at her, even managed a smile. "How long–?"

"Perhaps an hour. Someone came in to see us. A rat in a red robe."

"A rat?"

"Well, whatever they are."

He smiled, reached out and squeezed her arm. "They hit you too?"

"I got off lightly." She touched the side of her head, which was tender. "But they mashed my suit's smartware. The thermostat's gone."

He laughed gently. "Wondered why you were getting so intimate."

"Fool. I would have snuggled up whatever, okay?"

He winced, tried to sit up. She helped him. They sat side by side against the back wall, his arm around her. His head fell onto her shoulder, and when she peered down at him she saw that his eyes were closed.

She looked across the cell at Olembe. He hadn't moved in all the time they'd been there, and for a second she wondered if he was dead. Then she detected the slight rise and fall of his bull-like chest.

Oddly, she felt a quick stab of relief. Even though a part of her would not mourn his death, she wanted him to live. Dead, he would never find out what pain he had caused her, would never meet his deserved punishment.

During her last week on Earth, she had put together the package that would eventually, one far off day, spell Friday Olembe's nemesis. She had accessed an old UN data file on a fugitive war criminal, broken the encryption and copied it to a personal pin. Then, working in her room well into the early hours, she had patched in Friday Olembe's personal details, erasing all trace of the identity of the original war criminal so that to all intents and purposes it was Olembe who had given the order for the execution of the five hundred Moroccan civilians.

It would never have convinced people on Earth, of course, where the original records would have pointed up the dissimulation. But hundreds or thousands of years later, with only the UN data pin to go by, it would be compelling evidence to a fledgling colony that they had a mass murderer in their midst.

She had planned to splice the data into the core smartware system just as soon as everything was up and running, introduce the details of his spurious past into his personal identity entry and wait for someone in administration to make the discovery. Now, things were on hold. She might never get the opportunity to enact her revenge—in which case she would have to think of some other form of punishment for the bastard.

Meanwhile, she tolerated his odious presence.

Carrelli coughed, rolled over onto her side and groaned. She tried to push herself onto all fours and failed. Kaluchek left Joe and moved across to the medic, taking her shoulders and easing her onto her back. Her beautiful, oval ballerina's face was marred by a growing contusion that discoloured her left eye and cheek.

Carrelli sat up, shuffled to the wall next to the sleeping Joe and slumped against the brickwork. She closed her eyes, breathing hard.

Kaluchek touched her hand. "You okay?"

Carrelli opened her eyes and smiled at her. "Nothing broken, I think. You and Joe?"

"I'm fine. Bastards smashed my suit controls, is all." She looked at Joe. "I think he's okay. He came round a while ago. I think he's sleeping now."

Carrelli frowned.

"Is that bad?" Kaluchek asked, heart leaping.

"It might not be good. It is hard to tell."

"Joe's tough. He'll be fine."

Carrelli smiled. "You like Joe a lot, don't you?"

Kaluchek found herself blushing like a schoolgirl.

Carrelli touched her hand. "That's nice. Joe's a good man. Look after him, okay?"

Kaluchek smiled, and wondered what exactly the medic meant by that. Did she intend not being around for much longer? The thought frightened her: the cool, intelligent Italian was a foil to Olembe's illusions of power.

Across the cell, Olembe cursed under his breath and rolled onto his back. He blinked up at the ceiling for a second or two, then propped himself up on his elbows, taking in the bars and the corridor, then looking around at his fellow prisoners.

He sat up, moved to the bars and leaned against them, as if putting as much distance as possible between himself and the other three—which suited Kaluchek fine.

He wore a face like thunder. "Well done, Carrelli. Fucking ace tactics. Look where it got us. We should have attacked the bastards when we had the chance."

Carrelli stared at him, calm. "I think we did the right thing, Friday."

He looked incredulous. "The right thing? You kidding? What if the bastards had killed one of us back there?"

In reply, Carrelli pointedly looked from Joe to Kaluchek, and back to Olembe. "It looks to me, Friday, as if we're all still alive."

"Yeah, but for how much longer? How long before they decide we're a threat and execute us?"

At this, the Italian smiled. "I don't think they will do that, Friday. You're being overdramatic. They have more to gain from keeping us alive."

Olembe looked disgusted. "We've listened to you long enough, Carrelli. From now on we do what we should have done in the beginning. We're bigger and smarter than these fucking animals. Let's show it."

He would have gone on, but Joe groaned and hung his head between his knees. Carrelli moved quickly to examine him, peering into his eyes and taking his pulse.

"Joe?" Kaluchek said, heart racing.

He smiled weakly. "I'm fine, Sis. Well, I feel like shit, but…"

Carrelli knelt before him and nodded. "You'll be fine. Just take it easy."

He smiled. "Will do. Give me a comfortable bed and I'll go back to sleep."

Kaluchek moved closer to Joe and put an arm around him, easing him to her and staring defiantly across at Olembe.

Joe said, "Any water? I'm thirsty."

Olembe said, "Water? You kidding, Hendry?"

They froze at a sound from beyond the corridor. Sliding bolts cracked like gunfire and the door swung slowly open.

## 2

THE PRISON WAGON slid along the ice canal, heading south. Ehrin and Kahran huddled in the darkness of the cart, shivering. Neither had their padded jackets and the sub-zero temperature cut to the bone. They held each other, gaining little warmth but some sense of comradeship.

Kahran said, "The most important thing to remember is that we need to get out as soon as possible. The last thing we want is to anger Cannak and the Inquisitors. We admit our mistakes, claim drunkenness as Sereth advised, and apologise. We must remember that our personal feelings are of little account. Do you understand?"

Ehrin nodded. "I'll try to smile at Cannak when he's strutting before the Inquisitors."

"Good, do that. But no heroics, Ehrin. Do you promise?"

Ehrin nodded. "Of course. the sooner we're out of there, the sooner we can aid Havor."

"And that's what's important." He stopped. "Hello, I think we've arrived."

The wagon had slowed. The susurration of the runners on the ice was replaced by the panting snorts of the zeer. Ehrin heard shouts, then the opening of a timber gate. Seconds later the wagon started up again, moved a short distance, then stopped.

"Take heart, Ehrin," Kahran said. "We're closer now to the truth than we ever were before. Remember that."

The doors of the wagon opened. Four guards climbed aboard without a word and grabbed Ehrin and Kahran as if they were lifeless goods to be unloaded. Ehrin was dragged to the ice, striking his knee painfully on the ground. Kahran was hauled out after him, protesting feebly.

In the darkness Ehrin was aware only of the intense cold rising from the ice, the dark shapes of the Church militia and the pain knifing through his kneecap.

He was dragged through a door, down a long, dark corridor, and thrown into a cell. A second later Kahran joined him, fetching up against the far wall. Ehrin helped him into a sitting position. The old man was dazed, his eyes frightened.

He tried to smile. "This brings back painful memories, Ehrin."

Ehrin gripped his hand. "This time things are different. We'll soon be out of here. Then—"

"Then we'll show the bastards, eh, Ehrin?"

Ehrin smiled, cheered by the old man's spirit.

He looked around the cell. A barred window was set high up in the back wall, way out of reach. The only other things in the cell beside themselves were a rusty bucket and a pile of straw.

He had expected to be left here a while, possibly hours. He was startled, minutes later, when the cell rang to the report of bolts being shot. The door swung open and four silent guards—perhaps the same four who had arrested them—marched in, took Ehrin and Kahran roughly by the arms and dragged them from the cell.

The guards had perfected their technique. They held their victims a few inches off the ground, so that their gripping fingers dug painfully into the prisoners' armpits. By the time they reached the second chamber, Ehrin had lost all feeling in his arms.

They were marched into a brightly lit room. Something about it sent a shiver through Ehrin's soul. Its walls were white, as if recently painted, and the slabbed floor sloped slightly towards a sink-hole in the corner.

Two chairs awaited the prisoners. They were odd chairs, as terrifying in their way as was the rest of the room. Their arms were equipped with semicircular manacles, and their backs were open frames, through which the spine of the prisoner could be accessed.

But perhaps the most frightening thing was Kahran's reaction. The old man, following Ehrin into the room, said under his breath, "Oh, mercy upon us..."

The chairs were set back to back. Ehrin was strapped into the chair facing the door, Kahran into the second. The manacles secured his wrists to the splintered timber armrests. Then the guards left the room.

Kahran said, "They're trying to frighten us, Ehrin. They wouldn't... they wouldn't go through with..."

Ehrin interrupted. "You've been here before?" Despite himself, he tried to make the question light-hearted.

"Only once," Kahran said, and fell silent.

The door opened and a tall figure in black strode into the chamber. It was the Elder, Velkor Cannak.

He strode around the chairs in the centre of the room, the Book of Books lodged under his left armpit. He regarded the stone slabs beneath his feet as he paced.

The Elder's expression of smug supremacy, barely suppressed, was what angered Ehrin most.

"Gentlemen," Cannak said at last, "it is unfortunate indeed that we meet again in such circumstances. However, I need not detain you for long. I require, quite simply, a number of truthful answers to a few straight questions. I am sure that men of your learning will oblige me. After which, we can all repair to our respective homes."

He continued pacing, around and around the seated pair.

"I am sure you are both aware of the reason for your presence here."

"Isn't this a little excessive," Kahran interrupted. "So we baited you back on the skyship. I thought the Church was bigger than—"

Cannak laughed, silencing Kahran.

"A little theological debate, even with people as ignorant as yourselves, never troubled me," Cannak said. "But I think you know that the charge of sacrilege is the least of your worries."

Ehrin looked up and said, "I don't know what you're talking about."

Cannak paced. It was no doubt a practised ploy, to disconcert the prisoner, destabilise his focus. "No? Are you quite sure? Cast your minds back, if you will, to our last night out on the western plains. Recall the thunderclap, the streak of light through the air—the meteorological effect, you called it?"

"What of it?" Kahran snapped.

"You investigated. You found something. You were gone for quite a while. I thought little of it at the time. Only later did I begin to wonder..."

"You're talking in riddles, Cannak," Kahran said.

Ehrin hoped that Cannak would not notice the beads of perspiration gathering on the fur of his snout. The Elder suspected, that much was clear. Perhaps the militia had searched the hangar after the arrest, and found Havor?

Cannak slowed his pacing. His tread became deliberate as he said, "In that case I shall endeavour from now on to speak plainly. While out on the ice, you made contact with aliens. I suspect that the expedition to the western plains was nothing more than an excuse to rendezvous with these creatures. I intend to learn the truth of your contact. What do they want here, and how did you establish first contact with them?"

Ehrin shook his head. "You're wrong, Cannak."

"You made an excuse to take the freighter across the ice, looking for whatever it might have been that caused the thunderclap. You were gone for over two hours. During that time, I suspect you contacted the aliens and directed them towards Agstarn, for they were captured a day later by tribesmen, heading for the mountain pass."

Kahran laughed. "This is ridiculous, man!"

Ehrin heard a note of relief in his friend's voice. If aliens had been discovered by tribesmen, then perhaps the militia had not yet discovered Havor.

"What I want to know," Cannak said, his footfalls as regular as a metronome, "is what they want in Agstarn? Why are they here? Are they the van of an invasion force?"

"For mercy's sake," Kahran said with infinite forbearance, "what aliens? I thought Church tenets held that we were the one and only sentient race in creation? Or did God get it wrong, Elder?"

This had the effect of halting Cannak's pacing. He was behind Ehrin, on Kahran's side of the room. Ehrin could well imagine the look upon his thin face as the Elder said, "Oh, my dear Mr Shollay, you will live to regret your heresy, indeed you will!"

Cannak was silent for a time. He moved into Ehrin's view, his receding chin lodged on his chest in contemplation.

At last he said, "You refuse to admit that you are in league with the aliens?"

Kahran was silent, and Ehrin followed his lead.

"You deny even making contact with the aliens upon the ice plain two evenings ago?"

Cannak paced. The silence stretched.

"I will leave you for five minutes, so that you might reconsider the wisdom of your silence. When I return, I will not be alone. I shall be accompanied by two Inquisitors. I will question you again. If you maintain your lies, they will proceed to practise certain physical procedures upon your persons which might persuade either one of you the benefit of candour."

He strode from the room and the timber door shut solidly behind him.

"Two different races of aliens?" Ehrin could not keep the humour from his tone. "Isn't that an embarrassment of riches?"

"I wonder what brings these second aliens to Agstarn?" Kahran said under his breath.

"Perhaps they heard about the famed hospitality and tolerance of the Church."

Kahran smiled. "No wonder Cannak is desperate to learn the truth, Ehrin! Imagine his fear—everything he has ever held as true, subverted by the aliens' arrival. Oh, isn't it wonderful?"

The door rattled open. Suddenly serious, Kahran said, "Say nothing, my friend."

Two black uniformed Inquisitors strode into the cell, followed by Cannak. The Inquisitors' bulk seemed to fill the chamber. Ehrin wondered if they had been selected because of their height and girth. Perhaps they were specially recruited from the tribesmen of the plains.

His idle speculation ended when Cannak said, "Well, gentlemen, have you had time enough to reconsider your obdurate stance?"

Kahran said, "What do you think, Elder?"

Cannak paced, around and around. The Inquisitors had taken up positions on each side of the door, staring straight ahead as if the prisoners did not exist.

Cannak said, "Did you make contact with aliens on the ice plains on the evening of the 5th of St Belknap's month 1280?"

Ehrin said, "We saw no one. We returned to the dirigible after seeing nothing of—"

"When you rendezvoused with the aliens, what were your instructions, and what do the aliens want on Agstarn?"

"Go to hell, Cannak!" Kahran cried.

Instantly Cannak said, "Start on this one!"

Ehrin closed his eyes. He heard the Inquisitors move from the door, and step around him. Then he heard the sound of ripping material, and Kahran's feeble grunting as he tried to resist their attention.

Tears had formed in his eyes, and he wanted to raise his hands to dash them away. The manacles prevented movement. He opened his eyes, allowing the tears to track down the fur of his cheeks.

Cannak had taken a small folding chair and placed it before the door. He sat down, positioning himself so that Ehrin was between him and Kahran as the Inquisitors went about their business.

He addressed Ehrin in little more than a murmur. "My friends will perform upon the person of Kahran Shollay a procedure known in their trade as the Devil's Wings. Put simply, two lateral vents are opened in the back of the subject, between the second and third ribs on each side of the spine. A rib is then removed, snapped off, so allowing the entry of an expert hand which takes first the right lung and pulls it through the opening so that it resembles, with a little aesthetic licence, the wings of a devil. It is, I am assured, an exquisitely painful process. The subject is conscious all the while and, when the second lung is pulled through the ribcage, and punctured on the broken rib along with the first lung, death is assured but slow in arriving. A suitable end for the godless, my friends… However, if at any stage it comes over you to cease your lies, you will survive with your lives." He paused, then, and nodded to the Inquisitors.

Kahran yelled, "We know nothing, you bastards!" and Ehrin could only close his eyes and sob.

Kahran screamed as the Inquisitors sliced the flesh between his ribs. Ehrin heard a snap then, like the breaking of a branch, and Kahran's pained cries saved Ehrin from hearing the second break.

Cannak raised a hand, a signal for the Inquisitors to pause there.

"We can bring an end to this business if you simply admit your complicity..."

Kahran said, between racked breaths, "Cannak, may you burn slowly in your hell—"

Kahran screamed. Ehrin heard a slushing, liquid sound—for all the world like the noise his father's hand had made when removing the giblets from the feast-day fowl—and then an odd rushing of air as Kahran's lung was pulled out and punctured on the shattered rib. The old man yelled, and then panted, and then coughed up what sounded like fluid, and Ehrin could only close his eyes and vow one day to kill Cannak with his bare hands.

He opened his mouth to say something, concoct some story about collusion with aliens that would stay Kahran's torture for a while—but too late.

Kahran's cries ended abruptly.

He sensed movement behind him, as the Inquisitors stood up. He heard their murmured report to Cannak, "Dead."

Cannak regarded the Inquisitors with rage. "You fools. You claimed that death would come slowly!"

Ehrin could not make out the Inquisitor's murmured reply. Something turned to ice within him, and then rage. He leapt forward, attempting to get at Cannak, hurt him before the Inquisitors did their business on him too.

The chair held solid, restraining him.

Cannak merely smiled, then said, "You are either supremely foolish, Mr Telsa, or entirely innocent. But I don't think it's the latter." He hesitated, then said, "Very well, there is another way we can go about this. We will evince the truth from the aliens, shall we?" He nodded to the Inquisitors. They came into view and unfastened the manacles, hauling Ehrin to his feet and dragging him towards the door.

"Where are you taking me?"

"Where else, Mr Telsa, but to your friends? We will have them tell us whether or not you are guilty as charged."

He was bundled from the cell, but not before squirming in his captors' grip and looking back at Kahran's body. His lungs spilled from his shattered back, and his head had slumped forward in death.

The Inquisitors dragged him down a long corridor, turned into another, his feet trailing, their fingers digging into the flesh of his armpits. He could feel their desire to do to him what they had done to Kahran, their frustration at this interruption of their bloody business.

He thought of Sereth, then, and had the irrational urge to shout at her, to scream that this was the logical extension of her Church's authoritarian rule.

They halted outside a tall timber door. Two guards stationed beside it turned and shot six bolts, then stood back with rifles at the ready as the Inquisitors kicked open the door and pushed Ehrin across the threshold.

They followed him inside, along with Elder Cannak, and the door was secured behind them.

They were in a short corridor, on the other side of which was a barred cell.

Ehrin had expected to find that the aliens were like Havor—having only Havor as a guide to the appearance of aliens—but in that he was very wrong.

In the cell before him were four huge creatures, their bald flesh an unnatural pink—all except one, who was as black as Havor. They were perhaps half as tall again as his people, and were watching him with small, animal-like eyes. But the most offensive thing about these creatures was their stench, like turned zeer milk and faeces combined.

One of the aliens, a little less pink than the other two, though not as dark as the fourth, stepped forward and stared through the bars. It had long fur upon its head, and tiny, ugly facial features.

Then, to Ehrin's amazement, the creature spoke to him in the language of his people.

## 3

SERETH JASPARIOT SAT on a window seat in her father's study and stared out at the winter-gripped city. The grey was darkening, and the mansion buildings on the far side of the street were slowly merging with the night.

She jumped and turned at a sound from across the room. Her father had stopped on the threshold, surprised at finding her in his sanctum. She wanted to tell him that this was where she had come as a little girl, when awoken by frightening dreams. The solidity of his books, and what they represented, had always calmed her.

Her father, never tall even in his prime, looked even shorter tonight. He seemed slumped, shrunken within himself.

"Sereth, my dear." He limped across the room, embraced her with frail arms and slumped into his armchair. She saw, then, that he was weeping; globular tears had caught in the fur of his cheeks.

"Father?"

"I was at the penitentiary, Sereth. I sought out Governor Kaluka and asked him if the vile rumours were just that, scandalmongering by the lower orders bent on sedition. How could alien beings descend from the sky and step upon God's ground?"

She knelt before him and laid a hand on his lap, as thin as the cloth-covered spar of a scarecrow's limb. "Father?"

"Kaluka blustered at first, but I saw through him. At last he admitted it. Four strange beings, animals, had indeed been captured beyond the western mountains."

Sereth opened her mouth, but words were beyond her.

"Animals?" she said at last. "Not intelligent beings?"

"Animals in that they resembled nothing I had ever seen before; but they were undeniably intelligent."

Sereth gasped. "You saw them?"

"When Kaluka admitted that he had them locked up in the western tower, I demanded as the prison chaplain to visit the creatures. Being a mere civilian, he dared not deny an official of the Church."

Sereth shook her head. "But did not God say that we of Agstarn were the chosen ones, that no others beside ourselves should be granted the gift of sentience?"

He returned her stare bleakly. "So it is written, my child."

"And yet you saw these creatures with your own eyes?"

"I entered their cell. They were... they were appallingly ugly, Sereth. For the most part they were furless, other than for tufts of hair upon their heads. Three of them were as pink as a newborn's anus, the other as black as night. But most distressing was their size; Sereth they were fully half again as tall as ourselves."

She swallowed; she felt nauseous, as if teetering on the edge of a bottomless precipice.

"Did you speak with these creatures?"

He shook his head. "I admit that I was speechless in their company, though they did communicate amongst themselves in deep, dull tones."

"They did not attempt to harm you?"

"They were peaceable, and had been throughout their incarceration."

She shook her head. "But they might have been animals, still. What evidence have you that they were sentient, reasoning beings?"

"They wore clothing, my dear, strange garments embedded with tiny machines, the like of which we have never seen before. The Governor claimed that they appeared to be even more technologically advanced than ourselves."

Sereth stood quickly and walked to the window. She thought of Ehrin, and how he would no doubt delight in this news, and she silently cursed him.

She turned to her father. "And what will happen to these creatures? The Church won't let it be known that such beings exist, surely?"

"Of course not. My guess is that they'll be executed as godless heathens, their carcasses donated to the Church medical researchers for dissection. But Hykell has yet to decide upon their fate."

She was silent for a long time after that, watching her father as he dabbed at his damp nose with a soiled handkerchief and blotted his eyes.

"Does that make the Church right, father? Does that mean the word of God can be trusted?"

He looked up. "I beg your—"

"I'm sorry, father, but if alien beings come to Agstarn, intelligent aliens, then what of the veracity of the Book of Books?"

He held his head in his hands, his expression woeful. "It has... has yet to be decided. The Book is but the *received* wisdom of the Lord, communicated through the prophet Kahama. But Kahama was but mortal, and prone to error. This visitation does not, cannot, call into question the other tenets of the Book of Books and the Church's wise teachings."

She wanted to believe his words, but the manner of their delivery, the very state of her once proud father, suggested that even he did not believe what he was saying.

She felt as if her world were falling apart.

She thought of her fiancé, and how much she wanted to feel safe in his arms just then. "And Ehrin? With Hykell so busy with the aliens, I doubt he will have decided on Ehrin's fate, father?"

He looked up, and his expression was pained. "What?"

"Hykell made his pronouncement late this afternoon, just after the aliens were imprisoned. It was Velkor Cannak's doing. He is convinced that Ehrin and his friend Kahran Shollay had a hand in the arrival of the aliens while out on the plains. Apparently they heard the arrival of an airborne craft, which they said was a meteorological effect at the time, and they went out to investigate."

"But I was there, father. They certainly had nothing to do with any alien visitors!"

"Cannak claims otherwise. At any rate, Hykell ordered the arrest of Ehrin and Kahran at first dark. I didn't want to distress you further, Sereth."

She could not stop her tears. "Have the militia been for them yet?" She moved to the door.

"Sereth, don't be rash. There is nothing you can do."

"I want to be with the man I love, father. I want to prove his innocence."

He called her name again, but she ignored him and slammed the door. She ran down the stairs, almost slipping in her haste, and snatched her skates from the table in the hall. She spent a long minute pulling them on and fumbling with the laces, before tottering upright and dragging open the door. The icy blast that greeted her had the effect of clearing her mind and stiffening her resolve. She would get to Ehrin before the militia, and if needs be she would be arrested with him.

She skated north at speed, to the edge of town where Ehrin had his grim place of work, the long mill building of which he was so proud. Tears came to her eyes as she thought of him, and froze on the fur of her cheeks. When she dashed her hand across her face, the frozen tears fell through the air like tiny jewels.

On the ice canal leading to the foundry, she saw in the distance an approaching wagon drawn by a team of zeer. She passed alongside it, wondering as she did so if it could be a prison wagon—and then dismissed the thought. Ehrin and Kahran were respected citizens, and would not be made to suffer the indignity of being hauled off to jail like drunken hoodlums. They would be approached by a High

Church official, surely, and politely requested to accompany him to the council chambers...

She came to the foundry entrance and was about to haul on the bell-pull when she noticed that the big double doors were standing ajar. Her heart leapt. At this time of the evening, with the shift over and the workers gone home, the doors should be locked.

Fearfully she stepped inside.

The vast cavern of the foundry was in darkness, and the silence was intimidating. Orienting herself and crossing towards the stairs, stepping carefully lest she bark her shins on the anvils and girders she knew made an obstacle course of the factory floor, she came to the wooden steps without mishap and hurriedly ascended to the offices, and from there to Ehrin's attic rooms.

"Ehrin!" she called optimistically as she pushed open the door. She stood on the threshold, staring about her, heart tolling like the bell for evening prayers. A lamp burned beside his favourite armchair, and his books and papers littered various desks and tables. The room spoke so much of Ehrin's character that his absence was cruelly emphasised.

She thought back to their last meeting, that afternoon. She had warned him of his impending arrest, so he would have been a fool to remain where a Church official would easily find him. Therefore he had taken her words to heart and hidden himself.

But where, she asked herself as she hurried from the attic and tapped down the stairs. The offices offered no place of concealment, and while he might conceivably have hidden himself somewhere in the vast foundry, a more obvious place would be the hangar... It came to her suddenly that he might even have taken flight aboard one of his skyships, but she dismissed this. Even someone as headstrong and recalcitrant as Ehrin would not risk flight when the charges against him were so meagre.

Having said that, if Velkor Cannak thought him in league with the aliens...

But how would Ehrin know of Cannak's suspicions, she asked herself as she moved carefully across the foundry towards the vast hangar doors.

Then it came to her that the only reason he would have to take flight in a skyship would be if he were guilty, if he had indeed, that night out on the ice plain, come across aliens whom he had aided and abetted.

She laughed nervously. She was being fanciful. She had more faith in Ehrin than that; a stubborn radical he might be, but stupid he was not.

As she crept through the darkness, the thought of aliens sent a chill up the fur of her spine. She felt, unaccountably, under threat. From a workbench she fumbled for something with which she might arm herself, and found a short, sharp chisel, which fitted snugly into her palm and offered reassurance disproportionate to its size.

A faint light spilled from the open door of the hangar. When she reached the threshold, she saw that an oil-lamp had been dropped on the floor and was guttering as the last of its fuel seeped across the concrete.

The sight of it confirmed her worst fears. Could this be Ehrin's lamp, taken from him on his arrest?

She picked it up and proceeded into the hangar, the great shapes of the skyships casting mammoth shadows across the walls.

She had no way of knowing if any of the dirigibles were missing, but the hangar doors at the far end of the chamber were closed. Surely, if he were fleeing, he would not have had time to shut them behind him?

So perhaps he was still hiding in one of the dirigibles?

But which one? The *Expeditor*? She crossed to it quickly and stepped through the hatch into the gondola's lounge, which was empty. She hurried along the corridor, checking the cabins on the way. Finding nothing, she moved to the control room. "Ehrin," she called under her breath. "Ehrin!"

She left the *Expeditor*, holding the lantern high and casting her gaze around the dozen other stilled skyships. Her eyes alighted on the largest dirigible in the hangar, the scarlet freighter that had accompanied them across the ice plains. The door of its cargo hold, she saw with a start of joy, stood open a fraction.

She ran towards it and slipped inside, then stopped. At the far end of the hold, she made out an effulgent golden craft like a stylised teardrop. She moved towards it slowly, the light of her lamp playing across its surface.

It was unlike the gondolas that belonged to the other skyships, but what else could it be? Perhaps another of Ehrin and Kahran's inventions, a secret prototype?

She walked around the ship, searching for some kind of hatch. She found a triangular viewscreen on one flank, but it was black and impossible to see through. She paused, then raised her fist and knocked on the glass. "Ehrin, are you in there? Ehrin, it's me, Sereth!"

She waited, her heart thumping. How she wanted Ehrin in her arms now. How she wanted his reassurance that all would be well...

A noise made her jump. Something mechanical sighed, back along the flank of the vessel. She turned and saw a section of its golden panelling ease out and upwards. She started forward. "Ehrin, you don't know how—" she began, then screamed.

Something was standing in the entrance to the golden ship, staring out at her.

Before she could unfreeze herself and command her limbs to move, the creature darted for her and grabbed her upper arms. Its grip was painful and, as much as she struggled, she was unable to free herself.

The creature pushed its face close to Sereth's, and she almost passed out. Its visage was beyond ugly— it seemed malformed, crumpled and hairless and blackened, as if it had suffered some terrible injury.

"You know Ehrin?" it said, its accent grating.

She screamed, "What have you done to him?"

"I have done nothing." Its snout was horribly flattened, its nose smeared halfway across its face. It breathed noisily. "He was taken, with Kahran."

"Taken?" was all she could say.

"I saw them arrest him and Kahran, drag them outside. I need to know where they were taken."

"Why? What do you want with—"

It shook her, silencing her questions. "You are a friend of Ehrin?" it asked.

"A friend? I'm his fiancée! We—"

"A female?"

She grunted. "What do you think?"

The monster blinked. "I'm sorry, but I think you all look alike to me."

She realised that she was still grasping the tool she had picked up in the factory.

The creature had relaxed its grip on her. Quickly, without thinking, she raised her hand and swung the chisel with all her might.

Gasping, she stared at what she had done. The handle of the chisel emerged from the alien's chest and blood trickled from the wound and down its silver suit.

The monster's reaction startled her. She had expected it to fall, or even to attack her. It did neither, but instead grimaced at her. With its free hand, it plucked the chisel from its chest as if it were nothing but an insect-sting.

It cast aside the chisel and gripped her even tighter. "Listen to me!" it said as if the attack had not occurred. "Ehrin, Kahran and I are working together. We are friends. You have nothing to fear from me. I need to find out where Ehrin and Kahran are being kept. Then, with luck, I can free them."

"Free them?" she shook her head. "But they'll be freed in days..." She stopped herself. So Velkor Cannak was right. Ehrin and Kahran were in league with the aliens, some of whom had been captured. In which case, the Church was unlikely to free Ehrin and Kahran within days.

The alien said, "I need Kahran now. It is vital to my plans that I free them. Do you know where they are being held?"

She wanted to cry. She was shaking with fear and she realised, with a hot flush of embarrassment, that she had lost control of her bladder. The fur on the inside of her legs was hot with urine.

She wept. "In the central penitentiary." She recalled what her father had told her. "In the western tower. It's the most secure block there is."

The alien monstrosity blinked at her. "You are telling the truth?"

Something battled within her. She loved Ehrin, that she could not deny; but was her love for him sufficient to accept his alliance with these monstrous forces?

She wept as she said, "Of course I'm telling the truth! Don't you think I want Ehrin free as much as you do?"

The creature bared its oversized teeth in a horrible snarl, then dragged Sereth into the gloom of the golden ship. It pushed her along a narrow corridor, into a small triangular room fitted with two horizontal couches and other black accoutrements.

The alien forced her into one of the couches, then strapped her in so that she was unable to move. It pulled something from the silver suit that clothed its body, and held it out to her. In the gloom she could only make out a dark plate.

"Touch it!" the alien barked at her. "Now tell me, where are Ehrin and Kahran?"

She touched the plate with trembling fingers and said, "In the Church penitentiary, the western tower."

"Do you know where it is from here? Can you direct me?"

She wanted to laugh and cry at the same time, and tell the creature that it would not get a dozen yards along the ice canal before some citizen alerted the authorities. "You can't possibly go by foot!"

"I said, can you direct me?"

She nodded. "Yes, yes, of course. It's—"

"Not now," the alien said. "Show me, okay?"

She felt something lurch in her stomach. It wanted her to accompany it into the centre of the city...

"We can't go by foot. We'd be arrested—"

The creature gave a loud grunt and flung itself into the opposite couch. It strapped itself in with one hand, and with the other reached up and tapped something above its head.

Sereth screamed. The ship was moving, rising from the floor of the freighter's cargo hold and turning slowly on its axis. Sereth raised her head, peered along the length of her body to a long, narrow viewscreen beyond her feet. She saw the inside of the hold swing dizzily. The golden ship was approaching the doors, hovering a matter of yards above the floor. As she watched, it came to the doors, nudged them open and passed through.

The alien grunted, pulled a black frame from the ceiling and entwined its arms about it. "Put your head down, girl. Hold on tight."

The ship lurched. Serith screamed. Despite his command, she raised her head and stared through the viewscreen. They were approaching the wall of the hangar at speed. "No!"

The nose of the ship hit the wall and it crumbled outwards, falling bricks striking its carapace with deafening blows. Seconds later the ship passed through the foundry wall and hovered a yard above the ice canal amid a cloud of settling dust, its sudden emergence creating panic along the ice canal. Sereth saw people scatter in fright, and spooked zeer rear up and bolt away down the canal.

"Now," said the alien, "which way?"

Sereth pointed south, and instantly she was thrust back on the couch. She screamed in fear as the ship accelerated and shot up and over the rooftops of the city with impossible speed.

# 4

KALUCHEK STARED IN amazement as Carrelli stepped forward, gripped the bars and spoke to the rats.

She had always thought that there was something different about the Italian medic. Carrelli had seemed to stand apart from the rest of the group, coolly observing without comment; she'd known things in certain situations that she had no right to know. Kaluchek had put it down to the fact that she was the only survivor of the original maintenance team, and had received extra training, but that didn't account for her intuitive assumptions that had always proved correct... and now this. This changed things, though Kaluchek couldn't work out quite how things were different, now.

It was an odd and unsettling experience, watching the Italian-speaking rat. She had always spoken a quiet, attractively accented form of English, never raising her voice. Now, as if forced by the language itself, she leaned forward and almost retched up a series of strangulated barks, high pitched and imperative.

Kaluchek looked quickly at Joe, who was open-mouthed in amazement at the Italian's performance. Across the cell, Olembe was pop-eyed with surprise.

The rats appeared equally taken aback. The small alien in the colourful tunic dropped into a crouch, staring at Carrelli with large eyes, snout open to reveal a set of white, needle-sharp fangs. Behind it, the red-robed alien stepped back into the doorway.

Carrelli ceased her linguistic contortions and paused, as if awaiting a reply. Cautiously the small alien took a step forward and snapped out a quick yelp.

Carrelli replied in kind, and the rat launched into a volley of yips and barks.

It was interrupted by the robed alien, who yelped at the smaller rat, and then turned and addressed the astonished guards. The latter sprang forward and clutched the small rat by its short arms, almost lifting it off the ground.

The robed rat stepped forward, dropping into a crouch and sidling into the corridor, appraising Carrelli slantwise from massive, dark eyes.

It barked, and Carrelli replied.

The small alien, gripped by the guards, screwed itself round to face the robed rat, and spat a series of high-pitched barks.

Carrelli turned to her fellow captives and smiled. "I've made it clear that we come in peace, and are no threat to them or their way of life. But I get the impression that our very presence here, the fact of our existence, has upset things in some way."

"How the hell—?" Olembe began.

"Not now," Carrelli said. "I think our arrival has stirred up some kind of social unrest. Jacob here seems open to the fact of our arrival, while Red Robe is violently opposed."

Joe said, "It's called Jacob?"

Carrelli smiled. "That's what I call it. The coat it's wearing," she explained.

Before she could go on, the small alien—Jacob, Kaluchek thought—barked at Carrelli, who nodded and replied at length.

Whatever she said had the effect of incensing Red Robe, who sprang forward and almost lashed out at her through the bars in rage, literally spitting in anger.

Without turning, Carrelli said, "It's calling us... devils, phantoms... at any rate, evil creatures that do not exist—"

Olembe cut in, "What matters, Carrelli, is who's running the show here? Natty dresser or red riding hood?"

"Who do you think, Friday?"

"Christ, I knew it. You've really landed us in the shit now, Carrelli."

She turned and stared at him. "There was absolutely nothing I could have done to appease those in power, Friday, okay?"

He just shook his head. "So what do they do with devils on this ice ball?" he sneered. "Burn them at the stake?"

Kaluchek pressed herself closer to Joe and clutched his hand, fear turning her stomach. She wished Olembe would just shut it, let Carrelli do the talking.

Carrelli turned to Red Robe and barked.

The rat stepped forward, inserting its dripping muzzle through the bars, and snarled at her. Its obvious anger gave Kaluchek the creeps.

"What the hell is it saying, Carrelli?" Olembe asked.

Carrelli just shook her head, but from Kaluchek's position she could see the expression of shock on the medic's face.

Jacob yelped something, a single exclamation, and began a series of bucking contortions in a bid to free itself from the grip of the guards. They held on tight, and Red Robe barked a command, at which the guards hauled the struggling alien towards the outer door.

"What did they say?" Olembe demanded.

Carrelli turned to him. "Red Robe threatened us with death, torture on some kind of frame..."

"Jesus!" Olembe cried.

Kaluchek felt suddenly sick. Joe gripped her hand and held on tight, then drew her to him.

Seconds later a muffled explosion rocked the very foundations of the jail. Kaluchek and Joe, seated on the floor, fell suddenly to their left. Carrelli, standing beside the bars, staggered like someone in an earthquake and fell to her knees. The rats in the corridor tipped into a struggling heap, yelping and barking as one.

Seconds later Kaluchek heard a second blast, sharper though not as earth-shaking. Alien cries came from beyond the corridor door, followed by a fusillade of what might have been rifle shots, echoing deafeningly in the confines of the building. The guards released Jacob and pulled weapons from their belts, short antique-looking pistols. They slipped through the door, almost slinking like the animals they resembled, and moments later Kaluchek heard screams as one rat fell in a spume of dark blood. Jacob leapt at the bars and clung on while Red Robe, cowering in the corner of the corridor, appeared to be gabbling prayers to itself.

Then the corridor wall disintegrated in a shower of pulverised stone and choking dust. When the dust cleared, Kaluchek stared at what was revealed.

In the settling silence, a tall creature—an alien unlike the others—appeared in the gaping rent where the wall had been. Beside it, tiny by comparison, was another rat-like being. As she watched, the rat sprang over the rubble and ran towards Jacob; she thought at first it was attacking him, then realised her mistake. The new alien was touching Jacob with solicitous paws, their snouts meeting and rubbing with what might have been affection.

Then the giant strode over the rubble in a single step, crouching to fit itself into the confines of what had been the corridor, and yelped at Jacob. The small alien looked up and replied.

Kaluchek was surprised by the giant's reaction: it bellowed, hitting out to strike the bars with a balled fist. It addressed Jacob again.

Jacob keened—that was the only word for it, Kaluchek thought. It flung back its head and howled into the air.

The giant barked, dragging Jacob from the bars and towards the rubble. Jacob cried out, gesturing back towards the imprisoned humans. The giant stopped for a second, looked back at the four in the cell and seemed to be considering.

Only later did it come to Kaluchek that things would have been very different if the giant had come to another decision.

The giant stepped forward and barked something at Carrelli. She stepped back and the alien aimed a weapon at the bars. It fired, and a bar ignited and melted down its length like a candle. The gap was just wide enough for Carrelli to squeeze through, followed by Olembe, who had more difficulty. Kaluchek helped Joe to his feet, taking his weight and easing him across the cell and through the bars.

The giant, its duty to Jacob discharged, hurried from the corridor.

Ahead, on the piled rubble, Jacob turned and gestured for the humans to follow. Then it scrambled away, gripping the paw of its recently arrived friend.

Carrelli led the way, stumbling over the rubble. The giant was ahead, firing its weapon through the ruins of what had been the jail. The rats returned fire, Kaluchek hearing the whining ping of ricocheting bullets striking off masonry. In the distance she made out the bobbing heads of the militia as they appeared above the debris and took aim.

The giant grabbed Jacob again, shook it and yelped. By way of a reply, Jacob pointed down a corridor still intact. The giant barged its way through the opening, followed by the others. Seconds later it came to a cell, blasted open the door and stooped to enter.

Kaluchek and the others came up behind it, staring past the bulk of the giant. In the tiny cell, a rat was bound to a chair. It was clearly dead, the victim of torture. Its lungs had been pulled through the smashed ribs on either side of its spine. Its muzzle gaped, frozen horribly in a silent scream.

Jacob moaned and looked away. The giant alien touched the dead rat once, on the head, with a gesture that, from a hand so massive, was at once touching and absurd.

Then it turned and squeezed from the cell, beckoning the others to follow. Her heart racing, Kaluchek gripped Joe by the hand and ran after the giant through the tumbled ruins of the jail towards a source of grey light in the distance.

The closer they came to the outer wall of the jail, the greater the opposition they encountered. The giant had evidently blasted its way through numerous rooms and corridors on its way to the cells; the ruins of the jail provided a network of partially standing walls behind which the militia concealed themselves and fired at will.

Kaluchek ducked as bullets whined around her. The giant returned fire with its blaster, turning piles of debris to blazing slag and accounting for dozens of screaming rats with each shot. To her right, Olembe dodged the bullets; Kaluchek found herself willing him not to get hit, amazed that in the heat of the moment thoughts of revenge were still uppermost.

Joe staggered along beside her, breathing hard and struggling to keep up. She slowed her pace, held him all the tighter.

The spectacular escape was all very well, she thought, but she hoped that the alien had thought through what they might do when they'd fled the jail. They would still be in a hostile city, surrounded by aliens after their blood, and the even greater barrier of the encircling mountains.

Seconds later the giant staggered as a bullet ripped into its shoulder, a gobbet of meat the size of a fist exploding from its back, narrowly missing Kaluchek. Amazingly the giant continued running, firing its blaster with its free hand while its left arm hung useless on tattered shreds of muscle.

The firing ceased, suddenly, and an eerie silence prevailed. A cold wind blew into the ruins, eddying a heavy fall of snow around their running forms. Kaluchek was shaking, whether from cold or fear she had no idea.

The giant came to a high, buttressed wall through which a ragged gap had been blasted. It pressed itself against the masonry, holding the remains of its left arm to its side with its right hand and grimacing in pain. It peered around the corner, into a cobbled courtyard, and said something to itself in a language quite different to that of the rats.

Kaluchek followed its gaze and saw, standing in the centre of the courtyard, the squat teardrop shape of a small golden spaceship.

She looked at Joe, who was staring at the ship and grinning like an idiot. They embraced, Kaluchek tremulous with hope.

The giant shouted a command, gestured with its uninjured arm and led the way at a sprint across the cobbles to the ship. Kaluchek heard the whine of gunshot as they fled. She ducked reflexively, dreading the thought of failing so close to their goal. Shots rang off the carapace of the ship, scoring silver streaks across its golden livery.

The giant came to a hatch and touched a panel, and the entrance eased open with painful precision. The giant turned and laid down a barrage of fire while the others sped inside one by one, first Jacob and its mate, followed by Olembe and Carrelli. Kaluchek and Joe dived aboard, then the giant alien.

The hatch eased shut and Kaluchek found herself weeping with relief.

The alien pushed its way past them without ceremony and strode down a short corridor to what was clearly the control room. Unlike the flight-deck of the *Lovelock*, which had been brightly illuminated and finished with clean, bright surfaces, the interior of this ship was matte black, its contours of markedly alien design, with strangely rounded surfaces that put Kaluchek in mind of the chitin of a giant beetle.

The alien dropped into one of two horizontal couches and hauled from the ceiling an arrangement of jet black rods and spars which reminded her of nothing so much as the antlers of a moose. It gripped the frame with its good arm, then turned and yelled something to Jacob.

As they watched, the rat scrambled between the control couches and hauled open a storage unit, emerging seconds later with a square of black material which it passed to the giant.

On closer inspection, Kaluchek saw the full extent of the alien's injury. It appeared that the whole of its shoulder had been blown away, severing arteries, which pumped black blood like engine oil across the surface of its silver suit.

The alien took the material and applied it to its injured shoulder.

Carrelli barked at Jacob. The rat looked up at her and replied.

"What?" Olembe asked.

Carrelli said, smiling, "Jacob calls it a magic healer."

"Those two know each other?"

Carrelli shook her head. "They've met. I don't know the full story."

Kaluchek was about to ask her how she knew the language of the rat people, but at that second the ship powered up and rose, wobbling precariously from side to side. They hung on, swaying. Jacob's mate whined in fear and clung to it, eyes wide in fear. Jacob spoke to it, in tones Kaluchek took to be reassuring.

Through the triangular forward viewscreen, she saw the remains of the jail fall away, to be replaced by the snow-filled grey of the sky. The giant was grimacing with pain as it handled the frame.

Carrelli crouched beside the couch and spoke to the alien in urgent tones.

The giant snapped a reply.

Carrelli said, "It came here on a mission, to destroy some weapon. I'm not sure what. However, for some reason it was unable to locate the weapon."

"Where's it taking us?" Olembe said.

Carrelli spoke to the alien as the ship tilted nose-down and accelerated away from the ruined jail, low buildings flashing by on either side. The giant concentrated on its controls, then replied.

Carrelli turned to them. "It's returning home, to the world adjacent to this one."

"They have the technology to help us find a habitable world," Kaluchek said. "Could you ask it—"

Carrelli looked at her. "The only problem is, it's not sure it will survive long enough to complete the journey."

"Jesus!" Olembe cried. Kaluchek glanced at the giant's shoulder, where viscous blood seeped from under the edge of the so-called magic healer.

Carrelli spoke to the alien, and it gestured with its head to the second couch. She slid into it, barking questions. The alien replied. The Italian nodded and pulled a second frame from the ceiling, fingering control studs and gripping the frame with both hands.

Beside Kaluchek, Joe slid to the floor and sat with his back against the bulkhead, watching what was happening in a daze. She lowered herself down beside him.

The rats huddled together between the couches, looking from the giant to Carrelli and back again.

Carrelli frowned as she wrestled with the controls, barking at the giant in its own language. The ship wobbled as it sped over the city. She cursed in Italian as they missed clipping an airship by a matter of metres. They were climbing now, the city mansions falling away on either side and the dark mountains looming ahead. The scene through the forward viewscreen was dotted with colourful airships, which seemed to be accelerating in order to avoid collision.

Carrelli screamed at the alien, who was slow to reply. Kaluchek glanced at it. Blood was pumping steadily now from beneath the healer, spreading in a syrupy slick across its chest and over the couch. The alien's face appeared slack, its great flat eyes distant.

She felt a sudden overwhelming fear. To have come so far, only to die in a crashed alien spaceship...

Carrelli yelped at the giant again, then cursed in Italian. The giant turned its head, gazed across at her with dimming eyes. It spoke quietly, then glanced between the couches at Jacob, and addressed the rat.

Jacob flung its head back, opening its muzzle in a howl of anguish.

On the first control couch, the giant's right arm slackened, losing its grip on the frame which bobbed back on hydraulics and resumed its original position flush with the ceiling.

Kaluchek could see, from the opacity of the giant's eyes, that it was dead.

Jacob rushed forward, clutched the giant's arm and keened.

Olembe said, "You can fly this thing, Carrelli?"

She stared through the screen, her features set with concentration as she moved the frame minimally, thumbing controls and reading numerals from a tiny console that bobbed on an umbilical before her.

"I'm doing my very best, Friday."

They were screaming towards the foothills, the city receding in their wake. Ahead, the serried steel-grey ramparts of the encircling mountains seemed to rush at them with alarming speed. Carrelli eased the ship into a steady climb, following the incline of the mountains towards their peaks. Kaluchek and the others tipped, clinging to handholds to stop themselves rolling.

Joe closed his eyes, tipped his head back and laughed.

"What?" Kaluchek said.

"Fifteen years ago, on Mars, I was aboard the shuttle that narrowly missed clipping the observatory on the top of Olympus Mons. This brings it all back, Sis."

"A thousand and fifteen years ago," she reminded him, taking his arm.

They were screaming up the side of the summit, the snow-capped peaks rushing by in a blinding avalanche.

Olembe called out, "Hope silver suit told you where its homeworld was, Carrelli?"

She didn't spare him a glance, just concentrated on the controls and replied, "There was no time for that, Friday. Anyway, that doesn't matter now."

She turned and looked at them. "The ship isn't functioning at maximum efficiency. I can't work out what is wrong. But it might just be capable of getting us to the next tier."

Kaluchek felt something tighten around her heart, a quick throb of hope followed by fear that they might not make it all the way.

"Look," Carrelli said, indicating the forward viewscreen.

They looked. They were flying almost vertically now, and ahead of the ship the grey cloud cover was shredding, giving way to a deep blue.

The rat Carrelli had named Jacob rushed to the screen and stared out, gripping a handhold and chattering to its mate. It pointed, and Kaluchek saw the reason for its excitement. Directly ahead of the ship, spiralling through space with an immensity that took the breath away, Kaluchek made out the next tier—the third from bottom, she calculated— and the one above that, and, in the distance, the faint curl of the tier above the central sun. As she stared, the great primary burned with an actinic glare, the brightest object they had seen for what seemed like a long, long time.

The sight provoked a strange reaction from Jacob's friend, or perhaps not so strange. It rushed into the corridor, hiding its eyes behind its paws and gibbering to itself in fear. Jacob, conversely, was drawn to the sight of the celestial wonder, pressing its snout up against the viewscreen and staring out in silence.

The ship punched through the last of the cloud cover, emerging into space between the tiers, and sunlight flooded the flight-deck with blinding illumination.

Kaluchek laughed. "It's like the summer sun back home," she said to Joe, "after a long hard winter..."

Olembe turned to Carrelli and said. "Now, you intend to tell us how you know their lingo?"

She stared at the controls, gave a minimal nod. "ESO implanted the original maintenance team with neuro-smartware."

"You're joking—it was still in its experimental stages years ago when the plug was pulled."

She went on, "ESO kept working on it, perfecting it, or getting it as damned near perfect as possible. One of the subroutines was a decoder." She touched her right temple with long fingers. "I also have various logic systems that help me process possibilities, integrated smartware slaved to my cortex."

"Jesus Christ," Olembe said. "You're a cyborg."

"I wouldn't say that, Friday. I'm implanted. Augmented, if you like."

Kaluchek said, "So that's why..." She shook her head. "I don't know. You knew things. Worked them out so fast it seemed unnatural." She realised something. "The symbol on the ziggurat's door—"

"It was nothing unnatural," Carrelli said, "just very powerful, parallel processing."

"What else have you got in there?" Olembe asked with suspicion.

Before Carrelli could reply, Kaluchek said, "Christ, Olembe. What's your problem? We should be thankful Gina's augmented, for fucksake!"

He smiled. "Hey, I'm just curious, is all. Just want to know what other surprises to expect."

Kaluchek felt a flare of anger. "You asshole, Olembe."

Carrelli cut in, "That is all, a decoder, a logic sub-routine, improved hearing and vision, limited telemetry systems." She smiled. "Don't worry. I'm still human."

"We aren't worried," Kaluchek reassured her. "It's just that some people," she looked across at Olembe, "can't take being second best."

"Shut it, Kaluchek," Olembe began.

"Look," Joe said, pointing through the forward viewscreen.

The command had the effect of silencing them. They all looked.

They were approaching the third tier, a string of beaded worlds, green and blue and ochre, with between each separate landmass a band of lapis lazuli shimmering in the sunlight—the dividing seas.

Carrelli said, "I'm not going to risk trying to make it to the fourth tier. We're lucky to have got so far. I'll try to get us down in one piece, and maybe then we can work out what the problem is, okay?"

Joe said, "That sounds fine to me."

"Okay, hold on tight." Carrelli repeated the command in rat for the benefit of Jacob and its mate. "This might be a bumpy landing."

They held on as the spaceship slipped into orbit around the third tier. A minute later Kaluchek made out—an impressionistic blur through the sidescreen—a wide swathe of brilliant green vegetation shot through with the vast, serpentine coils of a river.

She gripped Joe's arm and closed her eyes.

## 5

ELDER VELKOR CANNAK was a pious man, and he believed that anyone who opposed the Church—that is, opposed the word of God—was by definition evil.

This made the suppression of dissent, the imprisonment, torture and execution of dissidents, the logical consequence of a state run by the Church for the greater glory of God. For the good of the people, who for thousands of years had enjoyed unparalleled prosperity under the rule of the Church, severe measures from time to time had to be imposed. Anarchy ruled before the Church came to power, with innocent citizens the victims of the unscrupulous and the power-hungry. The Church had stopped all that, imposed its rule, and Agstarn had reaped the benefits.

Unfortunately, there were still anarchists and heretics like Kahran Shollay and Ehrin Telsa who denied the existence of God and the right of the Church to rule.

The torture and death of Shollay brought Cannak no personal pleasure; in fact, he found the entire episode somewhat distasteful. More frustrating was

Shollay's reluctance to admit the truth, that he and Telsa were in league with the alien invaders.

When he confronted the aliens with Telsa, he was alarmed to learn that the pink ones spoke their language. This suggested a conspiracy long in the making, and that the arrival on Agstarn of the pink ones was no accident but the vanguard of a well-planned and orchestrated invasion.

The alien spokesman had even attempted a clever ploy when addressing Telsa. It had said that they came in peace, and wished the Agstarnians no harm. Telsa, for his part, had been disingenuous with his display of amazement.

The truth, Cannak knew, was that Telsa and Shollay had been instrumental in bringing the vanguard of the alien invasion to Agstarn, that night out on the western plains, and no degree of deception would conceal the fact from an Elder as dedicated as Cannak.

And then the arrival of the black alien had added confusion to his neat hypothesis; what part did this giant play in the invasion, with its destruction of the penitentiary and its rescue of Telsa and the pink ones?

Cannak himself was fortunate indeed to have survived the penitentiary's demolition. He'd managed to slip from the corridor as the gunfight began, but found himself pinned down by cross-fire as the aliens made their escape. A stray blast from the giant's weapon had brought masonry tumbling down around his head, though by the grace of God he had suffered merely superficial cuts and bruises. As the pink ones led by the giant made their escape, Cannak had followed at a distance, his robe of office stained with dust and his own dark blood.

He'd arrived at the courtyard in time to see the last of the aliens flee within the ship. He screamed at the useless militia to disable the flying machine, to do all within their power to bring it down as it rose, unsteadily, into the cold air. They had loosed off volley after volley of bullets at the thing, but it appeared impregnable. With despair he watched it rise, clear the perimeter walls and accelerate over the city towards the mountains.

He considered his options for perhaps five minutes, before deciding on a course of action. It was radical, but there was no other way of countering the threat posed by Telsa and his alien invaders. From the smouldering ruins of the penitentiary he took a Church wagon to the penthouse suite of Prelate Hykell and informed the venerable Elder of the momentous events of the past two hours.

Then, tentatively, fearing the Prelate's outright refusal, he made his suggestion.

Hykell considered his words for a long minute, his gaze abstracted.

At last the Prelate asked, "And who would lead the mission?"

Cannak straightened. "I would, Elder."

"It would be dangerous. By all accounts the godless giant was well armed."

"I will have God on my side," Cannak pronounced, and felt a thrill of pride as he did so.

"If you succeed, all Agstarn will hail your exploits, Elder Cannak."

The very idea made Cannak's head swim. "I will endeavour to discharge my duty to the state and to the glory of God."

At last Hykell inclined his head. "Go, and may God go with you, Elder."

Cannak rode from Agstarn in a wagon hauled by eight zeer, the faster to take him to the Church's mountain redoubt. He had time to summon two scientists, both Church officials, whom he briefed as they rode through the foothills.

An hour later they passed through the buttressed walls of the redoubt, slowed by numerous identity checks, which, while gratifying to see being upheld, nevertheless frustrated Cannak's wish to pursue the aliens. Every minute wasted here increased the likelihood of the pink ones' eventual escape... And who knew what that might mean for the future of Agstarn?

At last they were admitted into the inner chamber of the fortified redoubt, into the very hub of the laboratory, which, for fifteen years, had housed the Church's most terrible possession.

Cannak had last seen the deathship—as the Zorl had called it—fifteen years ago, when Telsa senior had piloted it from Zor to Agstarn. Cannak and other Church officials had travelled with the ship, while scientists had attempted to fathom the weapons systems. It had been Cannak's idea that they should test the weapons on the return journey—the ziggurat upon the western plain being the obvious target.

Cannak recalled the thrill of watching the beam lance towards the edifice, and the disappointment as it withstood the onslaught and remained intact. They had tried again, this time aiming at the column that connected daily with the ziggurat, and this time they had succeeded in destroying the lower portion of the mechanical tentacle.

For the past fifteen years, though, the ship had been concealed in the bowels of the redoubt while Church scientists worked to learn more about its fearsome capabilities.

Now Cannak stepped over the threshold of the hangar, flanked by the scientists, and stopped in awe at the sight before him. The deathship almost filled the chamber, a thing of stark and brutal magnificence, combining the predatory lines of a mountain raptor with the sleek grace of a snowbird.

He gave a short speech to the assembled technicians, who for years had worked upon the ship's secrets, hardly thinking that one day it would take flight. They cheered as he ordered the vessel to be readied for take-off, and he felt a strange power fill his chest as he realised that his idea, his words, would soon unleash the might of the deathship on its quest to track and destroy the godless ones.

As he climbed the ramp, escorted by eager young pilots dressed in the black uniforms of the Church's science corps, the roof of the hangar was winched open, and he paused to stare up into the grey sky.

On the bridge of the deathship, he addressed the crew.

"We are united in the eyes of God, upon a righteous mission into the unknown. What we will discover, beyond the grey, only God knows, but be assured that we are in pursuit of evil on behalf of all that is good in existence." He nodded and smiled at the assembled crew. "Let the flight commence."

He sat in a padded seat to the right of the captain as the ship lifted with a mighty roar of engines, seemingly floating on a cushion of air, then leaped through the roof of the hangar. He was pushed back into his seat as the ship accelerated, covering the distance between the foothills and the mountain peaks in seconds.

Cannak stared into the grey, and he knew fear.

He believed in the word of the Book of Books. He believed that they were the chosen ones of God, that Agstarn was God's true land, and that all others, and all other lands beyond theirs, were illusions created by malign forces opposed to the true God. But what terrible, illusory lands might lie beyond what he had known for all his life?

To the pilot he said, "Are you able to track the renegade ship?"

The pilot smiled easily. "We're locked on to its ion signature, Elder."

Cannak turned to the scientist seated to his right. "The weapon is primed and ready to use?"

The scientist smiled an affirmative. "We have a dozen missiles at our disposal."

Cannak could hardly contain his excitement. "Inform the gunner to await my command," he said.

He stared through the long screen that fronted the bridge, and as he did so the grey suddenly vanished. His old eyes, accustomed by years of grey and only grey, found it hard to adjust to what now lay before the ship.

The sky had changed colour, from grey to the deepest indigo, and then...

He stared, as did the crew with him on the bridge, and a collective gasp filled the air. This, then, was where the illusions began.

Ahead he witnessed a bright fiery ball, and twisted around it what appeared to be a vast rosary, and

Elder Velkor Cannak knew he was gazing upon all that was evil in the universe.

## 6

FROM HIS GARDEN in the mountain-top phrontistery at Yann, Watcher Pharan had an uninterrupted view of the world as it spread to the horizon in every direction. He had never considered it anything less than paradise, and this evening it seemed especially so. Had the massed lobes of the ko trees ever been greener; had the great river Phar—after which he had been named, long ago—ever seemed bluer and more sustaining of the life that teemed in the rainforest? He thought not, and for perhaps the hundredth time that day gave thanks to the Creator.

Life was beauteous and bountiful, and the fact that Pharan was coming to the end of his own physical existence made his appreciation of it all the greater.

From contemplation of the land, he turned his attention to the night sky. He rose from his chair and hobbled across the lawn to where his scope was set up before his armchair. He settled himself, as he had done every evening at this time for the past fifty cycles, and bent to the eyepiece. A warm breeze stirred his gown, playing over his scales. Far off, a nightbird sang a gentle lullaby.

The sight of the helix, resplendent in the early evening light, never failed to bring a tear to his eye and fill his chest with a mixture of emotions: wonder at the vastness of the construct, awe at the fact of its existence, curiosity at the mystery of its provenance.

As the world turned slowly and the sun set over the rainforest, the last light caught the tier above his own, underlighting the string of multiple worlds and seas that swept around its vast upward curve. He wondered at the strange beings that inhabited these other worlds, and pondered on their ways and customs. As ever, these thoughts led him to the most perplexing question of all: why had the Creator initiated the chain of events that began with the Constructors building the helix and continued with their stocking the worlds with life of every type? What was the purpose of such a grand project?

For many cycles he had taught his acolytes the way of the Calique: that the motives of the Creator were shrouded in mystery that one day might, or might not, be revealed. More importantly, every day he had taught that what was important, what was paramount, was the appreciation of the wonder of existence, the delight of small things, and the reciprocation of kindness to one's fellow creatures. All else, all craving of material possessions, of wealth or power, was a distraction that would turn one's head from the essential truth: that the ultimate gift was the gift of one's blessed existence.

He turned his scope on its well-worn cycle of the heavens. He tracked the upward sweep of the helix, and then the downward curve for as far as it went. Then, feeling the thrill of apprehension that always assailed him at this point, he turned his scope to the space between the tiers, at the deepening mysterious blue that was rich with distant, tiny suns. He was scrupulous in his observation of the heavens, but as ever saw nothing of note.

He was a Watcher, and it was his nightly duty to scour the heavens.

A hesitant throat-clearing alerted him to the fact that he was not alone.

He turned. Sela stood upon the lawn, her bare feet crushing fragrance from the grass. She carried a pot of herb water, which would help to keep him awake until the early hours, when his shift of sky-watching would be over, and a Watcher elsewhere on the mountain would resume the constant vigil.

Sela wore the green gown of the graduated acolyte. She was not only his favourite pupil, but his best, combining modesty of being with sharpness of intellect. She wore her crest swept upright and tied with ko bark, denoting that she would soon enter the Guild of Healers.

Pharan would miss her when she finally left to take up her post in some far off village, if, that was, she departed before he met his demise: the two events would be soon, that he knew for certain.

"Watcher, your herbs."

"Set it down on the arm, child."

She placed the pot on the wide arm of his chair, then asked, "The Watching goes well?"

He smiled. It had become a ritual between them, this catechism, a means by which she extended her stay in his high garden, so that she might stare in awe at the magnificent brass scope aimed at the heavens. It gave him, too, the chance to appreciate the inner beauty and goodness of his acolyte.

"The Watching goes well, Sela. The wonder of creation fills the soul with gratitude."

"Watcher," said Sela after a pause. "There is one thing."

This was not part of their nightly ritual, and he smiled at his acolyte in encouragement.

"Watcher, I will miss you when I leave. For so long we have been one, you have given me all the wisdom you possess. The parting will be difficult."

"But new experiences await you, child. The new supplants the old, as the scriptures state, and all is to be appreciated with eyes as receptive as those of a newborn."

She smiled and nictitated her large eyes. "I was wondering if... that is, when I return to visit my siblings at holiday times, I might come to visit you, too?"

A chasm of sadness opened within him, and he reached out and laid a shaky, scaled hand upon her arm. "Child, time moves on, does it not, and takes all with it? We are born, we live in full appreciation of what has been granted us, and then we take our leave."

She nictitated again, the lower shutters blinking upwards to momentarily occlude the pink orbs of her eyes. "Watcher?"

He let out a breath. "Sela, the Creator has decreed that my time on Calique is short. I am soon to pass on."

She opened her mouth, perturbed. "So soon?"

He gave a chuckle. "I am almost one hundred cycles old."

"But even so—"

"The stones have foretold the end, Sela. But it is an end not without event." He considered for a second, then rose slowly and said, "Stay here. I will show you."

He crossed the lawn, his passage raising scent into the warm night air. He hobbled into his study, a great hole in the rock scattered with charts and old books, and even the odd plate covered with stale food.

He found his stones in their gourd and carried it out to where Sela was standing patiently beside the scope, her slight form dwarfed by the antique intricacy of its brass and leather housing.

He gestured to the lawn and she sat quickly, cross-legged. More slowly, he lowered himself and faced her.

He shook the gourd. "Every day for the past cycle," he said, "I have cast the stones and received the same foretokening. Watch."

He rattled the stones in the gourd, their percussion pleasing to his ear. He tipped the gourd. Six stones spilled out, tumbled across the grass and came to rest revealing planes which showed three active symbols—Setting Sun, Full Cup, Running Hog—and three abstract—Ultimate Achievement, Heat, Quiescence.

He smiled, "So you see, my child, a satisfactory end, but one which is wrapped with incident."

She looked up at him. "Have you cast further within each symbol for a more concrete foretokening?"

He smiled, and lied to her, for the first time in his long acquaintance with the acolyte. "I have not. It is enough to know what the stones tell me here."

She inclined her head in understanding. "You have been kind with your time, Watcher. I have kept you from your duties." She rose gracefully, then helped him to his feet.

"Sleep well, Sela."

"I will bring your herbs for five further evenings before I leave, Watcher. Each one will be an honour."

He watched her move from the lawn and take the stairway that wound down inside the mountain to the acolytes' dormitory, an ache of sadness within his chest.

He resumed his seat before the scope, but paused before resuming his duties. Despite what he had told Sela, he had cast further within each symbol, intrigued to know more about the manner of his passing: it was the incongruous Heat symbol that had piqued his curiosity, for it was an odd sign to have among the five that obviously told of his passing.

His further casting had been more definite: before his death he would see great things, and his death would be violent, and he would meet his end at the hands of an outsider, moreover an outsider who professed to do the duties of his God.

And it would all happen within the next five days.

How could he have burdened such an innocent soul as Sela's with news of this import?

He bent his head to the scope's eyepiece and resumed his search.

An hour passed, then two. He sipped his herbal water, felt it revitalise his tired system. His mind strayed to the portent of the stones, and he chastised himself for not concentrating upon his task.

His fate was of little concern beside the correct scanning of the heavens.

It was perhaps a minute from the third bell, which would spell the midpoint of his shift, when he saw it. He gasped, felt shock rock him like an attack of ague.

That for which the Guild of Watchers had been established, the event which the scriptures spoke of as the ultimate in the history of Calique... it was happening, there in the night sky above the sleeping rainforest, and on his shift. He was mistaken, of course. A firefly had lodged itself upon the lens of his scope, tricking his tired brain and raising his hopes.

But what firefly scored a trail across the heavens like this, trailing fire in its wake as it descended? He swung the scope, tracking the fall of the hallowed craft towards the rainforest. It fell at an angle, which levelled out as it approached the mountain. He could not make out the object itself, just the fiery signature it trailed through the night.

As he watched, the fire went out to reveal the vessel itself, a golden craft that fell through the treetops at an acute angle and vanished from sight. He expected an explosion, or some sound to denote its landing, but evidently the craft still flew on below the high treetops, for from time to time Watcher Phar witnessed, along the route of its flight, the canopy shake violently with the ship's passage.

He watched with rapture, his old heart knocking in his chest. At a point perhaps one day from the mountain, the movement in the forest canopy ceased, suggesting to Pharan that the vessel had come to a final halt.

There could be no mistaking the event, could there? He was not going mad in his final few days? But the stones had forecast that great things would precede his demise, had they not?

He gathered himself, stood and hurried, as fast as his old legs could carry him, towards the interior steps. He plunged into the shadows, relieved only every ten lengths by flickering candles. He was grateful that no one else was abroad this late to witness his flustered state. It would be enough to stand shaking before the Venerable Kham and endure his incredulity.

He arrived at the door behind which the Venerable had his rooms. He would be sleeping now, sleeping the innocent sleep of the holiest Caliquan on the mountain. Pharan hesitated before he knocked, but the miracle of his discovery gave him strength.

The door was opened by an acolyte, and Pharan rushed past him to the door which gave on to the bedchamber. He said, "Rouse the Venerable. Great things are astir. I must have an immediate audience."

He had dreamed of this day for most of his life, and now he was giving orders as if he were some uncouth ignoble. "My apologies, but it is of the gravest matter of importance that I speak with Venerable Kham."

The acolyte bowed, slipped into the bedchamber, and seconds later emerged. "Please, enter."

Pharan did so, attempting to control the shaking of his limbs.

Venerable Kham was sitting up in his bed-chair, blinking himself awake. "Pharan? What brings you flapping in like a nightbird?"

Pharan fell to his knees. "Venerable Kham, it has happened. They are here. I witnessed their fall but minutes ago."

Venerable Kham merely stared at Pharan. "And you are not mistaken? A dream, maybe?"

"I was awake with herbs, and alert. I saw the fall."

"Within close reach?"

"A day away, by my estimation. To the north, beside the fourth loop of the Phar." Pharan cleared his throat. "I hereby request to mount a caravan, to meet the Fallen and take them to the Sleeper."

These were the words that every watcher down the cycles had dreamed of pronouncing before their Venerable Master, and it had fallen to Pharan to speak them.

The Venerable inclined his head. "Your request is granted. I will call the acolytes to order. You will leave with the dawn."

Euphoric, Pharan returned to his garden and assembled his scant belongings for the journey to meet the Fallen.

## Ten /// Calique and the Sleeper

### I

HENDRY AWOKE AND opened his eyes. Sunlight, striking through the ship's forward viewscreen, warmed his face. He was overcome with a sudden and overwhelming sense of well-being. The events on the ice-bound planet seemed a long way off. The attack of the alien militia, even though he could still feel the pain, was an event that seemed to belong to a much earlier chapter of his life. Perhaps it was the sunlight, he thought, betokening an end to their troubles—an end to their search for a habitable world.

He was aware of someone beside him, curled sleeping with a hand across his chest. Then again, he thought, perhaps he felt so good because he had found Sissy Kaluchek.

He sat up, careful not to disturb her. Carrelli was lying on the control couch, arms enwrapped about the curious frame, which more resembled a beetle's chitinous outgrowth than anything mechanical.

On the opposite couch, the giant lay dead and rigid, like the bas-relief of a knight on an ancient sarcophagus.

Between the couches, the two lemur creatures were asleep, hugging each other.

Through the viewscreen Hendry made out the serried, vertical boles of what looked like immensely tall palm trees, with the dense cover of their foliage high overhead. Carrelli was easing the ship through the forest, the snout of the vessel nosing aside tree trunks as if they were stalks of grass.

Olembe was sitting against the far bulkhead, watching her. "What gives, Carrelli?" Evidently he too had just woken up.

She glanced across at him. "I've cut the main drives. We're hovering on auxiliaries. Havor was afraid that the Church might follow us in their own ship—well, the ship they appropriated from his people."

"Havor being the alien?" Hendry asked, indicating the dead giant.

Carrelli nodded. "His people are the Zorl. They inhabited the world neighbouring the lemur's world. The Church rule the latter."

"And our guests oppose the rule of the Church?" Hendry asked, glancing at the sleeping lemur and its mate.

"So I understand," Carrelli said.

Hendry imagined life on a world where the truth, quite literally, was hidden; how might the race of a world shrouded in perpetual cloud come to any true understanding of its place in the universe?

Olembe said, "What now?"

"We land," Carrelli said, "somewhere hidden from the Church ship, if they have indeed followed us. And then we explore this place."

"Perhaps," Hendry ventured, expecting Carrelli to dash his hopes, "this might be the Earth-like world we've been looking for?"

She smiled. "Perhaps you're right, Joe. My telemetry says that the atmosphere's breathable, and the temperature's thirty Celsius. It's too early to tell yet, but it looks good."

Olembe said, "Of course, it might be inhabited already."

"That's always a possibility," Carrelli conceded.

"In which case we simply move along to the next one," Hendry said, countering the African's pessimism.

"Okay," Olembe said, "so we find a habitable world. What then? How do we work out how to get the colonists up here?"

Carrelli eased the ship through the forest, staring through the screen. She said, "Our first priority should be finding somewhere suitable to settle. After that we can debate our next move."

Olembe pressed, not to be sidetracked. "It's always best to plan ahead, Carrelli. If we only have this ship, which according to you isn't functioning at full capacity, then it's going to be a long hard job ferrying three thousand colonists up two tiers."

Hendry said, "You've forgotten the umbilicals. There might be more."

"I'm working on the assumption that we can't rely on them," Olembe said. "I'm looking at a worst-case scenario."

Carrelli smiled to herself. "Let's just land and see what kind of place this is, and then consider the future, okay?"

The lemurs were waking. Jacob blinked, looking around at the flight-deck, its large eyes lingering on the humans. Its gaze settled on the corpse of the alien, and it opened its mouth in a silent gesture. Hendry could only guess at what thought processes were going on behind those discus-like eyes, but he chose to interpret the alien's reaction as grief. Beside Jacob, its friend came to its senses and sat up suddenly, clutching Jacob in evident alarm.

Hendry raised a hand and smiled. "Tell them we're friends, Gina."

Carrelli spoke to the lemurs, who replied. They conversed for a few minutes, the flight-deck filled with their high-pitched dialogue. At last the lemurs turned to stare up and out of the viewscreen.

Carrelli said, "I've told him what we're doing, where we are from. I don't think he fully understands the concepts of individual planets." She shook her head. "Which is understandable. Until a few days ago, apparently he had no idea that his world was just one of many on the helix. Their Church taught that their world was a flat platform floating in a grey void."

"Its friend seems to be finding the experience harder to accept than Jacob."

Carrelli said, "His name is Ehrin, at least that's the phonetic equivalent. His... I suppose we'd call her his fiancée, is Sereth. Ehrin opposed the Church. As for Sereth, I get the impression that she was a believer."

Hendry regarded the two alien creatures. They were perhaps a metre tall, and were standing now, small claws touching the frame of the viewscreen as they stared out in wonder. It was difficult to conceive that they had lives as rich and complex as his own; perhaps, he thought, that was because they so resembled animals, and animals with some resemblance to terrestrial fauna. He wondered what they made of the humans, pink furless giants who until now they had never even dreamed might exist.

Beside Hendry, Sissy Kaluchek yawned, murmuring to herself. She blinked up at him, smiled. "Hey, you," she said. "Where are we?"

Hendry gestured through the viewscreen. "Looks like paradise to me, Sis. And according to Gina, the air's breathable."

"Let's not get too carried away," Olembe said. "For all we know this place is inhabited by man-eating sentients."

"Lighten up, for Chrissake," Kaluchek said.

He shrugged. "Look at the track record. Two races discovered, and have either held out the olive branch? One set of bastards set about killing us, the other would have done—"

"So," Kaluchek said brightly, glaring at the African, "third time lucky, yeah?"

"In your dreams, girl," Olembe murmured.

They were interrupted by movement across the flight-deck. The lemur called Ehrin left the side of his partner and moved to the control couch bearing the giant's body. He leapt up onto the couch—his movements, though he was bipedal and walked upright, as agile as those of a chimpanzee—and squatted beside the alien, gazing down at the hairless, wrinkled face.

Hendry watched, confident in his correct inter-pretation of the creature's reactions as those of sadness. The lemur-analogue might have been alien, his race evolved in circumstances wholly different to those that had prevailed on Earth, but there seemed to be a commonality of emotion between the two. He wondered then if this was a universal constant, and, if so, whether it might indicate the possibility that extraterrestrial races, no matter how seemingly different, might have points of contact which would augur well for the future relations between the various species that dwelt upon the helix.

No doubt Olembe would call him an unrealistic romantic.

Ehrin was silent, staring at the dead alien. His mouth moved silently, before he looked up and spoke to Carrelli.

She nodded and replied.

Ehrin lifted its paw in an indecipherable gesture and yelped.

Carrelli returned the sounds, then said in English to the others, "Ehrin has asked that when we land, the first thing we do is dispose of the remains of the alien, Havor."

Hendry said, "We owe our lives to the alien's arrival." He recalled what had happened back in the cell when Ehrin had appeared to suggest that the humans should be freed. "Tell Ehrin that we are grateful for what he and Havor did for us."

Carrelli spoke to Ehrin, then said, "I asked what the Church would have done to us. Ehrin said that they would have certainly put us to death."

"Some Church," Olembe grunted. "Let's just hope we've left our old superstitions back on Earth to rot along with everything else."

Carrelli smiled. "The selection process for the mission hopefully reduced the chances of fanaticism, Friday." She shook her head. "We have enough to divide us and cause potential conflict, being human."

Olembe smiled. "Amen to that."

Ehrin's mate, Sereth, snapped something across the flight-deck, and Ehrin leapt from the couch and joined her. They yipped at each other in lowered tones.

For the last few minutes the ship had travelled through shadow, the forest canopy high above occluding all trace of sunlight. Now Carrelli eased the ship down, bringing it in to land with a diminishing whine of auxiliary motors.

As the ship settled, Hendry stood and moved to a sidescreen. There was little undergrowth surrounding the landing site, just the surrounding boles of the towering trees and the occasional, spectacular shrubs bearing blooms of vivid scarlet and yellow stripes.

Kaluchek asked Carrelli, "And you say the air's breathable? We can go out without the hoods?"

"The air's fine, but I'm not as sure about the local fauna. Let's be careful out there."

Olembe found the blaster the alien had used to such effect, as sleek and black as the rest of the ship. He checked its controls, hefted it and said, "Open the hatch. I'll cover you."

Hendry was first out, with Kaluchek at his side. They walked down the ramp and set foot on the sandy soil. He took her hand and smiled, then cracked his faceplate and pulled down his suit's hood. He breathed, laughing at the incredible perfume that filled his head: flowers, honey, and something so alien and spicy it defied description.

Ehrin and Sereth came next, holding hands like the two humans, Sereth cautious as if expecting an attack at any second. Carrelli followed them and Olembe came last, holding the rifle on his hip and scanning the limited horizon of the clearing.

Hendry heard distant birdsong, a high mellifluous carolling. He saw something flit through the air on multicoloured wings: an insect the size of a bird. The sunlight was largely shut out here, but the odd rapier streak did penetrate the canopy, slicing the aqueous half-light into sections full of floating pollen and spores.

Ehrin released his mate's paw, hurried forward to the edge of the clearing and squatted on the ground. He reached out and touched the ground, then began scooping the sandy soil into a mound. Only then did Hendry understand what it was doing. He joined the alien, along with Kaluchek. They fell to their knees and began digging, their much larger human hands far more successfully displacing the loosely packed earth. At one point Ehrin looked up at Hendry, and pulled its lips back in a rictus more like a snarl than a smile, and Hendry smiled in return. Carrelli joined them, calmly sweeping handfuls of the golden demerara soil to expand the long pit. Only Olembe remained standing, covering their grave-digging duties, while across the clearing Sereth squatted on the ship's ramp, gazing about her with big eyes.

They returned to the ship, and between Hendry, Carrelli and Kaluchek, they managed to ease the giant's considerable bulk from the flight-deck, along the narrow corridor and down the ramp. Ehrin scrambled alongside, a skinny arm reaching up to clutch Havor's radiation silvers.

They laid the alien's body in the shallow grave, and then stared down at it, at a loss what to do next. Kaluchek plucked a flower from a nearby shrub, placed it in the giant's great fist and said to Ehrin, "It's what some of us do on our planet."

Carrelli translated. Ehrin flicked his head, then stared at Havor and spoke, the litany going on for a minute before he paused, then knelt and began shoving the displaced soil back over his friend's recumbent form. The others helped, and minutes later the makeshift funeral was over.

Olembe called out, "If you're quite through over there, I suggest we get on with what we're here to do."

Kaluchek moved away from the grave. "Which is?"

They gathered at the foot of the ramp. Olembe said, "The first job is to work out what's wrong with this crate—you said it was dysfunctional, Carrelli?"

She nodded. "Havor told me what was wrong, but the mechanical terms he used didn't translate. He also told me that Ehrin helped fix the ship. Ehrin was some kind of engineer, back on his own world."

"So if we want to get back to the colonists on the first tier, we have to do something about the ship," Olembe said. "Which, with no materials and Christ knows what tools, will be a miracle."

Carrelli spoke to Ehrin, then turned back to Olembe. "He replaced a component in the main drive." She indicated a hatch on the ship's flank. "We'll have to take a look and see if we can do anything."

Kaluchek said, "We need food, right? I don't know about you lot, but I'm starving. I mean, we can't stay in paradise if we can't eat. Me and Joe'll look for food while you repair the ship, okay?"

Carrelli smiled. "Take the blaster. Don't go far. Bring back anything you think might look edible."

"Who's going to play guinea pig?" Olembe said.

Carrelli said, "Who else? Don't worry, my augments wouldn't let anything poison me."

Olembe, with grudging reluctance, gave up the weapon to Hendry. As the others moved along the flank of the ship, Carrelli quizzing Ehrin, Hendry and Kaluchek looked around the clearing. She pointed. "How about this way? I saw a hill through the trees, bathed in sunlight. We might be able to take in the lie of the land from there, okay?"

"Lead the way."

She strode across the clearing and Hendry followed, cradling the rifle and gazing ahead of Kaluchek at the gap in the trees. They left the landing site and made their way through the forest, and Hendry thought back to a time, years ago, when he'd taken Chrissie to Australia to show her the place of his birth. They had spent a week in the Dandenong forest east of Melbourne—this was before the forest succumbed to blight—and its vast towering trees, its air of serenity, the golden sunlight filtering through the treetops, all put him in mind now of this alien forest. Sylvan and tranquil, he thought, pushing away the sudden vision of Chrissie lying dead in the cryo-unit and concentrating on the slim form of Sissy striding through the forest before him.

At one point she knelt and played the palm of her hand across the ground in a wide sweeping arc. "Look at this stuff, Joe. It isn't grass. It's like velvet, golden-green velvet."

He squatted beside her, watching her as she stared in fascination at the moss-like growth. There was something refreshingly childlike in her expression; he felt his stomach lurch when she looked up and smiled at him.

She took his hand, almost pulling him to his feet. They hurried through the trees, apprehended by wonder on all sides, from strange colourful flowers that floated through the air below diaphanous bubbles, to a variety of insect that cycled past them with an arrangement of wings like a paddle-steamer's wheel. They saw tiny, darting silver creatures like lizards, which left shimmering images of themselves in their wake, evidently a survival mechanism, and animals like frogs, which inflated themselves to the size of footballs and retched noisome venom at their prey.

"Look, Joe," she said, indicating a low-lying bush replete with small round fruit like melons. She picked one, holding it on her palm between them.

"Well, it certainly looks delicious."

"Gina will soon tell us," Hendry said.

"Perhaps I could try just a little?"

"Best not to. It might look great, but at the same time it might be poisonous." He went on, "And even if it wasn't harmful, it might not be any use as a foodstuff."

At her frown, he said, "Not all proteins are like those on Earth. If the molecules are reversed in relation to our own..." He shrugged, "then the edible food of this world would pass through our system and we wouldn't be able to metabolise it."

"But if we could..."

He smiled. "Then I'll name it Kaluchek fruit, after its discoverer."

She smiled, looking around her at the shimmering golden forest. "I hope this place isn't already inhabited. Wouldn't it be wonderful to start a colony here?"

He pointed to a patch of sunlight, and standing in it the moss-covered outcropping of rock Kaluchek had seen earlier. They approached it, leaving the shade of the forest and stepping into warm sunlight.

She leaned against the rock, turned to him and smiled. She said nothing, just smiled, and then reached out a hand to him.

She was small, and seemed very young and beautiful, and sudden desire flipped in his belly like a live thing. He took her hand and she pulled herself to him, her lips so urgent that the contact was clumsy, bruising. He laughed, slowed her, took her face in both hands and kissed her lips, her cheeks and eyes.

Then she pulled away quickly and, before he could fear that he'd offended her in some way, she was twisting and struggling from the confines of her atmosphere suit and finally standing before him, at once small and vulnerable and yet elementally powerful in her nakedness.

Something caught in his throat, a sound like a moan. He dropped the blaster then pulled off his atmosphere suit, suddenly urgent, and when he fell into her embrace the touch of her flesh was electric.

She pulled him down on top of her onto the soft carpet of moss, then rolled so that she was straddling him, then took him and eased herself down around him. He slipped into her, amazed by her warmth and wetness, and she let out a loud cry of laughing joy and arched her back, riding him for minutes until he emptied himself and cried with the exquisite release.

After the animal act came the tenderness. She held him to her, stroking his face, his body. He felt dizzy, overcome with desire and at the same time a vast protective sense of caring for this woman.

He recalled Su, then, and how that had turned sour, and involuntarily he superimposed on this nascent relationship the experience of how that first one had failed—and then looked into Sissy's wide dark eyes and banished such heresy from his thoughts.

"Jesus, Sissy..."

"I felt it when we met, Joe. I can't explain it. The attraction... Christ, I wanted you from the very first time we met."

He stroked her hair. "I never even considered it. You were... unattainable, too young... or rather I was too old—"

"As if that matters!"

"And I hadn't had anyone for years..."

She whispered into his ear, "Me too."

He felt a sudden kick of joy, then; she was making him happy for the first time in... in God knew how long. And he felt a sudden surge of optimism. If this world was safe, and not already inhabited, and they could transport the colonists up here, then what a paradise it would be.

She rolled away from him laughing, stood and scrambled up the outcropping of rock, and it struck Hendry that there was something gloriously outrageous in her naked athleticism on a new world so far from Earth.

He stood and followed her, feeling the wind on his exposed flesh, the sunlight striking his head and shoulders.

She was poised at the rock's very summit, one knee bent, the other leg braced against the incline, and Hendry was struck speechless by the sight of her. He joined her, slipped a hand across the globe of her bottom, delighting in the spontaneous smile of complicity and affection she turned on him.

Side by side they surveyed the world.

They were high now, and from here the forest fell away down a long sloping escarpment, so that it seemed as if the whole hemisphere of the planet were laid out before them. Sissy laughed, and Hendry joined her in sheer joy at the sight.

The rolling forest top extended for as far as the eye could see, and a great river looped lazily through brilliant verdure on its unhurried journey towards the horizon.

She turned and pointed. In the distance he made out a sudden mountain erupting from the forest, a feature that seemed too regular to be natural. He scanned its height for any sign of features that might suggest habitation, but found none.

And, over everything, the golden sunlight prevailed.

She took his hand. "How are you, Mr Hendry?"

"Amazing," he whispered, and then wondered whether he should be feeling guilt at experiencing such rapture so soon after losing his daughter.

His grief made the rapture all the greater, as he held Sissy to him and gazed out over her head.

She stiffened suddenly, and swore, and the swift transformation alarmed him. His heart kicked sickeningly. "Sis?"

"Oh, Christ, Joe. Look."

His imagination conjured so many dire possibilities, in the second or so before he saw where she was pointing, that when he did see her cause for alarm he was almost relieved. It wasn't some malign Serpent come to spoil their Eden, but then again perhaps it was.

The black ship swept in low over the forest like some kind of vast manta ray. It was perhaps a kilometre away, moving slowly over the treetops as if searching for prey.

She looked at him. "It's the Church's ship, right?"

He nodded, grabbed her hand. "Come on!"

They fled down the rock and slipped at the bottom on the velvet moss. They snatched the bundle of their atmosphere suits, Hendry remembering the blaster, and sprinted into the cover of the forest, pausing long enough to dress before resuming their flight.

Sissy stopped, grabbing him. "Joe!" she said. "Christ, Joe, which way now?"

He gazed about him at the serried tree trunks, which offered an identical vista in every direction.

Then he laughed with relief and pointed. The golden-green moss had retained the smudged imprint of their passage, diminishing ellipses leading back to the clearing.

He took her hand and ran.

Minutes later he made out the teardrop shape of the ship through the trees, and the oddly reassuring sight of Carrelli and Olembe discussing something in its shadow. They both looked up as Hendry and Kaluchek emerged from the forest at a run.

"We have..." Kaluchek began, fighting exhaustion, "we have company. A ship. About a kay away, closer, and coming this way."

Carrelli instinctively looked up, attempting to view the ship through the occasional rent in the canopy.

"You think they've managed to trace us here?" Olembe asked.

Carrelli shook her head. "I don't know. Havor told me they could trace the ion trail, but I shut down the main drive a hundred kays back... I'd say this was a lucky guess on the Church's part." She paused, then said, "I hope."

Olembe reached out and snatched the blaster from Hendry's grip. "You saw the damage this thing did. Just let the ship get near us and I'll..."

Carrelli glanced at him. "If we see the ship, we let it pass, okay? It'll be armoured. The blaster might penetrate it, but it might not. And we can't take the risk of alerting them to our presence."

Olembe nodded. "Okay, but if they have tracked us..."

From the ship, Ehrin emerged carrying a tool. Carrelli barked at him, and the effect of the words was instant. He dropped into a crouch and moaned, his teeth chattering together in a gesture that might have denoted fright or fear as he gazed up through the treetops.

Olembe said, "Ask it if there are more weapons aboard the ship, okay?"

Carrelli turned to Ehrin and relayed the question. Ehrin barked his reply and scurried back into the ship.

Carrelli shook her head. "As far as he knows, that's the only weapon Havor carried. He said he'd search the ship for more."

Kaluchek said, "What now?"

"Not much we can do, sweetheart." Olembe looked at her atmosphere suit, then glanced at Hendry. "Hey, ain't that cute? You two've swapped name tags."

Hendry looked down, only then realising he was wearing Sissy's suit, which had expanded to accommodate him.

Kaluchek stared at the African, refusing to be cowed, and said, "And fuck you, Olembe."

Carrelli said, "Okay, okay... So, what do we do? We sit tight, I think is the phrase. The ship is as hidden as we can possibly make it."

Hendry looked up. He could see gaps in the canopy, patches of blue light where golden spears of sunlight penetrated the submarine gloom of the clearing.

Then he heard the sound of the approaching ship, a low drone at first, climbing to an ever-present roar that drowned out Olembe's imprecation and silenced the birdsong in the immediate area.

Seconds later Hendry made out a succession of flickers high overhead, the effect of the passing ship occluding the sun.

Instinctively he dropped into a crouch, Kaluchek and Carrelli beside him. Olembe remained standing, the rifle propped on his hip, his face turned up to track the ship's progress high above them. He was perspiring freely, great beads of sweat the only indication that he, like everyone else, was feeling the pressure.

The ship seemed to take an age to pass. The very noise of its engines was like a threat; Hendry imagined the ship as some predatory animal, playing with its minuscule prey. Sissy smiled at him, and it was all he could do not to pull her to him and kiss her.

The sound diminished gradually, the roar receding, and minutes later the ship disappeared from sight. The birdsong started up again, signalling the resumption of normality.

Hendry released a breath. Carrelli said, "I think that if they had seen us, then they would have fired. Havor said that the ship did not belong to them. There is the chance that their pilots haven't fully mastered its monitoring capabilities."

"Thank Christ for that," Olembe said.

"I wonder how long they'll keep on searching," Hendry said, "and if they'll land and send the militia after us."

Carrelli looked at him. "The Church fears losing its power, according to Ehrin. They wish to eradicate all evidence that alien races exist. Their holy book claims that their kind are the only ones, God's chosen people."

"Where've I heard that before?" Olembe said.

"So…" Carrelli continued, "I don't think they will give up the search that easily."

"We might have to destroy the fucking thing if we want to stop them," Olembe said. "Does your lemur friend know if our ship carries integral weapons?"

Carrelli shrugged. "He doesn't know much about the ship at all. The technology is way beyond anything his people have even dreamed of."

Olembe turned and spat against the carapace of the golden ship. "And pretty damned in advance of our science, too."

Hendry indicated the open hatch in the flank of the ship. "How are you getting on with repairs?" He looked at Carrelli. "What's the problem?"

She stared into the hatch and said, "The ship suffered damage on its initial landing on Ehrin's world. They managed to patch something together—it was a simple engineering problem, nothing major. The ride up here blew the same part. The trouble is, we don't have anything like the appropriate technology to repair it."

"We're looking at cannibalising other parts of the ship," Olembe said, "but without the tools to do so..." He shook his head. "Imagine Neanderthal man, trying to repair a bicycle in the desert."

Hendry glanced at Sissy. She had drifted away from the group—a tendency he had noticed when Olembe was holding forth. She was walking towards the forest, staring, her body language suggestive of her straining to hear something.

She stopped and turned quickly. "Shut it, okay? Listen!"

Olembe opened his mouth to protest, then fell silent as Carrelli laid a hand on his arm. Heart pounding, Hendry listened.

Kaluchek turned and ran back towards them, moving into his arms. He looked out above her head, towards the forest and the noise.

It was a grunt, a great snorting expiration, as if whatever was making the sound was labouring under a great weight.

Seconds later, as they watched, the ponderous headpiece of a vast creature emerged between the boles of the trees and peered in at them, the lids of its old eyes blinking myopically.

"What," Olembe said, "in Christ's name is that?"

Hendry's immediate reaction was relief. He had feared some rapacious, taloned beast, not this overblown turtle-analogue, the expression on its face combining great wisdom with grandfatherly kindness.

It advanced its bulk little by little into the clearing and stopped before them, sighing dolorously. It did resemble a turtle, Hendry saw, but without a shell; it was wide and solid, its bulk vaguely elephantine, even its grey skin pachydermous.

Hendry was wondering if Carrelli spoke extraterrestrial turtle, when he made out the slight, silvery creatures riding upon its back and realised his mistake. The creatures were perhaps a metre tall, but perilously thin, and moved in bursts as swift as quicksilver.

They slipped from the beast and moved around the clearing, seating themselves on the ground in a semicircle. One of their number advanced to within a couple of metres of Carrelli and raised a clawed hand.

They were, he saw, like bipedal lizards, silver and scaled and fleet of movement. So much for this being a virgin world...

The leading creature spoke, its voice a whistle so high Hendry could hardly hear it.

Olembe laughed. "Reply to that, Gina," he challenged.

Without glancing at him, Carrelli inclined her head to the alien and began to whistle. It was an impossible sound to come from a human throat, and only then did Hendry realise that it was her augmentation producing the noise.

The lizard creature replied, and then fell silent.

Carrelli turned to the rest of them, a baffled expression on her face. "He is Watcher Pharan, and he wishes us felicitations, and welcomes us to the world of Calique." She paused, then went on, "His people have been awaiting us for millennia, he says, and he will be honoured now to lead us to the Sleeper."

# 2

WATCHER PHARAN WAS in a heightened state of consciousness when he slipped from the back of the sharl and approached the Fallen across the clearing. It was as if he had sloughed the infirmity of old age, as if his mind were again as crystal clear as that of the acolyte he had been ninety cycles ago. His every sensation seemed sharpened, his vision whetted by the blessed events in which he was participating. It would be the stuff of legend, and would surely enter the scriptures, never to be forgotten by the generations that studied on the mountain.

He reminded himself that there was ritual to observe. It was all very well considering the future and his place in it, but that was immaterial: what mattered now was that he conduct himself with propriety; he was, after all, the ambassador of the Calique.

A dozen acolytes dismounted from the three following sharls, moved around the clearing in the prescribed semicircle and seated themselves. They were the finest pupils of the mountain, with Sela seated immediately to his right.

He gazed across the clearing, hardly daring to believe that the day had come. The Fallen were a curious species. They were tall and bulky and slow moving, with oddly flattened faces and strangely textured skin, without scales; their flesh reminded Pharan of the raw meat that lay beneath his scales, which he had seen only once following an accident. How must they live from day to day, he wondered, with no outer protective covering?

As he watched, the four tall beings were joined by two small, furred creatures that resembled nothing so much as gerekos, the mischievous tree-dwelling creatures that inhabited the forest. They left the golden ship and hurried across to the taller beings.

Then one of the tall Fallen left the group and, with painful exactitude, stepped towards Pharan.

He glanced right and left, and only when he was satisfied that the acolytes had arrayed themselves in the symbol of holy munificence—the stylised cup of the Creator—did he step forward and raise a hand.

He spoke his name, and welcomed the Fallen to Calique.

The spokesperson of the Fallen spoke his language, though inexpertly. "I am," an unintelligible sound, "and my friends and I come in peace."

Pharan gestured, excitement mounting in his thorax, and then informed the spokesperson that it was his duty to lead the Fallen to the Sleeper.

The Fallen spokesperson listened, and then inclined its head slowly. It turned and spoke to its fellows in a low, slow language that Pharan found hard to conceive might possibly convey the necessary information.

Pharan dropped into a squat, which a day ago might have caused him pain; he felt nothing now but exultation.

The spokesperson sat down, crossing its thick limbs. Slowly, cautiously, the others joined it and sat down to either side. Last of all came the furry creatures, which dropped into squatting positions and stared at him with huge dark eyes.

The spokesperson said, "You spoke of the Sleeper. Please tell us more." Its grasp of the language was rudimentary, and hesitant, but by concentrating fully Pharan understood its meaning.

It was written in the scriptures that the Fallen, when at last they arrived on Calique, might be ignorant of their mission. The scriptures claimed that the Fallen might even be ignorant of the Sleeper, and the grand saga of the Sleeper and the Caliquans.

It was Pharan's noble duty to enlighten these strange beings.

"Many thousands of cycles ago," he began, "the Sleeper did fall to earth aboard a magnificent jewelled vessel; I say the Sleeper, though of course he was not known as the Sleeper then..."

Pharan proceeded with the story, as it was laid down in the scriptures.

The jewelled vessel was seen first by a lone acolyte meditating upon the mountain-top, who reported seeing a fiery coal descend from heaven and come to rest in the forest, three days north of the phrontistery. The Venerable at the time, one esteemed Baraqe, had foreseen the event in the stones, though further casting had failed to impart what future events might lie beyond the fiery coal's arrival.

He sent out a caravan consisting of his wisest teachers and a dozen of the finest acolytes, and three days later they reached the place where the coal had landed.

They were amazed to find not some nub of meteorite but a complex vessel studded with winking jewels, though the vessel had suffered on impact: its skin was dented, many of its jewels lost, and oily smoke issued from within the craft. As they watched, a hatch opened, and a strange beast staggered forth and collapsed upon the ground.

Their first reaction was revulsion, for the beast was hideous in the extreme; but revulsion was swiftly followed by compassion, for was not the beast one of the Creator's creatures, and in need of succour?

The being was injured, bleeding badly, its limbs shattered, and suffering who knew what terrible internal injuries? With much effort, for the creature was twice as tall and three times as heavy as the largest Caliquan, they managed to ease it onto the back of a sharl and made their way back to the phrontistery.

For the next cycle the teachers and acolytes of the mountain nursed the creature back to almost full health. Through much of its bedridden recuperation, it was attended by an acolyte name Heth, who as well as ministering to its physical needs, undertook to guide its spiritual welfare too.

To this end, Heth taught himself the creature's language, and spoke of the scriptures, and the supreme Creator of all that the universe contained.

It was from Heth that the story of the creature entered the scriptures and came to be passed down the generations.

There were no terms for many of the creature's more technical words, for the Caliquans were not a mechanical, tool-wielding race, and therefore much of what the creature told Heth was translated with approximate phrases and words.

The creature—its true name was too complex for Heth to transliterate—was one of a team of world-menders, that is, beings who moved about the helix with the duty of restoring what was not perfect. There were many worlds on the helix, and over the multiple cycles of their existence, things became worn, mountains lost soil, rivers dried up, food trees died. The team of noble world-menders moved from world to world around the helix, ensuring that all was perfect, harmonious. They also aided the many races of the helix, in many ways. It was a fine profession, which brought much prestige to those who carried it out. However, one day as the world-mender was going about its business, a fault developed in the interior of the creature's jewelled vessel—perhaps its heart failed, or its brain suffered fever; at any rate, the vessel fell from the skies and crashed upon the soil of Calique.

According to scripture, the creature, when well enough to regain its feet, returned to the vessel and inspected it, and decreed it dead; he mourned its passing, for he could not leave the planet now, nor could he communicate with his fellow world-menders.

However, there was hope that one day he might be reunited with his kind.

He took Heth, accompanied by Heth's teacher, into the jewelled vessel and showed them a long object, very much like a passing box in which acolytes and teachers alike were placed before burial. The creature explained that he would place himself within the box, and sleep for many cycles, and tell the box to wake him only when another craft fell from the skies to the soil of Calique. He instructed Heth to tell his people to watch the skies, and, when a vessel fell to earth, to be on hand to guide the Fallen to where he slept. Then he would awake and be returned to his people, via the craft of the Fallen.

That was the story according to Heth, which was recorded in the scriptures, and which brought great merit to the people of Calique, for to aid a strange creature in its hour of need, without thought of gain or benefit to oneself, was the finest act a being could accomplish.

Pharan recounted the story to the strange, long-haired spokesperson of the Fallen, who leaned forward and listened intently, from time to time turning slightly to relay the account to its fellows, who evidently did not understand the language of Calique.

"And so, now, it is my duty to lead you to the Sleeper," Pharan finished triumphantly.

The spokesperson made a gesture with its head, which Pharan found unusual. It spoke to its fellows, two pinky-brown creatures and one as black as a gourd, and they all spoke together, with what might have been called animation if the term could be applied to creatures who moved with great lethargy.

The spokesperson faced Pharan, and asked, "I take it that the Sleeper was of the race that was responsible for the building of the helix."

Pharan listened well, and worked out the clumsy words, and said, "We do not know whether the Sleeper belonged to the beings known as the Constructors. This was not recorded by Heth."

The spokesperson moved its head again, and said, "If the Constructors sent out world-menders, then did the Constructors themselves dwell on a world that was part of the helix?"

Pharan thought through the question and replied, "The scriptures surmise that this is so, but which world exactly is a secret known to none."

The spokesperson spoke to its fellows, and its words caused much excitement among the slow-moving creatures. Each one of them had something to say, even the small furry creature, though in a language faster than the honey-flow tongue of the tall ones.

At length the spokesperson turned to Pharan and said, "We would be honoured to be taken to the Sleeper. With good fortune we might be able to assist in his return to his own people."

The very idea sent a shiver of excitement through Pharan. He said, "Then all is agreed. If it is convenient, we shall leave immediately."

The spokesperson conferred with its people, and again much debate was entered into. At last it spoke to Pharan, "We have decided that two of us shall accompany you. The others must remain and work upon various repairs to our ship."

Pharan gestured, and spoke to his acolytes, relaying the joyous information that their mission was to continue to the shrine of the jewelled vessel.

But first, said the spokesperson, its people must eat.

Pharan, curious as to the feeding habits of these strange people, stood beside his sharl and watched as one of the Fallen stepped into the rainforest and returned some minutes later bearing fruit in its arms. This bounty it placed before the spokesperson, evidently in some form of ritual. While all the Fallen looked on intently, the spokesperson tasted first the greer fruit, then a shod-berry, followed by a kurl. It ate slowly, very deliberately, speaking to its fellows as if discussing the merits or taste of each fruit.

Then they waited, staring at the uneaten fruit on the ground, and Pharan wondered at their strange rituals.

Perhaps five minutes later the spokesperson turned to the others, and moved its head again, and stretched the lengths of skin that surrounded its mouthpiece, and the others made odd low repetitive noises and fell upon the fruit and devoured it quickly, or as quickly as these slow-movers were able.

Pharan watched it all, for soon he would make his observations known to Venerable Kham, and then write up his experiences, and perhaps with luck the events of his final days might find their way into the inviolable texts of the sacred scriptures.

Five minutes later the spokesperson announced that the chosen two were ready to leave the clearing. These two included the spokesperson itself and a Fallen not unlike the spokesperson, in that it was the same shape and shade and had the same dark substance growing long upon its head.

As they mounted the sharl, the spokesperson—after exchanging words with the black

Fallen—asked Pharan if they might encounter any dangerous animals while on the trek north, to which Pharan replied that Calique was not a world of danger.

They set off, though not before the second Fallen who would make the pilgrimage first embraced—and joined mouthpieces—with one of the Fallen who was to remain behind.

Then Pharan mounted his sharl, and gave the order for the trek to resume, and as they left the clearing and plodded north through the forest, he gave thanks to the Creator for the wonder he was experiencing.

# 3

HENDRY WATCHED THE strange procession leave
the clearing. Sissy and Carrelli rode upon the first
animal, while the alien who had introduced himself
as Watcher Pharan rode upon the second. Two further animals, each bearing six insectile lizards,
brought up the rear.

There had been a heated debate as to who should
accompany Carrelli to the tomb of the Sleeper. The
medic had suggested first that Hendry join her, but
Sissy had objected to that, stating in no uncertain
terms that she had no desire to be left behind with
a couple of aliens and Olembe. At that, Olembe had
volunteered to accompany Carrelli himself, which
Carrelli vetoed on the grounds that they needed
someone to remain behind to work on the ship. By
a process of elimination, Sissy had found herself
dragooned into making the trek.

"Can't you go by yourself, Gina?" Sissy had
asked.

Olembe laughed. "Lovesick already?"

Carrelli intervened. "It makes sense to go in pairs.
These people seem friendly enough, but all the same

they are aliens. Joe, you work on the ship with Friday, okay?"

Hendry would rather have made the trek himself, but for the sake of diplomacy he acceded to Carrelli's wishes.

As the last of the animals disappeared through the forest, Olembe returned to the ship, attended by the alien called Ehrin, and inspected the open hatch in its flank.

Hendry was still coming to terms with what he had shared with Sissy back in the forest, viewing his memory of the unexpected passion as if it was an episode in a dream. It was the culmination of days of increasing affection for the quiet, yet occasionally outspoken, Inuit woman. He was amazed that it had come to a head so soon, and with such rapidity. He had been alone, and then through some mysterious and wonderful fusion, like alchemy, he was no longer alone. At least, that was how it felt. His future had been uncertain, haunted by the absence of someone he had assumed would always be there. It seemed now that Sissy had in some odd way replaced Chrissie, and while euphoric at the turn of events, at the same time he could not help but feel guilty that he was beginning to enjoy life again while Chrissie was dead.

Tears stung like acid in his eyes as it came to him that Chrissie would surely approve of his liaison with Sissy.

Olembe pulled his head from the recess in the side of the ship. "I need a hand here, Joe."

He indicated a mass of fused circuitry and a fifteen-centimetre column of blackened steel, which looked as though it had exploded. "Our lemur friend here told Carrelli that this was the problem. Don't ask me what the hell it is. I'm fucked if I know."

"But we need to replace it, right?"

"Yeah, but with what? I'm a nuclear engineer, not a mechanic. Anyway, I need to get it out first. Hold this while I work it free, okay?"

Hendry grasped a hank of charred wires while Olembe struggled to free the burst cylinder with something that resembled a monkey wrench. While they worked, Ehrin climbed nimbly up the sloping side of the ship and perched on a golden fin, watching them work. From time to time it gestured and chattered to itself.

Hendry caught its glance and winked, not expecting a response and not getting one. He was aware of the creature's rank animal smell, its quick respiration.

He said to Olembe, "Supposing we do get the ship running again, we need to find an uninhabited Earthlike world before we go back for the colonists."

Olembe nodded. "Pity the lizards turned up. This place pretty much fits the bill, little of it we've seen."

"I wonder how different the neighbouring worlds might be? Think about it—how many hundreds of worlds are crammed onto each tier? They can't all be occupied."

Olembe, head thrust into the hatch, paused in his work to shoot a glance at him. "No? What if the Builders populated each one when they built this place? What if we aren't welcome here? We gate-crashed, remember."

"You're one pessimistic bastard, Friday."

The African laughed. "Just pointing out how it looks to me."

Hendry looked up through the treetops. The great arc of the helix's next tier curved through the clear blue sky, so vast that its extremity was lost to sight. He considered its enormity; not only its physical construction, but the notion behind it. What the hell had the Builders intended—a zoo, a haven? He said as much to Olembe.

"How about," Olembe said, grimacing with the effort of loosening the cylinder, "a lab experiment? They gather specimens of alien races from around the galaxy, build this Petri dish and populate it, and watch the extraterrestrials fight it out."

"I don't buy it," Hendry said.

"Why not?"

He smiled. "Maybe I'm just a bleeding-heart liberal romantic, but I like to think that a race advanced enough scientifically would be pretty morally and ethically advanced too."

Olembe snorted. "Wishful thinking. Who says altruism is a universal constant?"

"Who says evil is?"

Olembe shook his head. "We're talking aliens here. Who can guess their motivations? What might appear evil to us might be intended as something else entirely by the aliens themselves."

"Granted. But I still think that they didn't build the helix in order to watch a bunch of aliens fight it out."

"And I'll expect the worst-case scenario until I'm proved wrong."

Hendry glanced at Ehrin and said, "What do you think, friend? Why were you brought here?"

Ehrin just blinked giant eyes at him and opened its muzzle in what might have been a snarl.

Olembe stopped work and glanced at the lemur creature. "I wonder if they know? I mean, do they have creation stories, myths, about great ships that came from the skies and took their people to another land?"

"Maybe we should get Carrelli to ask it when she gets back."

Olembe smiled. "Maybe by then she'll be a lot closer to solving this damned riddle, if she's managed to wake this Sleeper. Maybe we'll know whether the Builders are benevolent zoo-keepers or sadistic voyeurs." He swore and yanked the cylinder free. He held it up to Ehrin and said, "You know where we can find something just like this, a kind of replacement, yeah? To fit in here? Go fetch, boy."

Ehrin merely blinked at him.

"I reckon the only hope is to cannibalise the ship. I'll check later. Meantime, how about a fruit break?" He crossed the clearing to the pile of fruit and came back with a selection. They sat against the flank of the ship and ate. Ehrin chattered, ran off up the ramp and disappeared inside.

Olembe looked at Hendry and said, "So you and Kaluchek are getting it on, right?"

Hendry glanced at him. "What? You don't approve? Think I'm too old?"

"Hey, I'm no moralist, pal. Good luck to you, while it lasts. It's just that... I'd like to know something, is all."

"What's that?"

Olembe paused, spitting out a mouthful of black seeds. "Why does your squeeze treat me like shit, Joe? And don't say you haven't noticed."

Hendry nodded. "Of course I've noticed."

"She's racist, right? She can't get her head round why an African, from the continent that's given nothing to the world—cos that's a perception that a lot of people held back around the end of the twenty-first century—gets to be aboard a life-saving mission to the stars, yeah?"

"It's not that, Friday."

Olembe spat. "And don't say, how can she be racist when she's half-coloured herself? It's a typical ignorant white man's remark I've heard a hundred times before!"

"Screw you, Friday. I know what racism is. I was married to a Japanese woman, okay, and she hated every colour but yellow."

Olembe looked at him. "So… what's the Eskimo's problem? She acts like she's got an icicle stuck up her arse every time she talks to me."

Hendry looked away, determined not to be provoked by Olembe.

Olembe went on, "Look, you're fucking the bitch, Hendry. What the hell gives?"

Hendry turned, angered now. "She told me, Friday. Okay?"

Olembe stopped chewing, glanced sidewise at Hendry. "Enlightening. Very fucking enlightening. She told you… so what the fuck did she tell you?"

Hendry stared at the African and said, "She ran a check on everyone on the maintenance team when she was in Berne." He paused, surprised to find that he was enjoying getting back at Olembe like this.

"She came up with something about you, about what you did back in West Africa."

"Christ... Jesus Christ, man."

Hendry turned and looked at Olembe. He was staring off into the distance, biting his bottom lip. At last he said, "How the hell did she find that out?"

Hendry shrugged. "Hacked into some UN smart-ware files. I don't know the exact details."

"UN files? How the hell did the UN know about that?"

Hendry looked at Olembe, puzzled. "That's their business, Friday. They monitor wars, war crimes. They probably had observers at the trial."

Now it was the African's turn to look puzzled. "Hendry, what the hell are you on about?"

"The order you gave, sanctioning the execution of the prisoners, the five hundred Moroccans."

"Jesus Christ!" Olembe pushed himself to his feet, striding into the centre of the clearing and turning. He hurled a fruit at the ship, where it hit the golden carapace with a ripe splat and slid to the ground.

He approached Hendry and pointed. "I don't know what the hell she's been telling you, Joe. But that's a lie, you got me? A fucking goddamned lie!"

"Sissy seemed pretty convinced."

Olembe was shaking his head, vehement. "I didn't do that. I wouldn't... Christ, what kind of monster do you think I am?"

Hendry opened his mouth, thought through Olembe's reaction, and said, "So you didn't give the order—"

"I was never in the fucking army, Hendry!"

"But you're hiding something."

Olembe just stood there, staring at him. He looked, Hendry thought, tough and aggressive, and yet at the same time vulnerable. At last he said, "Joe... I trust you, okay? You just sit around, taking it all in. You've lost your daughter, and do you moan about it?" He shook his head. "You're cool, Joe."

Hendry wanted to protest that though he might not bewail his loss, he still felt it deeply; Olembe's assessment of his reaction to Chrissie's death demeaned his grief. He said nothing, but waited for the African to go on.

"You're right," Olembe said, "I did something back then, but I didn't massacre five hundred fucking civilians."

Olembe began striding back and forth across the clearing, nodding to himself as if rehearsing the lines he would say to convince Hendry.

"Okay, Joe... this is what happened. This is the truth. I'm not proud of what happened, but it isn't as bad as massacring civilians..." He stopped and dropped into a crouch before Hendry. "This was '94, right? Last year—I mean, what would have been last year... Anyway, the war in Africa was over. What was left of the Republic of West Africa was trying to recover, pull itself from the shit. Everything was chaotic. It was every man for himself, okay? Bear that in mind. I was working in Lagos, on the coast. A shit job in an oil-fuelled power station. It was a hand-to-mouth existence. The government hadn't paid us for three months. I went shooting game for food—I had a wife and two kids to feed." He stopped there, hung his head, and

Hendry wondered if he was thinking about the wife and children he had left behind on Earth. "Anyway, I had this brother working in the north, at the fusion plant in Abuja. We were close, we'd studied at Lagos together—nuclear mechanics—before he got a grant to study in the US ten, twelve years ago. When he got back, he landed himself a top post at a nuclear station in Abuja."

He paused, stopped his striding and looked at Hendry. "Then last year, a few weeks before the ESO call up, my brother came down to Lagos to see me. He knew how hard things were down south. He gave me money, enough to keep me and the family alive for a few months."

Hendry said, "What happened?"

"He was staying with us, on leave from Abuja. We went out shooting one day, me and my brother and a couple of friends. Bag a bit of game to supplement the rations, right?"

Olembe fell silent. He dropped into a squat on the golden moss, staring at his big fingers interlaced to form one great knot. He looked up, into Hendry's eyes. "I didn't shoot him, Joe. It was a friend. An accident. My brother got between the gun and an antelope... He died instantly."

"And..."

Olembe was shaking his head, smiling. "And we covered it up, buried my brother and didn't tell the police."

Into the following silence, Hendry said, "What was your brother's name?"

Olembe smiled. "You're no fool, Joe. What do you think? Friday Olembe."

"You took his identity?"

"I didn't plan to, not until the ESO call up came along, forwarded to my place via Abuja. I opened the file and read the offer and... it came to me in a rush. I could do the job. I was a qualified nuclear engineer. What could be simpler? I was to report to a government department in Lagos, where I'd be security checked, my ID verified—"

"So how did you get through that?"

Olembe smiled, held two fingers up before his face and rubbed them together. "How do you think? I gave a couple of officials the equivalent of a year's wages—paid from my brother's account—and they passed me as Friday Olembe."

Hendry nodded, then said, "You left your wife and children?"

"Don't sound so fucking censorious, Joe. Do you have any idea what life was like in Lagos back then? You would have done the same—and yes, it tore me up, it was the hardest decision in my life, even harder than taking my brother's identity. But desperation breeds even greater desperation, Joe. I left my wife and kids—with enough money to see them okay—but don't think for a second that that doesn't eat me up in here, Joe, because it never stops hurting like hell."

Hendry nodded. "I believe you," he said, and wondered at what Olembe had done. Perhaps he was influenced by his new-found feelings for Sissy—but how could anyone leave a wife and kids just like that?

Olembe stood, moved back to the ship and slumped down beside Hendry. "So that's how I'm here, while every last fucker we knew—my wife and kids and their descendants, if they ever had any—are long dead and gone."

Hendry heard sweet birdsong echoing through the forest. It worked like a balm, comforting.

He said, "So why would Sissy fabricate that evidence against you? Make out you were a war criminal?"

Olembe sighed. "Search me, man. Maybe it's simply this, she doesn't like the colour of my skin."

Hendry thought about it. He said suddenly, "Where did your brother study? You said he went to the US?"

"Yeah, LA."

Hendry said, "So did Sissy. She graduated from LA in '83."

Olembe was nodding. "My brother... yeah, it'd be around then."

"It might be a coincidence... but you never know, they might have met—"

"And something happened, and Kaluchek held a grudge ever since?"

Hendry shrugged. "It's possible."

"So how come she can't tell I'm not really Friday. Joe?"

Hendry shrugged. "People change a lot in twelve years. She remembered the name, not the face... I don't know."

"Crazy. I thought the bitch had it in for me."

Hendry said, "Don't say anything. About your brother, LA, or what Sissy told me about the war crimes. I'll ask her what happened. Maybe we can straighten things out between you two. We need to pull together if we're to get back to the colonists."

"Okay, okay, Joe," Olembe said. "Do your stuff and we'll all be happy families again."

"Just keep off her back and I'll do my best to get to the bottom of this."

"Fine." Olembe stood and indicated the entrance to the ship. "I'm going through the ship from top to bottom, see if I can come up with something I can hammer into shape."

Hendry watched him go. "Friday—one thing. Who were you before you were Friday?"

Olembe grinned. "You really want to know? I never liked the name. It was my father's. He called his first-born after him. Cyril, man. Can you believe that?"

Hendry smiled. "I won't tell anyone, Friday."

He settled back against the warm metal of the spaceship, considering Sissy Kaluchek and what might have happened in LA all those years ago, twelve subjective, a thousand real-time.

He closed his eyes and anticipated her return. Birds called, soothingly, from the surrounding forest.

# 4

EHRIN CROUCHED INSIDE the hatch of the space-ship, hugging his shins and watching the two aliens—humans, they called themselves—as they talked for a long time in the clearing.

One sat against the ship, while the other, a giant black creature, strode back and forth, gesturing animatedly. Ehrin watched with wonder, amazed at the fact that the words these beings spoke—slow, slurred sounds—could mean anything at all.

Everything about the humans filled him with awe: their appearance, their size, their level of technological accomplishment, the fact that they had arrived here—according to their leader, Carrelli—from a planet way beyond the helical system of worlds.

And to think that mere days ago he had been mired in the ignorance that affected all the citizens of Agstarn. To them, Agstarn *was* the world, with even the plains beyond the mountains a distant, shadowy realm; to them, the word of the Church, of the Book of Books, was the ultimate arbiter of the reality of existence.

He had never believed the version of reality promulgated by the Church, but he had to admit that in lieu of belief there had been a vast absence—how could he possibly have known what might have existed beyond Agstarn?

The reality had rocked him to his core. Staring through the spaceship's viewscreen at the vastness of the helix—his brain processing the view little by little, first the sun, then the tier immediately above them, and then all the other tiers and the miniature worlds like beads upon them—he had been overcome with a strange emotion that made him first weep and then laugh aloud.

He had tasted victory then, a euphoric sense of righteousness that his opposition to the Church and its draconian ways was justified. He wanted to show Velkor Cannak the helix, laugh in his face as he viewed the Elder's horror. That was impossible, of course, but he could *imagine* Cannak's disbelief, his refusal to accept the visual evidence of the helix. He wondered if Cannak were aboard the deathship, or if fear of what he might discover beyond the cloud cover of Agstarn had tempered his need for revenge. Ehrin liked to imagine that the Elder had boarded the deathship, and that his faith was now being undermined by the sight of the helix dominating the heavens.

He wished Kahran had lived to share his sense of victory, and Havor had survived so that he might have achieved his goal of destroying the deathship.

Perhaps that should be his goal now, he thought. Somehow, despite the seeming impossibility, he should help to bring about the destruction of the feared deathship. Perhaps that might be the first step in a much larger, more ambitious goal: to bring the truth to the people of Agstarn, to open their eyes after blinkered centuries of ignorance to the fact of the helix and their place upon it.

It would be a fitting tribute to his good friend Kahran Shollay.

His throat constricted as he thought about the death of the old man.

Kahran would have revelled in the series of conceptual thresholds Ehrin had crossed, and been amazed by the latest revelation: that there existed somewhere in this forest, asleep for centuries or even longer by some process he couldn't even guess at, a being who was linked in some way to the creators of the helix.

He looked up. The two humans had finished their conversation. One of them, the tall darker being, moved up the ramp into the ship, his big fingers touching Ehrin on the head as he passed. He wondered what it might mean—perhaps an instruction to follow.

Dutifully he climbed to his feet and entered the ship. The human moved around the flight-deck, clearly looking for something.

He glanced at Ehrin and spoke, the sounds impossibly slow. The being held something up, before his face. It was the fractured cylinder he had lovingly fashioned in the foundry, a seeming age ago.

The human pointed to it, then gestured around the ship.

Could he be asking if there were another component like it somewhere in the ship, Ehrin wondered.

Ehrin gestured no, and said that he had made the device back on his homeworld, but the human just stretched his lips and shook his head, continuing his search.

He passed down the corridor and Ehrin followed, intrigued by the being's search.

They came to the rear lounge, and there Ehrin found Sereth. She was curled on the floor, staring through the viewscreen with a blank expression. The human moved around the lounge with his usual slow precision, then said something to Ehrin, stretched his lips again and moved back down the corridor.

Ehrin remained in the lounge, watching Sereth. He felt a stab of guilt, and at the same time frustration. He had tried to comfort her on the flight from Agstarn, but fear had made her unreasonable and argumentative.

At last she turned her head and looked at him. "I didn't want to come here," she said.

"I'm sorry, Sereth."

She gestured with her muzzle. He could see the fear in the dilation of her pupils. "You are enjoying all this, aren't you? The company of these monsters, the illusion of... of wherever we are. You think this proves that you were right, don't you?"

He moved his head in a pained negative. "They aren't monsters, Sereth. They're very different to us, and we might never understand them, but they aren't monsters. They have... compassion. They helped me bury Havor."

"He was another monster!"

"He helped to save my life, Sereth."

"For his own godless ends! Perhaps it would have been best if you had died with Kahran."

He stared at her, anger a naked flame in his chest. "Do you really mean that? You'd rather have had me tortured to death by the Church's Inquisitors?"

She stared at him. "It would have saved all this, Ehrin."

"All this? You mean the truth?"

She barked contemptuously. "The truth? This is a lie, Ehrin, a godless illusion. It says in the Book of Books, chapter three, that the anti-god will confront the strayed with illusion, that the one true world is Agstarn, the one true faith the Church—"

"Superstition used by a corrupt and powerful Church to keep itself in power, Sereth. All lies. We're like minuscule insects at the bottom of an ice pond, who by some miracle climb out and behold another order of reality. Some can't take it and scamper back into the darkness. Others blink at the light and try to make sense of it."

She cried out. "But God did not intend this! It's an evil illusion." She stood and approached him. "Can't you see, Ehrin, you're being lured into something against your will, by beings we don't understand, for their own ends. I loved you, Ehrin. I don't want to see you harmed..." She reached out, touched his coat with her claws.

It was a difficult thing to do, but he did it. He pushed her paw away and said, "There is no God. I am here because I want to be here. I am not being used. I want to know the truth. That and only that is what is important to me."

She looked at him, and said at last, "More important to you than me, Ehrin?"

"Sereth, Sereth..." He looked into his heart, then, and knew the truth, that he no longer loved the woman who stood imploringly before him. His infatuation with her had been a manifestation of his other, younger self, a self blinded by the clouds of Agstarn, the blinkered social mores of a society ruled by deceit and lies.

He said, "I want to share the truth with you, Sereth. I want you to stop fearing, to open your eyes and apprehend the truth. The Church lied to us. Cannak and Hykell and all the others are evil."

Sereth spat, "No! My father is a good man, a great—"

"Your father is a deluded fool blinded by ignorance."

She attacked him then. She leapt at him and tried to scratch his face. He grasped her wrists, flung her back into a sunken sofa, where she sprawled sobbing and stared up at him.

"Your Church is evil and murderous and deserves to perish," he said.

She cried, "I loved you, Ehrin!"

He moved to the exit. "And I loved you, Sereth." He turned and hurried from the lounge, pulling the hatch shut behind him. Her sobs followed him all the way down the corridor.

He stopped at the top of the ramp, a sickness in his stomach. Much as he disliked the idea of hurting Sereth, he knew the pain he felt was provoked by his memories of the good times they had shared, the love. All that was over now, part of another life. It was odd, but beyond the pain he experienced a sense of achievement, a sense of freedom at being able at last to state his views. He felt suddenly liberated from everything that had held him back, as if Sereth had been the last connection to the lie that was Agstarn.

He looked around the clearing. The humans were kneeling on the ground beside the engine nacelle again, working with the tools they had found aboard the ship.

The big being saw him and gestured with something, and Ehrin saw that it was a square of metal that the humans were attempting to fashion into a cylinder. Ehrin joined them, fell into a squat and watched.

At one point he gestured to the tool container beside the humans, and lifted out a shaped wrench, which he thought more suited to the job.

The humans looked at each other, commented in their odd retarded language and stretched their lips. They took the wrench and continued their work.

Perhaps an hour later they had shaped the metal to their satisfaction, and then began the process of fixing it to the starboard manifold.

Ehrin squatted on the fin and watched them, and from time to time the humans looked up and stretched their lips and spoke to him. And Sereth had said these beings were evil.

The sun was setting by the time they finished the job and sealed the hatch. The humans spoke to each other again, and both of them stared up at the gaps in the canopy overhead.

They sat beside the food they had gathered, gestured Ehrin to join them, and passed him a large round fruit. He ate, watching these strange creatures as they chewed slowly, and listened to their odd words. He wished the other human was present, the being called Carrelli, so that he could take part in the conversation and tell these people about his world, and ask about their own home planet.

The sun went down and the light in the clearing dulled to the colour of old gold, and the humans talked on while they ate.

Ehrin thought about the deathship, and Agstarn, and how he might bring the truth to the people of his world.

# 5

KALUCHEK SHIFTED UNCOMFORTABLY as she sat, legs astride, behind Carrelli on the broad back of the slowly lumbering beast—sharls, Carrelli said they were called. "The sooner we arrive, the better," Kaluchek said. "I'm getting saddle sore."

Ahead, the insectile lizard who called himself Watcher Pharan slowed his mount so that he was riding alongside Kaluchek and Carrelli. He spoke in a rapid burst of flute-like sounds.

Carrelli nodded her understanding.

Kaluchek asked, "What was all that about?"

"He asked if we were comfortable. I assured him that we were... and asked how far we were from the Sleeper's ship. He said that we should arrive in about five, six hours. Before nightfall anyway."

Behind them were two slowly plodding beasts, each carrying six tiny quicksilver aliens. From time to time the aliens had taken it in turns to dismount, dart forward and scale the mountainous flank of Kaluchek's sharl. They would sit staring at her and Carrelli for a few seconds, their large pink eyes nictitating unsettlingly from the bottom up, before dismounting again, fast as an eye-blink, and returning to their mounts.

Now Carrelli passed a fruit over her shoulder. She had been trying various berries and pod-shaped things all afternoon, picking them *en passant* from overhanging branches. "Try these. I'm sure they have a mildly soporific effect."

"The best thing I've heard all day," Kaluchek said, taking a handful of the berries. They were sweet, with a pungent acid aftertaste.

She was still sore at being separated from Joe. She would rather Olembe and Carrelli went in search of the sleeping alien, leaving her and Joe back at the ship to have some fun. But she saw things from Carrelli's point of view. Olembe knew a bit about mechanics, and needed someone to help him repair the ship.

Last night they had halted at sunset and slept in a clearing pretty much identical to the one they had left. The golden moss had proved a surprisingly comfortable bed, and the temperature never dropped below a clement twenty-five Celsius, according to Carrelli's atmosphere suit.

Kaluchek had lain on her back and stared through a rent in the canopy at a tier of the helix that swept overhead. She assumed it was the second tier, the one they had left, as the planet they were now on, Calique, was turning away from the sun and so was therefore facing *down* the spiral. She made out oceans glittering in the sunlight, and the alternate sections of massed land, which were individual planets. To think that down there somewhere was the place where they had very nearly lost their lives...

Then her thoughts had turned to Joe, and the miracle of her finding him, and she'd forgotten all about vengeful rats.

She'd turned to Carrelli and asked to use the radio on her atmosphere suit. She wanted to hear his voice, receive the assurance that he was okay. She explained that the damned rats had mashed hers.

But Carrelli had said it would be best to maintain radio silence. If the Church ship were still in the vicinity...

"Sure. Sorry," Kaluchek said, feeling like a schoolgirl reprimanded by the head teacher.

Now, rocked by the swaying motion of the great turtle-like animal, sedated by the fruit Carrelli had given her, Kaluchek thought about Joe Hendry again. For the first time in years, she could look ahead, plan her life with someone. She saw a colony thriving on a world like this one, next door or not far away, and herself a vital part of it; married to Joe, maybe with kids.

She sat upright, wondering if it was an effect of the fruit that was turning her head all mushy. She'd never given a thought to kids in the past, and she'd known Joe only a matter of weeks, give or take a thousand years...

Carrelli was saying, "...between you and Friday?"

"Mmm?"

"I said, why the antagonism between you and Friday?"

"Goes back a long way," she replied, almost unconscious now.

"Tell me."

"Rather not."

"It's getting to the point where your animosity is disturbing the rhythm of the team. I don't want it to affect the outcome of the mission, Sissy."

"Won't," she said. "It's fine. I'll ignore him from now on, 'kay?"

Carrelli looked over her shoulder. "You promise?"

"Promise. Cross my heart."

She felt suddenly woozy, and lay back on the leathery hide of the animal. Its broad back was accommodating. She could lie down, face up, without fear of falling off; her legs were bent awkwardly on either side of Carrelli, but the drug dulled her mind to any discomfort. She stared up at the scintillating spokes of sunlight spearing through the canopy for what seemed like hours. At one point she became aware of voices, alien voices, like duelling flutes, and opened an eye to see Watcher Pharan riding alongside, talking to Carrelli. She closed her eye and minutes later slipped into unconsciousness.

She woke with a start and sat up, disoriented, wondering where the hell she was. Then it came to her. She was riding a turtle on a planet called Calique with an Italian dyke and a lizardly insect named Watcher Pharan...

She wanted to be back with Joe, holding him in her arms. She laughed to herself. Here she was, in all probability one of only a few human beings left alive in the galaxy, on the mission of a lifetime, and all she could think about was the guy she loved. She didn't know whether to commend or castigate herself.

The effects of the drug had worn off. She felt bright and alert. The sun was going down, laying a patina of honey over everything she could see.

Carrelli looked over her shoulder. "You back with us, Sissy?"

"That was a pretty strong... whatever it was. Where are we?"

Carrelli smiled. "Not far to go now. Another hour maybe."

Kaluchek nodded, glancing ahead at the lumbering beast bearing the tiny form of Watcher Pharan. She nodded towards the alien. "What were you two talking about?"

"I was asking it about the Sleeper. What kind of alien it was, if it said anything about the Builders, their motives."

"And?"

Carrelli shook her head. "All this happened long ago," she said. "Thousands of years ago. There were no written descriptions of the Sleeper ever made—or rather, Watcher Pharan suspects there were at the time, but that these have been lost from the scriptures."

"Lost? Sounds odd."

"That's what I thought, but I have a theory. The Sleeper is so alien, so relatively ugly to these people, that the Teachers—they're almost like priests, you might say—suppressed the Sleeper's description in order to make the Sleeper more mysterious, god-like."

Kaluchek thought about it. "And where exactly do we fit into it? I mean, who do the Caliquans think we are? Some distant cousins of the Builders?"

Carrelli shook her head. "All they know is what they've interpreted from what was written down, that the Sleeper said that one day a race of beings would fall from the sky and come for him or her. It had to happen sooner or later, Sissy."

"And what do they expect from us? I mean, what do they expect us to do when we come to the Sleeper?"

Carrelli shrugged. "That was hard to determine, Sissy. I think, but I'm not sure, that they credit us with motives that will remain always mysterious to them."

"So what's in it for them?" she asked.

"As far as I can make out, the act of leading us to the Sleeper is reward enough. I know this sounds corny, but they seem a wholly altruistic people."

Kaluchek looked at the tiny alien perched upon the back of the leading animal. "They have a whole religion based around the Builders and the Sleeper?"

"They revere the Builders for obvious reasons, and I think they see the Sleeper as a holy relation of these godlike beings. For centuries the Caliquans have been watching the heavens for signs of our arrival."

Kaluchek smiled. "What'll we find, Gina?"

Carrelli was a second or two before answering. "Answers, perhaps. The reason the Builders built the helix? That would be rather nice."

Kaluchek laughed. "Yeah. The stuff of fairy tales. We'll probably come across nothing more than the rusted wreck of a spaceship."

Carrelli glanced over her shoulder and smiled. "Do you know something, sometimes your cynicism reminds me of Friday."

"Christ, don't say that, Gina." She shook her head. "It's just that I'd rather expect the worst, and if it doesn't happen... well then, that's great." Just like I never expected to come across Joe Hendry, she thought; just like I told myself that all men were bastards.

"Did you ask Pharan about the neighbouring worlds, Gina? Does he know if they're inhabited?"

"I asked. He doesn't know. They've had no contact with alien races, until the Sleeper came along, and then us. They're a... I was about to say they're a backward people, but that would be grossly unfair. They're a race that have turned their back on materialism, on technology, and embraced the way of the spirit. So they haven't developed vessels to explore the neighbouring worlds. They look inward, not outward."

Kaluchek considered this. "And they haven't been visited by their neighbours. That might mean the worlds on either side aren't inhabited."

"Or it might mean that they are, but their citizens do not have the means or the inclination to cross the oceans."

"I just want to find a warm, Earthlike world where we can settle and live in peace without making a mess of it."

The Italian smiled. "I'll second that, Sissy."

Minutes later the air was filled with shrill ululations, and on the leading animal Watcher Pharan raised his hands and called out, his cry taken up by those Caliquans riding behind. Kaluchek turned to see the insect-lizards dancing about on the backs of the stoic sharls, hands raised, great cerise eyes nictitating in what might have been religious euphoria.

Ahead, through a gap in the boles of the trees, she made out the object of their frenzied veneration.

The great ship had felled a whole swathe of forest with its forced landing, pushing down trees in an oddly beautiful and symmetrical fan shape around the blunt end of its nose-cone. The forest had regrown around it, new trees giving the impression that the ship was imprisoned; custodial vines snaked over its surface, as if pinning it to the forest floor. The ship itself had suffered an extensive fire in the aftermath of the crash-landing, its silver carapace excoriated and blackened.

The Caliquans had erected a stairway to the open hatch of the ship, constructed from logs, the rustic architecture of the stairs contrasting with the ornate, almost baroque, lines of the ship.

An air of sanctity hung over the scene. Kaluchek wondered if she would have felt it had she not known of the Caliquans' reverence of the ship and what lay within it.

They were entering an artificial clearing now, and over the tops of the surrounding trees Kaluchek could see that the sun was setting on another day— or rather, she thought, the planet itself was turning on its equatorial axis, bringing night to this hemisphere as it turned towards the outside of the helix.

The caravan halted. Watcher Pharan slipped from his mount and approached the stairway. He performed a series of gestures, so fast Kaluchek could hardly make them out, then knelt and lowered his face to the forest floor.

He stood and gestured, raising his arms high.

The other Caliquans left their sharls and hurried to either side of the stairs, creating a guard of honour down which Kaluchek and Carrelli would have to pass to board the ship.

"I've been thinking about the Sleeper," Kaluchek said. "Surely the Builders would have noticed the loss of the ship and come for the Sleeper ages ago."

Carrelli nodded. "The same thing occurred to me."

"And?"

Carrelli said, "Perhaps they did. Perhaps the cold sleep unit—or the ship's equivalent—is empty."

"And the Caliquans have been venerating an empty casket all along?"

Carrelli smiled. "Couldn't that be true of all religions?"

Kaluchek shook her head. "Maybe... But I like the Caliquans. I find it sad."

Carrelli touched her hand. "They have faith. That's what is important. It gives purpose to their lives and makes them what they are."

"Isn't that even sadder? They might be worshipping the empty casket of an advanced alien race."

"Like I said, it gives their life meaning. It's responsible for their being so good, being so anti-materialist. They live at one with their world." Carrelli shrugged. "By comparison, what have we done, other than wreck our own planet?"

Kaluchek smiled. "You saying we should live like Buddhists and venerate the Builders?"

Carrelli laughed. "Of course not. We should live lives of conservation and venerate our eventual homeworld."

"Sounds fine to me."

Watcher Pharan advanced towards them between the lines of his acolytes. He paused before the great snuffling nose of the sharl and looked up at Carrelli with his blinking pink eyes. He spoke quickly, gesturing with his thin arm towards the ship.

Carrelli replied, bowing her head.

She turned to Kaluchek and said, "Pharan says he will escort us as far as the ship. We will enter by ourselves. Protocol, apparently, does not allow for us to be accompanied when we approach the cask of the Sleeper."

Kaluchek dismounted, sliding down the toughened hide of the sharl and landing on the golden moss. With Carrelli beside her, she followed Watcher Pharan towards the stairway leading up to the ship, passing down the aisle of twittering acolytes.

Pharan stopped at the foot of the stairs, turned and gestured for them to proceed. Carrelli spoke to him quickly, nodded and climbed. Kaluchek followed, the timber stairs creaking beneath their weight.

Behind them, Pharan and the acolytes started up a piccolo piping, filling the forest with its joyous sound.

As they reached the top of the stairway, they were dwarfed by the ship's great curving flank rising above them, its fire-blackened panels skeined with vines. The arched entrance hatch, three times their size, gave on to a great cavernous hall, which might have been the cargo hold.

They paused on the threshold, overcome with the size of the ship and its cathedral silence. The baroque design of its exterior was repeated within, with no straight lines in evidence, all angles rounded. It was not what Kaluchek had expected from a spaceship, after the starkly functional architecture

of the *Lovelock*. Here the lavish whorls that decorated the bulkheads, the tubular design of the
corridors leading off, struck her as excessive, the
product of an aesthetic entirely alien.

She wished Joe were with her to experience this
incredible place. She could fully understand why
the Caliquans considered it so hallowed.

Carrelli glanced at her. "This way?" the medic
suggested, gesturing down a corridor that led in the
direction of the nose-cone.

They moved across the floor of the hold, their
steps echoing around them, and entered the tubular passage. There was something intestinal in its
refusal to adhere to straight lines; it seemed to
meander through the ship, rising and falling on its
way forward. After ten metres the light from outside gave way to shadow, and Carrelli illuminated
their way with the flashlight of her atmosphere
suit.

The curving walls of the corridor were decorated
with the same whorls and curlicues as the hold, less
a series of deliberate patterns than what appeared
to be an accidental arrangement or natural designs,
like frost patterns.

Ahead, the corridor lightened. Carrelli stopped
abruptly, and Kaluchek almost collided with her.
"What?"

"I think this is it," Carrelli said in a whisper,
switching off her wrist-mounted flashlight and
pointing ahead.

They were on the lip of what appeared to be a
great sunken amphitheatre, illuminated by the
slanting rays of the setting sun, which poured in
through a 180-degree arrangement of viewscreens.

Cradles hung from the domed ceiling, their material frayed and rotted with the passage of centuries. What might have been banks of com-terminals, more like the dusty grey cases of giant beetles, circled the flight-deck beneath the viewscreens. An absolute silence hung over the place, almost forbidding them to defile it. Kaluchek was aware of the rasp of her breathing.

Carrelli pointed, as if not wanting to spoil the perfection of the silence.

In the centre of the flight-deck, below them as they stood on the threshold, was a raised plinth and upon it a long cask or catafalque. It was, as Kaluchek had expected, nothing like their own cold sleep units. As if intended as the centrepiece of some alien cathedral, it was bulbous and decorated with a bas-relief of abstract design, like Mandelbrot fractals made three-dimensional.

Carrelli stepped down into the well of the amphitheatre. Kaluchek followed.

Like pilgrims they approached the cask and climbed the steps of the plinth. At the top they paused and gazed down at the catafalque. Carrelli reached out, traced the patterns with long fingers. Kaluchek did the same, the rococo metal surprisingly warm beneath her fingertips.

Carrelli moved around the cask, trailing fingers as if searching for some mechanism whereby to open it. Kaluchek looked for anything that might indicate an operating interface, technology she might recognise. There seemed to be no heat-responsive sensors, nothing as crass as touchpads or verniers.

She looked around her, at the rearing domed ceiling of the flight-deck, and wondered at the creatures that had operated this bizarre craft.

Across the cask, Carrelli touched something. Kaluchek cried out as the lid of the cask cracked. She stepped back in alarm, almost losing her footing on the top step of the plinth and tumbling down.

She reached forward, gripped the rim of the cask, and stared into its interior as the lid slid back along its length.

Carrelli looked up and across at her. "That's your answer," she whispered. "That's why the Builders never came for the Sleeper."

Kaluchek stared down at the collapsed bones on a bed of dust, a neat configuration that illustrated the shape of a tall biped, with more ribs than a human, thicker limb bones and a great domed skull with a jutting nose and jaw-line.

"System malfunction," Carrelli said, "or perhaps it succumbed to its injuries, despite the Caliquans' ministrations."

Kaluchek shook her head. "What do we tell them? I mean, if they find out their revered Sleeper is dead…"

"I don't know," Carrelli said, surprising Kaluchek. The cool Italian medic usually had an answer for everything.

Carrelli stepped down from the plinth and moved around the perimeter of the flight-deck, examining the hunched arrangement of the com-terminals.

Kaluchek joined her. "What are you looking for?"

Carrelli glanced up. "I'm not sure. Some means of accessing information, however that might be achieved. It might be a case of touching everything and hoping—as I did up there."

Kaluchek nodded. "Aliens do things differently," she murmured.

Carrelli smiled and continued her search.

Kaluchek moved around the flight-deck in the opposite direction from Carrelli, counter-clockwise. She ran her hand over the bulging surfaces, furred with centuries of dust. She recognised nothing similar to any smartware systems she had worked with; for all she knew, the globular consoles might have been examples of extraterrestrial art.

She paused to look out over the forest. The sun had gone down, and the light was aqueous now, golden green. She could see Watcher Pharan and his acolytes seated around the foot of the stairway in a semicircle, heads bowed.

She wondered suddenly what Joe was doing, and desperately wanted to be with him.

She reached out to touch a protuberance on the surface of a console—which looked like a toad on a rock, she thought—and immediately pulled her hand away, shrieking with alarm and examining her tingling fingertips.

"Sissy, what did you do?"

Kaluchek turned to Carrelli, and was amazed to see something hanging in the air between them. She could see Carrelli through it, the Italian's expression mirroring her own, open-mouthed with surprise.

The image was indistinct, like a poor holovision, but Kaluchek could make out what appeared to be a three-dimensional representation of the helix, perhaps as tall as a human, floating in the air. It turned as she watched, a complex rosary of worlds spiralling around a central, burning sun.

Involuntarily, she stepped forward and reached out. As expected, her fingers passed through the fourth tier. She told herself that she felt a slight tingle, but nothing more.

As if in a daze, Carrelli moved around the rotating helix. "Some kind of... map," Carrelli said. She stepped forward, reached out.

Instantly, her head snapped back and she cried out as if in pain. Instead of retreating, however, she took another step forward, then another, passing through the tiers until she was standing inside the spiralling helix. Her torso took the place of the sun, which continued to burn, filling her with radiance.

"Gina!" Kaluchek called out.

Carrelli opened her eyes. She seemed to be in rapture. She reached out, touching the tiers, her fingers playing an arpeggio across the span of worlds. "*Magnifico*," she sang.

She turned, her fingers running up and down the spiral, her head flung back.

Kaluchek retreated, fetched up against the console with a start and stared. "Gina?"

As if from a great distance, Carrelli replied, "I'm fine, Sissy. More than fine. I'm... I'm accessing information... it's random, patchy. Corrupted. The ship crash-landed here three thousand years ago. I can't control what I'm finding out—I just accept what I receive! Oh, the wonder..."

"How come you...?" Kaluchek began. "I felt a jolt, nothing more."

Rapturously, Carrelli shook her head. "My augments... I seem to be picking things up through my smartware implants." She closed her eyes, flung back her head.

When she opened her eyes again, she was staring at Kaluchek. "Enough, Sissy! I've had enough. Can you... whatever you did to activate it, turn it off..."

Kaluchek found the reptilian protuberance, reached out and once more felt the jolt. She turned quickly. The image of the helix flickered out of existence, and Carrelli, suddenly divested of the wondrous image, slumped to the deck.

Kaluchek rushed over to her, cradled Carrelli in her arms and checked her pulse. She was alive, breathing normally. Kaluchek's panic subsided. She wondered what she had felt, then: alarm for Carrelli that she might be dead, or fear of being left alone aboard an alien ship in an alien rainforest. As Carrelli's eyes flickered open and she smiled up at her, Kaluchek felt a quick hot flush of shame.

"You okay?" she asked redundantly.

"Fine. I'm fine. God, the... sensation. I don't know... I've never felt anything like it before. I was... I was *flooded* with information. Much of it..." she shook her head. "It was meaningless, just beyond the threshold of my comprehension. But some of it..." She shook her head and laughed aloud.

"Some of it...?"

Carrelli moved away from her, sat cross-legged on the deck and hung her head, as if recovering from shock. She looked up suddenly, smiling. "Sissy, the image of the helix is a kind of registry, an index."

Kaluchek echoed the word.

"When I touched each world..." Carrelli went on, "I don't know how, but I could access information about it, technical information, its status—things like its atmospheric constituents, mass, gravity… I even," she laughed "in some cases I even knew what beings inhabited the worlds, but the knowledge was like a dream, the information fleeting, elusive. Then there was more…" She stopped speaking, hung her head and touched her temples with graceful fingers.

When she looked up again, she seemed to have calmed herself, controlled her breathing. She said, "Towards the end, I learned about the ship itself, its pilot. The Sleeper was an engineer, one of a team whose job it was to service the helix." She screwed up her eyes, as if fighting for recall. "They were… I can't recall their names, this race of engineers, but they weren't the Builders. They were… sub-contractors, if you like. They worked for the Builders."

"And the Builders?" Kaluchek asked. "Did you learn anything about the Builders?"

"I… I learned that they still inhabit a world on the helix," she said in little more than a whisper. "The Builders… that's not what they call themselves, but that's how my smartware translated their name… they inhabit a world on the fourth tier. That is, on the tier above this one. They are an ancient race, the oldest of all the known races in the galaxy. They are… I received the impression that they are… perhaps dormant, or suspended, or in some form of hibernation. They are so old that their flesh is…" She shook her head in frustration, "I didn't understand what I was receiving, but I had the impression that they were in hibernation because their flesh was weak, whatever that might mean."

She smiled at Kaluchek and said, "Help me up. Then activate the image again."

"You sure? I mean—"

"Do it. I'll be fine."

Kaluchek nodded. She assisted Carrelli to her feet, then moved to the console and hit the protuberance. Carrelli approached the helix, reached out and seemed to grasp a planet on the fourth tier. "This is their world," she said in a hushed voice, and pointed to a world on the tier below, almost directly underneath the first. "And this is Calique."

She moved into the middle of the helix, reached out and ran her hands across the tiers. She shook her head. "It's strange, but the effect isn't as powerful this time. I'm getting the same information, and the rapture is reduced." She laughed. "But it's still incredible…"

Kaluchek stepped forward cautiously and reached out, touching a world with her fingertips. Again she felt a slight, tingling sensation, like pins and needles, but nothing more.

She looked at Carrelli. "You don't know why they built the helix and brought the extraterrestrials here?"

Carrelli dropped her arms and stepped from the helix. She crossed to the console and touched the control, and behind her the helix winked out of existence.

She shook her head. "That was what I wanted most to learn," she said. "Why? But I couldn't access that information, Sissy."

She moved from the perimeter of the flight-deck and approached the plinth. As Kaluchek watched, the Italian climbed the steps and paused at the top.

Kaluchek hurried up the steps of the plinth and stood beside Carrelli, staring down at the remains of the dead engineer.

Then Carrelli reached into the cask. Her fingers gently moved aside what might have been a collarbone, then reached out and picked up something. As Carrelli withdrew her hand, Kaluchek saw a pendant glittering in her grip.

"What is it?"

Carrelli held it up before them. "Call it a badge of office," she said, and Kaluchek saw that dangling on the chain was a miniature golden helix—with, incredibly, a small glowing sun somehow suspended at its centre.

Carrelli looked at her. "I'd like to keep it as a souvenir, but..."

"But?"

"I know someone who would appreciate it even more."

Kaluchek smiled. "Watcher Pharan?"

"Who else?"

"But what will you tell him...?" She gestured towards the bones. "You can't..."

Carrelli was shaking her head. "The Caliquans are a good people. I knew that before, but when I touched the facsimile of their world, that was confirmed. I'll give him this memento, tell them that they must keep up their vigil until the day the Builders descend and reward them for their altruism. I'll say that the Sleeper still sleeps, is not yet ready to awaken."

The light from beyond the flight-deck was dying with the setting of the sun, and Carrelli activated her flashlight and said, "It's time we were getting back." She looked at Kaluchek. "We have a lot to talk about. Whether we remain on this tier and try to find a suitable world, or move up to the next one and locate the Builders."

Kaluchek said, "We can't stay here, Gina... not when we know where the Builders are." She shook her head. "That would be impossible. We need to know why, how..."

Carrelli smiled. "That's what I think, too. Come on, let's get back."

They retraced their steps through the ship, following the elliptical disc of Carrelli's flashlight until they came to the cargo hold, then paused at the top of the crude timber steps and gazed down.

Kaluchek wondered if she had ever seen a sight more beautiful. The clearing was bathed in dying sunlight, fringed by tall trees and scented by a million colourful blooms. In pride of place at the foot of the steps stood the tiny, expectant forms of the Caliquans, silvery and ethereal, staring up at them with huge pink eyes, their insectile arms raised as if in supplication.

They descended the stairs, Carrelli leading their way, and when she reached the forest floor she held out the pendant at arm's length and spoke to Watcher Pharan in his fluting tongue.

Instantly, the acolytes behind Pharan fell to their knees and pressed their faces to the golden moss, while Pharan himself set up an exultant ululation. He reached out and took the pendant, staring at the magical fiery sun at its centre, then placed it reverently over his head and settled it on his chest.

He called to his acolytes and they rose and hurried to their mounts, so many quicksilver blurs. Watcher Pharan spoke to Carrelli again, and she replied. He mounted his sharl, and Kaluchek and Carrelli climbed aboard theirs. Slowly, the sharl turned and plodded from the clearing and entered the twilight word of the forest.

Carrelli said, "I told Pharan that the Sleeper awoke and addressed us, said that he wished them to treasure the pendant as a token of his gratitude."

Kaluchek smiled. "The story will become myth, in time; your lie a source of wonder."

Carrelli stared ahead. "As I said earlier, Sissy, what matters is faith."

Kaluchek smiled to herself and they fell silent. As they passed a tall shrub a little later, Carrelli reached out and grasped a handful of berries, and seeing that they were the soporific fruit, Kaluchek did the same. Tired anyway, she found that with the sedative of the berries she was soon on the edge of sleep. She lay back, lulled by the rocking motion of the sharl, and was soon asleep and dreaming.

Carrelli woke her a short time later—at least, it felt like a short time. She opened her eyes and blinked, dazzled by bright sunlight penetrating the canopy of foliage high overhead.

"Sissy. Time you woke up."

Kaluchek struggled into a sitting position, rubbing her eyes. She seemed to have been asleep for a matter of minutes, and yet she felt fully refreshed, even invigorated. She wondered if it was something to do with the drug.

"It's morning, Sissy. You've been asleep for hours."

"Morning?" she repeated idiotically.

"Here," Carrelli said, passing her a fruit. "It's almost all water. You need to drink in this heat or you'll dehydrate."

Kaluchek took the fruit and began peeling it, and instantly a cascade of cool water splashed across her hand. She lifted the fruit to her lips and took a mouthful of cool, scented fluid.

"How far are we from the ship?" she asked. She had wanted to say 'from Joe', but Carrelli would only have smiled her motherly smile at her.

"I estimate six hours," Carrelli said. "Maybe less."

"Do you think they'll have fixed it?"

Carrelli glanced at her over her shoulder. "Let's hope so. I have faith in Friday. I know you don't like him, but he's determined."

Kaluchek bit her lip, deciding not to tell Carrelli what else he was. "Even if the ship's up and running," she said, "do you think we can make it to the next tier?"

"I don't see why not. We made it so far. Of course, it's not settled yet that we're definitely going. The others might veto the idea. Rather than risk the flight, they might rather remain here and find a habitable world."

Kaluchek shook her head. "Not Joe. I know him. He'll want to find the Builders. I can't speak for Olembe. But even if he's against the idea, that's three against one. The majority wins."

Carrelli smiled to herself. "Let's just see what they say, okay?"

Kaluchek fell silent, watching the tall trees of the forest pass slowly, the lumbering sharl ahead with the tiny figure of Watcher Pharan perched upon its back. She grabbed a bunch of fruit that Carrelli had passed safe earlier, handed one to the Italian and ate as she thought of Joe, waiting for her.

Carrelli's estimate of six hours was conservative. Less than three hours had elapsed when Watcher

Pharan turned upon his mount and chirruped to Carrelli.

"We're almost back at the ship," she said. "Five minutes."

Kaluchek looked ahead, through the tall trees at the vista of golden sand. Minutes later she made out, a deeper shade of gold against the sand, the crouching shape of the alien ship, with Joe and Olembe seated beside it.

As the procession of sharls and their riders entered the clearing, Joe stood quickly, waved and hurried across to meet them.

Kaluchek couldn't help herself. She slid from the back of the sharl and dropped into his arms. It felt so good, so natural, that she resented the time she'd spent away from him—even if she had beheld wonders.

"It's so good to have you again, Joe." She looked up, into his eyes, wanting him to respond with similar sentiments. He looked at her, something questioning in his eyes, his expression almost curious.

"What?" she said, her stomach tight.

What if he'd had second thoughts about her during her time away? What if that bastard Olembe had turned him against her? But she was being paranoid. She should credit Joe with more humanity than that.

He shook his head. "Nothing. It's great to have you back." He pulled away and regarding her at arm's length. "Well, tell me all about it."

She stared into his smiling face. "It was amazing, Joe. I mean…" She looked across at Carrelli. "Are you going to tell them?"

Olembe had stirred now and joined them, unable to keep himself away from the excitement.

Watcher Pharan darted from his mount and approached Carrelli. They spoke for a while, before touching hands. The Watcher then turned towards Kaluchek and the others, lifting both arms briefly in what might have been a farewell gesture.

In an instant it was upon its mount, and then the procession started up once again. Kaluchek watched the sharls carrying the tiny aliens back into the forest.

"Well?" Joe said.

Carrelli said, "First, what's the status of the ship?"

"We repaired the mechanical fault," Olembe said. "We powered up the ship's smartware, as well as we could, and it seems to be running at around eighty per cent efficiency."

Joe said, "As far as we could tell, that is. It's an alien system. Much of it was familiar, but I might have missed signals for systems failure."

Carrelli nodded. "That's fine. Well, we have a decision to make…"

Olembe said, "What the hell did you find out there?"

Carrelli gestured to the ship, and led the way across the clearing to the ramp. She sat down, massaging her calves.

There was movement from the entrance to the ship, and Kaluchek saw Ehrin and Sereth peering out. Carrelli beckoned them, and Ehrin came and sat beside Carrelli. Sereth, cautious, remained where she was and squatted on the ship's threshold.

Carrelli said, "What would you say if I told you we found out where the Builders are hiding themselves?"

Joe smiled. "You're not kidding, are you?"

Kaluchek felt something melt in her chest as she looked upon his wonder. She shook her head. "It was incredible, Joe. We entered the ship and found the Sleeper. It was dead, but then Gina—"

"I interfaced with some highly advanced smartware system," Carrelli said. "It was... I guess it was a simple directory. The ship was a maintenance vessel, operated by a race that worked for the Builders. I found that the Builders themselves have a planet almost directly above this one on the next tier."

She turned and spoke to Ehrin in his own language, and the effect was marked. He sat up, his muzzle open, eyes wide, then spoke rapidly to Carrelli. She smiled and replied, then turned to Joe and Olembe.

"So, gentlemen, what do we do? We've found a temperate tier. We could explore the next worlds along on either side, think about settling here and fetching the colonists—"

Joe cut in, "Or we could take a trip to the next tier and seek out the Builders."

Carrelli nodded and looked around the group. "Those are the options. What do you think?"

Olembe said, "If we could make it to the next tier without the Church's ship intercepting us..." He shrugged. "Then I'm all for pushing on."

Oddly, Kaluchek found herself feeling annoyed that Olembe had fallen in with her own opinion. She looked at Joe, praying that it wouldn't be him who raised objections. She was relieved when he said, "I agree. If the Builders are up there, then I want to meet them. Sissy?"

She smiled. "I'm with you. I mean, how can we look for a colonisable world when the people who built this place are so close to us? I'd always be wondering what we might have missed."

Carrelli turned and spoke to Ehrin and Sereth.

Ehrin stood quickly, leaning forward. He fired off a question at Carrelli, and listened to her reply wide-eyed. He turned to Sereth and spoke. She replied, barking at him, then turned quickly at slipped into the ship.

Ehrin followed her.

Kaluchek said, "What was that about?"

Carrelli shook her head. "Ehrin is with us. He wants to meet the Builders. He told Sereth and she... She's finding all this hard to take, to say the least." She looked around the clearing. "So we'll go, but we'll be very careful about it. My guess is that the Church ship is miles away by now, but even so we'll set off through the jungle on auxiliaries, okay?"

She led the way to the ship, followed by Olembe. Joe was about to step onto the ramp, but Kaluchek stopped him. She pulled him to her. "One last kiss on the planet where it first happened," she said, exhilaration flowing through her.

He kissed her, then looked around at the forest and pulled her up the ramp.

Carrelli and Olembe were strapped into the pilots' couches, going through pre-flight checks. There was no sign of Ehrin or Sereth. They strapped themselves into seats set into the bulkhead, close enough together to allow contact. She reached out and touched his fingers, feeling apprehension despite herself at the thought of ascending to the next tier in a patched together alien ship.

Thirty minutes later, Carrelli said, "Well, everything seems to be functioning pretty well. Let's hope your repair holds."

"Amen to that," Olembe said.

Behind them in the corridor, Kaluchek heard a commotion, the high chatter of Ehrin and Sereth. She turned, expecting to see them enter the flight-deck.

Joe touched her hand and pointed through a sidescreen. The aliens had left the ship and were standing in the clearing, facing each other, evidently arguing. At one point Ehrin reached out, grabbed Sereth by the arm and tried to drag her back to the ramp.

Sereth exploded, lashing out at Ehrin and screeching so that she could be heard inside the ship. Then she turned and sprinted off into the forest.

Kaluchek was aware that they were watching an alien drama, and though she was unable to understand the nuances of the discord, the salient facts were obvious. She looked across at Joe, and wondered if he too was feeling a vicarious melancholy as he apprehended Ehrin's dilemma.

Ehrin started after his mate, then stopped. He reached out a hand, called out and waited.

Then he dropped his hand and looked back at the ship. He hesitated, torn between two desires, and at last made his decision. He hurried back to the ship and scampered up the ramp.

Carrelli said, "Sealing the hatches. Okay, let's power up. Auxiliaries activate. Standby, Friday."

"A-OK."

The ship vibrated, shaking as the engines came to life.

Ehrin joined them on the flight-deck, found a seat and strapped himself in. Joe smiled across at him, and the alien open its muzzle in what might have been a reciprocal expression.

"This is it," Carrelli said. "Okay, hold on. Here we go…"

The ship rose unsteadily, rocking like a boat in a storm. Carrelli managed to equalise the lift, gripping the frame and scowling with the effort. Seconds later, the ship rose higher with a lurch. Carrelli eased the ship forward, through the trees. Like this, cautiously, they proceeded for perhaps an hour.

"Okay," Carrelli said. "Hold on back there."

Seconds later they crashed through the treetops, moving from shade to dazzling sunlight. All around was a sea of green, and to their right a wide river looped towards the horizon.

Then the ship tipped, flipping Kaluchek's stomach, and accelerated at an incredible speed. Calique vanished beneath them, and immediately ahead, through the forward viewscreen, appeared the great arching parabola of the fourth tier, its length marked with alternating sections of ocean and thicker bands of land.

Joe gripped her hand as they accelerated way from Calique.

# 6

Sereth fled into the rainforest, her only thought to escape Ehrin and the aliens.

He had changed. He had become someone else, a being Sereth no longer knew, as different to her as were the aliens. He had always been a little different, she knew, which perhaps was what had attracted her to him in the first place—but she wished she could have told the impressionable girl she had been back then, on first meeting the illustrious Ehrin Telsa, where her infatuation with him might lead.

The aliens, the minions of the anti-god, had turned his head with this illusory quest for the truth, and were leading him ever further astray. Now they were ascending to the fourth tier of this hell, to rendezvous with the evil creatures responsible for the creation of this illusion. That had been enough for Sereth, that and the fact that Ehrin had said that he had *loved* her. She felt the same for him—she had loved him, once, but no longer.

It would be better to be alone and lost in this forest than to be imprisoned with the aliens aboard their cursed spaceship bound for perdition.

She halted in her flight and looked about her.

Then she heard it, a roar she at first ascribed to a wild animal. Her heart skipped, before she realised the truth. The sound was the engine of the alien spaceship, a crescendo of noise that soon became deafening even at this distance. The ground seemed to shake beneath her feet, and the cacophony of the engines became the only reality. She fell to her knees and covered her ears, and dropped her hands only when the roar diminished. She listened until the sound died in the distance, and thought of Ehrin aboard the ship with the aliens and their doomed mission to meet the Builders. When she climbed to her feet, she realised that she was crying.

Through a gap in the foliage overhead she glimpsed a section of the helix. She was a long way from Agstarn, wherever that might be now. She felt a keen sense of loss, a longing to be in her father's apartment, to be surrounded by all that was familiar—the ice of the city, the reassuring grey skies—rather than this sultry forest and the dazzling sunlight that penetrated the foliage and irritated her eyes.

But this was all an illusion, she told herself, a mirage conjured to lead her from the truth.

But if that were so... If this *were* an illusion, if she were living a dream, then where in reality was she? In some limbo world of hallucination, instilled in her mind by the anti-god? Might she in fact still be in Agstarn, but tricked into believing she was elsewhere?

She touched the bark of a tree. It felt solid enough. The golden moss beneath her feet felt real. Perhaps she really was here, but that *here* was what was not really real. Perhaps *here* was what the anti-god had created to lure the unsuspecting away from God's one truth.

She didn't know which was the more frightening, that the illusion was in her head, or that this place was a creation of the anti-god.

But the creatures that inhabited this world? They had seemed, from what she could make of them from their actions, and from Carrelli's reports of what they had said, to be peaceable creatures, if deluded. If she could find them, then perhaps she might learn from them whether this world had substance in fact.

She set off in the direction she had seen them take.

Even as she went, scampering through the golden forest, a part of her was aware of the flaw in her reasoning. How might she petition the truth from a race of beings who might themselves, unknowingly, be part of the illusion created to snare the pious? She pressed on regardless, wondering if it were only the desire for the company of others, whoever they might be, that made her seek the insect creatures.

After a short while, she realised that she was hungry and thirsty. She had not shared the fruit gathered by the aliens, although Ehrin had eaten without ill effect. Perhaps, if she found the silver insect beings, they might be able to provide her with something more substantial than fruit.

She stopped, listening. In the distance she thought she heard a snort, one of the grey creatures clearing its great proboscis. She set off in the direction of the sound, then stopped again to listen. This time she made out the laborious shuffle of the animals as they made their slow way through the forest, and seconds later she glimpsed the grey hide of a beast between the trees.

She surprised herself with her relief at coming across the caravan.

For a minute she ran alongside the procession, concealing herself behind the trees, and only when she drew near the first animal, carrying upon its back the spokesman of the silver insects, did she step from the cover and stare up at the alien.

It saw her and called something in its high impossible language, and the beast beneath it plodded to a halt. The being spoke to her, gesturing with a thin, stick-like arm.

She said, "I... I'm lost. I need food..." before realising the futility of her words.

The silver spokesman fluted something to the beings seated on the animals behind it, and they replied in kind. The spokesman blinked its huge pink eyes at her, then gestured to the place beside him high on the back of the animal.

For some reason she could not identify, though the alien was like nothing she had ever seen before, she did not feel threatened by him as she had by the other beings.

She accepted his invitation, and with difficulty scaled the flank of the animal and at last perched beside the spokesman.

He instructed his mount to proceed, and then turned and addressed her.

She gestured her incomprehension, opened her mouth to show her tongue and indicate that she intended no threat, and wondered how she might communicate to these aliens the essence of her plight.

They processed slowly through the forest. The alien talked almost continuously to her, indicating trees and bushes with its many-fingered hands, and Sereth could only make gestures that she hoped might convey that she was listening.

At one point, a couple of hours into the journey, the alien plucked a bunch of red berries from a shrub and offered them to Sereth. Despite her earlier caution, she took them. Her mouth watered at the very thought of eating, and though she was unaccustomed to berries—they were rare in the winter climes of Agstarn—she popped one into her mouth, and then another and another as she found their taste more than pleasing. They were sweet, like frosted-tubers, and soon she had consumed the entire bunch.

Shortly after that she began to feel drowsy, and then a great lethargy descended over her, a sensation that was not at all unpleasant and rendered her physically unable to move a muscle. Mentally, too, she was affected, filled with a strange euphoria that made light of the fact that she was experiencing an illusion, in the company of weird alien creatures, her future uncertain.

All she could appreciate was the languor that cushioned her, the strange beauty of the surrounding rainforest. Even the sudden thought, as she drifted into unconsciousness, that this might be another of the anti-god's ruses to beguile her and subvert her piety, did not trouble her as she thought it might.

Seconds later she was sleeping upon the back of the plodding beast.

She awoke instantly, alerted by the high whistle of the alien beside her.

She opened her eyes and stared about her. The sun was low on the horizon, where before it had been high. Had she slept for most of the day?

They were no longer in the forest, but climbing a narrow track up the side of a mountain that thrust itself vertically from the surrounding land. As they climbed, they rose above the level of the treetops, gaining a startling view of the green ocean of foliage stretching to the horizon, with the bright blue radiance of a river coiling sinuously into the distance.

Then all was darkness as they entered what appeared to be the mouth of a cave. Here, in the twilight gloom, the aliens descended their mounts and Sereth did the same, wondering where they might be taking her. The spokesman indicated ahead, and she made her way along a wide tunnel, which turned, eventually, into a flight of steps seemingly carved through the heart of the rock.

Burning torches illuminated the way, casting flickering shadows across the black walls. The steps were tiny, made for feet much smaller than hers, and she had difficulty climbing. She found it best if she proceeded on all fours, gaining speed and safety this way.

The light increased, and she looked up to see that the stairs terminated in a great dazzle of sunlight. She slitted her eyes and climbed, at last coming to the top of the carved stairway and standing.

She looked around, her eyes adjusting to the glare, as the spokesman and the other aliens emerged from the mountain and gathered around her.

She had had no idea what to expect when she came out into the sunlight, and at first she doubted the evidence of her eyes.

She was standing on a level section of the mountainside, perhaps as wide as a square in Agstarn city. But this was not what caused her to stare in wonder and disbelief.

Standing before her was the reassuringly familiar figure of Elder Velkor Cannak.

Her heart swelled with sudden joy, and then she experienced confusion. Perhaps this was yet another illusion, sent down to plague her sanity.

The Elder advanced, arms outstretched, and Sereth found herself rushing towards him. He held her, and she luxuriated in his familiarity, the heady scent of his fur, his reassuring words after the high warblings of the aliens.

"I... I was taken, Elder. The great alien took me! I wanted nothing to do with their scheme."

Cannak worked to soothe her. "Child, child, I know. You are blameless. We are beset by evil working against all that is right and good. But, as we know, the truth will prevail."

She drew her head away from him and gazed at his smiling face, feeling tears welling in her eyes.

Behind him, she made out others of her kind, Church militia in familiar uniforms—and behind them, perched upon the mountain greensward, a great, black ship.

"Where are we, Elder? What is this place?" She indicated the mountain, and then pointed to the spectacular sweep of the helix high above. It dominated the heavens like an abomination, where by all that was right a grey pall should exist.

"The dwelling place of evil creations, my child." He took her shoulders. "Worry not, for the end is in sight. When we trace Ehrin and the alien interlopers, and bring them to justice, then we will return to Agstarn and all that is good." He looked into her eyes. "Where are they, child? Do they conceal themselves in this unholy forest?"

She shook her head. "They left this world in their ship, many hours ago."

Cannak snapped a command to one of the militia to power up the ship and ready it for immediate departure, then turned to Sereth. "Do you know, child, where they were bound?"

She felt her heart swell with joy, and something else. She would be instrumental in bringing an end to Ehrin's misguided quest; she felt the delight of revenge as she said, "They are bound for the world above this one, Elder Cannak. They intend to locate the beings they think created this evil illusion."

Cannak's grip tightened on her shoulder. "*Directly* above this one, on the fourth tier? Are you sure of this?"

She nodded. "They told me. One of the aliens, the one that spoke our language. It discovered where the Builders dwelt, and they set off to their world."

Cannak barked a laugh and reported Sereth's words to a uniformed militiaman. Then he turned to Sereth and said. "Board the ship. Settle yourself for the journey. Soon, child, thanks to you, we will make Ehrin and his followers see the error of their ways."

She hurried across the grass towards the ramp of the ship, hearing Elder Cannak bark instructions to the militia. At this she stopped and turned. "Elder?"

She looked past him at the small, silver insectile aliens who had gathered on the margin of the sward and were staring at the visitors with their innocent pink eyes.

Cannak said, "They are an ungodly illusion, my child. Is it not written that all who oppose the one truth shall perish?"

She turned and hurried towards the ship, and on reaching the ramp cast one glance back at the militia and the tiny aliens. Her people were drawing their rifles, and taking aim, and she saw the spokesman of the aliens step forward and address the leading militiaman.

Elder Cannak gave the order to fire, and the militia swept their spitting weapons across the phalanx of twittering insects, and she saw the spokesman raise his arms in what might have been a defiant gesture, or one of joy at his ascension. The aliens fell, then, and all was silent.

Sereth hurried into the ship, recalling the Elder's words of justification, and wondered what punishment might in time be meted out to Ehrin and the other godless aliens.

## ELEVEN /// PILGRIMAGE

HENDRY HAD OFTEN thought that there was no finer sight than planet Earth as seen from high orbit, the vast orb reflecting the light of the sun and the features of the planet, familiar after a hundred shuttle runs, spread out silent and serene far below. But he had to admit that the view of the fourth tier of the helix, the string of worlds demarcated by sections of glittering oceans, would take some beating.

They had travelled for half a day through vacuum, not once entering the darkness of space. Now they approached the fourth tier, the sun just visible above the parabola of worlds before them.

The comparison with Earth inevitably dragged Hendry's thoughts back to the time he had returned home after a long shift, to pick Chrissie up from boarding school in France and spend precious time with her before duty dragged him away again. They had been the best times of his life; simple days spent laughing with his daughter, watching the changed child she had become in the weeks he had been away and marvelling at his fortune in having her.

Before melancholy set in, he felt Sissy squeeze his hand and he was catapulted back to the present. She was smiling at him, her expression almost daring him to dwell on his loss.

He recalled his conversation in the clearing with Friday Olembe, and wondered what his brother had done to make Sissy hate him with such a vengeance. If, that was, he had surmised correctly in thinking that they must have encountered each other at university in LA in '83.

He would find some opportune time in the days ahead and ask her, and find some way of telling her that her vitriol was misplaced, that Friday was innocent. For the sake of the mission, as well as for their own sakes, a line had to be drawn under their hostility.

He smiled at her and enjoyed the show through the forward viewscreen.

A while later, just as Hendry was beginning to doze, Carrelli swore.

Olembe glanced across at her from the co-pilot's couch. "What?"

"We're being followed. The ship's not visible, but I'm picking up its signature. I guess it's around six hours behind us, and closing fast."

"How long before we reach the fourth tier?"

"I estimate... around two hours."

Kaluchek leaned forward, restrained by her harness. "What do we do?"

Carrelli shook her head grimly. "There's very little we can do but continue onwards."

Olembe glanced at her. "The ship's armed. We could make a fight of it if they get any closer."

Carrelli looked at him. "I'm not familiar with the operating system, Friday."

He grinned. "What do you think I was doing while you were enjoying your jaunt in the forest back there? I'm pretty sure I could give the bastards a shock or two."

Carrelli thought about it, then said, "Only as a very last resort, Friday. Only if there's no other option. We don't know our weapon's capability. We might be committing suicide if we open fire."

Olembe nodded. "Agreed. Only as a last resort."

Carrelli turned to Ehrin and relayed the gist of the information to the alien, who hung in his harness and stared at her with his huge, inscrutable eyes, his mouth open in what Hendry had come to interpret as apprehension.

Carrelli looked back at Hendry and Kaluchek and said, "As a precaution, I'm not heading for the Builder's world. I'm sure they can look after themselves, but I'm not taking the risk."

"What's the plan?" Kaluchek asked.

"We land on the neighbouring world and hide up for a while. Only when we think the danger has passed, and the Church's ship has given up its search, do we proceed." She looked round the small group. "Does that make sense?"

Hendry nodded. "Sounds fine to me."

Olembe agreed. Kaluchek said, "It isn't as if we're in any rush."

Carrelli told Ehrin of her plan, and he responded with a single, sharp bark.

"That's agreed, then," she said, and stared at the rapidly approaching band of worlds strung out before them.

Hendry glanced across at Sissy. She was staring through the viewscreen. He saw her as she was in the forest clearing, two days ago, naked and smiling at him with love and abandon. He closed his eyes, never fully sleeping but drifting in and out of semi-consciousness as the ship roared through the void.

A diminuendo in the pitch of the engine brought him upright with a start. Sissy was yawning, stretching her arms. Carrelli and Olembe were muttering between themselves.

The architectural immensity of the helix was no longer visible through the viewscreen. All that could be seen was land, over which they were flying at speed. Hendry peered through a sidescreen, down at what looked like a mass of some kind of vegetation, though like none he had ever seen before. It thrashed, as if by its own volition or as if stirred by a fierce gale; individual strands, pale tendrils without leaves or branches, whipped back and forth. All was bathed in bright sunlight, and above the spaghetti-like vegetation were what looked like... he called them spinnakers, as they resembled the bellying sails on yachts he recalled from his youth, though these were vast diaphanous membranes pushed at incredible speeds by the prevailing winds.

Kaluchek said, "It's... *alien* down there," and laughed self-deprecatingly at the inadequacy of her description.

Hendry looked through the far sidescreen. They were lower now, and on the horizon to the right he made out the scintillating expanse of an ocean. Beyond which, he surmised, though not visible, was the world of the Builders.

Carrelli said, "Okay, we'll attempt to bring the ship down on the coast, in the cover of whatever those things are down there."

"Is the Church ship still following?" Kaluchek asked.

"It was until an hour ago, when we passed round the light side of the world. I cut the main drive around then. With luck, it'll have difficulty tracing us. And if we can conceal the ship from view... Anyway, here goes. You ready, Friday? Careful now, dampen the auxiliaries by half and ease her down."

Hendry watched the writhing mass of etiolated tendrils dance back and forth, as if trying to grab the ship. Only now, with the vessel coming down along the coast and the tendrils waving high above them and to their left, could he fully appreciate their height. They towered over the ship by a hundred metres, each one as thick as the bole of an oak, only supple and terminating in what looked like a mass of smaller, equally agitated tendrils. This world made the forest of Calique seem positively homely.

Carrelli reported, "Telemetry says that it's another breathable atmosphere down there, though the gravity's lighter."

"Wonder what kind of crazy aliens live on this world?" Olembe said.

Carrelli pointed through a sidescreen. "Perhaps that's your answer."

She indicated one of the spinnakers Hendry had seen earlier, a vast bellying sheet heading out to sea.

"You think that's sentient?" Olembe asked.

"Who knows?" Carrelli said. "We're on a helix containing ten thousand-plus worlds. Anything might be possible."

In seconds they crossed the terminator, twilight coming down almost instantly. Stars appeared in the night sky above, and for a second Hendry could imagine he was back on Earth, watching the stars from his seat outside the old Mars shuttle—until he saw the waving fronds temporarily occluding the unfamiliar constellations.

"Hold on," Carrelli said. "We're coming in to land. This might be..."

They hit the ground with an extended squeal of metal on what might have been rock, the ship slewing like a tea tray on ice. Hendry saw a mass of pale boles rushing towards the viewscreen, and then their forward momentum was halted abruptly as they sheared through the vegetation. The ship came to a halt, while tendrils came down around them like felled trees. The ship rocked under the impact, then settled. Silence descended.

Hendry looked out through a sidescreen. The sea was perhaps a hundred metres away, through a vista of rocking tendrils, dappled and lapping quietly in the starlight. Above the ocean, the spinnaker things drifted with the wind, eerie and majestic.

Olembe unfastened himself from the couch, stood and stretched, peering through the screen on three sides. "We couldn't have concealed ourselves better, Gina. We're almost surrounded by the tendrils."

Carrelli said, "I stocked up on fruit back there. Help yourselves. I don't know about you, but I'm tired."

Kaluchek slipped from her couch. "I found some bunks back there," she said, grinning at Hendry. She took his hand and tugged him along the corridor to the rear lounge, closed the door behind them and turned to him.

"Do you think we're safe in here, or will the others come barging in?"

He laughed. "I think they might guess what we're up to."

"Oh, and what's that?"

But her arch innocence was betrayed by her haste to get out of her atmosphere suit, and seconds later she was naked and in his arms.

They made love in the sunken bunker, with the thick boles of the tendril plants a matter of metres from the viewscreen. This low to the ground, the tendrils swayed hypnotically, though Hendry was only minimally aware of the fact as Sissy straddled him and eased herself down with a moan.

Later, arms about each other, they slept.

When they awoke, almost simultaneously, a couple of hours later, Kaluchek grabbed his arm and said, "Look, Joe…"

Something in her tone alarmed him. Disoriented, he struggled upright and stared through the viewscreen.

What looked for all the world like a tree-frog, but the size of a ten-year-old child, was suckered to the screen and staring in at them.

# 2

HENDRY DRESSED QUICKLY and followed Kaluchek from the lounge to the flight-deck. "We've got company—" she began.

Olembe turned to her. "We've noticed." He indicated the forward viewscreen, which was plastered with the emerald green, pot-bellied creatures.

Carrelli was in her couch, staring up at the screen. "We haven't seen the Church ship since the first sighting," she said. "I suggest we just sit it out and bide our time."

"For how long, Gina?" Kaluchek asked. "I mean, they're persistent. They'll orbit the planet, waiting for us to make a move. And when we do..."

Hendry said, "How long can we wait it out? How long will the fruit last us? And we don't know if there's anything edible on this world."

Gina looked at him. "I'll go out and scout around."

Olembe gestured to the reptiles stuck to the viewscreen. "With our green friends out there showing such interest?"

Gina regarded the creatures. "Well, they look harmless enough."

"So did the lemurs at first glance," Olembe said. "Sorry, Ehrin."

If the alien heard his name, he gave no indication, just remained staring through the screen at the underbellies of the tree-frog analogues.

Carrelli rolled from the pilot's couch, stood and approached the viewscreen. She remained watching one of the creatures for a minute as it stared in at her with bulbous, unblinking eyes. Then she reached out and placed her palm flat against the surface of the screen, perhaps half a metre to the alien's left.

Seconds later the creature moved, adjusted its stance on the glass with a glutinous unpeeling of its suckers, and matched Carrelli's gesture, placing its thin-fingered paw against the outside of the viewscreen in a mirror image gesture.

Carrelli looked back at them. "I know it isn't proof positive, but I think that suggests some level of sentience."

Hendry stared at the nearest creature's eyes, watching him. He counted at least a dozen frogs decorating the viewscreen now, and more were appearing all the time to stare in at the strange new arrivals.

"I agree with you, Gina," Kaluchek said. "They don't look aggressive to me." She looked across at Olembe, challenging him.

He said, "So you're volunteering to go outside?"

Hendry said, surprising himself, "I'll go. You said the atmosphere's breathable, Gina?"

She nodded. "Be careful. Take a weapon."

"I'll forage around for anything that might look edible."

Olembe handed Hendry the blaster. Kaluchek said, "I'm coming with you."

He didn't argue. "We'll be back in five minutes. We'll try not to stray far from the ship."

"If possible, stay within sight," Gina said, reaching up to the controls and opening the hatch.

Hendry passed down the corridor, Kaluchek behind him, and paused on the threshold. The first thing he noticed was the temperature, a sultry gust of heat that hit him like a wave. The air was moist and freighted with a rich cloying scent, not unlike rotting vegetation, though not so unpleasant.

Then he heard the wind, a high musical sound as it soughed through the swaying vegetation.

He looked along the length of the ship, noting at least fifty frog creatures adhered to the carapace. They were stuck fast, it seemed, anchored against the high wind.

He glanced at Kaluchek and she nodded.

He stepped from the ship onto loamy topsoil, which gave a little beneath his feet. The wind tugged at him, its warmth reminding him of Melbourne's north winds in his youth.

Kaluchek touched his arm and said, "Look, aren't they beautiful?"

He followed her gaze upwards. A flotilla of the spinnakers he had seen earlier sailed overhead and passed out to sea, vast and silent as they rode the winds.

Hendry turned and regarded the closest creature clinging to the ship. As if in response, it moved itself, one suckered foot at a time, to face him. It blinked, turned its head to Kaluchek and belched.

At least, it seemed like a belch, though Hendry doubted this when the creature repeated the sound and continued with variations, like some kind of laryngeal bassoon.

Kaluchek gripped his upper arm. "Christ, Joe, is it trying to communicate?"

Hendry looked up, movement alerting him. The other creatures adorning the ship had moved to stare down at the interlopers.

The first creature turned its head and belched to its neighbour.

"I wonder if Carrelli can talk tree-frog," Kaluchek said.

"I don't doubt it," Hendry replied, looking around at the phalanx of thick stalks that hemmed the ship on three sides. He gestured to Kaluchek and they moved along the length of the ship, drawing alongside the forward viewscreen. He could see Carrelli peering out at them from between the mosaic of frogs.

He gestured to the closest vegetation and set off with Kaluchek, aware that an audience of curious frogs was watching his every move.

He examined the tendrils. They were soft, fibrous, and those lopped by the nose of the ship were oozing a sickly pale ichor. He looked around, but the floor of the forest was notable for its absence of anything else resembling vegetation.

"I wonder if the tendrils are edible?" he asked Kaluchek.

"Let's take some back and see what Carrelli makes of it."

He selected a tendril damaged by the landing, breaking off a long strip of the pulpy fibre. He didn't envy Carrelli her tasting session.

They returned to the hatch, watched every step of the way by the curious natives. Once inside they hurried down the corridor to the flight-deck. This time human eyes turned on them, expectantly. Hendry deposited the section of unappetising tendril on the couch. "The bad news is that this is the only stuff that looks remotely edible," he began.

"And the good news?" Olembe asked.

"The natives are friendly, or at least seem to be. One even spoke to me."

"Well," Kaluchek said, "it belched."

Carrelli turned and stared at the frogs on the viewscreen. "I'm going out there. Anybody else?"

Olembe grunted a laugh. "This I must see. Gina in conversation with a frog."

Carrelli looked at the lump of tendril on the couch. She broke off a piece and sniffed it, then experimentally slipped it into her mouth and chewed. She kept her expression neutral and reported, "It has the texture of overcooked pasta."

"And the taste?" Kaluchek asked.

"The taste of... it's difficult. Maybe sweet seaweed with an unpleasantly bitter afternote."

"You'll make a great restaurant critic," Olembe said, "when the colony's up and running."

"But is it edible?" Hendry asked. The thought of living off the tendrils for who knew how long didn't exactly appeal to him.

Carrelli shook her head. "I'll tell you in five minutes," she said. "Okay, let's see what these creatures have to say for themselves."

She led the way down the corridor, Hendry following her with Kaluchek and Olembe bringing up the rear. Ehrin, Hendry noticed, remained inside, watching them through the sidescreen.

Carrelli stepped cautiously from the hatch. Hendry and the others joined her. Perhaps a hundred frogs clung to the ship now, watching them. Hendry indicated the frog that had addressed him; at least, he thought it was the same creature. They were, to the untutored eye, very much alike.

Carrelli stepped forward and lifted a hand. The alien blinked at her. Seconds later, it gave vent to a rumbling series of eructations.

Carrelli bent her head, frowning. The alien fell silent and remained watching her closely. She looked at Hendry and shook her head. "The smart-ware's having difficulty with this one. It's a language, but so tonal it's almost impossible to decipher."

She smiled to herself. "Well, I'm getting something. Fragments. The creatures are curious. What are we doing here? It... it asked a question. There's a word that translates as pilgrimage. I think they want to know if we're embarking on a pilgrimage."

"Christ," Olembe said. "Religious frogs now."

Carrelli dragged a sleeve across her sweating brow. "Pilgrimage? Quest? Trek? I don't know... maybe vital journey is closer to what it means."

"Ask it if it can be more specific," Kaluchek said.

Carrelli nodded and stepped forward. She opened her mouth. Hendry thought that the few sounds that emerged did not quite have the resonance of the native's pronouncement, but they were a pretty impressive approximation.

She said, "I've asked what it means by pilgrimage, and to where."

The creature responded. Carrelli listened attentively, head bent close. When the alien fell silent, she straightened up, frustrated. "Something about across the divide. They are to go by... it used a specific word, a noun, which is meaningless to the smartware program. I'll try again."

Overcome by the cloying heat, Hendry sat down on the loam, leaning back against a truncated stump of tendril and watching Carrelli attempt to communicate with the frog-like extraterrestrial.

The alien speaker was joined by others now, an echelon of beings determined, it seemed, to aid her understanding. They belched in relay, as if explaining or amplifying their cousin's pronouncements.

At a lull in the chorus, Carrelli turned to the others with an excited expression.

"What?" Kaluchek said.

"The noun... it refers to the sail-like membranes." She pointed out to sea, where the spinnakers, silver ellipses highlighted in the illumination of the stars, floated serenely on the high winds.

"With first light, the rising of the sun... the creatures here will summon the... the sails... and ride them to the other land... except it's not the other land, but something greater, more important, the hallowed land, maybe. They ride to the hallowed land once in a lifetime."

The alien spoke again, and Carrelli's eyes widened and she laughed aloud. She turned to the others. "They will soon be embarking on a pilgrimage to pay their respects, give their thanks, to the Guardians."

"The Guardians?" Hendry echoed.

"They are not materialistic creatures," Carrelli reported. "They have no concept of the word 'build', and so don't employ the word Builders. Their Guardians are our Builders."

"Jesus Christ," Olembe muttered under his breath.

Carrelli paled suddenly. She turned and hurried towards the ship's entrance, then doubled up before she made it and vomited her meal of tendril across the loamy ground.

Olembe said, "I guess that answers one question, friends. The local delicacy isn't for us."

Kaluchek hurried across to Carrelli and assisted her in to the ship. Olembe followed and Hendry sealed the hatch after them. Behind him, the assembly of aliens had set up a continuous croak as if in humorous comment.

On the flight-deck, Carrelli lay back on the couch and mopped her brow. "I'll be fine, Sissy. The augments filter the toxins, so they won't poison me. It's just unfortunate that they can't filter the bulk of the tendril." She smiled. "There is still only one wholly efficient means of doing that."

Hendry said, into the following silence, "The natives asked you if we were going on the pilgrimage." He paused, looked around the group. "Does that suggest to you that they expected us to use the sails to do so?"

Carrelli nodded. "That's the impression I received, Joe."

Kaluchek shook her head. "But would it be possible? I mean… how the hell would we go about it? They said something about summoning the sails…"

Carrelli said, "If they could do that for us—"

"Hey," Olembe said, holding up both hands. "So we go sailing off into the sunset with the vague hope of arriving on the other side of the ocean...? I think I'd rather take my chances with the bad food here and the Church ship, thanks."

Hendry thought of sailing over the ocean on a membrane...

Carrelli was saying, "They have control over the sails. I surmise it's some kind of empathic link with the creatures."

"The creatures?" Kaluchek cut in.

"The sails are alive," Carrelli said. "Animals. The aliens... they call themselves the Ho-lah-lee... control them, ride them. Continually, groups of Ho-lah-lee ride the sails across the ocean to pay respects to the Guardians."

Kaluchek said, "If we could ride the sails... that'd be the answer, wouldn't it? I mean, the rats on the Church ship won't be looking for us aboard the sails, will they?"

"Hold on. Let's think abut this." Olembe looked around the group. "Okay, it's one option. But there's the danger involved, right? Accidents, for Chrissake. What if... I don't know... what if the sail we rode in came down in the ocean? They're animals, right? What if one died mid-flight, what then? We'd be dead and the colonists back at the *Lovelock* would be in the same position we were in when we landed. We owe it to them to be cautious."

Carrelli nodded. "Friday's right." She thought about it. "The obvious answer would be to split up. Some of us go with the sails, if that's possible, while someone stays with the ship."

Olembe nodded. "I can fly this thing. I know how it works. I volunteer to stay here. Keep in radio contact, and if you don't make it—"

Hendry said, "And what if the Church ship's monitoring for radio signals?"

Carrelli said, "We'll contact you only in the event of an emergency, okay?" She looked across at the African.

Olembe nodded. "Fine by me."

Carrelli turned to Hendry and Kaluchek. "How about it?"

"I want to sail over the ocean," Hendry said. "I wouldn't miss it for the world."

Kaluchek nodded. "I'll second that."

Carrelli turned to Ehrin and explained the situation, and in due course the alien replied. Carrelli smiled. "Ehrin's coming too. Okay, I'll go out there and see if we can hitch a ride."

Hendry watched her go, wondering what the alternative would be if, for some reason, they were unable to sail the spinnakers. He put the question to Kaluchek and Olembe.

The African shrugged. "Then we sit tight and wait, and at some point try to make it across the ocean in the ship."

"And just hope the Church ship isn't in the area," Hendry said.

"Jesus," Kaluchek said, "I'd rather take my chances with the sails."

Hendry moved to the viewscreen. Its extraterrestrial patterning had diminished now as more of the creatures moved off to join their fellows in conversation with Carrelli. She stood beside the ship, backed by the ocean, and addressed the phalanx of alien amphibians.

Hendry was aware of his heartbeat as he watched. Their future, he knew, depended on what happened over the next few minutes. Kaluchek joined him and placed a hand on the small of his back.

Carrelli's audience came to an end. She inclined her head, lifted a valedictory hand and moved back to the hatch.

Kaluchek prayed quietly under her breath. They turned to face the corridor.

Seconds later Carrelli entered, smiling. "It's on," she said. "The Ho-lah-lee will summon a sail for us. We set off at sunrise."

# 3

THE SEA WAS blood red. The sun, rising at a right angle to the ocean, filled the dawn sky with coppery light.

Hendry stepped from the ship and paused in wonder at the view. The light was incredible, illuminating the scene before the ship. More than a hundred Ho-lah-lee had assembled on the foreshore. They stood upright on the littoral loam and in the shallows, gazing out to sea in a silence he guessed must be part of some ritual obeisance. One or two raised their arms, and after a minute a concerted sound issued from the creatures, a bass note that for some odd reason struck him as profoundly moving.

He walked with Kaluchek to the edge of the sea, Carrelli and Ehrin close behind. Olembe stood on the ramp of the ship, watching them.

A Ho-lah-lee moved from the mass of creatures at the water's edge and spoke to Carrelli. She replied, then turned to Hendry and Kaluchek. "They will now perform the ritual of the summoning. Many of them are embarking on the pilgrimage today. We must wait our turn."

As if at a silent signal, the assembled Ho-lah-lee raised their arms as one, and another silence descended upon the gathering. Hendry looked into the sky. Directly above, the tendrils waved in the wind, great lazy sweeps that seemed, because of their great height, retarded like the ebb and flow of marine flora.

"Look," Kaluchek whispered, pointing.

High above the tendrils, Hendry saw the first sail. It drifted in over the vegetation, then descended suddenly and with slow majesty. It was, he saw, vast—perhaps a hundred metres high and almost as wide. On closer inspection it appeared silver, though the tendrils could be seen through its membrane as if through an opaque lens. It was, he thought, the strangest animal he had ever witnessed.

The sail came in low over the shallows, then slowed itself by some unknown feat of aerodynamics and paused long enough for a dozen Ho-lah-lee to scramble aboard. They climbed up the concave inner curve of the sail, and seemed to hang suspended as the sail took off again, allowing the wind to waft it out to sea and higher into the air. Soon it was a rapidly dwindling speck against the brightening sky.

"And there's another, and another..."

They were coming in threes and fours now, a slow procession of the incredible extraterrestrial beings, dipping over the tendrils and slowing above the shallows. Little by little the crowd of Ho-lah-lee diminished as they climbed aboard and took off on their once-in-a-lifetime pilgrimage.

A Ho-lah-lee approached Carrelli and spoke to her. She translated. "The next sail is for us. According to the Ho-lah-lee, it is an ancient sail, which has made the journey a thousand times before. It will be honoured to convey us to the hallowed land."

Hendry turned and watched a great sail dip over the tendrils, its bellying curve catching the sunlight in a rouge filament like a sickle. It swept in low, slowing and coming to a halt a few metres from them. The Ho-lah-lee spoke again and Carrelli said, "We simply climb aboard and the sail will do the rest. Don't climb too high, though, or we'll be in danger of tipping the creature."

As the closest to the sail, Hendry waded into the shallows and climbed aboard, turning to help Kaluchek after him. The membrane gave beneath his feet, like the surface of a slack trampoline, and he wallowed for a few paces before coming to the concave inner sweep of the curious creature. He reached out, and was amazed to find that his palms adhered to the diaphanous surface as if glued—and yet he was able to pull his hands away with ease. He climbed, then turned and found himself supported by the membrane. He lay back as if in a hammock and watched Kaluchek ascending until she was beside him. Carrelli came next, followed by Ehrin, and they settled further down the curve. Last of all came two Ho-lah-lee, who laid their heads against the membrane and closed their eyes as the sail rose and moved away from the shore.

The sail climbed, and the land sank away beneath them. The ship became ever smaller—Olembe on the ramp a tiny stick figure, waving a hand in the air—until it was a golden sliver almost lost amid the tendrils that crowded the foreshore.

They rose rapidly, their ascent dizzying, in total silence. Hendry recalled a balloon ride in his youth, and his amazement at the lack of noise. As was the case then, now they were moving with the wavefront of the wind: the only sound was Kaluchek beside him, laughing to herself in exhilaration.

He scanned the skies for any sign of the Church ship. The heavens above the tendril forest were a cloudless bright blue, a shade deeper than any sky on Earth. All that could be seen in the depthless blue were a hundred elliptical specks as the sails headed out to sea.

He examined the surface of the sail. It appeared to be a jelly-like substance, shot through with tiny silver filaments like veins. He craned his neck, straining to see to the top edge of the creature, but he could detect no evidence of sensory organs, or a knot in the flesh that might denote the locus of a cortex. He reminded himself that his was an alien creature, a very alien creature, and he would be foolish to expect its physiology to conform to terrestrial norms.

They were rising all the time. The ocean glittered below, and the land they had left was on the horizon now, a fringe of waving tendrils that seemed kilometres distant. Hendry looked left and right, and made out a flotilla of a dozen nearby sails, all bearing their cargo of tiny frog-like Ho-lah-lee. He wondered how many years this had been going on, and what form their pilgrimage took when they reached journey's end.

Journey's end... He doubted it would be his journey's end, but merely a stage upon the way. The thought of returning to the first tier for the colonists, having to avoid the lemur militia and any other dangers that might be lurking, filled him with apprehension. There was a long way to go before that, though: the finding of a suitable, empty world, the planning of how best to go about ferrying the colonists up the tiers...

Kaluchek reached out and touched his arm. "What are you thinking, Joe?"

He smiled. "Journey's end," he said. "But we've really only just begun."

"It's as if we've been travelling for ages," she said. "I'm tired. I want to settle down, start the colony."

He looked at her, at the beautiful woman he was coming to love, and wondered at the secrets hidden behind her open, smiling face. He wondered how someone so loving could harbour so much hate. What had happened all those years ago in LA, between the man who had been Friday Olembe and herself?

"Sissy..."

She looked up at him, smiling radiantly. "Mmm?"

He reached out and knuckled her cheek. "What happened?" he asked.

Her eyes narrowed. "I don't..."

"At university in LA. You met... Friday Olembe, right? What happened?"

She stared at him, her expression mystified, and he wondered suddenly if he'd got it horribly wrong. Then she said, "How do you know?"

"I don't. That is, I know something happened— to make you feel the way you do towards Friday. But I don't know exactly what."

She looked away, shaking her head, pain in her eyes.

"You don't have to tell me, Sissy. If it's too… if it's something you don't want to share. But," he paused, wondering how to phrase what he had to tell her, "but I think there's something you should know about Friday."

She stared at him. "I know all I need to know!" she said with a flare of anger. "I know what he did to me, how he, how…"

Her face collapsed, her mouth pulled into a pained rictus, and she was crying, sobbing silently. He reached out and cradled her in his arms, rocking her. "Sissy, listen to me, I need to tell you… You've got to know."

She looked up, shaking her head. "What?"

"It wasn't Friday," he said, then corrected himself, "That is, it wasn't the man we know as Friday Olembe."

She pulled away, eyes wide, as if accusing him of some terrible complicity with the man who had destroyed her life all those years ago. "Sissy, he took the identity of Friday Olembe a year ago. Friday was his brother, a nuclear engineer like himself, but who studied at LA in the eighties, while you were there."

"Olembe told you this?"

He nodded. "I asked him about his past. I wanted to know if he really was responsible for the war crimes, as you claimed. I questioned him. He took it the wrong way, told me about the crime he *had* committed, in taking his brother's identity."

She shook her head. "I don't understand."

So he told her about the shooting accident, and Friday Olembe's call up from the ESO, and how his brother had seen the opportunity to steal his identity.

"And you believe him?" Kaluchek asked.

Hendry nodded. "He was telling the truth, Sissy."
He shrugged. "Anyway, I put two and two together, realised something must have happened between
you and Friday's brother back in LA."

"Something *happened*? Christ, do you want to
know what *happened*? The bastard raped me. I was
eighteen. A virgin. He *raped* me!"

"It's okay. It's over. That was a long time ago."
He held her.

"And you try to tell me that it wasn't Olembe!
The man I've been hating all these years, been planning to destroy... Christ, it kept me going, Joe. I
dreamed of the day I'd finally get even with the bastard! And now you're trying to tell me..."

"Sissy, Sissy... It's no good hating. It doesn't help
you! It destroys—"

She spat at him, "What do you know about
hatred, Joe!"

He stroked her cheek. "I hated, Sissy. I hated
Su for leaving me, leaving me and Chrissie. And
leaving us for some crackpot terrorist organisation. I hated her with all my strength. And do
you know something? It didn't make me a very
nice person. Hate corrodes. It corrupts the good
person you could become if you release the
hatred, let go, look ahead and learn to live
again."

She was sobbing on his shoulder now. "But he
hurt me so much, Joe. The bastard took so much
away from me and almost killed me in *here*!"

"I know, I know. But you've got to let go."

"I dreamed of the day I'd take revenge on him.
Nothing else mattered."

"You were imprisoned in the past, fantasising about a future act that could never be as satisfying as the dream."

She stared at him. "I never got that revenge, Joe. It... it feels like something's missing."

"Sissy, Friday Olembe died a thousand years ago, in the shooting accident in Nigeria. He got what he deserved."

"But he never knew the pain he caused me!"

He stroked her cheek. "Who knows? Perhaps he did. He had plenty of time to look back and regret." He shook has head. "But that doesn't matter now. All that's in the past. Put it behind you. Look ahead." He smiled. "You have me, if that's any compensation."

She smiled through her tears. "You're a good man. Joe, I love you so much."

He held her.

She looked up at him. "And Friday. I've spent so much time hating him... I don't think I could stop, just like that. And he is the brother of the man who—"

"You can't hold him responsible for his brother's crimes, Sissy."

She murmured, "I know that, Joe."

"You have to try to stop feeling the hate, okay? Later, when all this is over, tell him what happened. Apologise." He smiled, to forestall her protests. "You'll feel better if you do, okay?"

She shook her head, her gaze distant. "I don't know, Joe. I need to think about it," she said in a small voice.

He hugged her to him and kissed the top of her head.

A little later she said, "Tell me what happened in Africa, Joe, when Friday's brother was shot..."

They rode on, and he told her Olembe's story from the beginning. She listened in silence, reliving the death of the man she had hated for so long.

Hendry held her and watched an armada of sails waft through the clear blue sky.

Later, she rooted about in the pouch of her atmosphere suit and pulled out a handful of squashed berries. "I saved these for a rainy day," she said quietly. "They're... well, I don't really know what they are, but they knock you out, put you under." She smiled at him. "I could do with that right now."

Hendry looked back in the direction they had come. The coastline had vanished. He twisted around and stared through the blurred lens of the membrane. The sea stretched ahead for as far as the eye could see. He wondered how much longer the journey might last.

"Try some?" Kaluchek asked, proffering the berries.

He smiled and nodded, and allowed her to feed him the sweet mush. She ate the rest, and leaned against his chest, and minutes later Hendry felt himself drifting off, his thoughts becoming fuzzy, his body relaxing.

In his dreams he was with Chrissie, except that she was not Chrissie but Sissy... At least, some of the time she was Chrissie, at others she was his small Inuit lover. Their identities morphed, segueing from one to the other. Then, as he dreamed that he was making love to the strange hybrid, he was pierced by a shaft of guilt that brought him awake, crying out loud.

He sat up, trying to pull himself away from the membrane, then recalled where he was and slumped back. Sissy was curled beside him, sleeping. He felt the residuum of the guilt sluice from his consciousness, and wondered why he was torturing himself like this. He smiled; the answer was obvious, really. He had never really got over the guilt at Su's leaving him. He'd told himself that it had been his fault she had left, depriving Chrissie of a mother. Now Chrissie was dead and he was in love with someone very much like her, and by extension someone very much like her mother.

He shut off that line of reasoning and watched Carrelli climb carefully up the concave inner surface of the membrane to join them. Ehrin came too, nestling beside the Italian and watching her with its large eyes.

"You've been asleep for hours, Joe."

He indicated the berry juice staining his fingers. "Thanks to Sissy."

"We've almost crossed the ocean."

He turned and peered through the membrane. Far below he made out the long gentle curve of a shoreline, surprisingly normal after the tendrilled coast they had left. This one was a stretch of what might have been golden sand, backed by undulating green plains and, further inland, foothills rising gradually to a distant mountain range.

"Look," Carrelli said, indicating the sky all around them.

Where before there had been perhaps twenty sails floating across the ocean, now the air was filled with them. Hendry counted fifty before giving up. The closest was perhaps a dozen metres from their own sail, a vast lens carrying its cargo of tiny Ho-lah-lee; others sailed high on either hand, hundreds of them diminishing in perspective to tiny silver parings.

"Convergence," Carrelli said. "We can't be far from the place of pilgrimage, wherever the Builders—or the Guardians—make their base."

Beside him, Kaluchek stirred to wakefulness. Hendry relayed what Carrelli had said. She stretched and yawned. "I hope we won't be disappointed," she said. "I mean, what if the Builders aren't at home, or don't want to see us?"

Carrelli smiled. "I think the very sight of where they dwell will be amazing enough, even if we don't find out anything about them." She gestured at the converging sails. "It's enough of an attraction to bring the Ho-lah-lee in their thousands, at any rate."

They were passing over the coastline now. Far below he could see the gentle lap of the ocean on the golden sands, for all the world like something from a terrestrial holovision programme.

Not so familiar, though, were the herds of animals grazing on the foreshore. They were long-legged and spindly, with tiny heads bearing a disproportionate array of ramified antlers.

Hendry looked ahead, through the membrane, for any sight of where the Builders might reside. The hills rolled on for what seemed like hundreds of kilometres, with not an artificial construction in sight.

Ehrin touched Carrelli's sleeve and spoke. She replied. For ten minutes they exchanged mysterious words in the abrupt, barking language. Hendry watched their faces for any sign of a familiar expression, but even Carrelli betrayed no emotion as she spoke, and Ehrin's furred snout and massive eyes conveyed nothing.

At last Carrelli turned to Hendry and Kaluchek and said, "Ehrin wants to bring the truth of the helix to his people. He says the Church has ruled with lies and cruelty for too long. He would like our help in bringing change to his world."

Kaluchek smiled. "How would we do that?"

Carrelli shrugged. "Perhaps it's not our place to get involved in the political struggle of other races. I don't know. We'd have to discuss that when the colony is set up, the legislature functioning."

"Perhaps tell him that we are all for the dissemination of the truth, and against the rule of tyranny," Hendry said, "and leave it at that."

Carrelli nodded. "I'll give him hope," she said, "without definite promises."

Hendry watched her relay the words to Ehrin, and wondered if the politicking had begun already, the mealy-mouthed compromises and half-truths that had been part of human interaction since time immemorial.

"Am I imagining it," Kaluchek said a short time later, "or are we losing height?"

Hendry gazed down. The land was closer now. The grazing animals, spooked by the arrival of the sails, started nervously and set off across the plain, the herd moving as one with the gestalt empathy of a shoal of fish.

Hendry turned and stared into the distance, and then saw it.

It stood in the distance on a plateau of land in the shadow of the mountain range, a towering ziggurat of perhaps fifty levels, its baroque bronze surface refulgent in the morning sun.

The sight of it filled his throat with an odd, choking emotion.

There could be no mistaking that this was their destination: all around the massed sails were converging, the leading sails settling to earth before the edifice, the Ho-lah-lee dismounting and prostrating themselves in euphoria at the climax of their pilgrimage.

Kaluchek gripped his arm. "Joe, Joe... isn't it beautiful?"

Hendry wondered why it was so affecting; it was simple, and vast, its rounded architecture was pleasing to the eye—and all this taken together, along with the knowledge of what it represented, made it a thing of wonder.

Kaluchek whispered, "What kind of beings would have made the helix, Joe?"

He shook his head. He could not imagine them physically—it was almost as if he dared not imagine the Builders incarnate for fear of being disappointed with the reality, if or when they revealed themselves. No creatures of flesh and blood, however impressive, could do justice to the immense achievement of the helix.

Their sail swept low over the plain, slowing as it went. To either side, sails came down and their Ho-lah-lee passengers alighted on the grass, gazing in awe—at least, that was how Hendry interpreted their goggle-eyed stares—at the towering immensity of the ziggurat before them.

Their sail slowed and came to a sedate halt. Hendry eased himself from the membrane's embrace and shuffled down the curve, jumping the last two metres to the grass and turning to assist Kaluchek, Carrelli and Ehrin. Then the sail rose like a curtain to reveal the bronze magnificence of the ziggurat.

For long minutes, all they could do was stand and stare in silence.

The Ho-lah-lee, thousands of them, were filing towards the ziggurat in a slow procession, heading for an arched entrance in the base block of the edifice and then passing silently inside.

Kaluchek took his hand and they began walking.

They were a hundred metres from the great entrance when Carrelli said, "Do you feel it, or is it only me?"

Kaluchek nodded. She put her fist to her lower chest. "Here."

Hendry felt it too. It was hard to describe—a kind of euphoria that filled his chest, a physical sensation like a wall of sound drumming against his diaphragm, only in silence. Power, he thought; some resonating power that communicated itself in some way from the Builders of the helix to its lowly inhabitants.

He wondered if this was how believers might feel in the presence of their god.

He was eager to see inside, over the heads of the massed Ho-lah-lee. The archway loomed, the interior shadowy. They came to the threshold, slowing as the press of aliens created a brief bottleneck, and then they were inside.

Hendry opened his mouth as he stared. He had had no idea what to expect, and might have been disappointed if merely told what he would behold when inside the ziggurat. But the reality was different, and staggering.

They were in a vast chamber, the greatest space he had ever experienced bounded by walls, and when he looked up, following the lead of the thousands of Ho-lah-lee before him, he saw that the rising levels of the ziggurat were hollow, creating a dizzying, diminishing perspective that seemed to rise to the stratosphere and beyond, to penetrate the very core of the universe.

But perhaps more moving still was the great bronze oval that stood in the centre of the chamber. It was perhaps fifty metres high, a perfect ovoid that throbbed with silent power; it seemed to thrum and throw at him an ineffable force, almost forcing him backwards, and yet at the same time drawing him forward in awe.

Before them, the Ho-lah-lee parted as if by some silent command, and the humans, accompanied by Ehrin, stepped towards the effulgent oval of bronze.

Hendry glanced at Kaluchek, surprised by her expression of mixed wonder and fear, though realising that these emotions were what he felt, too.

They came to the foot of the ovoid and paused, and in his heart Hendry knew that whatever happened now could only be an anticlimax.

And then Carrelli reached out and touched the bronze of the great ovoid, and then passed through the surface. She turned, smiling, and beckoned them after her. They obeyed – stepping through the wall as if it were gossamer – and found themselves in a chamber filled with sourceless light. He was aware of Kaluchek by his side, clutching him as if in fear, and aware too of his racing pulse.

Carrelli stood before them, and as they watched she transformed, became something other than what she had been, and seconds later they stared at a column of light that limned a vague humanoid form, the features of which were now indistinct.

A voice, though not Carrelli's, issued from the living light.

"Welcome," it said. "We have been awaiting your arrival for many millennia."

## 4

AFTER THE EXCITEMENT of the chase came the disappointment of losing the quarry.

"I'm sorry, Elder," the pilot said. "We have lost the ship's signature. We traced it to the world below, and then it simply vanished."

"Then search the world!" Cannak thundered. "It's vital that we locate and destroy the ship, do you understand that?"

"Of course sir, but..."

Cannak glared at the trembling pilot. "But? But what?"

"The world, sir. It's covered in... in vegetation a hundred yards high. The ship might be anywhere among it. A search would take weeks, and then might not be successful."

Cannak considered the options. "Proceed to the next world, the home of these illusory Builders. Ehrin and the interlopers will make their way there at some point. We will be waiting for them."

"Very good, sir."

That had been hours ago, and Elder Cannak had quelled his rage and retired to his cabin, where he had immersed himself in the Book of Books.

The heretic Ehrin would not escape justice, he thought, thanks to Sereth. The irony of the betrayal was beautiful; it would be a shame that she could not reap the rewards of the righteous, but the fact was that he could not trust her silence when she returned to Agstarn. The crew of the deathship, on the other hand... they were trained priests, versed in the deceit of the anti-god, who knew what they were experiencing for the illusion it was.

He read, in chapter seventy-three of the Book of Books, that the pious should be wary of bogus gods, that the anti-god was a master of deception and that what seemed to be real might often turn out to be no more than a trap to snare the unwary believer. That, he realised, was an apposite description of their present situation. They were travelling through an illusion, a vast construct of evil made to entrap the believer.

They would destroy the base of the so-called Builders, and then they would track down Ehrin and his cohorts and their ship and destroy them too. No word of their exploits must reach the impressionable of Agstarn, for fear of dissent and opposition to Church rule. Elder Cannak knew from experience that there were factions in society who would take advantage of unrest to foment their own godless agendas.

Ehrin and the aliens would be destroyed like the heretics they were. This evil illusion would dissolve, and Elder Cannak and the deathship would return to Agstarn in glory.

A soft tapping at his door interrupted his thoughts.

"Yes?" Could it be the pilot, come with good news? "Come in."

A timorous snout appeared around the edge of the door. Sereth Jaspariot peered in, blinking. "Elder Cannak, please forgive my interruption. I... I hope you don't mind, but I had to see you."

Cannak laid aside the Book of Books. "Child, enter. Don't be shy. My door is always open. How can I be of assistance?"

He gestured to a spare seat and Sereth sat down, glancing uneasily through a viewscreen at the sea passing below.

"Something worries you?"

Sereth avoided his eyes. "Elder... One can act correctly in the eyes of God, and yet find oneself in confusion and doubt."

Cannak smiled. "A common dilemma of all citizens," he reassured her. "The way of the righteous is not easy. God calls for sacrifices, and hard decisions. If in your heart you know that you made the right decision in the eyes of God, then any doubts are illusions..." He smiled and gestured through the viewscreen, "Just as all without is illusory..."

"Yes, Elder, but..."

"What troubles you?"

"Elder, I made the right decision, I know I did, in telling you. But... but I fear for Ehrin, and for all his sins hope that he will survive this episode and repent."

Cannak stared at her. "You fear that he might be executed as a heretic, is that right?"

She lowered her head and whispered, "Yes, Elder."

He gave his most reassuring smile. "Sereth, it is the ship he rides within that I must see destroyed, and the godless aliens who ride with him."

"Then... then you will spare Ehrin?"

"I am a man of compassion. I do God's duty, and our God is a God of boundless love."

"But," she began, before she could stop herself.

"Yes?"

She shook her head. "Nothing, Elder."

"But..." he said, "you were wondering about the aliens upon the last planet, the insects who gave succour to the godless?"

She looked up, clearly terrified now. In a tiny voice she said, "Well, yes, Elder Cannak."

"Child, they were but an illusion. They had no substance in reality. They were a trap of the anti-god. Do you carry with you the Book of Books?"

"Of course, Elder. In my cabin—"

"Then return there and study it, specifically chapter seventy-three. There you will find explanation enough."

She stood and lowered her head and made for the door. "Yes, Elder, and thank you."

He sat for a while when she had departed, and was about to return to his study when an urgent rap sounded upon his cabin door, and a young priest looked in. "Elder, the captain requires your presence. We have discovered something."

Cannak stood and hurried after the priest. "Something? What, specifically?"

"I... I can't rightly say, Elder. A building, a great building."

He entered the bridge and stared through the viewscreen. The ship was hovering over a vast plain, perhaps twenty feet from the ground. Directly ahead he saw a rearing golden edifice, and he had to check his initial impulse to marvel at the construction. The captain came to him. "Sir, we have evidence that this was their destination."

Elder Cannak hardly heard the words. The sight of the ziggurat was, he had to admit, staggering. But then, he reminded himself, what did he expect from the anti-god, who could create any illusion to turn the heads of the innocent?

He found his seat and sat down. "What evidence?"

"Elder, look…" The captain snapped an order. A screen dropped from the ceiling, and seconds later an image of the ziggurat appeared. The captain pointed out four small figures making their way towards the entrance of the imposing edifice. "This is a recording, made some ten minutes ago. It shows Ehrin and the aliens."

Cannak leaned forward, pulse racing now that he saw the captain was correct.

"Elder," the captain said, "we could fire now, destroy the entire illusion…"

Cannak watched as the godless quartet entered the archway of the ziggurat. He raised a hand. "Not yet, captain. They will emerge in time, and we will be waiting for then." He turned to the young priest and ordered him to find Sereth Jaspariot and bring her to the bridge.

He looked from the small, recorded image of the ziggurat to the real thing, rearing magnificently on the plain, and anticipated the final confrontation with the godless Ehrin and his cohorts.

Minutes later Sereth appeared on the bridge and crossed to him, looking fearful. He smiled to put her at her ease. "Sereth," he said, "we have located Ehrin and the aliens. All that remains now is to find their ship."

She inclined her head. "Yes, Elder."

"You have already excelled yourself in the eyes of God, child. But I wish of you one further mission."

"How can I be of assistance, Elder?"

"When Ehrin emerges, we will hail him and demand he tell us the whereabouts of the golden ship. You will speak to him, claim that we have threatened your life if he does not give us the information."

Sereth stared, wide-eyed, at Cannak. He smiled. "A ruse only, to test his loyalties, child."

She said quietly, "I fear he will call your bluff, Elder. His love for me died when he fled Agstarn."

Elder Cannak laid a compassionate paw upon Sereth's head. "We shall see, my child. We shall see."

He returned his eager gaze to the entrance of the ziggurat and waited.

:

# 5

HENDRY STOOD BETWEEN Kaluchek and Ehrin in the chamber of light, staring at the figure that, until moments ago, had been Gina Carrelli. She existed now in a column of light much brighter than that which surrounded them—a human figure, though no longer recognisable as the Italian medic.

Hendry was the first to find his voice. "What have you done to Gina?"

"She will come to no harm," the calm, avuncular voice reassured. "She will be returned to you when the audience is over, with no recollection of her ordeal."

Kaluchek said, "Why Carrelli?"

The light responded, "We have... employed... Gina Carrelli to facilitate your arrival at the helix."

It explained, Hendry thought, Gina Carrelli's peculiar abilities—her adept translations, for one; her uncanny facility with alien technologies.

Kaluchek was shaking her head, as if in wonder. "For how long? I mean, for longer than we have been on the helix, right?"

The light pulsed, replied, "We have employed members of your race for perhaps two hundred years before the launch of *Lovelock*."

Hendry opened his mouth to speak, but found that no words would come. He had questions aplenty, clamouring for expression, but where to begin?

Kaluchek spoke for him. "Employed? You mean, used? To what end?"

"Used," repeated the light. "Employed. The terms are similar, though we did not coerce; we merely encouraged individuals whose mindset was already attuned to our ways and views."

Hendry glanced to his left. To his surprise, Ehrin was speaking to the column of light—and no doubt, he thought, receiving replies in his own tongue. He reminded himself that he was dealing with a race far in advance of humanity's paltry achievements.

Kaluchek said, "Who are you?"

The figure in the light spread its arms. "We are the Builders. That will suffice. Long ago we called ourselves by a different name, but almost as long ago, since the construction of the helix, we have known ourselves as the Builders."

"You built this, the helix..." Kaluchek whispered. "But the science, the technology..."

Hendry sensed that the figure in the light was smiling indulgently. "We are an ancient race. We achieved a high level of technical expertise many hundreds of thousands of your years ago. For twenty thousand years we laboured at building the helix piece by piece, planet by planet."

"But... why? " Hendry found himself asking. "For what purpose?"

The light pulsed, bathing them in its radiation. "In our early days," it said, "we ranged the galaxy in our ships of exploration. We were a young race in a relatively young universe. We wanted company, but instead we found evidence of civilisations that had grown, attained technological sophistication and then destroyed themselves. Again and again we found the same. It was as if sentience was obeying some pre-ordained pattern, you might even call it a deterministic law of nature; as if the fight for survival dictated that enmity and wars were the only solution to conflicts. Oh, occasionally we did find races that had survived—that had either never attained a level of technology whereby they had the ability to self-destruct, or had attained it and then devolved before they could commit racial suicide. In both cases, we found races that had never had the opportunity to attain their full potential."

Hendry said, "Which is?"

"Which is," said the light, "the ability, the understanding, to live with their world, their planet, in balance and harmony, with a reciprocal understanding of mutual needs. Worlds are holistic systems that require respect and compassion. Again and again we discovered materialistic races with no comprehension of this universal truth."

"So you—" Kaluchek began.

"It was too vast a task to monitor and aid the many races spread across the face of the galaxy. We knew we had the wherewithal, the experience, to shepherd nascent races through their times of trouble, to even influence their philosophies in a bid to guide them to the truth. But our resources were stretched. We could aid only a dozen or so localised races, which would have been better than aiding none at all, but still far from satisfactory. Then our engineers suggested a radical solution."

"The helix," Kaluchek said.

"It was the perfect answer, the means of storing, if you like, thousands of different worlds in a compact series of self-contained environments. For centuries we planned the construct, and over millennia went about building it, and populating it as we went."

Hendry shook his head. "How did you... populate it? Invite races to relocate, kidnap them?"

"We had various methods of saving races from themselves. Some we simply took from their planets without their knowledge, races locked in conflict who would have resisted our interference; it was a simple task to translocate viable communities like this, pre-technological races who within a few generations would have supplanted memories of their homeworld with myths. Other, more sophisticated races we contacted by other means, consulting enlightened individuals, building a core community of like-minded people to found colonies devoted to non-materialistic coexistence with their new environments. Yet others, like yourselves, we seeded with—I suppose you might call them memes, ideas, philosophies—and then encouraged the technology to enable them to find the helix themselves."

Hendry said, "The reason astronomers didn't detect the helix back on Earth—"

"We... you might say we masked its presence, cloaked its luminosity, until we judged the time to be right."

"So our arrival here," Kaluchek said, "was... intended?"

"That is so. Many things might have stood in the way of your reaching the helix. Thanks to subversives amongst your race, you almost failed to make it."

"And if we had perished in space, as the terrorists intended?" Hendry asked.

"Then," the light responded in a regretful tone, "we would have mourned your passing, moved on and looked for another race suitable for our requirements."

A long silence followed these words. Hendry glanced at Kaluchek. He turned to the light and said, "Suitable? What do you want from us?"

"Over millennia, we have employed races to... I suppose you might call it govern the helix, and the various races upon it. Govern, guide, assist, call it what you will... as well of course as maintaining the technical integrity of the structure."

"Like the Sleeper we found in the rainforest on Calique?" Kaluchek said.

"He was a Maerl, a race we employed thousands of years ago."

Hendry shook his head in wonder at the vast scale of things that the figure in the light mentioned so casually. "But what happened to the Maerl? Why did they cease to govern?"

The light said, again with the suggestion of a smile, "All races pass on, attain an understanding with the universe—you might call it an empathy or union—which then predisposes them to turn their thoughts to philosophies and modes of existence other than the materialistic. They no longer have the inclination to maintain technological systems, or to govern. They evolve, you might say. The Maerl was one such race. Ho-lah-lee was another. Fifteen thousand years ago, for three millennia, they maintained the helix."

The light paused, and the silence lengthened, and Hendry considered the idea of the human race, so recently responsible for the destruction of its own homeworld, being handed the task of monitoring others.

He gestured. "Are we suitable?" he asked. "I would have thought—"

The light cut in. "You are suitable *now*," it said gently. "It took you millennia, and you almost perished along the way, but thanks to your inherent... call it survivability... and with a little assistance from ourselves, you have achieved a level of understanding whereat we are happy to instruct you in the governance of the helix."

In awe, Kaluchek said, "Gaia... It was you, you gave us the idea of Gaia."

The light almost laughed at this. "Gaia was always present, a universal truth. We merely gave you the intellectual wherewithal to perceive the truth."

"The governance of the helix," Hendry repeated. "The task must be... almost impossible."

"Nothing is impossible, my friend. It will take time, and effort, and there will be failures along the way, but we will always be here to assist."

Kaluchek said, "But... you no longer wish to undertake the task yourselves?"

The light pulsed. "We are no longer able to undertake the task. We long ago ascended from the state of the physical to something higher, something exalted. In time, and with effort, other races upon the helix will ascend with us. It is destined. It is the way of the universe."

Hendry said, "How many races exist on the helix?"

"At present, a little over six thousand, though there is room for many thousands more. Over the millennia, they will arrive."

"We need to transport the colonists from the first tier, find a suitable world," Kaluchek said.

"This will be arranged. We have ships, and this world is available for your use."

Hendry looked at Ehrin, his muzzle working as he spoke. The light explained, "I have answered all his questions, reassured him that he will return to his people and bring enlightenment to their clouded world. With your help, of course."

Kaluchek said, "And now?"

"Now," said the light, "you will return to the plain, and face the future, when a new era for humanity will begin."

They were the last words Hendry and Kaluchek heard the Builder pronounce, for the light surrounding the figure diminished, flickered and died, and once more Carrelli stood before them, eyes closed, before slumping to the floor.

## 6

HENDRY AND KALUCHEK helped Carrelli to her feet between them and, each taking a shoulder, walked her from the chamber, seemingly passing through the wall of solid bronze and once more into the vast base of the ziggurat. Ehrin trotted alongside, a hand protectively clutching Carrelli's leg. A thousand amphibian faces gazed up at them as they emerged, and the Ho-lah-lee parted to allow them through.

Dazed, Carrelli said, "What happened? What happened in there?"

Kaluchek laughed. "Where to begin?" she asked.

They passed from the ziggurat and onto the plain, and halted in shock at what they saw there. Ehrin uttered a pained yelp of terror and Hendry felt an icy fist of dread punch him in the gut. "Oh, Christ," Kaluchek said quietly to herself.

Perhaps a kilometre away, hovering over the plain, was the Church ship. After the radiant white light of the chamber, the black ship seemed to suck all light and hope from the air around it.

Hendry's first instinct was to dive back into the chamber, but the sound that filled the air stopped him.

It was an amplified series of barks, issuing from the ship. Ehrin stepped forward, muzzle open in consternation.

Kaluchek looked at Carrelli. "What did they say?"

Carrelli cocked her head, listening. She said, "They want to know where our ship is. They're... they've told Ehrin that they have Sereth. They say they will put her to death if Ehrin doesn't tell them the whereabouts of the ship."

Ehrin stepped forward, both fists raised as if in rage against the ship and its crew.

Carrelli barked at him. They conferred, and Ehrin turned back to the ship and barked at the top of his lungs.

Kaluchek said, "What did you say?"

"I told him to ask for assurance of Sereth's safety. He will tell the Elder—a high Church official—that he will divulge the whereabouts of the ship only if Sereth is released and returned to him."

Ehrin came to the end of his speech and waited, staring up at the ship.

The response was slow in coming. When it came, at last, booming out over the plain, Carrelli translated.

"They have agreed. They will release Sereth. They have warned Ehrin that if he does not keep his promise, then they will kill all of us."

Kaluchek shook her head. "But if he tells them where the ship is—"

Carrelli glanced at her. "I thought you and Olembe were mortal enemies, Sissy?"

Kaluchek glanced at Hendry. "We were," she said in a whisper.

"Don't worry about the ship, or Olembe," Carrelli said.

Ehrin barked again, and started forward. From the underside of the Church ship, a column emerged, for all the world like the ovipositor of some stinging insect. Seconds later a tiny figure dropped from it, picked herself up and hurried across the plain towards them.

Ehrin moved to meet her and they embraced in the shadow of the ship.

The Elder's barks rolled over the plain. Carrelli said, "He's demanding Ehrin's side of the bargain, now."

Ehrin looked up, still holding Sereth, and called out to the Church ship.

Carrelli smiled.

"What did he say?" Hendry asked.

"What I instructed him to say," Carrelli replied. "That our ship is on the shore of the planet directly across the sea from the ziggurat."

Kaluchek shook her head in mystification. "But you could have told them anywhere..."

Carrelli laughed. "It doesn't matter, Sissy," she said, "because the ship is no longer there."

"Then where—?" Hendry began.

He was answered a split-second later when the radio on his atmosphere suit crackled into life and Olembe yelled at them, "Get back into the ziggurat, fast!"

Carrelli barked to Ehrin and Sereth, and they began running.

Hendry grabbed Kaluchek and almost dragged her back into the arched entrance. He glanced over his shoulder. Carrelli was right behind them. Behind her, still fifty metres from the entrance, Ehrin and Sereth were desperately sprinting towards them.

Hendry dived into the ziggurat and rolled to his left, activating his radio and shouting, "Olembe! How the hell—?"

"Carrelli called me an hour ago!" the African replied. "Now shut it while I sort the bastards!"

An hour ago Carrelli had been transformed by the white light, controlled, as she had been for who knew how long, by the Builders. Was it they, then, who had summoned Olembe?

His thoughts were interrupted by the deafening crack of an explosion. He risked a glance outside. A ray from the ship had pulverised the ground a matter of metres behind the scampering figures of Ehrin and Sereth. They fell, scrabbling, and picked themselves up. Hand in hand and yelping with fear, they sprinted towards the ziggurat. Another ray lanced from the ship, striking the metalwork beside the entrance with a deafening clang. Hendry yelled at them to dive and roll, before a third ray accounted for them. Seconds later they reached the ziggurat and fell to the ground, and Hendry made a grab and pulled them to safety.

The third ray struck the body of the ziggurat above them, and Hendry was aware of the irony. Ehrin's people, however long ago, had been saved from themselves by the Builders, and now they were unwittingly attempting to destroy their saviours.

Another explosion shook the edifice. Hendry imagined the towering blocks of the building tumbling down around them. He was about to grab Kaluchek and drag her outside when another explosion, this one many times louder than the first two, rent the air. A great actinic flash blinded him. He rolled over, clinging to Kaluchek, who grabbed him and moaned against his chest.

He opened his eyes and stared through the entrance. The view was at once devastating, and oddly beautiful. He thought his vision had been slowed, or some processing function of his ravaged mind retarded, for the manta-ray shape of the Church ship was tilting to starboard in a great ball of flame and sliding from the air, impacting with the ground in slow motion. It crumpled, imploding in on itself, as if passing through the very surface of the plain, and all the while subsidiary explosions were blooming about its falling carcass, the sight followed seconds later by a cannonade of detonations.

Hendry rolled back into the cover of the entrance. Beside him, Carrelli was clutching Ehrin and Sereth beneath her arms like children.

He activated his radio. "Olembe? Olembe? For Chrissake..."

There was no reply.

Had the mad bastard, unable to fathom the alien weapons system, rammed the ship with his own? It would have been a gesture unsurprising from someone as bellicose as Olembe.

"You don't think...?" Kaluchek began.

"I can't reach him. I wouldn't be surprised."

The explosions outside had ceased. All he could hear now was the frantic sound of burning. All around them, curious Ho-lah-lee were climbing to their feet, wandering through the entrance and viewing the aftermath of the confrontation.

Hendry stood, pulling Kaluchek to her feet. Her atmosphere suit was torn, her face dirty and bruised, and she had never looked so wonderful.

They stepped cautiously through the arch and stopped to look upon a scene of absolute destruction.

The ship was a scattered mass of molten slag, white hot in places, trailing palls of smoke like the pennants of a defeated army.

Hendry looked among the debris for any sign of the wreckage of the smaller ship.

Carrelli was staring up at the surface of the ziggurat, and smiling. Hendry followed her gaze. The bronze edifice appeared pristine, untouched.

Kaluchek gasped, released his hand and stepped forward. Hendry stared through the drifting smoke, to the plain beyond the wreckage.

There, sitting on the grass with its nose-cone excoriated by the explosions, was the golden ship. As he watched, filled with an odd euphoria, the ramp opened and Friday Olembe staggered out. He slumped onto the ramp, his back against the entrance, and just about managed to lift a hand in greeting.

Kaluchek turned to Hendry. "Joe, I've got to tell him. Apologise, okay?"

He smiled, and touched her cheek. He watched her turn and walk away. She paused before the wreckage of the Church ship, then gazed through the rising smoke towards Friday Olembe, who was climbing to his feet. She set off again, around the debris, to make her necessary and long delayed reparations.

Hendry sat down, his back against the warm bronze of the ziggurat, next to Carrelli, Ehrin and Sereth. Through the smoke drifting from the wreckage, he watched the two small, human figures face each other. Seconds elapsed. They were speaking. Olembe reached out. Kaluchek stepped forward, and they embraced.

## Twelve /// The Time of Changes

I

EHRIN SHIVERED IN the doorway and watched a procession of zeer-trucks make their way along the ice canal, waiting for a break in the traffic so that he could cross to the lighted building opposite. He braced himself against the cold, his teeth chattering. After the heat of the upper tiers, the sub-zero temperatures of his homeworld struck him as alien and inimical. He thought of the rainforests of Calique, and then the warm plains of the homeworld of the Builders, and something ached within him like nostalgia.

The humans had set him down in the mountains surrounding Agstarn two nights ago, promising that they would do what they could to help him. What that might be, Ehrin could not envisage. The overthrow of the Church would be a long and weary business, prone to failure, but he had contacts in the city who were just as opposed to the Church's rule as he was.

Last night he had stayed in a safe house on the edge of the city, and recounted with barely concealed excitement his adventures to a hastily convened coterie of friends and fellow atheists. They had heard him out in silence, their expressions conveying wonder, hope, and in a few instances incredulity. Indeed it was a far-fetched tale he told them, a subversion of every tenet of life on Agstarn, even if one did not believe in the truth as promulgated by the Church. It was hard to take in, but Ehrin's standing in society, his known opposition to the ruling elite, and the veracity and detail of his description of the helix and the life that existed on the other tiers, had won over even the most hardened sceptics.

Now he was moving on to another safe house, there to meet friends in business whom he might rally in opposition to the Church.

Tomorrow he would rendezvous with Sereth in a quiet coffee house in an industrial district of the city. She had come with him as far as the outskirts of Agstarn, and then they had parted company and she had made her way to the house of a friend. She had prepared a cover story for her absence: it would be known that she had entered the penitentiary with the alien giant, but she would claim that she had been concussed in the resulting mêlée and had wandered the ice canals in an amnesic fugue, until her senses had returned and she made her way back to her father's penthouse.

She had been quiet during the flight to Agstarn aboard the Builders' ship, clinging to him and weeping. She had undergone severe hardship during her time away from home, physically but also mentally. As a believer, the overturning of her safe way of life, of everything she had held to be true, had proved traumatic. She had hardly spoken a word to Ehrin during their return journey, avoiding his questions, his reassurances that all would be well in time.

He had wondered, and wondered still, how much her silence was the result of guilt—for the appearance of the deathship before the Builders' ziggurat must have had something to do with Sereth. Had she guided Cannak to the homeworld of the Builders? If so, then he could not guess what pressures might have been placed upon her...

Before him, a gap appeared in the caravan of zeer-trucks. Ehrin stepped from the doorway and skated across the ice canal. It was early evening, in mid-winter, and the cold wind seemed to sharpen itself on him like a thousand knives. Even the protection of his padded jacket did little to warm him. He would be thankful of the warmth of the safe house, a mug of tisane and a hot meal.

He came to the doorway, unfastened his skates and rang the bell. Seconds later a servant opened the door, glanced once at Ehrin and turned away without a word, leaving the door open. Ehrin slipped inside while the servant hurried down a corridor and into a far room.

Seconds later a large-bellied, prosperous man appeared at the end of the corridor. He appeared nervous, as if to approach Ehrin might in some manner infect his person with the insidious virus of apostasy. This was, according to his last contact, a rich rope-maker whose grandfather had been put to death many years ago on the orders of Prelate Hykell. There was no love lost between the magnate and the Church, according to Ehrin's contact. The industrialist would convene a meeting of powerful fellow sceptics, to plan ahead... Or so said the contact, though the man appeared decidedly hesitant now that the time had come to turn grand words into action.

He gestured at Ehrin, motioning him into the room with a quick paw. "Make yourself comfortable," the man said, barely bringing himself to meet Ehrin's gaze as the renegade entered the room.

"Excuse me while I attend to business. The others will be arriving soon." He gestured to a samovar of tisane and a plate of cold meat and bread.

The door closed firmly on Ehrin and he ate, warming his hands on a cup of tisane.

He wondered how much the magnate had been told of Ehrin's adventures, and if his nervousness was a result of finding stories of other worlds and races hard to stomach. It was all very well to oppose the draconian rule of the Church, but some people were almost as fearful of the uncertainty of change.

There was a loud rapping on the front door, followed by a shout. He heard the servant's footsteps, and then the amplification of the voices as the door was opened.

He stood quickly, spilling tea. A delegation of disbelievers would not have drawn attention to themselves with such raucousness.

He was making for the door when it burst open and six Church militiamen swarmed into the room, weapons levelled. Before he could move, two burly guards had him by the arms, then two more took his feet, and like this he was carried struggling from the house. Of the industrialist there was no sign.

He saw a prison wagon on the ice, shackled to six snorting zeer, and a second later he was tossed unceremoniously into the back and the doors slammed shut behind him. The familiar darkness brought back memories of his last experience of a prison wagon, and what had transpired then.

He thought of Kahran, and wondered then if his tears were for his dead friend, or for himself.

He hardly had time to gather his thoughts and wonder who might have betrayed him, before the sound of the wagon's runners skimming over ice changed suddenly. Now they were scraping bare cobbles, and he knew he was approaching the precincts of the penitentiary.

A minute later the doors were flung open, and a hand reached in and grabbed him by the ankle, yanking him out and onto the hard floor without thought of his safety. He gasped as his head struck the cobbles, and vice-like hands gripped his arms and legs. He was borne like a carcass down a series of corridors until at last he arrived at a barred cell, into which he was tossed. The door slammed with finality. An ominous silence filled the cell. He stared around, and what he saw brought a bolus of bile to his throat.

The cell was bare, but for one fitting—a chair bolted securely to the stone-slabbed floor, a chair with straps upon its arms and in its back panel a gap through which the Church torturers might do their deeds.

Rather than contemplate his immediate future, he occupied his thoughts by wondering who of the so-called disbelievers had betrayed him. Certainly there had been many present the night before who might have found his tale of interworld travel hard to take, but his contact had assured him that all had been vetted and found trustworthy... But obviously not. The Church had infiltrated the meeting. Or perhaps the industrialist had been responsible...

Then another, more alarming thought occurred to him, though he tried hard to dismiss it. Sereth had known where he was heading when he left her. Perhaps she, aggrieved that all her certainties had been subverted by his actions, had alerted the authorities? Their leave-taking had been hurried, with Sereth hardly able to bring herself to look him in the eye. Even so, he found it hard to believe that she would so callously betray him, for perhaps a second time.

His thoughts in turmoil, he started when the thick wooden door creaked open, and two black-clad Inquisitors entered, followed by a familiar, red-robed figure.

Some scared, irrational part of his mind half-expected to see Velkor Cannak confront him, back from the dead to mock his plight.

The figure standing before him was Prelate Hykell, his face expressionless. "Indeed, it is Ehrin Telsa himself. I hardly believed the reports of your return."

Ehrin rose to his feet, staring at the Prelate. How might he save himself, he wondered; what ploy might he adopt to spare his life?

"You boarded the golden ship with the monster and its cohorts, and now you are back. Bent upon invasion, perhaps, and upon undermining the rule of the Church."

The Prelate waited, but Ehrin gave no reply.

"Whichever, you will die, but not before we have extracted from you the truth."

"The truth?" Ehrin burst out. "You couldn't handle the truth!"

"The truth of what happened when you left Agstarn, of the whereabouts of Elder Cannak and the deathship."

"The truth," Ehrin began, feeling himself shaking uncontrollably, "is that Cannak is dead, the deathship destroyed, and soon the true nature of the universe will be known to all who live in Agstarn and beyond."

Hykell bared his sharp teeth. "The true nature...? You have no conception of the truth, you blasphemer." He gestured, and the Inquisitors grabbed Ehrin and forced him into the chair, strapping his wrists secure with leather thongs, then standing back and awaiting, with ill-concealed eagerness, Hykell's next instructions.

Even though all evidence suggested otherwise, he could not believe that he would die. The thought was too overwhelming, too vast to accept. Shaking, he spat at Hykell, "I beheld the truth and your puny Church stands futile before it, a corrupt regime of power-mad zealots who know nothing of the true nature of the universe!"

There, he had said it, and saying it he had certainly signed his death warrant, though the satisfaction that coursed through his being then filled him with euphoria and a feeling almost akin to triumph.

Hykell leaned forward, staring at him, "Do you not fear death, you fool?"

"More than the fear of death, I rejoice in the fact that your Church is doomed. I might die, but I will die in the knowledge that you and everything you represent will be swept away when the people learn the truth."

Something appeared then in Hykell's eyes. Was it doubt, even fear? Whatever, Ehrin felt suddenly heartened.

Then Hykell said, "I will take great pleasure in watching you die, Ehrin Telsa."

And Ehrin tried to laugh, but instead choked on a sob.

Hykell was about to instruct the Inquisitors, but at that second a knock sounded on the timber door. For a heady, hopeless second, Ehrin wondered if the humans had arrived—the humans who had vowed, on leaving him, that they would do all they could to help his cause. Might they have invaded and come to effect a dramatic rescue?

But when Hykell opened the door, Ehrin saw only an armed guard in the corridor outside. They spoke briefly, in low tones, and the effect was immediate and startling.

Hykell swept from the cell, the Inquisitors with him, but not before he turned to Ehrin and said, "We will return, Telsa..." Ehrin felt he was about to say more, issue some grand threat or petty jibe, but the Prelate bit his lip and hurried down the corridor.

The door thundered shut behind them.

Ehrin heard footsteps beyond the door, as guards passed the cell with indecipherable shouts.

He hung his head and closed his eyes. He had been spared death, this time, but knew full well that he had been granted only a stay of execution.

## 2

SERETH APPROACHED THE mansion where her father lived, fearful of the reception that might be in store. She would have to lie to her father, something she had never done before. She feared that he might see through her fiction, but told herself that that was highly unlikely. He would believe that she had suffered concussion and wandered the ice canals for a week, rather than gone off in some alien interworld ship, even if prison officers had told him the latter.

She took off her skates, pulled open the door and slowly climbed the stairs to the penthouse suite. She was aware that her physical state would attest to her tale of concussion and amnesia: she had lost weight, and looked thin and bedraggled. Mentally, too, she had suffered. Everything she had believed true and good had been proven to be a lie, and evil. What the Church had done on the homeworld of the Builders... The thought of Elder Cannak's deception was enough to make her sick.

She had seen the truth, and she knew that everything would be very different from now on.

She reached her father's rooms and tried the door. It was locked. A part of her was relieved that she would not be forced to face him immediately. She took a key from her pocket and let herself in, then crossed to the window seat and stared out at the darkening city.

More than anything else, she was consumed with guilt. Ehrin had been right all along. The Church was repressive, not a force for good; and there did exist beyond the confines of Agstarn a vast if inexplicable series of worlds. And yet, even though the evidence of her own eyes had told her this, she had betrayed Ehrin and the humans to Elder Cannak.

She wanted to tell Ehrin this, to explain her confusion at the time, in a bid to absolve herself, and yet at the same time she was fearful of his reaction.

She heard slow footsteps on the stairs beyond the door, and straightened herself with apprehension.

The door opened, and the bent, weary figure of Bishop Jaspariot appeared in the doorway. He was hunched within his padded greatcoat, and the sight of the tiny, pathetic figure made Sereth want to cry.

He stopped in his tracks, staring at her with disbelief through his tiny glasses. "Sereth?" It came out as whisper.

"Father!" she said, advancing.

He fell into her arms, and she was amazed and startled at his frailty.

"But I thought... a guard said you were dead, caught in the crossfire." He sobbed and gripped her.

"I... I was concussed. When I came to my senses, it was night. I didn't know where I was. I wandered the canals, confused. For a week I stayed in a workers' hostel... I couldn't remember my name, where I lived..."

He was shaking his head, hardly taking in her words for the fact of her miraculous survival.

"Thank God!" he cried. "Truly, He rewards the virtuous."

She hugged him again, so that he could not witness her pained expression.

He pulled away and stroked the fur of her cheek. "I was so fearful, Sereth, my darling. I feared that you were dead, and worse..."

She stared at him. "Worse?"

"One guard said he thought he saw you board the alien's ship, though he couldn't be sure. He did see Ehrin Telsa board, though, along with the alien prisoners."

She gripped his hand. "I was spared that fate," she said. "But I fear for Ehrin—"

"He was in league with the invaders," her father interrupted. "He deserves whatever comes to him."

"Father, I know Ehrin is innocent. He was forced against his will," she heard herself saying. "He had no say in the matter."

He was smiling at her. "Well, we shall soon find out, Sereth."

"Find out? How...?" She trailed off, a horrible suspicion forming.

Her father confirmed it. "Ehrin Telsa was arrested two hours ago. He had returned to Agstarn, no doubt to further aid the aliens in their invasion."

"No! Ehrin wouldn't..." Her mind raced. She clutched her father's frail hands. "I need to see him, father. I must!"

"My child, Ehrin is not the man you knew. His head has been turned by evil ones."

She said, "I want to see him, father. It is a right of all prisoners, is it not, to receive visitors?"

"Sereth, in the circumstances, I am sure that Prelate Hykell has Ehrin in the securest custody. Visitation is out of the question."

She seized his shoulders, desperate now. "You must help me. Take me to the penitentiary. You know where Ehrin is imprisoned. Take me there!"

"Child, are you out of your mind?"

She dropped her arms and backed off. "Father, if you refuse me this wish, then... then I will leave, and this time never return. If you do not take me there, then you will never see me again."

His eyes were moist behind the thick lenses of his glasses. He stared at her forlornly.

"Father, I swear..."

"I can take you to the penitentiary, but it will be of little help to you. They will not allow you to see Ehrin."

"Take me, father!" She had gripped his shoulders again and was shaking him.

She stopped herself, then almost apologised.

He said, "You are young and foolish, Sereth."

She wanted to tell him that he was old and foolish, that she had seen more than he might ever conceive possible.

He relented. "I will take you as far as the penitentiary, but it will be in vain."

She almost dragged him from the room. On the way she found her jacket and pulled it on. At the foot of the stairs she strapped on her skates and opened the door. After the warmth of her father's rooms, the cold pounced like a vengeful thing. The ice canal was in darkness. Overhead, the grey cloudrace obscured the truth.

She took her father's hand and tugged him into the canal, and they headed south towards the penitentiary.

She had no idea what she might achieve when she arrived there. Perhaps her father was right, and her mission was futile. But, at least, she would know in her heart that she had tried to see Ehrin... whatever they might do to him.

She remembered Kahran, and choked on a sob.

If she could somehow get word to Ehrin, tell him that she loved him, that she would do all in her power... She tried to blank from her mind the impossibility of the situation.

Ahead, the monolith of the penitentiary loomed before the distant jagged peaks of the mountains, the prison cold and forbidding as those enclosing ramparts. A few lights showed in the tiny, slit windows, highlighting the dreary grey façade.

They came to the gatehouse, a token and futile thing now that the wall beside it was a pile of rubble, thanks to the ministration of the alien's golden ship. Two guards stood on duty before the rubble, shivering in the icy wind.

Her father showed his pass to the guard in the gatehouse, and the massive timber gate was duly hauled open to reveal the ice-free cobbled courtyard beyond.

They unfastened their skates and Sereth took her father's hand again, pulling him towards the arched entrance set into the sheer wall of the building. A guard stood sentry beside the door, something in his stance suggesting increased vigilance.

Her father showed his pass again, but the guard barred his entry. "No visitors. A directive from the Prelate. You might enter, Your Grace, but the girl..."

"But..." her father began feebly. Then, surprising her, he went on, "The girl is not a visitor. We have work to do in the records office. Important work, might I add." He paused, then added, "If you doubt the word of a bishop, then ask Prelate Hykell himself."

The guard looked doubtful, and finally gave way and stood aside. They hurried past him, through the timber door and into a long corridor. As they walked, Sereth took her father's hand and squeezed.

They turned down another corridor, towards the west wing. Minutes later they heard shouts from up ahead, and Sereth's heart raced. A guard ran past them, followed by another, then two more, all armed. For a fleeting, hope-filled second, Sereth fantasised that perhaps Ehrin had managed to escape.

They heard shouts from another part of the prison. Up ahead, where a window opening was let into the thick wall, Sereth beheld a curious phenomenon. The corridor was lighted, as if the glow of a torch was illuminating it from without. She wondered if the prison were on fire.

Activity was all around them now, as more guards left their posts and made for the courtyard.

They hurried on. Ahead, she made out the collapsed walls and piled rubble created by the giant alien just one week ago. To reach the cells where Ehrin was imprisoned they must pass outside again and through another exposed courtyard.

Sereth halted in her tracks as she realised that the light outside the penitentiary was not a localised affair.

She began to run again, her father exclaiming as she pulled him along after her.

They came to the rubble and hurried around it, and across the courtyard. It was bathed in a curious light, the like of which she had never seen before. Her father was frozen in his tracks, muttering frenzied prayers to himself.

Sereth felt something swell within her chest—fear, but also hope.

She dragged her staring father through a jagged rent in the inner wall and down a corridor towards the dungeons.

"Now where is Ehrin?" she cried at him when they were within the relative gloom of the dungeons.

Feebly he gestured to the right, along a narrow corridor.

They turned, Sereth running. They came to a great timber door. Her father nodded.

The corridor was empty, free of guards. Sereth flung herself at the timber, crying, "Ehrin!"

A second later a disbelieving voice replied, "Sereth? Sereth, is it you?"

"Ehrin, I'm here!" She battered at the door with tiny fists.

She turned a beseeching stare upon her father.

He looked at her, then turned and fled, and Sereth let out an anguished wail.

"Sereth?" Ehrin cried.

"Ehrin... I'm here. I'm sorry. For everything. I didn't believe you. I was a fool. I'm so sorry. Believe me when I say I love you, please believe me, and forgive me."

"Sereth!"

"I will do all I can to save you," she cried, horribly aware that her promise might be futile.

"Sereth, what's happening? The light?"

A sound from behind her made her heart leap. She turned, expecting to see a guard.

It was her father, standing before her, holding out a hand. She stared.

"Take it, child. I have seen enough to... Take it!"

Hardly daring to believe her eyes, she reached out and took the key. With useless fingers she inserted the key into the lock and attempted to turn it. The mechanism was stiff, ungiving. She cried aloud, expecting to be found out at any second.

Her father eased her aside, took the key and turned it in the lock.

The door swung open. Sereth cried out as she beheld Ehrin, believing that the Inquisitors had already begun their work.

Ehrin stared at her, eyes massive. She ran at him, fumbled with the straps holding him to the arms of the chair. In seconds she had them free and Ehrin was in her arms.

"Come, we have no time to lose."

"What's happening?" Ehrin asked as they hurried from the cell.

"I... I can't begin to explain," Sereth said. She was aware that her father was following them as they fled down the corridor towards the courtyard.

Before they came to the breach in the wall, her father halted them with a shout.

They turned. He was staring at them, an indecipherable expression on his ancient face. Sereth saw in his eyes the death of faith, and at the same time the light of love for her and all she represented. He removed his greatcoat and held it out to Ehrin. "Here. Take this. You will need it. Pull the hood over your head, and you might escape detection."

"Father!"

"Hurry! The guards will soon be ordered back to their posts. Now go."

Ehrin struggled into the greatcoat and pulled the hood over his head. She took his hand and headed for the courtyard, coming into the miraculous light. The yard was thronged with milling guards, all staring in wonder at the sky. Sereth looked over her shoulder and saw the tiny shape of her father within the corridor, then she turned and hurried on.

They crossed the courtyard, then passed beneath an archway that led to the outer yard. Here a similar chaos reigned; it seemed that the entire staff of the penitentiary had left their post the better to behold the aerial phenomenon.

Across the cobbles, perhaps just fifty yards away, was the rubble of the breached outer wall. Beyond were the ice canals, the promise of escape and freedom.

They ran, clambered around the rubble. They heard shouts, but did not pause to learn if the cries were intended to halt their flight or to comment upon the wondrous light.

Sereth felt her heart pounding as they moved from the precincts of the prison and came to the ice canal. She had her skates around her neck, but Ehrin was without his. To save time, she did not stop to put them on. Soon the ice would melt, and skates would be the first of many things they would be able to do without.

Holding onto each other, they made their precarious way along the canal and down a side-alley. Here they paused, panting, laughing exultantly but not without fear.

They faced each other. Sereth reached up and removed the hood from Ehrin's head, and it was evident from his reaction that he had not looked up into the sky before now.

He did so, and bared his teeth in awe.

She followed his gaze.

Overhead, the immemorial grey clouds of Agstarn, the cover that had hidden so much from the citizens for so long, were dissipating, dissolving as if by magic, to be replaced by a beauteous, effulgent blue. As they watched, the clouds turned ragged, driven by a high wind, and parted to reveal the great spiral arcs of the helix as it wound upwards to the distant, life-giving sun.

"They kept their promise," Ehrin whispered to her, and they set off through the city of Agstarn towards the temporary refuge of the mountains.

The time of changes had begun.

# 3

HENDRY AND SISSY Kaluchek left the control room housed within the core of the ziggurat. They took the elevator up to the central chamber, then walked from the ziggurat and boarded a ground-effect vehicle.

Sissy drove, reminding Hendry of the time, which seemed like years ago now, when they had left the wreck of the *Lovelock* and ventured across the ice wastes of the first tier.

He considered what, with the aid of the Builders, they had just done.

She looked across at him and smiled. "What are you thinking, Joe?"

"I'm thinking about Ehrin, and Sereth, and what might be happening down there."

"We should pay them a visit, in a while."

He smiled. "In a while, yes," he said. And what might they find down there, he wondered? A city in chaos, torn by revolution and civil war, or made safe and peaceable following the downfall of the Church?

Sissy braked the vehicle and they climbed out, stood side by side and stared down the incline towards the valley. What looked like the beginnings

of a small town were in the process of being constructed beside a winding river. Hendry recognised
the containers from the *Lovelock*, the beetling
shapes of the ground-effect trucks moving from the
hold of the Builders' ship.

And there were people, thousands of people,
moving about their appointed tasks in the skeleton
of the nascent colony. They were human, and the
sight of them never failed to fill Hendry with joy
and at the same time melancholy.

Off to the side of the growing township was the
designated grave-garden, where the thousand
colonists who had not survived the journey, including Chrissie, would be laid to rest.

He felt a hand take his. She squeezed.

"This is where it all starts," she whispered.

There was so much to do in the weeks, months
and years ahead... in the millennia ahead, if they
were to discharge their obligation to the Builders.

He opened his mouth to speak.

"What?" Sissy said.

"What trust," he said at last, moved almost to
tears. "We made a mess of it the first time, and yet
they give us a second chance. What trust."

In the valley below, Hendry made out the tiny
forms of Olembe and Carrelli. They were sitting
side by side on the greensward, taking a break from
erecting the habitat domes.

Hendry lifted a hand and waved, then set off with
Sissy to join them.

It was year zero, and New Earth was coming to
life.

## ABOUT THE AUTHOR

Eric Brown's first short story was published in *Interzone* in 1987, and he sold his first novel, *Meridian Days*, in 1992. He has won the British Science Fiction Award twice for his short stories and has published twenty-five books: SF novels, collections, books for teenagers and younger children, and he writes a monthly SF review column for *The Guardian*. His latest books include the novella, *Starship Summer*, and the children's book *An Alien Ate Me for Breakfast*. He is married to the writer and mediaevalist Finn Sinclair and they have a daughter, Freya.

His website can be found at:
*www.ericbrown.co.uk*